My cell phone rang just as I was getting into bed, but, according to plan, I let the call go straight to voice mail. I fluffed my pillows, switched off the light, and closed my eyes.

But only until enough time had elapsed for me to retrieve the message.

"I know you're up there," Billy said. "And if you don't come down and talk to me in the next two minutes, I'm going to give you my best Stanley Kowalski impression until you do."

He wouldn't. He *couldn't*. He—

"Daaanaaaaa!"

Oh crap.

"Daaaaaanaaaaaa!"

I jumped into a pair of jeans and raced down the stairs to discover Billy leaning against the mailboxes in the outside foyer. Grinning, he mouthed the words, *What took you so long?*

I unlocked the front door and opened it just wide enough for us to converse without having to shout through the glass. But he was too fast for me. Instantly my back was against the door of my super's apartment, and Billy was kissing me and kissing me and kissing me. . . .

Until the super's mangy little mongrel started yapping frantically and hurling its body against the other side of the door. We froze, eyes locked.

"You are *not* invited upstairs," I said.

"Then come outside and sit with me on the stoop for a while. Tell me about this harrowing evening of yours."

The last thing in the world I wanted to do was discuss my harrowing evening. "Honestly, it's not important. Besides, it's twenty degrees out there." I'd run downstairs too quickly to grab a jacket.

He opened his and cocooned me inside it, and my brain turned to pudding while I let him guide me out the door. We settled on the top step with me sitting between his legs, both of us snug in his coat. "See? Nice and warm."

Warm, my ass. It was hot as hell out there.

PERFECT ON PAPER

JANET GOSS

NEW AMERICAN LIBRARY

NEW AMERICAN LIBRARY
Published by New American Library,
a division of Penguin Group (USA) Inc.,
375 Hudson Street, New York, New York 10014, USA
Penguin Group (Canada), 90 Eglinton Avenue East, Suite 700, Toronto,
Ontario M4P 2Y3, Canada (a division of Pearson Penguin Canada Inc.)
Penguin Books Ltd., 80 Strand, London WC2R 0RL, England
Penguin Ireland, 25 St. Stephen's Green, Dublin 2,
Ireland (a division of Penguin Books Ltd.)
Penguin Group (Australia), 250 Camberwell Road, Camberwell,
Victoria 3124, Australia (a division of Pearson Australia Group Pty. Ltd.)
Penguin Books India Pvt. Ltd., 11 Community Centre,
Panchsheel Park, New Delhi - 110 017, India
Penguin Group (NZ), 67 Apollo Drive, Rosedale, Auckland 0632,
New Zealand (a division of Pearson New Zealand Ltd.)
Penguin Books (South Africa) (Pty.) Ltd., 24 Sturdee Avenue,
Rosebank, Johannesburg 2196, South Africa

Penguin Books Ltd., Registered Offices:
80 Strand, London WC2R 0RL, England

First published by New American Library,
a division of Penguin Group (USA) Inc.

First Printing, March 2012
1 3 5 7 9 10 8 6 4 2

NAL REGISTERED TRADEMARK—MARCA REGISTRADA

LIBRARY OF CONGRESS CATALOGING-IN-PUBLICATION DATA:
Goss, Janet, 1957–
Perfect on paper/Janet Goss.
p. cm.
ISBN 978-0-451-23569-5
I. Title.
PS3607.O853P47 2012
813'.6—dc23   2011044645

Set in Adobe Garamond
Designed by Elke Sigal

Printed in the United States of America

For Edgar, my long-suffering husband

PERFECT ON PAPER

CHAPTER ONE

TONGUE AND GROOVE

Under ordinary circumstances, I could ring a doorbell as well as anyone. Nothing to it—one push, mission accomplished.

But not that Sunday afternoon on Perry Terrace. My hands had begun to tremble when I'd boarded the downtown R train at Astor Place, and they were fluttering like hummingbirds by the time I arrived at Bay Ridge Avenue a seemingly endless nineteen stops and forty minutes later. I poked at the bell multiple times, jabbing and missing, jabbing and missing, like a cyclops devoid of depth perception.

Not to mention common sense. I was taking a risk just by being there. But there was where I was, standing on the threshold of the "3BR, 2B, spac liv rm w/ det gar!" on Perry Terrace, about to take the grand tour.

If I could just manage to make contact with the damn doorbell and gain access.

Not that I had any intention of relocating to Brooklyn, any more than I was attending Bay Realty's Sunday afternoon open house in order to check out the property on Perry Terrace. I was there to check out the real estate agent, Renée Devine—who happened to be the daughter of the former love of my life.

As I could have predicted, my risk-averse best friend deemed my fact-finding mission a singularly boneheaded idea when I'd mentioned it during our regular morning phone call.

"Renée Devine is going to take one look at you and rip your face clean off," Elinor Ann said.

"That's not going to happen. She won't even recognize me. We met only once, for maybe ten seconds, when she was barely a teenager. Don't forget—I haven't seen her father for twenty years." Twenty-one years, to be precise. Literally half my lifetime. Long enough, one would think, for me to forget all about Ray Devine. Long enough, one would hope, for Ray Devine's daughter to forget all about me. "I figure she'll be so busy extolling the virtues of the spacious living room or the detached garage that I'll be lucky to get five minutes with her." Which was all the time I needed, I calculated, to discover her father's whereabouts.

"Funny; a detached garage would be a drawback in Pennsylvania. Too far to lug the groceries—especially in winter. You city folk can be so backward."

"Oh, please. You hayseeds out there in Kutztown have detached garages all over the place. You just don't call them garages. You call them barns, and you park your tractors in them." I love Elinor Ann, my best friend ever since we were thirteen and sharing a bunk bed at summer camp. We have absolutely nothing in common. Luckily for her.

"And another thing," she said. "Even if Renée Devine doesn't recognize your face, don't you think your name might jog her memory?"

This was a strong possibility. Based on what Ray used to tell me, Renée's mother, Rhea, invoked my name with great frequency in those days. Evidently she was given to hollering, "You're having an affair with Dana Mayo, you bastard!" every time he'd arrive home late from work, which was pretty much every night, all winter long and well into the spring, twenty-one years ago.

But it was a possibility that had already occurred to me, which was why I would be attending Bay Realty's Sunday afternoon open house under an alias and in partial disguise.

"Simone Saint James," I introduced myself, presenting one of the business cards I'd designed on my computer the previous afternoon. They'd turned out great. Renée Devine would never suspect I wasn't a canine behaviorist—unless one of the other prospective buyers showed up with an out-of-control mongrel, or the card somehow got wet and smeared ink-jet toner all over her white cashmere turtleneck.

Renée Devine had turned out great as well, which in my experience isn't always the case with the daughters of handsome men. But Ray's strong features were softer on her, and she'd been lucky enough to inherit his perfect, pearly teeth, and his wavy, sandy brown hair, and—

Oh man, I thought, frozen in place in the hallway. *I'm still hung up on this girl's father—so much so that now* she's *even starting to look good to me.* And I'm straight. Really straight. Elinor Ann had been right all along. No good could come from this mission. I should have stayed home on East Ninth Street with the Sunday *Times.* I'd have finished both the regular and the diagramless puzzles by now. *And* avoided being ambushed by memories of my first love and his perfect, pearly teeth, and his wavy, sandy brown hair.

My own wavy, dark brown hair was stuffed underneath a wool newsboy cap, concealing my most distinguishing feature. Bloodred lipstick, a shade I'd ordinarily dismiss as overly drag queen–esque, turned my mouth into a Pop Art cartoon. Black-framed reading glasses, which I'd recently been forced to purchase in order to distinguish between the sixes and the eights in crossword squares, completed the masquerade. Ray's daughter would never associate this exotic (if I did say so myself) stranger with the dreaded Dana Mayo, besmircher of her father's good name.

———

"So happy you could make it!" Renée smiled, then wrinkled her exquisite nose and rolled her sparkling blue eyes toward the staircase leading to the second floor. "The homeowners have requested that we all remove our shoes before touring the interior. New white carpeting in the bedrooms." She led me to a lineup of footwear in the foyer. Still in a bit of a daze, I managed to tug off my boots and add them to the row.

"Note the sunken living room," she said, indicating the space with a practiced sweep of her right arm. She pointed in the direction of her stocking feet. "And these would be the tongue-and-groove floors I mentioned in the Web listing."

Oh they would, would they now? I thought, suppressing a smirk. I couldn't help myself. Hoity-toity figures of speech unleash the inner snob in me. So do errors in spelling and punctuation. In fact, my inner snob had been having a field day with Renée Devine for the better part of a week, because she hadn't merely covered the specs of the house in her Web listing, but had gone on to describe the neighborhod [sic] she'd been born and raised in as having it's [sic] own unique flavor, with the added bonus of highly rated school's [sic].

A couple emerged from the kitchen with questions about the appliances.

"Mr. and Mrs. Voronokova," Renée introduced them. "From Russia."

"Belarus," the wife corrected, with a look that made it obvious that referring to a Belarusian as a Russian was akin to mistaking a Puerto Rican for a Dominican in my part of town.

"But now we liff Brighton Beach," the husband added. I pegged them as likely claimants to the spike-heeled alligator slingbacks and the slip-on Gucci knockoffs on display in the foyer. Overhead, a robust temper tantrum, accompanied by desperate shushing sounds, explained the Three-Bears-like row of Adidas lying nearby. The pale pink suede Uggs, therefore, must belong to Renée.

After a brief conference about the age of the refrigerator, the Brighton

Beach Belarusians returned to the kitchen, and I took a deep, steadying breath. "You know, Ms. Devine—"

"Please—Renée."

"Renée. It's just—well, I realize 'Devine' is probably an awfully common surname, but—"

She laughed. "There must be a million of us in this borough alone."

Talk about an understatement. I'd hit what seemed like at least that many dead ends searching for her father on the Internet before thinking to search for his offspring instead. It wasn't until I'd googled "Renée" plus "Devine" plus "Bay" plus "Ridge" plus "Brooklyn" that I'd finally happened upon the right picture of the almost-right face. "It's just—I was wondering . . . Well, twenty or so years ago, I was the manager of a little dress shop in SoHo. It was right next door to an art gallery. . . ."

"Prints on Prince! Oh my god! My folks worked there! Ray and Rhea!"

I'd been employed by the gallery as well, but I didn't want her putting two and two together, which explained the bogus career in fashion administration at the boutique next door. "I was sure I noticed a family resemblance. You're a dead ringer for your mother."—*Not,* I silently added.

"Funny, most people think I look just like my dad. He's the one who actually worked in the store; Mom was one of their printmakers. She's still at it, as a matter of fact. Has a gallery up on Fifty-seventh Street showing her work, and she's still teaching lithography over at Queens College."

"Terrific." *And what's Dad up to these days?!!! What what what what what???* I silently added.

She grinned. "You're not going to believe this, but Mom remarried a couple of years back. To a guy named Sam Polster." She paused to let the effect of her words sink in. "I mean, isn't that a scream? Her new name is Rhea Polster!"

I'd figured that out already, and of course I saw the humor in it, but I was much too close to my ultimate goal to offer more than a polite chuckle. Besides, I had become understandably fixated on the word "remarried." "Oh. Uh . . . I'm sorry, but I had no idea. And, uh . . . well, I don't mean to be intrusive, but, uh . . . when did your parents divorce?"

"Oh. Uh . . . they didn't. Dad is, uh . . . no longer with us."

As soon as she spoke the words, I knew I was doomed. Not because Ray was dead—which was undeniably traumatic in its own right—but because of my lifelong inability to handle life's curveballs.

The thing is, I suffer from a supremely embarrassing condition, one that's as uncontrollable as it is unseemly. A condition I would go so far as to call my bête noire. A condition that would certainly cause Renée Devine to declare herself my lifelong enemy from that awful day forward.

I must have turned whiter than the new bedroom carpeting, because she laid a steadying hand on my shoulder. "Simone? Simone? Are you all right? *Simone!*"

For a split second, I thought there was literally such a thing as the Twilight Zone and that I'd crossed over to it, but then I remembered that *I* was Simone and finally managed to snap out of my stupor.

Big mistake.

I burst out laughing.

According to the psychotherapist I once consulted out of utter desperation, reacting to tragedy with a show of hilarity is not as unusual a response as one might imagine. Unfortunately, there's no official name for the syndrome; no way for the sufferer to gasp the words, "I'm a victim of Rabelaisian-Inversion-Disorder, or RID, and I'm in the throes of an attack!" and reap sudden sympathy from formerly outraged bystanders. Instead, one is forced to simply stand there and endure all manner of shocked and withering gazes, all the while convulsed in helpless paroxysms of mirth. To call it mortifying would be a raging understatement. At that moment, all I wanted to do was sink deep down into the living room floorboards and take up permanent residence there, in between the tongues and the grooves.

Renée froze, staring at me with the expected shocked, withering gaze, while I tried to compose myself.

"My god," I finally managed. "I am so, *so* sorry to hearrrr . . . *bwah hah hah hah hah hah!*"

This encounter was *so* not going the way I'd imagined it would while riding the R train.

Meanwhile, Ray Devine was dead, as in No Longer of This Earth. The demigod to whom I'd pledged my undying love day after day, month after month. The archetype to whom I'd compared all my subsequent boyfriends, none of whom had measured up. No one would ever love me the way Ray Devine had loved me, and now he was dead.

And pretty soon I would be, too, judging by the look I was getting from his daughter.

Eventually Mrs. Belarus came to my rescue, bringing a glass of water from the kitchen. I would have kissed her, but I was clenching my jaw too hard to form a pucker. After I'd choked down a couple of swallows, I managed to get myself under control and find my voice.

But now that I'd found it, the challenge lay in what to do with it—a challenge I failed miserably.

"Rhea Polster," I croaked. "That's just about the funniest thing I've ever heard. I mean, what are the odds?"

Renée looked at me as if we'd just arrived at the prom wearing identical gowns.

"Guess it's time to be going," I said, gauging the distance from my spot in the sunken living room to the front door. I estimated it to be, oh, about seven hundred miles or so.

The sound of voices at the top of the stairs signaled that now was the optimal time to flee the premises. Not only would the Adidas family create a diversion, but Renée would be less likely to strangle me in the presence of additional witnesses. With a nod to Mr. and Mrs. Belarus and a tight-lipped smile for my would-be real estate agent, I headed toward the foyer, and freedom.

A young couple, writhing toddler in tow, reached the bottom of the landing just as I was stepping into my second boot.

"They did a fabulous job on those upstairs bedrooms," Mrs. Adidas said. "Aren't you going up there to have a look?"

"No, I—I—I—"

She peered at me more closely. "Ma'am? Are you all right?"

Of course I wasn't all right. Ray Devine was dead. Plus the bitch had called me ma'am.

I didn't respond in words, but she got her answer anyway—in stunning fashion. I bent over and, in one interminable instant, unleashed a torrent of puke, the bulk of which landed directly inside Renée Devine's pale pink suede Uggs.

"Ugh," said the toddler.

CHAPTER TWO

IDOL WORSHIP

It would have been convenient to blame the entire, humiliating incident on my former coworker, but Lark was only partially responsible for my trip to Bay Ridge.

"I'm in love," she'd confided over lunch two Wednesdays ago, the day I'd found myself in Chelsea and decided to drop by the gallery where I used to work—ostensibly to see their latest installation, but really to catch up on gossip.

"I'm happy for you," I told her, although Lark was so ridiculously stunning and youthful and all-around perfect that it was pretty much impossible not to be happy for the girl every second of every day. "Do I know him?"

She blushed, so adorably that the German couple at the adjoining table stopped eating and beamed at her. "It's . . . Sandro."

"Sandro Monte*vecchi*?"

She frowned. "You look upset."

I was upset. Not as upset as I would have been to hear that Lark had fallen head over heels for the Antichrist, but only by the narrowest of margins.

In short, the man was a snake—an unctuous ogler who made me feel like running home to shower if he so much as glanced in my direction. Plus he was much too old for her—*and* a rotten artist, even if he was the gallery's biggest moneymaker. The public seemingly couldn't get enough of his altarpieces designed to mimic the Byzantine style—only his painted panels depicted celebrities, not saints. Naked celebrities, complete with halos.

And that wasn't even the worst of it.

I leaned forward. "Lark, trust me on this. You do *not* want to get involved with a married man."

"Oh, Dana. I know you're right. But—"

But I already knew what she was going to say. "The time you spend with Sandro is the only time you feel genuinely happy. And he tells you how much he worships you a dozen times a day, even if it's only over the phone."

"But—"

"You meet for drinks in some crummy, out-of-the-way bar where there's no possibility of running into anyone he knows, and it feels as though you're sipping champagne at the Waldorf," I continued. "And if you can arrange a couple of extra hours together, it's as luxuriant as a three-day weekend at some cute little B and B in Montauk. Am I right?"

Her pale blue eyes widened. "How do you know all that?"

I just sat there, sipping iced tea while she figured out for herself exactly how I knew all that.

"Oh my god," she finally said. "You had an affair . . . with *Sandro*?"

I would have burst out laughing, or shuddered in horror, but Lark needed guidance, not derision. "Of course I didn't," I told her. "But back when I was your age, I got involved in a . . . similar situation. And I know you don't want to hear me say it, but these things never work out."

"But—"

"I mean it, Lark. They never, ever do. No matter what Sandro might be promising you."

Her eyes welled with tears, and within seconds she was sobbing uncontrollably.

Swell, I thought, handing her my napkin and scrupulously avoiding the outraged glares of the German couple.

"I'm not trying to upset you," I went on, pretending not to hear the impassioned *ach*s coming from the next table. "But I wish someone had told me what I'm telling you now."

Not that it would have made a bit of difference. I would have simply sat there, nodding energetically, all the while thinking, "But you don't understand. This is true love."

Which, no doubt, was exactly what Lark was thinking that very moment as she sat there, nodding energetically.

That was when I realized there wasn't a thing I could say to change her mind. All I could do was pacify her—and brace myself for dozens more conversations identical to this one for the foreseeable future.

She dabbed at her eyes with the napkin, chin quavering. "I swear I never meant for it to happen. But Sandro's so talented. And mature."

Wrong on both counts, I thought to myself.

"He told me he's never met anyone like me."

This year, I thought to myself.

"And then he told me he and his wife haven't gotten along for ages now, and they're going to get a divorce any second, and—"

"Well, then, there's nothing to cry about, is there?" I said, suppressing the urge to lunge across the table and shake her until she came to her senses. "Once Sandro's divorce is final, there'll be nothing to stand in your way."

"I . . . guess not."

"Then don't you think you should wait until that happens before you get any more involved with him?"

"I . . . guess so."

"Lark, I know so. And if Sandro really loves you, he'll think so, too."

She reached across the table and squeezed my hand. "Oh, Dana. I am *so lucky* to have you for a mentor."

God knows it hadn't been my idea. But one morning Lark had materialized behind the front desk at the gallery, and by nightfall she'd managed to convince herself I was mentor material.

"What makes you think so?" I asked her, wondering what had possessed me to invite the new girl out for a drink to celebrate her first day on the job.

"You seem so . . . like—you *know* things."

Boy, is this girl lucky I'm not a guy, I'd thought at the time. Lark was a fine-boned beauty, with enormous, trusting blue eyes and a blond, super-short haircut that would be unflattering on just about anyone alive but only served to accentuate her delicate features. My boss had hired her for the receptionist's job on the spot, before she'd spoken a single word.

"Of course I know things," I replied. "I'm older than you."

Twice as old, in fact, but really it felt like five times that, since I couldn't possibly have ever been as young as Lark Darling.

"But you get to work with clients. And you're a real artist—somebody at work told me you're a painter. And—and I love your necklace. I bet you even have your own apartment, with a lease and everything."

"Well, sure I have my own apartment."

"Where?"

"East Village."

She clapped her hands together in delight. "*See?* You're exactly who I want to be!"

It was no use arguing with her. I'd been drafted.

Although to be honest, I hadn't minded all that much. In fact, I hadn't minded in the least. There's nothing quite so flattering as seeing yourself reflected in the shining eyes of your most ardent fan.

But it was more than that. It was impossible to dislike Lark. She was so eager, and lovely, and solicitous. She spent her idle moments sewing tiny beads onto a black satin clutch bag she was customizing with a leaf pattern, and she left a faint trace of honeysuckle in her wake as she ushered clients in and out of the gallery. In short, she inspired protection.

I ultimately decided that the least I could do for the girl was convince her that Sandro would be a tremendous waste of her time—about fourteen months, if history repeated itself. But before I could make my case, I had a few questions for Ray Devine. If anybody had experience seeing himself reflected in shining eyes, he was the man.

Or, more accurately, he'd been the man.

Rounding the corner of Perry Terrace, I leaned against a mailbox to catch my breath, shaking my head in disbelief. Of all the ways I'd imagined the morning would turn out, this scenario hadn't even made the list.

I descended the steps to the Bay Ridge Avenue station just in time to witness a Manhattan-bound R train disappear into the tunnel.

Thanks a lot, Lark, I thought to myself.

Because of course this entire, humiliating incident wasn't just partially her fault; it was entirely her fault. Ever since that lunch two Wednesdays ago, I hadn't been able to stop thinking about Ray Devine.

Mainly to keep reminding myself that our relationship bore absolutely no similarity to Lark and Sandro's.

Because that just couldn't be true, or it would mean I'd wasted half my life holding out for someone who would love me the way Ray had.

But what if it was true?

I sighed and took a seat on a battered wooden bench at the end of the subway platform. What did it matter now? Ray was gone, and maybe that was all the answer I needed. Maybe it was time to forget about the past and move on with my life. After all, I was a mentor now. I was supposed to be older and wiser. People—well, Lark, anyway—looked up to me.

An elderly woman passed by and gave me such a concerned, pitying look that I had to wonder if she'd borne witness to my meltdown at Renée's open house a half hour earlier, even though I didn't recall seeing her there. "Ma'am?" she said. "Are you all right?"

I nodded and smiled reassuringly. Of course I was all right. But why was half the population of Brooklyn calling me ma'am all of a sudden?

Another train roared into the station and I boarded the rear car, taking a seat across from two girls around Lark's age. The taller one looked like a younger version of myself, with her wavy hair and long, skinny legs clad in tight jeans. She looked unhappy. She probably had an older man of her own, who was currently making her life miserable. I gazed across the aisle at her, hoping to convey my support with a single, comforting glance. I wished I could be her mentor, too, sharing all my hard-won wisdom and experience.

That was when she looked up, met my eyes, and flinched.

I pretended not to notice when she gave her friend a subtle nudge and the two of them rose from their seats and moved to the other end of the car. But it wasn't until the train arrived at my stop and I caught a glimpse of myself in the glass of the subway door that I realized why they'd done it.

The bright red lipstick I'd worn to the open house was smeared halfway across my left cheek. And my fit of hysterical laughter had caused my mascara to migrate down my face in watery black streaks.

"Some mentor you are," I muttered under my breath, skulking toward home with my head down, eyes riveted to the sidewalk.

CHAPTER THREE

GULP

There was only one item on my to-do list upon arriving back home: Swallow the very last Quaalude in New York City. At least, I was pretty sure it was the very last one; the government had discontinued their manufacture decades earlier. Mine was definitely a bootleg. The ROHRER stamped on the tablet was missing its *h*, but at least they'd gotten the number right: 714.

The pill had been a graduation gift from my philosophy professor, Dr. Spatzman, who was known around campus—for good reason—as Space Man.

"I heard you're moving to New York City," he'd said on our last day of class, pressing it into my palm. "You'd better be prepared."

"For what?"

He stroked his goatee and stared into the distance. "There are so many answers to that question."

I'd been saving the Quaalude for ages, to be used in case of only the most dire emergency. I'd reached for it on various occasions, even held it in my hand with a water chaser at the ready, but I'd always returned it to the little enameled box I kept hidden in the back of my underwear drawer. It seemed that nothing the city of New York threw at me—not rats, not transit strikes, not even the Giuliani administration—would ever be catastrophic enough to warrant its ingestion.

But the shock of Ray's demise called for a Quaalude; a pharmaceutical Quaalude, optimally, but where was I supposed to find one of those— the Museum of Banned Substances?

"Drugs won't do you any good," Elinor Ann said, just as I knew she would, during our regular afternoon phone call. "Can't you just have a good cry and get it out of your system?"

"You're forgetting a crucial point. The last time I had a good cry, I was probably teething." I never saw much point in tears. Eventually they stopped flowing, and the source of your anguish was right where you left it—staring you straight in the face.

"Dana, please don't take it. It must be years past its expiration date. You could get sick—or die, even."

"By taking one potentially ineffective pill? I should have known better than to say anything to you. A piano could drop on your head and you'd turn down a Tylenol."

"That's not true. I'd take a Tylenol. Probably. Unless I was dead, which I most likely would be if a piano fell on me, and stop trying to change the subject."

"Okay."

"Oh no. You just took it, didn't you?"

"Uh-huh."

I was a bit surprised when a delicious stupor began to sink in almost immediately. Perhaps emptying the contents of my stomach into Renée Devine's boots had helped speed the process along. Or perhaps undernourishment, lack of sleep, and my stupefaction at her father's passing had combined to create a state of psychosomatic narcosis. In any case, I was soon gliding languorously from room to room, propelled by the strains of Nat King Cole's "Blue Gardenia."

This didn't last long, since I live in a two-room apartment, not counting the bathroom, and the song clocks in at just under three minutes. What now?

My eyes alighted on the *New York Times Magazine* at the foot of my bed. Of course—the crossword. I hadn't had time for it earlier in my haste to get to Bay Ridge, and taking it along for my ride on the R train had been out of the question.

In my opinion, everyone has at least one thing they do exceptionally well, and in my case, it's crossword puzzles. This is more a result of solving them every day—even the humdrum Monday-through-Wednesday run—than innate acumen or a stratospheric IQ. On Sunday mornings, it was my custom to sit myself down and, after the hard news and real estate sections, but before Styles, Arts and Leisure, and the Book Review, devote my undivided attention to filling in the squares—always in pen, ideally without errors, and preferably in under twenty minutes (which sounds impressive, unless one is aware that a Sunday puzzle is really just a Wednesday with a weight problem, and nowhere near as challenging as a Friday or Saturday).

But that day the clues seemed to hover in blurry streaks above the page; threes morphed into eights, and the grid strobed like op art. My reading glasses didn't help at all; a magnifying strength of 175, as it turned out, was no match for a "Rorer" 714. When I filled in 18-Down with SST ("Retired boomer"), only to realize its rightful place was one square to the right, in 19, I tossed my pen in disgust and reclined on the bed. There was nothing to do, I concluded, but ruminate on the late Ray Devine.

I'd begun to nurture a crush on him less than an hour after beginning my illustrious career at Prints on Prince, my first job out of the gate—and the only one I could get—when I arrived in town with my useless BFA in studio art and dearth of experience. He was cute. Really cute. But just unkempt enough to convince you that he never gave his appearance so much as a thought. And when he looked at you, he *looked* at you, and all of a sudden you felt like the wittiest, most desirable woman in downtown Manhattan, if not all five boroughs. Or maybe even the entire state. East Coast. Time zone.

Within a week or two I'd discovered the man was a walking testosterone bomb, one who held universal appeal. The other salesgirl and the gay guy who worked alongside Ray in shipping and framing had been instantly smitten as well. Plus the married (but not to each other) co-owners had issued him a standing invitation to join them in a threesome.

"Caligula himself would turn down that offer," he said after confiding in me one evening when I was stuck in the gallery until its nine p.m. closing. "Man, I hope there's no such thing as hell. I can just see myself arriving there and being ushered to a room with a heart-shaped bed. Bernie and Felicia are lying on it, naked, of course, opening up a tube of K-Y Jelly while Lionel Richie—the *real* Lionel Richie—croons 'Endless Love' in the background."

"Thanks a lot," I said. "Now I'm going to have to squeeze in a lobotomy over the weekend just to permanently delete that image from my mind's eye."

"He sounds dangerous," Elinor Ann said when I called Pennsylvania that night. "And what a thing to tell you about Bernie and Felicia!"

"Are you kidding? That's spectacular dirt. Everyone gossips about their bosses."

"I doubt that. You never hear me gossiping about my boss, do you?"

"That's because he's your father."

Back in those days, Elinor Ann was being groomed to take over the brass factory her family founded three generations earlier. She proved to be a natural.

"What I'm really concerned about is the health of this guy's marriage," she went on. "What's he doing hanging around the store so late? I thought you told me he worked ten to six."

"He was just keeping me company. There's no foot traffic in SoHo at that time of night, unless it's the weekend. You wouldn't believe how boring those last few hours can be."

"Yeah, well, I still think he sounds dangerous."

She was right, and I was stupid. And I stayed stupid for the next five months, while Ray went from keeping me company one or two nights a week to every night I worked late. I stopped bitching about being stuck at my post until closing and happily swapped my early shifts for the other salesgirl's late ones. I stayed stupid while his wife graduated from greeting me with a warm smile, to a disinterested nod, to a wordless glare.

In retrospect, I now realize Rhea declared all-out territorial warfare the afternoon she dropped off a set of lithographs with her daughter in tow. Renée burst through the door with a delighted "Daddy!" while her mother looked on in smug satisfaction. At the time I interpreted Rhea's expression as maternal pride, and chalked up her increasing remoteness to the vagaries of the female menstrual cycle.

None of this was playing well in Kutztown.

"You haven't talked about anything other than Ray Devine for the past half dozen phone calls," Elinor Ann accused. "You're in love with that guy."

"Don't be ridiculous! It's a harmless crush. Believe me, nothing's going to happen. Don't you think I know better than to squander my youth on a married man? And he's old, remember?"

"Oh, right. I keep forgetting. How old?"

"At least forty. Although he could easily pass for ten years younger."

"*Ha!* You *are* in love!"

"What I was *going* to say was that even if he *were* ten years younger, he'd *still* be too old for me, so *ha* yourself."

Then the gallery experienced a post-holiday slump, and Ray got laid off.

"I never thought you'd be the one to go," I told him after I heard the news. "Guess Bernie and Felicia can kiss their threesome goodbye."

"Guess business trumps pleasure. I make more money than anybody else on staff; it makes sense to get rid of me first." He shrugged. "You know, Dana, I'm really going to miss hanging out with you."

"Same here," I replied, wondering why he was staring at me so intently. It seemed I had an uncommon flair for staying stupid.

On his final day, we went out for a drink to celebrate his freedom.

Somewhere in between the fifth and sixth rounds, Ray blurted out that he loved me, that he'd been in love with me for months, only he'd refused to face facts until his wife started leveling a string of unfounded (at the time) accusations at him, but he didn't care about that—or anything, other than our evenings together in the gallery—but now that he'd been laid off, he might as well confess since we were never, ever going to see each other again, because the last thing he'd want to do was screw up my life, which was exactly what would happen if I got involved with the likes of him, which I should absolutely never, ever do under any circumstances.

Then he kissed me.

Next thing I knew, a year had gone by. I'd spent most of it on the phone with Ray Devine.

Yes, the phone. We considered ourselves lucky if we could arrange one afternoon a week together.

But who cared about the remaining hundred-and-sixty-two hours when she was gazing into the eyes of Ray Devine, listening to him tell her how wonderful and funny and talented and clever and beautiful she was?

Poor Lark, I thought to myself. I knew exactly where she was coming from.

And poor me. She wasn't any more likely to take my advice than I'd been at her age. Meaning I'd be hearing about Sandro for months—if not years—to come.

A frantic pounding on the floorboards interrupted my reverie: Vivian, my employer, the proprietress of the vintage clothing boutique on the ground floor. "Not today," I slurred, pulling a pillow over my head.

Today, Vivian insisted with her broom handle, refusing to let up.

I glanced over at my cat, blissfully stretched along the entire length of the radiator in the corner. If the pounding didn't bother Puny, it didn't bother me.

Five minutes later she was still at it. Vivian is a bullmastiff disguised as a petite, blond fairy-tale princess. Dockworkers would quail at her epithets. Oil company executives would shudder at her avarice. Bloods and Crips would advise her to peace out. One day someone will murder her, and the building's tenants will gather in hushed circles and ask one another, "What took them so long?"

Sadly, that day had yet to arrive. Once the bedroom floor stopped shaking, the phone rang. I let the machine pick up.

"Dana, what the fuck. I know you're home. I heard you come in. Answer your phone right now—I have fantastic news! Dana? *Dana!* All right, *fine.*" She slammed down the receiver.

Vivian's fantastic news was going to have to wait. I was still preoccupied with my devastating news.

I'd been the one to finally end it, although it took more attempts than I needed to quit smoking, which was—well, maybe only a million, but it

felt like more. I would march into one seedy, out-of-the-way bar after another and announce we were wasting our lives. I would never break up a
family. I didn't like the person I'd turned into. I wanted to actually sleep
with the man I was sleeping with. Along with assorted other clichés that
the girlfriends of married guys spew the way Mount Kilauea spews lava.

Ray would agree. And then he would lean in and kiss me, and I'd lose
my train of thought for the next couple of months.

I finally determined there was only one way to make a clean break.

"I'm going to pretend you're dead, and you're going to do likewise
with me, and that's the way it's going to have to be."

"Okay," he said.

"Because every time I see you—"

"I know. And you're right." He gave me a long, mournful look and
shrugged on his coat. "I've been saying it all along, Dana. You deserve
better than this—meaning me."

He disappeared through the door, and I slumped on my barstool,
mentally kicking myself for pretending to possess deep reserves of inner
strength, which, of course, I didn't.

And that was it, except for the hang-up calls, which started about a
month later, after a ten-pound weight loss had turned me into a living
Giacometti sculpture and I'd taken the Quaalude in and out of its box
several thousand times. A day.

I became convinced it was Ray on the line when I answered the phone
to silence, then a click, on two consecutive Thursdays, our traditional
seedy-bar, back-to-my-place afternoon. At first, I literally had to sit on my
hands to keep from calling back, even though the prospect of Rhea answering was equal parts likely and terrifying. But after a few months, the
calls became comforting. I'd know Ray was thinking about me, and, in
the only safe way he could, he was looking after me. He became my gold
standard, my exemplar, my invisible protector against bad boyfriends.

And God knows I'd had my share of them: the fashion-forward fop who left my bedsheets reeking of Chanel Égoïste. Or Mr. Frugal, who split dinner tabs right down to the penny. And who could forget the infamous Darryl, who'd presented me with a toaster one dismal Christmas? I might have dated my share of losers over the ensuing years, but with Ray Devine's unspoken opinion to guide me, I hadn't dated any of them for long.

It wasn't much, but it was better than being an adulteress—sort of.

The calls would come in clusters, sometimes as many as four or five a month, only to be followed by an interminable stretch of nothing. But eventually, they'd always start up again. I'd utilized all available technology to uncover the presence on the other end of the line, installing Caller ID (only to read the words "unknown number" on the screen) and dialing *69 ("out of range").

But I'd never really doubted who was calling. Now I had to wonder: Was my conviction nothing more than a case of wishful thinking? If Ray was no longer with us, then who was the mysterious caller who dared not speak his name—or any other words, for that matter?

I'd pondered the question through all nineteen stops on the journey back home. There'd been no other significant relationship dating from the time the phone activity had begun, no creepy stalker-type lurking around my building's front stoop. And even if Rhea had been the one keeping tabs on me, wouldn't she have stopped bothering once Ray stopped breathing?

I jolted upright and swung my feet around to the floor. Ray Devine was dead. I was never going to see him again. Ever.

And I'd needed to see him again. I needed answers. I needed to know if we'd really been in love; if he'd really adored me the way he'd claimed; if what we'd had together was as singular as I'd made it out to be for fully half my life. Because if the answer had turned out to be "no" to any of those questions, it would confirm the pathetic truth: I was unlovable, and therefore destined to lead a solitary existence—one that would be alleviated only by occasional, subpar swains who presented me with kitchen appliances on major holidays.

The phone rang again, and I looked at my watch. Twenty minutes had passed since Vivian's call, an astonishing display of self-control on her part. *What the hell?* I thought. I might as well find out about the fabulous Givenchy suit she'd stumbled upon at Goodwill, or the client who'd just tossed her a set of keys to the family compound in Saint Bart's, or whatever enviable endowment had fallen into her charmed lap this week. I reached for the receiver.

"Hello?"

Click.

Had the Quaalude just caused me to hallucinate the sound of a ringing telephone, or was something potentially paranormal going on?

Whatever the reason, my brain was sufficiently addled to inspire an action that was as brash as it was illogical. I punched in the digits I'd committed to memory twenty-one years ago but never had the nerve to dial. I held my breath while I waited for a voice to come through the line.

"Hello?"

Click.

Now I was the one hanging up. But for good reason.

Ray Devine was alive.

Before I could let the air out of my lungs, the phone jangled again. I grabbed it halfway through the first ring.

"I thought you were dead," I said.

"Why, Dana Mayo, that's just about the silliest thing I've ever heard in all my born days! Have you gone and lost your mind? Good heavens! Whatever would give you that crazy idea?"

In that instant, it became obvious that Quaaludes have a much shorter shelf life than I'd given them credit for.

"Hi, Mom," I sighed.

CHAPTER FOUR

YOU CAN'T MAKE THIS STUFF UP

I was never so relieved to have a mother with a laissez-faire approach to parenting. A more analytical model might have read into my statement and said, "Who's dead? Some *guy*? Some *old* guy? Some old *married* guy? Shame on you! If that's the kind of person you've been running around with, then you'd better pack your things and catch the next flight home, young lady!"

Or perhaps no mother could lay claim to such formidable powers of extrapolation. Even so, I felt a familiar pang of wistfulness for a more nurturing childhood when she happily shifted gears after the most amorphous of explanations:

"Sorry, Mom. Thought you were someone else."

"Well, I should certainly hope so! Now, I wanted to wrap up some loose ends regarding your father's birthday celebration."

What Lucinda Mayo lacked in parenting skills, she made up for in wifely devotion. The party was slated for April 1, and it was only the second week of November.

"Don't you think five months is a little early to—"

"It's his centennial!"

"I think it's more accurately referred to as a centenary." I was fairly sure both terms were equally acceptable, but my brain seemed to be hard-wired for passive aggression when dealing with my mother.

"Fine. Your father's one-hundredth birthday—how's that? Land sakes, you and your twenty-dollar words!"

Land sakes? I silently repeated, rolling my eyes skyward. Ever since she and my father retired down south, my mother's expressions have become increasingly antebellum, even though she's originally from Cherry Hill, New Jersey, and Florida is hardly the heart of Dixie. What would she come out with next? "My stars"? "Saints preserve us"?

"I've been thinking your father might enjoy having all his children in attendance," she went on. "But I thought I'd consult you first."

This was a surprise. Anything—or anyone—associated with either of the first two Mrs. Mayos gave her pause. Despite forty-three years of marriage, she still paced in the kitchen every time "one of your father's sons" gave him a call.

"That's your decision," I said. "I've never even met those guys." I was telling a half-truth about my half brothers—literally. I'd never laid eyes on Jeffrey ("Jeffer," in family parlance), the product of my father's second marriage, who was in his mid-fifties and sold real estate in Southern California. Tom, Jr. ("Tom-Tom"), the offspring from Dad's initial union, was a fine-art dealer who had just celebrated his seventieth birthday, lived in high style on the Upper East Side, and was one of my favorite people in the world—a fact I'd always assumed my mother was better off not knowing.

"Don't you think you'd feel a little strange having them there?" I said. "Especially Tom-Tom. I mean, isn't he two years older than you?"

"Great day in the morning! If that was the sort of thing I spent my time fretting about, I never would have married the Commodore in the first place!"

I declined to point out that fretting about exactly that sort of thing took up more of her time than tennis and Sudoku combined.

"Tell you what," I said. "You call Jeffer, and I'll sound out Tom-Tom."

"Aren't you sweet! You'd do that for me?"

"Why not? His number's been in my address book for decades by now. This is as good a time as any to get acquainted. I'll let you know how it goes in a day or so—tell Dad I say hi."

"I'm sure he says hi back!"

I was sure he did, too, but I couldn't help thinking it would have been nice for him to actually get on the phone and speak the word once in a while, and not just on Christmas and my birthday.

Not that he didn't love me. Of course he did. He'd fed and sheltered me and sent me to camp and college. He'd given my senior prom date the evil eye, handed me a damp towel after I'd returned home drunk and gotten sick in the downstairs powder room, then yelled at me the next morning—even though he was more upset with my having swilled wine from a box than the sin of drinking to excess. ("Rotgut makes the hangover that much worse, kid. Stick to corks.")

My father was pretty much over the whole parenting thing by the time I came along—although to be fair, he did wait to relocate the family headquarters from Westchester County to Florida until the day after I left for college. And having no childhood nest to retreat to turned out to be a blessing after I'd graduated and moved to the Village. I've long held that the best time to tackle New York is at the youngest possible age, when one has nerve and grit and the constitution to survive on an unrelenting diet of instant ramen and chocolate chip cookies from the 99 Cent Store.

"You look good, kid," Dad would tell me on my rare visits from college to the Estates at Waterway Village. "Now, take this," he'd invariably add, pressing Tom-Tom's phone number into my palm. "I expect you and your school friends will be going down to the city once in a while. If anything happens, at least you'll have somebody to call."

"Oh, Dad. Nothing's going to happen."

"Make your old man happy. Keep it in your wallet."

For once—twice if you count the boxed-wine tip—I'd listened to his advice. It turned out to be a wise decision after I found myself imprisoned in the Manhattan detention complex—more commonly known as the Tombs—one ill-fated spring break, when I was a dumb sophomore out on the town with my even dumber boyfriend, George Landis (or George Landis-in-Jail, as my half brother eventually renamed him).

"How could this *happen*?" Tom-Tom shrieked when I called collect from the pay phone in my holding cell. I couldn't tell if he was shrieking in shock or because he was struggling to be heard over what sounded like the wildest party north of Rio de Janeiro.

"My boyfriend bought a dime bag of pot," I whimpered, taking pains to avoid stepping on a junkie in full-scale withdrawal, who was sprawled at my feet doing a masterful impression of bacon frying on a griddle. "We were walking down Saint Mark's Place—"

"Oh, sweetie. I know we've never met, but take some advice from your big brother. You've really got to start dating smarter men. Why didn't he score in Tompkins Square Park like any reasonably intelligent person?"

I couldn't answer the question, but I had a feeling the image I'd been harboring of a stodgy old queen was about to undergo a radical transformation.

"You're in luck," he continued. "One of the best criminal defense attorneys in town is attending my little soirée tonight. He'll get your charges thrown out in no time. We'll be on our way just as soon as he changes."

"Changes?" I echoed, wincing at the word "criminal."

"Clothes, sweetie. It's a costume party. Really, how would it look if Marie Antoinette took the stand for the defense?"

I punched in two digits of Tom-Tom's number before remembering he was in London all week, bidding on Impressionist masterworks for assorted captains of industry. I made a note to call back later, then tried to remember what had been going on before the phone rang.

Of course: Ray Devine was alive.

"Guess Renée saw right through your Simone Saint James act," Elinor Ann said.

"Either that, or she tells everybody he's dead." For all I knew, scores of women had shown up at her open houses to make discreet inquiries about her father. I remembered Ray coming to work one morning, putting his hand in his pocket, and withdrawing a half dozen scraps of paper in bewilderment. They turned out to be phone numbers. A half dozen women from the gallery opening he'd attended the previous evening had slipped them into his pocket when he wasn't looking. He'd laughed about it. I'd stifled a pang of what I refused to acknowledge as jealousy.

Elinor Ann sighed. "You know, Dana, if you'd just thought to call him in the first place, you could have spared yourself an awful lot of trouble."

"To say nothing of sparing Renée's Uggs." I had a discomfiting mental image of her traipsing through the streets of Bay Ridge in her socks that would linger in my mind until Alzheimer's set in.

Thanks a lot, Lark, I thought to myself for at least the hundredth time since that mortifying episode. If she hadn't spurred my quixotic quest for self-enlightenment, Renée's boots—as well as my self-respect—would be intact.

"So, what's your next move?" Elinor Ann wanted to know. "Are you going to call Ray back?"

"Maybe."

"*Maybe?* After all that?"

"Maybe."

The thing was, after all these years, I wanted Ray to get in touch with me—and this time, to remain on the line long enough to speak. The way I viewed it, a salvo had been fired when I'd attempted to make contact. Now it was his turn. As any seventh grader would agree, those were the rules.

But enough time had elapsed since the double hang-ups that I knew the call wouldn't come that afternoon. And since the only thing I'd managed to keep down all day was a superannuated Quaalude, hunger was quickly becoming a more pressing issue than resolving an affair that was even older than the pill in my stomach. I grabbed a jacket and my keys and tossed a treat to Puny.

As soon as I reached the sidewalk, a sharp rapping on the glass of Vivian's storefront made it clear lunch would have to wait.

"Well, it's about fucking time," she said when I walked through the door of Chase, Manhattan, which is what she calls her shop. Chase is Vivian's last name, and even though she receives regular cease-and-desist letters from the similarly named bank, she refuses to heed them. ("I know my rights. As long as that comma's in there, they can go to hell.") She grabbed a formal gown off a rack and thrust it into my arms. "You've got to put this on right now."

"Can't we do it later? I'm starving."

"Are you kidding me? This is a never-worn fifties Balenciaga with sleeves."

I gathered this was a great rarity in the Balenciaga oeuvre, since she pronounced the word *sa-leeves*.

She rummaged underneath her desk and emerged with a digital camera. "I need to get a picture for the Web site. Hit the dressing room."

There was no point in arguing. Vivian's edicts were never subject to debate. Besides, I worked for her. Posing in her latest find came with the job. I'm tall and skinny enough to wear pretty much anything—once the bodice is stuffed to compensate for my triple-A cup size. Vivian was too tiny to serve as her own model; she stood barely five feet tall and wore sizes that ran the gamut from zero to double zero. Walking next to her made me feel like a Clydesdale clomping alongside a gazelle.

"Would you *look* at that beading," she said after I emerged from behind the velvet curtains to strike my pose. "I'll get four for it easy."

"Four thousand?"

"No—four dollars. What do you think?"

Not for the first time, it occurred to me I might be severely undercharging her for my work.

We'd met several years ago when I stopped by the shop for a glass of the free wine she was offering during Grand Opening week. "I live upstairs," I told her. "Directly overhead, as a matter of fact."

"God, I wish you'd move," Vivian said. "I'm already strapped for space in here. I'd love to knock through the ceiling and turn this place into a duplex."

"Uh, I don't think that's going to happen," I replied, a much more polite response than what I'd originally planned to blurt out, which was, "Try it, and I'll turn my living room into a round-the-clock salon for the tap-dancing community." I'd been in my apartment for fifteen years by then; the rent was less than half what my next-door neighbors were paying.

After sizing up my paint-spattered jeans and sweatshirt and obviously dismissing me as a potential client, Vivian immediately swooped down on a young Japanese woman who'd just wandered in, cocooned in fur and clutching an Yves Saint Laurent tote large enough to park a Hummer in.

"I've got absolutely the perfect thing for you!" She seized a sixties baby-doll shift and held it under the startled girl's chin. "It's gamine . . . No, it's naif! Audrey Hepburn by way of Swinging London! And only six twenty-five. It'd be absolutely adorable with these fabulous new-old-stock go-go boots I tracked down on my last buying trip. Now, let's see. . . . You've *got* to have these Lucite earrings. . . ." Without letting go of her customer's elbow, she worked her way through the shop to the rear dressing room, snatching accessories at every turn. The girl trailed after her, nodding energetically and wearing an ardent expression common to religious zealots and winners of large jackpots on *The Price Is Right*. I settled on a couch with my glass of wine, took out a pen, and started doodling on a napkin.

After I'd snuck a second glass of wine and finished my drawing, I called toward the back of the store.

"Uh—see you later, I guess."

"Probably." She gave me a dismissive wave without turning around.

Moments later she was standing at my front door, brandishing the doodle in my face.

"Is this yours?"

Oops, I thought. Stalling for time, I inspected the napkin. I'd drawn the customer, outfitted in full sixties regalia, and bracketed her with commentary in elaborate lettering: *Gamine* over one shoulder, *Naif* over the other. Below her feet, I'd written the word *Sucker*.

I'd only been riffing on Vivian's spiel, but I guess I'd hit a nerve.

"Sorry," I muttered. "Meant to toss that before I left."

"Are you kidding? This is exactly the right tone for my clientele—without the 'Sucker,' obviously. I've been thinking I should take out ads in some of the local freebie papers for a while now. . . . How much would one of these run me?"

I made a few quick calculations, factoring in the twenty or so minutes I'd spent on the drawing, the prospect of dealing with such an abrasive personality on a regular basis, the exorbitant price she was charging for the dress. . . .

"Two fifty a pop," I said, fully expecting her to cut the bid in half.

"Done. I'll need a new one every week. To tell you the truth, I was prepared to pay twice that."

She brushed past me into the apartment while I mentally kicked myself for lowballing the job. *Even so,* I thought, *I've just made a deal that will cover roughly half my monthly expenses. Maybe I could go part-time at the gallery in Chelsea. And—*

Vivian paused in front of a painting propped against the kitchen cabinets. "Is this yours, too?"

"It is."

She was looking at a still life I'd just completed: an experiment in unlearning everything I'd been taught by my art professors. Rather than follow their textbook advice—"start everywhere"—I'd painted the items one by one, finishing the bowl of lemons before moving on to the vase behind it, and so on. Only after each object was completed did I start in on the background, an elaborate floral tablecloth. The end result would have likely resulted in a D-minus back in school, but I'd had fun, and it satisfied me. Its lack of depth and disembodied forms made it look like the work of an untrained hand. And seeing as how the output from my trained hand had failed to make an impression on even a single Manhattan art dealer, I considered it an encouraging development.

"Can you do something like this with, say, shoes?" Vivian said. "I'd love to hang one over my desk in the shop. And maybe you could give me a couple for the dressing rooms—jewelry would be good. Patterned scarves, too. Be sure to put some flowers in the background—chicks love flowers." She paused. "You know, forget the ads for now. I'd rather be selling these paintings. I bet we could get seven fifty for one this size."

"Sounds great," I said, suddenly thrilled I'd stopped into the store for Vivian's cheap chardonnay. *Goodbye, boring gallery job,* I thought, making a mental note to whip down to Pearl Paint first thing in the morning for fresh supplies.

A few days after our initial encounter, I entered Chase, Manhattan, toting the first canvas, an ensemble piece featuring items culled by my new patron: a pair of red patent leather platforms, an animal-print scarf by

Vera, several Bakelite bangles, along with the requested floral accompani-
ment, a spray of forsythia.

"Perfect," Vivian said. "I'll get my hammer."

As it turned out, she didn't need it. A blowsy, middle-aged woman
draped head to toe in flowing white garments entered the shop and let out
a squeal of delight at the sight of my painting. "Fabulous," she declared.

"You've got excellent taste," Vivian informed her. "That's a Hannah."

"Hannah?" the woman said, which was exactly what I'd been about
to say.

"An outsider artist from northern Maine," Vivian explained. "Terribly
reclusive. She lives alone in the cabin she was born in, miles from the
nearest town. It's insanely primitive. The only source of water is a stream
on the property—do you know she's actually never had a hot bath in her
entire life? And she's eighty-two!"

"Unbelievable!" the woman said.

"Scads of dealers have traveled up there to woo her into showing pub-
licly over the last few years. Hannah wouldn't have anything to do with
them," Vivian continued. "But one of my pickers heard about her and
went to pay a visit, and for some reason she took to him—you'll never
believe this, but she served him a stew she'd made from root vegetables
and squirrels she'd trapped in the woods."

"Incredible!" the woman said.

"Oh, you can't make this stuff up. Authenticity can't be faked."

As much as I was enjoying Vivian's performance, I saw a potential
pitfall down the road. "If Hannah's so reclusive, then where did she find
those?" I said, pointing to the patent leather platforms.

"Photographs," Vivian replied. "I send up a new batch every month,
along with some food items she's grown partial to. She's absolutely crazy
about Cool Ranch Doritos."

"Astonishing!" the woman said. "How much?"

"To be honest with you, I hadn't really planned on selling this one. . . . Oh, what the hell. I like your outfit. Comme des Garçons really suits you. How's twelve hundred sound?"

"I'll take it!"

I had to fake a coughing fit to keep from laughing out loud.

"That's fraud!" Elinor Ann said when I called with news of my nascent career.

"That's much too strong a word for it," I parried. "It's . . . creative license. Plenty of artists paint under assumed names."

"Well, sure, but speaking of licenses, it doesn't say 'eighty-two' under 'age' on the one in your wallet. And as far as I know, you've never set foot in the state of Maine, let alone dined on squirrel. And the last time you took a cold bath was about twenty-five years ago, when Cabin Five decided to go skinny-dipping in Lake Wallenpaupack on that overnight camping trip."

"Details."

"This Vivian sounds dangerous," she said.

"Oh, stop. That's what you used to say about Ray Devine."

"*See?* She *is* dangerous!"

"So what was the fantastic news you couldn't wait to tell me?" I asked Vivian after the pictures for the Web site had been taken and I was struggling to free myself from the Balenciaga.

"Hannah sold two paintings yesterday. The opera gloves with the beaded purse and the orchid, and the rhinestone necklace draped over the watermelon backed by the row of hyacinths."

"Really?" Even I'd thought the watermelon might have rendered Hannah just a little *too* eccentric.

Vivian handed me a check. I reached for it, but she wouldn't release her grasp. I tugged for a moment, then finally looked down to discover I couldn't see her hand. Well, most of her hand. It was nearly obliterated by a massive diamond.

"Chad finally proposed!" she squealed. "Last night at La Grenouille!"

With anyone else I knew, such an announcement would constitute a momentous event, but in Vivian's case, engagements occurred more frequently than one-day sales at Macy's. Chad was a hedge fund manager Vivian had been dating for a grand total of five and a half weeks. In fact, he was her third hedge fund manager in as many years, and, improbably, her second Chad.

"That's—wonderful," I finally managed. "Congratulations."

"We haven't set a date, but—"

My stomach growled loudly enough to be audible in Midtown. "Listen, I'm really happy for you," I said, "but if I'm not seated in a restaurant within the next five minutes, I'm going to pass out. How about a late celebratory lunch? On me, of course."

"Are you out of your mind? Didn't you hear me tell you I was at La Grenouille last night? I'm not eating a fucking thing until Tuesday."

"Okay, well—thanks for the check. I'll get started on some new Hannahs in the morning. And congratulations again."

In response, she flashed her ring, fingers waggling. "Six carats!"

CHAPTER FIVE

SPEAK OF THE DEVIL

It was hard to muster much enthusiasm for Vivian's news. Two to three weeks seemed to be the average shelf life of her engagements. Eventually her suitor would commit an act so blasphemous that he'd be banished permanently from her zip code. The last one had been sent packing for the unforgiveable sin of being lowborn.

"What are you, eleventh in line to the throne?" I'd asked at the time. "Didn't you tell me you were from Ypsilanti, Michigan?"

"I am. But *he* claimed to be from Philadelphia's Main Line. Turns out his parents own a pizza joint in Paoli. Which is hardly a pedigree that's going to get my unborn twin daughters into Brearley, is it?"

It won't be long before Chad meets the same fate, I thought, making my way down First Avenue en route to lunch. But before his engagement ring was back in Cartier's display case, she'd find someone new who would not only meet her rigid standards of genealogical and physical perfection, but also have enough purchasing power to corner the market on the world's platinum reserves. Plus he'd enjoy gourmet cooking and bestowing expert, lengthy foot massages in his spare time.

The cliché was true: All the good ones were indeed taken. By Vivian.

Then again, I reminded myself as I made a left onto Seventh Street, she was interested in only the high-net-worth good ones. Therefore, it was still open season on the butcher, the baker, the candlestick maker. . . .

Or whoever drove that Dodge.

Parked in front of a boarded-up brownstone just east of the avenue sat a vintage panel truck that stopped me in my tracks. It had been restored to perfection, with rechromed bumpers and a two-tone paint job of cream and sea-foam green.

Hmm, I thought. *I would happily forgo foot massages and* ragoût de lapin braisé aux chanterelles *for a few spins around town in this baby.*

On the windowless rear sides of the truck, *J. H. Wheeler and Son* was painted in brush script, with three lines of smaller block capitals underneath reading RESTORERS OF FINE HOMES, WOODWORKING AND PLASTER, and MASTER ELECTRICIANS.

Hmm, I thought. *The light switch in my bathroom could really stand to be rewired.* Come to think of it, it was probably a major fire hazard in dire need of immediate professional attention.

This wouldn't be the first time I'd experienced love at first sight—of a vehicle. In college, I'd spent the better part of senior year attempting to determine the identity of the owner of a classic Falcon, parking my own classic, a Chevy inherited from Dad, as near to it as space would allow. Finally, with weeks to go before semester's end, fate intervened in the lot reserved for students.

"So *you're* 'sixty-four Sprint."

"So *you're* 'sixty-seven Camaro."

We spent the remainder of our academic careers with our pants down around our ankles, our cars and futures all but forgotten. We'd relocated to opposite coasts after graduation, but I'd held fast to the belief that automotive compatibility was as valid a basis as any for selecting a mate.

Further investigation was called for. I stepped off the curb to read the year printed on the truck's registration tag: 1948. I looked up at the brownstone, which had been a source of much recent speculation around

the neighborhood. After years of sitting empty, allegedly due to a dis-
puted estate, signs of renovation had begun to appear. Roofers had been
spotted replacing gutters and missing shingles. Mini-Dumpsters filled up
with chunks of rubble and were carted away. The old, cracked window-
panes were now covered with plywood, as was the door, which was se-
cured by a heavy chain and a massive padlock.

But on this day the padlock was clamped firmly shut, and I doubted
that any electrician, master or otherwise, had worked on a Sunday afternoon since the invention of the lightbulb. Therefore, J. H. Wheeler (or
Son) would not be found inside the building. It was time to get some
lunch.

As I came around the rear of the Dodge on my way back to the sidewalk, a loud grunt emerged from the cargo area, followed by snoring that
could have drowned out the Mormon Tabernacle Choir.

Swell, I thought. *J. H. Wheeler (or Son) lives in his truck. And he's got
some pretty serious sinus issues.*

"Well, you did mention that it was an awfully nice truck," Elinor Ann
said. "I'm sure there are worse places to live in New York City. Besides,
that doesn't necessarily mean the guy is homeless. He could just be taking a nap, right?"

"It's possible," I conceded. "But listen to this." I rose from the stoop
where I'd sat to make the call and went to hold the phone up by the
truck's rear doors.

"Oh, that's nothing. You should hear the way Cal shakes the rafters
after a big dinner."

"I've spent the last dozen Thanksgivings at your house, remember?
Not once has your husband's snoring been audible in the guest room. Tell
you what—hang up the phone, go in there right now, and open a window. *This* guy's snoring will be audible in your guest room."

"Honestly, Dana. No wonder you're single. You're the only woman I know who could fall in and out of love with a guy before she even lays eyes on him."

I had to acknowledge there was some uncomfortable truth to my friend's assertion. Maybe I was more like Vivian than I cared to admit, discarding potential partners at the speed of light. Maybe it was time to think for myself and shift my focus from a man's flaws to his attributes.

Just as long as he didn't snore like J. H. Wheeler (or Son). Or have joint custody of children under the age of, say, thirty. Or, most important of all, display any interest whatsoever in the crossword. I was never going to find happiness solving in tandem, calling out from the couch, "Honey, what's a five-letter word for neckwear?" The puzzle was my domain. And of course the word would be "ascot."

Okay, I thought. *That covers the flaws. But what words would appear on my list of attributes?*

Funny. Kind. Devoted. Smart, but not necessarily book smart. Impressive upper-body definition would be a plus, but not a requirement.

It wasn't all that long a list. So why was I still looking, twenty-one years into my search?

I pushed through the swinging doors of Fred and Ethyl's on Avenue A, my usual destination when dining solo. Run by a couple of former anarchists, the place was just a bit larger than a typical handicapped bathroom stall and dominated by a single communal table piled high with tabloid magazines. I took a seat at its corner, grabbed the *National Enquirer*'s annual Stars Without Makeup issue, and waited for Ethyl to come tell me what I'd be having for lunch. There was no menu, and the size of the kitchen severely limited the number of entrées—usually to one.

"Fred's doing a stew with garbanzo beans and chorizo today. Or we've still got some of yesterday's community garden pasta salad. . . . Wait a sec. I remember you. You're the one who picked all the onions out of your lasagna last week. Thought Fred was gonna come out here with a meat cleaver when I brought that plate back to the kitchen. You're gettin' garbanzos, girlie."

I nodded my acquiescence, then checked out my tablemates. At four thirty in the afternoon, the restaurant was practically empty. To my right, a doting Latina mother fed her toddler bites of lemon meringue pie. Directly across from me, an elderly woman in a Grateful Dead T-shirt was engrossed in the November issue of the AARP *Bulletin*.

Something about the back cover caught my eye. I squinted at it for a moment before I realized what I was looking at:

Undeniable evidence that God has an exceedingly warped sense of humor.

"Uh, do you mind if I take a quick glance at your magazine? I'll only be a second," I said.

"Help yourself. But you look a little young to be in the AARP, dear," she replied, sliding it across the table.

It was an ad for an investment firm, divided into three separate photographs. "Healthy," read the type over the first panel, which showed a distance shot of a sandy-haired man, becomingly gray at the temples, jogging lakeside with a chocolate Labrador retriever. "Wealthy," read the second one, which showed a tighter shot of the man pausing on the steps of an ivy-covered brick mansion to remove his mail from the shiny brass box attached to the front door. "Wise," it concluded, with a close-up shot of—who else?—Ray Devine, reading over a financial statement with a satisfied smile. "Why Not Ask Your Adviser About the Leading-Edge Retirement Portfolio Today?" suggested the tagline at the bottom of the page.

This guy was going to haunt me for the rest of my days.

All of a sudden I didn't feel nearly as bad about puking into Renée Devine's boots as I had that morning. Doing so at the communal table might have resulted in a permanent ban from my favorite restaurant. I wasn't sure whether my blood pressure had plummeted or skyrocketed, but either way, it was causing little black spots to hover before my eyes. I blinked hard a couple of times before turning to the third panel for a closer inspection.

He still looked good enough to call into question the long-standing doctors' advice about limiting one's intake of hard liquor and cutting out tobacco. Even in the unlikely event he'd quit both vices the day after our final encounter, there was no evidence that either substance had done any damage. In fact, if Ray's picture were to appear on the cover of a book entitled *Binge-Drink and Chain-Smoke Your Way to a Sizzling Dotage*, some publisher would have a zillion-selling title on his hands. The wrinkles were a little deeper, but they were laugh lines, not frown lines. The pale blue eyes were just as clear and the teeth just as perfect and pearly as they'd been two decades earlier.

In that instant, everything became obvious to me.

Nobody was ever going to eclipse his legacy.

No wonder I was still single.

But what was it about this guy that made him so hard to forget, anyway?

I thought back to my conversation with Lark. As much as it killed me to admit it, Ray's behavior back then hadn't been markedly different from Sandro's now, with the declarations of undying love and the giddy joy he instilled in me whenever he managed to get away for a few extra hours. And now Lark was dutifully following in her mentor's footsteps, living out the same plebeian cliché.

I don't know how long I was staring at the picture, but eventually I looked up and met the expectant gaze of the elderly woman across from me and found my voice—although it sounded nothing like the voice I'd left my apartment with. "Thanks," I squeaked, pushing the magazine toward her, feeling so light-headed that the colors in her tie-dyed shirt were oozing like the goo inside a lava lamp.

"Don't mention it." She lowered her glasses and peered at me. "You know, miss, you don't look so good. Are you all right?"

Of course I wasn't all right. I'd spent half a lifetime glorifying the memory of nothing more than a plebeian cliché. And it had to stop now, before it went on for another two decades.

After choking down enough garbanzo-and-chorizo stew to avert the wrath of Fred, I settled up with Ethyl and headed home. *Home,* I thought: the place where I was destined to live out my days, alone and unloved—until I died and was eaten by my cat—with nothing to comfort me but tattered memories of a man I hadn't spoken to since Mike Tyson was the reigning heavyweight champion of the world.

"Oh, get over yourself," I muttered under my breath as I rounded the corner of Seventh Street. "If there was ever a time to put your Twenty-Men-in-New-York theory to the test, this is it."

I'd long maintained that in a city of eight million, it was only logical to assume there must be twenty men I was capable of falling in love with. Obviously, there was no way of knowing if I'd meet fifteen of them or three of them, but all I had to do was meet one of them.

Which I'd done, of course, but since Ray had been married to Rhea long before my arrival in town, there'd been nothing to say over the ensuing years but, "One down, nineteen to go."

Maybe a drastic change of lifestyle was in order. Maybe rather than merely producing paintings as the reclusive artist Hannah, I should escape to the hinterlands and actually become her—communing with nature, finding peace in solitude, and painting rhinestone brooches to my heart's content, with nothing but the gentle woodland creatures to keep me company.

Whom I would then be forced to slaughter and make into a stew with root vegetables if I didn't want to starve to death.

———

The vintage panel truck was still at the curb as I neared First Avenue. I'd intended to pass it by without a glance, but I couldn't resist taking one last look.

There was a man standing behind it with his back to me, fiddling with the lock on the cargo doors.

Hmm, I thought. *One down, nineteen to go.*

But how to open a dialogue?

I recalled one of my father's favorite aphorisms: Never ask a question you don't already know the answer to.

"Excuse me," I said, "but I was wondering what year—"

The man swung around to face me, and in that instant both my hope and my Twenty-Men-in-New-York theory officially breathed their last. He was a behemoth, with greasy hair slicked back from a low forehead and a snaggle tooth that poked out from below his scraggly mustache. He grinned. The snaggle tooth, as it turned out, was one of the few remaining he could call his own.

"Can I help you, lady?"

"Uh—that's okay. It's just—I was wondering what year your truck was."

"Huh. I dunno. It's pretty old, though."

What a strange response, I thought. *How could the owner of such a magnificent vehicle not know what year—*

There was a nail file in his hand, rather than a set of keys.

"This isn't your truck, is it?" I said, feeling all the hopelessness and frustration of the day coalesce into a ball of fury.

"No, no—it ain't like that at all, lady. I was just—"

"Get the hell out of here!" I shouted, not even thinking about the nail file and how easily it could wind up embedded in one of my ventricles. "I'm calling 911 right now!"

Snaggle-tooth took off toward Avenue A, colliding midblock with a man laden down with shopping bags and heading my way. Apples scattered in all directions as the bags were shaken from his grasp, but instead of re-trieving them, the man dashed down the street in hot pursuit.

About five minutes later, after I'd gathered up all but the most dam-aged fruit, the stranger returned, still panting from the chase.

"Most of these are pretty bruised," I said, fervently hoping I was ad-dressing J. H. Wheeler (or Son), because then he would be indebted to me and have to—well, at least buy me a beer. Because J. H. Wheeler (or Son) was very, very attractive. And tall. And lanky, with aqua blue eyes and lots of thick, dark wavy hair. *God*, I prayed as I handed over the salvaged apples, *please make this guy hate crossword puzzles.*

"No problem," he said. "I owe you one. Actually"—he looked down the street toward Avenue A—"I owe you two."

"Guess he got away, huh?"

"Third time in as many weeks." He inspected the lock on the back of the truck. "Least he didn't do any damage this time around."

"Don't you think we should call the cops anyway?"

"Uh . . ." His eyes darted back to the truck. "That wouldn't be such a hot idea."

Swell, I thought. *Whatever's in that cargo space, it's a pretty safe bet it isn't tools or electrical supplies. It's probably contraband of some kind. Bootleg designer jeans. Or bricks of heroin.* Or illegal aliens, which would at least account for the snoring I'd heard earlier on my way to lunch.

But before I could flee, he smiled at me, causing me to conclude there was probably nothing more illegal in the back of the truck than an over-due library book.

"Forgot to introduce myself," he said, extending his hand. "Hank Wheeler."

"Dana Mayo."

"Listen, Dana—I know I already owe you, but do you think you could do me just one more favor?"

I didn't want to seem overly eager, so I said yes only once.

He looked up and down the street. "Well, the thing is . . . I need somebody to act as a lookout."

Swell, I thought. *The recently defected Cuban national soccer team is in that truck, and they're cooking up a nice big batch of methamphetamine.*

Then again, Hank Wheeler was tall enough for me to wear the highest heels I owned with no fear of towering over him, and he did an awfully nice job of filling out his T-shirt. I'd committed the number of my brother's defense attorney friend to memory all those years ago in the Tombs. What was the use in retaining valuable information if one never got a chance to use it? "Sure."

He dashed up the steps of the brownstone and quickly removed the padlock. "It'll only take a second." He returned to the rear of the truck and flung open its double doors.

The light was so dim back there, all I could make out were two shiny black dots. I didn't realize they were eyes until they blinked at me. I stifled a scream, then waited for my eyes to adjust to the darkness.

Once they had, I gasped. "Oh my god," I said. "That's the biggest dog I've ever seen in my life."

The dog said "Oink," forcing me to stifle another scream.

CHAPTER SIX

A DAY OF RECKONING

"That's Dinner," Hank said.

Swell, I thought. *I have* so *completely misjudged this guy.*

"I mean—that's his name," he clarified. I let out a silent sigh of relief. I'd never been one to turn down a rack of pork ribs, but had I been on a first-name basis with the entrée . . . well, I guess I'd fill up on side dishes.

Hank glanced up and down Seventh Street, which was deserted except for a couple making out on a stoop down by Avenue A. "I've been waiting for the tranquilizers to wear off before I try to get him inside the house."

"The tranquilizers?" Maybe I hadn't misjudged Hank Wheeler after all. Maybe he wasn't about to eat Dinner for dinner, but what would possess a man to administer downers to a pig? Come to think of it, what nefarious activity must this guy have resorted to in order to get his hands on such a large quantity of them? Dinner looked as though he tipped the scales at around two hundred pounds.

"It was the only way to get him into the truck," Hank explained. "Without being seen, that is."

"Without being seen? I would think even the most jaded New Yorker would take note of a pig under the influence."

"I reckon they would have—if they'd seen him."

As curious as I was to find out how Hank had managed to render a pig invisible, I was momentarily struck dumb by his use of the word "reckon." Who did this guy think he was—Brer Rabbit? The men I dated didn't reckon, they theorized. Or they hazarded guesses.

On the other hand, the men I'd been dating of late weren't nearly as attractive as Hank Wheeler. I thought back to my list of attributes. I was looking for smart, but not necessarily book smart. So far, so good.

"After he conked out, I rolled him up in an Oriental rug," he continued. "Got a buddy to help carry him."

Once again alarm bells clanged inside my head. Was I about to get apprehended for aiding and abetting in a pignapping?

"Don't you think a leash would have been easier on your lower lumbar?"

"A whole heck of a lot easier. Problem is, there's a city ordinance against folks keeping pigs—or any other barnyard animals. 'No pets with hooves,' is how they put it."

I hadn't been aware of the law, but it explained the absence of ovines in Central Park's Sheep Meadow.

By now Dinner had caught a whiff of the apples and was clambering to his feet. "Let's get this boy inside," Hank said, handing me a bruised McIntosh. "Tease him with this here apple, but don't let him eat it—and hang on real tight. He's sneaky. After I get the front door open, check to make sure nobody's coming down the street. Then toss it up to me."

I could just picture the headline in tomorrow's *New York Post*: POLICE POP PERPS IN PLOT TO PILFER PORKY. Hank ran up the brownstone's stoop, yanked open the door, and miraculously, I managed to side-arm the apple into his outstretched hand. Dinner scampered up the stoop in hot pursuit. *Not bad for the most nonathletic girl at Camp Arcadia,* I thought. Elinor Ann would have been astonished.

But not nearly as astonished as she became upon hearing I'd ventured into a deserted building with a complete stranger. A complete stranger who was involved in potentially illicit activity with livestock, no less—livestock the rightful ownership of which had yet to be established.

"What were you thinking?" she gasped when I called during the walk home to Ninth Street. "The guy could have been a serial killer!"

"Don't be ridiculous. Serial killers drive beat-up old Pontiacs, not art-fully restored vintage panel trucks."

"Well, that's a load off my mind. Tell me—when did you become such an expert on sociopathic behavior?"

"Oh, stop. You sound like somebody's mother." Not my mother, of course, but somebody's. My mother would have said, "Goodness gracious! A pet pig! That doesn't sound much like a man with a *real* job, dear."

"I still think you should consider yourself lucky, Dana. For all you knew, he could have been luring you into a house of horrors."

"Welcome to my house of horrors," Hank said once Dinner was happily gnawing on his apple in the foyer and the door had been pulled shut. His comment failed to alarm me because the house was indeed horrible. The walls—what was left of them—had been stripped down to their lathing, and the remains of the plaster that had once coated them now blanketed every surface. The central staircase was missing half the risers from its banister, as well as the occasional tread, and wires poked out from as-sorted holes in the baseboard.

But oh, what a house it must have been, and would be again someday. The floorboards were mahogany, and the ceilings were easily eighteen feet high.

"What happened to this place?" I asked, which seemed a more polite question than the one I wanted to pose, which was, "Do you own this entire building and, if so, how much did you pay for it?"

"Rumor is it was a—uh, house of ill repute—for the past couple of decades," he said. "Sure makes sense to me. The upstairs is chopped up into about twenty little bitty rooms. The property wound up getting seized by the city, and they finally got round to auctioning it off a few months back."

"Please don't tell me you managed to pick it up for a dollar."

He laughed. *Nice teeth,* I thought to myself. "Not hardly. Even in this sorry condition it went for—I don't know. Millions, I guess."

"You guess?"

"Oh, it ain't mine."

Briefly I wondered how many years the additional charge of breaking and entering would add to my sentence for pignapping, but then I recalled the words painted on the side of Hank's truck.

His eyes traveled up and down the staircase. "Yeah, this here house here sure is one big project."

Briefly I wondered whether a word nerd could ever hope to find lasting happiness with a man who uttered phrases like "this here house here."

"The owner's some kind of world-famous chef," he explained. "He's based over in Spain, but he's got a deal to open a restaurant on Central Park South next year." He shrugged. "Must be nice. Me, I'm just the contractor."

I was actually relieved to hear him confirm it. The idea that an attractive man—of greater-than-average height who wore no wedding band, flossed regularly, and drove an enviable vehicle—would also turn out to be landed gentry . . . Well, next thing I knew, Dinner would sprout wings and fly around the vestibule. Or my alarm clock would jangle me into disappointed consciousness. "Just the contractor" was perfectly fine. And I was sure that, in time, I would come to find his colloquialisms charming. Especially if he fell in love with me.

"Are you also the pig sitter?"

"Nope, he's all mine. Had the perfect setup for him, too—a first-floor apartment up there on East Twenty-ninth Street. It came with its own little private courtyard." Hank inclined his head toward Dinner. "I put one of them pet flaps in the back door so he could go in and out to his heart's content. I'll tell you, that was one happy pig." The loving expression on his face made me think that Hank Wheeler might well be a modern-day Saint Francis of Assisi—only better, since contractors aren't obliged to take vows of chastity and poverty the way I believe saints are.

"So what caused you two to relocate?"

He grimaced. "Last weekend the landlord went and moved his daughter into the unit right over mine. She looked out the window and—well, here we are. For now, anyways. What with all the work I got to do to get this place livable, that chef won't be leaving Spain anytime soon."

I glanced around the decrepit front hallway, taking in the assorted hazards that could maim or prove fatal to humans, let alone pigs. "Don't you think this environment's a little dangerous for him?"

"Not all of it." He grabbed my hand, causing all the molecules in my body to perform the macarena, then led me to a doorway covered with heavy canvas. "Come see our living quarters." He pulled back the cloth to expose a long corridor, dimly illuminated by a single anemic lightbulb. *This is it,* I thought, rewriting the headline in tomorrow's *Post* to read: ARTIST FED TO PIG IN GRUESOME THRILL KILL.

Then again, I thought, eyeing the bag of apples in Hank's other hand, *Dinner seems to be a vegetarian.* I allowed myself to be ushered down the corridor and into a room that would not have looked out of place on the cover of a decorating magazine showcasing the most over-the-top kitchens in the Northern Hemisphere. I was nearly blinded by the expanse of stainless steel countertops. Hand-painted porcelain tiles and futuristic appliances competed for my attention.

He pointed to a door adjacent to the glass-fronted refrigerator. "The butler's pantry is plenty big enough for my bed and his pallet. The two of us'll be fine in here until I get round to finding us someplace permanent."

What an understatement, I thought. *The entire von Trapp family would be fine in here.* Hank pushed a button, and a massive bamboo panel magically disappeared into the ceiling, revealing a lush, if unkempt, backyard. "I'll bury apples out there for him to dig up after dark, when nobody can see him."

"Bury them? How come?"

"To keep him busy for longer than ten seconds. Watch this." He reached for a felt ball that I surmised had been marketed as a dog toy, pulled an apple from the bag, and inserted it into a hollow pocket in the middle of the ball. He tossed it on the floor. Dinner expertly batted it with his snout until the pocket faced upward, then pounced on it with his front hooves. Out popped the apple.

"Impressive," I said. "You know, I think that was only five seconds."

"I reckon you're right. Pigs are real smart."

And so am I, I thought to myself, *for coming up with a concept as brilliant as my Twenty-Men-in-New-York theory.* Hank Wheeler was living proof of its efficacy. And he smelled great. It wasn't cologne—a man wearing scent had always been a deal breaker for me—but some sort of personal pheromone that made me want to rest my head against his shirt and inhale deeply.

"So tell me, Dana Mayo," he said. "You got a husband I should know about?"

"That depends. You got a wife I should know about?"

"Sure don't. Just my young son here."

"Does that mean Dinner's the 'Son' in 'Hank Wheeler and Son'?"

"Sure does."

What a relief. A pig was the kind of offspring I could handle.

Hank left his position against the countertop and began to approach me. "I'll tell you what, Dana. I sure am glad you happened by today. If you hadn't stopped that guy from breaking into my truck, I don't guess I'd have no tools right about now."

That was quick, I thought to myself. *His colloquialisms are already starting to grow on me.* "Where are you from, anyway?" I asked.

"Las Vegas."

"Las *Vegas*?!" Elinor Ann said as I ascended my building's front steps. "I thought you just told me he was a reckoner." She paused. "Dana, I don't think people reckon in Las Vegas. Now, please don't take this the wrong way, but—I think this Hank Wheeler might be some sort of con man."

"That's what *I* thought! But it turns out he's from just *outside* Las Vegas. He grew up on a farm. His family trained animal acts for the casinos."

"Okay, now I'm sure he's a con man. I'm going to log on to *America's Most Wanted* as soon as I hang up."

Despite my brain's best efforts to create a mental image of a young Hank Wheeler frolicking in the Nevada dust with assorted camels and elephants, I, too, had been overcome with skepticism at the time. Didn't ex-convicts invent revisionist stories about their childhoods while paying their debt to society, to be trotted out to gullible females shortly after parole was granted?

By now he was standing so close, I would have been able to count his eyelashes if I'd felt like it. But I had better things to do. I put those party-pooping, suspicious thoughts right out of my head and asked him if he'd ever met Siegfried and Roy.

"Just Siegfried."

Obviously any form of derisive outburst on my part would have completely ruined the moment, so I bit my lower lip and met his gaze. Dinner stirred from his post near the sink and trotted over. He nosed in between us and planted his hoof on my foot, pinning me to the spot.

Hank leaned in even closer, and I treated myself to another big whiff of pheromones. Man, this guy smelled better than God's breakfast. "What are you doing tomorrow night?" he said.

I suppose he could be telling me the truth about his upbringing, I thought to myself. *Elephants need room to roam.* "Uh . . . nothing . . . I reckon."

There. I'd said it. I'd reckoned. It wasn't such a bad word once one got used to it.

He grinned. I grinned back, which isn't easy to do with two hundred pounds' worth of pig crushing one's instep, coupled with the nagging suspicion that one's potential life partner is selling one a bill of goods. "Then how about you and me go out on a date?"

"I'd like that," I replied, all the while wondering whether I would be able to walk out of there without dragging my mangled foot behind me when the time came to make my grand exit.

"One more thing."

I raised my eyebrows.

"May we kiss?"

"Are you kidding me?!" Eleanor Ann sputtered. "Who does this guy think he is? Please tell me you turned him down."

"You can't be serious," I replied, tossing my keys on the kitchen counter. "Hank Wheeler is irresistible. You would have kissed him, too." I covered the phone to muffle the outburst I knew would follow.

"Calm down," I said. "All we did was get that awkward first-kiss-good-night out of the way early, before tomorrow's date."

"Where's he taking you?"

"No idea."

"So he hasn't decided yet. Tell me—what does he do with that pig while he's out on the town?"

"I'll get back to you on that Tuesday morning."

"Tuesday *morning*?"

"Relax. I'm not planning on sleeping with the guy. But if you feel like sitting by the phone until midnight or so, I'll call you the minute I get home."

"Fair enough."

"Any other questions?"

"Only one. What does Siegfried's buddy plan on doing with that pig when the Spanish chef turns up and asks for the keys to his house?"

"I was just thinking about that. You know that horse paddock behind your barn? It's been years since you've—"

"Oh, no you don't! If you think you're going to turn my property into the Kutztown pig sanctuary—well, then, you are *uninvited* to Thanksgiving dinner this year."

CHAPTER SEVEN

VIVA LAS VEGAS

Three weeks later I was staggering down the rancid corridor connecting the Times Square subway and the Port Authority Bus Terminal, balancing my duffel bag and two dozen Everything bagels and doing my very best not to inhale the urine-scented air. Small billboards lined either side of the passageway, roughly thirty percent of them advertising the investment group behind the Leading-Edge Retirement Portfolio. Images of a Healthy, Wealthy, and Wise Ray Devine greeted me at regular twenty-foot intervals as I made my way to the Bieber bus, bound for Pennsylvania and Thanksgiving dinner at Elinor Ann's. "Don't worry," his expression seemed to convey. "I'm still looking out for you."

I greeted him back with a silent *Ha!* It might have taken two decades, but at last I was free!

Just that morning I'd been awakened by another hang-up call, which had come as no surprise. All the major holidays tended to trigger Ray's solicitousness. *You can stop keeping tabs on me now,* I thought to myself when I passed the next billboard. *My new boyfriend is working out just great.*

And Hank Wheeler *was* my boyfriend—we'd been on seven dates by then.

———

"So, what's wrong with him?" Elinor Ann had asked after each one. "And don't tell me, 'Nothing.'"

"Well . . . I *did* notice he left the top off a felt-tipped pen," I answered the first time. "That dries out the nib. Terribly wasteful."

"Oh, come on."

"Well, what do you want me to say—he flirted with the waitress and got into a road rage incident on the drive back to Ninth Street? I can't help it if he's perfect."

And Hank Wheeler *was* perfect—always calling well in advance of when I expected to hear from him, chauffeuring me anywhere my heart desired in his spectacular truck, and performing astonishing feats of virility from the fourth date on. Under the circumstances, I could live with the occasional dried-out nib.

"I still think you should slow down, Dana. Just because I couldn't find him on *America's Most Wanted*'s Web site doesn't mean he's not on someone's."

"He is—the *New York Times*'s. A few years ago the House and Home section ran a spread about a row house he'd restored. The owner referred to him as the Brownstone Whisperer!"

Elinor Ann sighed. "I know. I saw it online. Just . . . be careful, would you?"

Pushing through the throngs of Thanksgiving Day travelers, I finally reached the gate and took my place at the end of the line. I carefully counted the people ahead of me and noted with relief that there were only thirty-seven of them. This was indeed cause for thanksgiving. I would make it aboard the first Kutztown-bound bus.

In fact, there was more to give thanks for than ease of transit and the perfect boyfriend. The previous afternoon, Vivian had banged on my ceiling with her broom until I went downstairs, where she'd presented me with a check.

"Hannah's got a patron," she announced.

I inspected the piece of paper in my hands. "Uh, I think you put too many zeros on this. I'm positive there were only two paintings left."

"There were. I doubled the prices—should've tripled them, but I'm too damn nice for my own good. Do you remember that fat chick in the Comme des Garçons getup who came in a while back?"

"How could I forget? She was my first customer."

"Well, she's on her way to becoming your only customer. She asked me to call her immediately whenever my picker got back from Maine with more Hannahs. And then she gave me this." Vivian waved a business card long enough for me to make out the words GALERIE NAIFS.

"She's a dealer?" I said.

"'Representing the Finest Examples of American Intuitive and Self-Taught Artists Since 1994,'" she read from the card.

It seemed I had finally arrived—at the outermost fringes of the art world.

And the outermost fringes were exactly where Vivian expected me to stay, judging by the way her fingernails obliterated the dealer's name.

"We'll stick with the fifty-fifty split," she said. "This could be big for us!"

Gee. Thanks a lot, I thought.

Then again, what if Elinor Ann's allegation turned out to be correct? If peddling outsider art of dubious provenance indeed constituted fraud, wouldn't Vivian be the one perpetrating it?

"Gee! Thanks a lot!" I said.

The couple waiting in front of me had been engaged in an argument ever since I'd joined them in the bus line. It had grown so heated, I was beginning to wonder if they were staging some sort of guerrilla performance piece.

"Drop it," he growled.

"Not until I find out who that call came from," she hissed. "Let me see your phone."

"I mean it. Drop it."

"It was your ex, wasn't it?"

After a while all that growling and hissing started to make my temples throb. I leaned forward to peer through the grimy pane in the door leading to the boarding area, but all I could make out were clouds of exhaust.

The gargantuan man who was first in line decided to make himself comfortable on the floor, landing with a loud grunt and setting off a chain reaction. One by one, all but the most germophobic passengers behind him followed suit. I joined them, balancing the bag from Ess-a-Bagel squarely on top of my duffel in order to ensure the greatest possible distance between the food and the dingy linoleum.

It was at that moment Hissing Woman managed to wrest Growling Man's cell phone from his grasp, yanking so hard that her arm ricocheted into my pile of luggage. I lunged for the food bag, but not in time to salvage the topmost bagel. It rolled an impressive fifteen feet or so, finally coming to rest in front of a pair of Converse All Stars worn by an impossibly cute guy at the tail end of the line.

He grinned, picked up the bagel, and pantomimed taking a big bite.

I grinned back, felt myself flush, then quickly lowered my eyes.

That didn't last long. I couldn't resist sneaking in a few more glances.

He had shaggy, dirty-blond hair that looked as if he'd cut it himself, exquisite full lips, and the razor-straight jawline common to underwear models and Olympic gymnasts. I decided he couldn't be much older than his mid-twenties, because he was dressed in the scruffy, post-collegiate uniform of cargo pants and a T-shirt under a T-shirt under a hoodie under a vest under a jacket.

There was just one problem. Every time I allowed myself another furtive peek at Scruffy, he was looking back at me, still grinning and twirling the bagel on his index finger.

This wouldn't do. I was already taken. By the Brownstone Whisperer.

Besides, I was old enough to be—well, maybe just his aunt, but that was bad enough. What the hell was wrong with this guy?

More to the point, what the hell was wrong with me? Now that I'd finally hit the boyfriend jackpot, there was no justifiable reason in the world to be flirting with someone nearly two decades my junior, even if he *did* have beautiful gray-green eyes and impressively large feet.

But was I really flirting? Or simply reacting, in an amused manner, to an incident involving a wayward bagel?

Scruffy mouthed, *Watch this,* turned toward the young mother in line behind him, and managed to deposit the bagel into her baby's diaper bag without either of them noticing. I giggled and gave him a thumbs-up.

Now I was flirting.

I needed a distraction, one that would neatly fill the twenty-or-so minutes between the present and the bus's departure time. Reaching into my bag, I pulled out the *Times* and opened it to the crossword puzzle.

But Scruffy was undeterred. He produced his own copy of the Arts section, flipped over its front page to reveal the grid, took out a pen, and mouthed, *Race you.*

You're on, I mouthed back.

It was one of the easiest puzzles to appear on a Thursday in quite some time, once I'd figured out the theme. In honor of Thanksgiving, the solver was supposed to draw little turkeys in some of the boxes, completing phrases like "Turkey in the Straw" and "Jive Turkey." In well under ten minutes, I laid down my pen and directed my gaze toward the back of the line.

Scruffy's head was still bent over the paper, but he must have felt my eyes on him. He looked up a few seconds later.

Wow, he mouthed when I displayed my completed grid. He held up his own puzzle. From a distance, it appeared to be about half-finished.

Good, I thought. *Not only is he too young for you; he's clearly an inferior solver. Plus you'd have to fight him for the crossword every morning. Now, put your puzzle—along with any absurd fantasies about a May-August romance—away.*

As I was stuffing the newspaper back into my bag, I couldn't resist one final peek in Scruffy's direction. He was still looking my way.

Save me a seat, he mouthed.

This is getting out of hand, I thought, pulling out my phone. Maybe if that big-footed whippersnapper down at the end of the line observed me exchanging endearments with my boyfriend, he'd get the hint and back off. Of course, I had yet to drop any actual hints, but that was beside the point.

It was obvious I'd awakened Hank when he picked up.

"I thought you'd be on the Thruway by now," I said. He'd told me he was going to New Paltz to have dinner with former clients.

"Change of plans. Too much driving. I decided to go help out at that soup kitchen over on the Bowery instead—be heading over there in about an hour."

How could I have been so fickle? Hank Wheeler was a paragon. A selfless, virtuous avatar of decency—who, it bore mentioning, had impressively large feet in his own right.

"That is so incredibly kind of you."

"Well, now, I wouldn't be so sure about that. I got what you might call an ulterior motive. Yesterday somebody tried to get through that padlock on the back of my truck again, this time with a pair of bolt cutters. I got a feeling it's the same guy who—well, I guess you could say he introduced us."

"I guess you could," I agreed, thinking back to Snaggletooth and the scattered apples. "So you're hoping he'll turn up for Thanksgiving at the Mission?"

"I sure am. It's my big chance to set that guy straight."

"I get it—no sweet potatoes for you until you cease and desist."

"Something like that. Although I got a feeling he's going to keep trying, irregardless of what I say."

His words—rather, his word—rendered me temporarily speechless. When it came to pet peeves, "irregardless" was my pick of the litter, even worse than the use of double modifiers such as "more smarter." Not that Hank's flawed vocabulary made him, well, less smarter than me. After all, he was rewiring an entire brownstone, and I couldn't even rewire a lamp. But had I been deluding myself into thinking I'd found the perfect boyfriend?

"You still there?" he said.

"Oh—sorry. I was just, uh, nothing." Under the circumstances, "nothing" seemed a better explanation than "questioning the viability of our relationship."

From the corner of my eye, I could see Scruffy still looking in my direction, which didn't help matters one bit. I started blushing, a condition I was powerless to reverse once the process had begun. Long before I could establish beyond a reasonable doubt that I was speaking with my age-appropriate significant other, I heard the rumble of an engine.

"Looks like my bus is getting ready to board," I told Hank. "See you Saturday night?"

"Can't wait. You know, I miss you already, Dana."

"Me, too." It was true. I did miss Hank Wheeler, regardless of his linguistic shortcomings. Why, just last Sunday I'd sat on the rickety staircase of the brownstone, marveling at the painstaking way he stripped paint—not to mention the exhilarating way his biceps tensed and the endearing way his dark hair flopped into his eyes—and thought how appropriately timed Thanksgiving was this year.

You need to grow up, I told myself. *Step One: no more flirting with youthful strangers. Step Two . . . ibid.*

Soon the driver poked his head around the door, which was temporarily blocked while the gargantuan man staggered to his feet, and surveyed the snaking line.

"I can only take fifty-two of you on this run. But don't worry, folks—we got another coach right behind this one."

I quickly began counting from my position toward the back of the line. Scruffy was number fifty-three: first in line for the second bus. He'd been trying to count, too, but now that the passengers were milling around in preparation to board, it was unlikely he'd come up with an accurate total. He raised his eyebrows, gave me a hopeful look, and shrugged.

I shrugged back, torn between relief and dismay, with dismay coming out on top. *You are a horrendous excuse for a girlfriend,* I told myself, all the while wondering whether Scruffy's eyes were more gray than green or the other way around.

As I reached for the bagel bag, Growling Man's cell phone rang. Unfortunately for him, it was still in Hissing Woman's coat pocket.

"You *shit*!" She brandished the glowing screen at him. "I *knew* it! How many times has she called? Wait—don't answer that. I don't want to know." She ripped her bus ticket into sixteenths, threw the pieces in Growling Man's face, and stalked off.

I scrupulously avoided looking to my right. Instead, I stared straight ahead, all the while wondering two things: what the Bieber bus line's policy was with regard to saving seats, and what the hell was wrong with me.

I finally inched my way through the door and up the stairs to the bus, where I was once again confronted with the sight of the gargantuan man. He was sitting in the front row, across from the driver.

The entire front row. He was occupying both seats.

I let out a sigh of what I told myself was relief and made my way down the aisle.

The last thing I saw before the bus pulled out was Scruffy's face through the grimy windowpane. He was waving goodbye.

CHAPTER EIGHT

AN INCONVENIENT TRUTH

My heart sank when the bus disgorged its passengers and I spotted Cal's pickup idling across the street. Elinor Ann must be busy at home with giblets or yams. I had nothing against her husband—he hit fungoes for the boys and stretched chicken wire over the herb garden and dutifully draped his wet towels on hooks—but trying to conduct a conversation with him was excruciating. Even if I were to enter the truck and say, "What a bus ride! Just after we crossed the bridge into Pennsylvania, it exploded and collapsed into the Delaware river!" Cal would probably respond, "That so?" Or maybe, "'Magine that." Or, if he was feeling particularly loquacious, "Don't that beat all."

Of course, I was partially responsible for the abyss between us, if only by virtue of being city folk—childless city folk, with a peculiar career trajectory and too many pairs of jeans, if that didn't beat all.

Which would be off-putting enough for most any Lebanon County farm boy, but the situation was compounded tenfold by Cal's being a living example of what can happen when rumspringa doesn't turn out the way it's supposed to.

"He's *Amish*?!!!" I'd said when Elinor Ann called after their first date, which had taken place so long ago that we were conversing on phones attached by wires to baseboard jacks.

"He *was* Amish. He grew up Amish. But he hasn't been Amish for the past seven years. I just told you, we met on a building site. His company's tiling and grouting bathrooms, and we got the contract for the grab bars in the tubs."

"He's *Amish*?!!!" I repeated.

"I know. Do you think it's too weird? Back in high school, rumspringa kids used to show up at Saturday night keggers once in a while, but after a year or so they were expected to go back home. They all did."

That was what I'd always heard: Burn up thy youthful abandon; then throw down thy six-pack, sell thy Stingray, and return to the fold. "Here's what worries me," I said. "I think only the most extreme partyer—or motor head—would enjoy it enough to give up his family."

"I'd be worried, too, if it were cars or parties he couldn't live without. But it's music. Cal says he left because he can't imagine a future without Cheap Trick. Or Tom Petty. Or Pink Floyd. Especially Pink Floyd."

"He gave up life as he knew it . . . to join the Kiss Army?"

"It doesn't sound quite like that when he explains it."

I could tell from her tone that she'd already made up her mind, that she was going to live out her days listening to *Dark Side of the Moon* with Calvin Burkholder.

He saw me coming from across the street and gave a half wave. I tossed my bag into the back of the pickup and braced myself for fifteen minutes of stilted silence, broken only by my wooden attempts at jocularity, which would be met with terse grunts.

"Hey, Cal—happy Thanksgiving!"

He immediately burst into tears—deep, hacking sobs that had me looking back to the era of terse grunting with wistful fondness. I fumbled for a tissue, but the best I could come up with was a bagel wrapper, which he accepted with gratitude. No two people have ever been more mortified.

"I'm sorry," he managed to say before burying his face in his hands.

"It's okay. Take your time." *But if you wouldn't mind, please try to wrap it up before the tension sets me off on a laughing jag,* I silently implored him.

I knew from past experience that holidays were tough on Cal, so I could only assume he was grieving the loss of his birth family, who'd been forced to shun him once he'd struck out on his own. Usually he coped with his feelings by going down to the basement and playing Creedence Clearwater Revival records, the songs seeping out from the heating ducts long into the night.

I sat there, missing Creedence Clearwater Revival with every fiber of my being, until he managed a few deep breaths and blotted his nose with the sleeve of his flannel shirt. Cal was a big man, at least six-four, with fair hair and skin that was currently fuchsia with embarrassment. A trio of preteen girls crossed in front of the truck and stopped in their tracks at the sight of him. One of them screamed; then they ran across the street, shrieking and giggling.

"Guess they never seen a lobster drive a truck before," he said, finally managing a wan smile.

"Cal—what is it?" *Get through this,* I commanded myself. *This is your chance to finally bond with your best friend's husband. If you succeed, you will never feel uncomfortable or ill at ease in his presence—or his house—ever again.*

Unless this has something to do with Elinor Ann, in which case you will never feel comfortable or at ease anywhere, ever again.

"It's Elinor Ann."

The fluids in my body stopped circulating.

"I mean—it's not like she's dying or nothing," he continued, thank *god,* "but she's got that—you know—that whatsis—"

That cancer? That brain tumor? Speak, you bastard!

"That algoraphobia. You know—where you don't want to leave the house to go nowhere."

"Ohhh—agoraphobia."

"Yeah—that's it. It's just"—he reached into the Ess-a-Bagel bag for another wrapper and dabbed at his eyes—"I don't know what to do for her. I don't know how to help her." The expression on his face was one of pure love. Under normal circumstances, I might have felt a tremor of jealousy, but now all I could think about was the word "algoraphobia," and whether it would be manifested by a fear of algorithms, or of the former vice president. Meanwhile, what made Cal think Elinor Ann had agoraphobia?

"She sounded just fine last week," I said. "In fact, she was in the car, driving home from the plant after work."

"That's not the problem—I looked it up on the Internet. She can get back and forth to her normal places. But they say over time, the circles get smaller." He sighed. "That's sure what's happening. She's down to the house, the plant, and the grocery store. That ain't even a circle—it's a triangle."

How had I not been aware of this? I thought, trying to analyze the past few months' worth of conversations. Elinor Ann was usually at home. Or at work. But she'd always been usually at home or at work, so why did I feel so guilty all of a sudden?

"And computers sure ain't helping," he went on. "UPS comes just about every week. If Land's End don't sell it, she ain't wearing it. She hasn't been to the mall in I don't know how long."

"So . . . what can I do to help?"

He shrugged and shifted into gear. "I dunno—get her to go somewhere? A square'd be better than a triangle."

She didn't look any different when I walked into the kitchen, which smelled the opposite of mine—all yeasty and cinnamony. Elinor Ann was tall and skinny like me, with a mouth too large for her face—but in a good way, a way that transformed her when she smiled. She wore her dark, straight hair in a cut common to suburban mothers: shorter in the back than the front, giving the impression that the wearer had been caught in a sudden back draft.

"What took you so long?" She beamed and we hugged, and for that moment I felt everything would be fine; tomorrow we'd jump in the car and go off antiquing to Macungie or Moselem Springs, singing along with the oldies station at the top of our lungs.

"You painted the kitchen."

"Cal painted the kitchen." He was a weekend dynamo, invariably involved in a home-improvement project designed to keep the hundred-year-old farmhouse from succumbing to the harsh Pennsylvania winters. The walls of the room were now the color of butter, with cobalt blue trim on the baseboards and glass-paneled cabinets. Not for the first time, I envisioned myself in a similar setting just down Route 737, rustling up breakfast for several hunky farmhands while my photogenic herd of alpacas grazed contentedly on the back forty.

"Nice job," I said. "Hey—you know what would look great in here? Curtains made out of vintage dish towels. Why don't we take a drive over to Adamstown tomorrow and check out the antique malls?"

"Tomorrow? Oh, I don't know about that. . . ."

We were interrupted when her sons thundered through the door in a blur of arms and legs and Phillies sweat gear.

"Hey, Aunt Dana." I bumped fists with her elder son, Angus—named after Angus Young of AC/DC at his father's urging—who had never been much of a hugger. Now, at sixteen, he would sooner swallow saltpeter than embrace his nominal aunt. Next I allowed myself to be crushed by eleven-year-old Eddie—named after Van Halen, but only because Elinor Ann had put her foot down and vetoed Jimi. ("No son of mine is going to bear the name of a dead junkie!")

"Did you bring them, Aunt Dana?" Eddie said.

In response, I lifted the bag of bagels off a kitchen chair, but before I handed it over, inspiration struck.

"You know, we won't be sitting down to dinner for at least a few more hours," I said. "How about we all go for lunch at Willy Joe's? The bagels will keep until tomorrow."

The boys, clearly in favor of my suggestion, turned to their mother. Willy Joe's was a hot dog stand, a local institution in nearby Allentown that all four Burkholders held in the highest regard.

"Oh, I don't think that's necessary," she replied. "Besides, I can't imagine they'd be open on Thanksgiving."

Right then I knew Cal had told me the truth about his wife's condition. Elinor Ann had always regarded bagels as mysterious, ethnic circles of empty calories, permitting only the Everything variety in her kitchen because, as she put it, "I suppose there must be some whole grains in there *some*where." In the past, she would have at least made a call to see if Willy's was open.

The boys reached into the bag, each grabbing bagels with both hands before retreating upstairs. "Save room for turkey!" I called after them.

Elinor Ann laughed. "That bag will be empty by suppertime, and they'll still have room for turkey. Now, which do you feel like doing?" She held up a colander of peas that needed shelling while simultaneously gesturing toward a row of unskinned potatoes on the sideboard.

"Both," I said, reaching for the colander.

I knew better than to bring up Scruffy, but he was still very much on my mind.

"Are you crazy?" Elinor Ann said once I'd raised the issue—a question I'd asked myself several times on the bus ride out, with inconclusive results. "What would possess you to flirt with some college kid?"

"He wasn't *that* young. Maybe mid-twenties."

"You're robbing the cradle!"

"Hardly. Besides, I just told you—nothing happened."

"Yeah, but I have a feeling something *would* have if you'd waited in that bus line another ten minutes." She paused. "You know, it's too bad you didn't get Scruffy's phone number. He sounds like he'd be perfect for your friend at the gallery—you know, the one who's seeing the married guy."

"Lark? No *way!*"

She rolled her eyes. "And this from a woman who claims to have met the perfect boyfriend."

"But—"

Elinor Ann shook her head slowly from side to side. "I don't get it, Dana. You're like some kind of Goldilocks in reverse. Ray Devine was too old. Hank Wheeler—finally—is just right. But along comes this Scruffy person, who sounds much too young for you, and—well, I can only imagine what would happen in New York next week if he'd made it aboard that first Bieber bus." She picked up her turkey baster in a way that spoke volumes and yanked open the oven door.

I had plenty of time to mull over Elinor Ann's words when the hazardous combination of turkey, four different kinds of pie, and Creedence Clearwater Revival kept me up half the night. *Was* I suffering from Reverse Goldilocks Syndrome, allowing inappropriate men to waylay me on the search for Mr. Just Right?

Of course I wasn't. Hadn't I pulled out my cell phone and called Hank the instant Scruffy had veered into overfamiliarity? And I'd call him again tomorrow. And after that, Elinor Ann and I would get in the car and set off for points unknown, and she'd be magically cured of her agoraphobia. Everything would be fine.

Everything had to be fine. Because Elinor Ann had a husband and children and a farmhouse and a brass factory, and if she didn't get better, what would become of all that?

I turned on the light and looked at my watch. Swell—three in the morning. Getting out of bed, I went over to the bureau to inspect the photograph sitting on top of it. It was my favorite picture of the two of us, taken on her wedding day, back when we were twenty-five.

"Boy, you know you're young when you're laughing so hard you can't breathe and you still look cute," Elinor Ann said from over my shoulder, causing me to jump.

"You scared me!"

"I didn't mean to. But I couldn't get to sleep, and I saw your light was on. I was wondering if you needed anything."

"No."

Just for you to be fine, I thought but didn't say.

She picked up the picture and smiled. "Remember how mad that photographer was when we ruined her shot?"

"How could I forget?"

"Tillie Tutweiler," we said in unison.

Elinor Ann hadn't realized it at the time, but she'd hired the bossiest, most thorough wedding photographer in the Lehigh Valley for her big day. We were already running more than an hour late when this particular pose had been staged, and my friend was a nervous wreck.

"Okay, Maid of Honor—I need you standing behind the bride, fastening the something-borrowed pearls around her neck."

Elinor Ann had sighed. "Do we really need to take another picture? There are an awful lot of people waiting downstairs in that chapel."

"Young lady, this is the most important moment of your entire life! You'll be glad you took the time when you get to be my age." Tillie had handed me the strand of pearls, and I'd dutifully shuffled into position.

But just as I'd been about to close the clasp on the necklace, Elinor Ann had let out a faint yet unmistakable grunt of suppressed laughter, and that had been all it took to send the two of us into hysterics.

"Man, was she furious," I said, remembering Tillie's malevolent expression while we stood there howling, frantically dabbing at each other's eyes so our mascara wouldn't run.

"At least it got her to finally put down the camera."

"Until she corralled the bridal party after the ceremony and held up the reception line for forty-five minutes."

"Oh god—don't remind me." Elinor Ann returned the photograph to the bureau and turned to face me. "Dana?"

Uh-oh, I thought, bracing myself for a well-meaning critique of my recent behavior that was bound to be both annoying and accurate. "Yes?"

"I hope you won't take this the wrong way, but . . . well, sometimes I look at that picture and I feel like you're the exact same person now that you were then."

"So, what's wrong with that?"

"Nothing, I guess. As long as you're happy. But don't you want—I don't know—more out of life?"

"Like what?" I said, going into defensive mode so quickly that I completely forgot I was talking to my favorite person on the planet. "A husband and two boys and a mortgage?"

She flinched, and instantly I felt like the biggest asshole in the entire universe. Or the biggest kid, which was apparently what I was destined to be for the rest of my days. "I didn't mean that," I said. "I'm sorry."

"No, I'm sorry." She smiled, shaking her head, and sat down at the foot of the bed. "You'd think I'd know better than to try to give you advice after all these years."

"Yeah, you would, wouldn't you?"

"I just . . . wish you had someone to share your life with, that's all."

"I do. I have you, don't I?"

We both knew I was being manipulative, but I guess it was late enough and the situation was fraught enough that neither of us cared, because it worked. I scooted next to her, and she hugged me and everything was fine—at least until tomorrow.

"Now, you're sure there's nothing I can get you?" she said.

"I'm sure. Although I'd really like a copy of that photograph if you don't know what to get me for Christmas this year."

"Of course." She hugged me again, then got up and waved as she backed out the door.

Way to go, Dana, I thought to myself. *Elinor Ann's the one with the problem, and she's the one counseling you.*

As usual.

But maybe tomorrow I could finally prove to her—and to myself— that I'd made some progress since that picture was taken.

Just before I turned off the light, I looked over at the bureau one last time. What could have caused that happy, hopeful bride to become agoraphobic? Motherhood? Aging? Gluten?

And how in the world was I ever going to fix it?

I sighed and flipped over my pillow, wishing an answer would magically present itself in a dream, but knowing better than to expect one.

I rose early the following morning—the better to hoodwink Elinor Ann into expanding her triangle to a square.

"Ready for Adamstown?" I said when I swung open the kitchen door.

She'd beaten me at the game. Pumpkin seeds covered two large baking sheets, and the countertops were obliterated by an ominous number of Tupperware containers. Cal slouched in front of a mug at the kitchen table, the picture of dejection.

"Guess I'll leave you gals to your hen party," he muttered as he rose to his feet. "The pickup could sure use an oil change."

I helped myself to coffee and took his place at the table. "I thought we were going antiquing," I said. "What's with all the Tupperware?"

"I had an overnight brainstorm," Elinor Ann replied, a little too brightly. "I've got everything I need right here for turkey potpies. We can start on the dough as soon as I get those seeds toasting in the oven—I promised the boys I'd make them weeks ago!"

"But—"

"Potpies'll be a much better dinner than boring old leftovers." She was bustling around like a mad scientist on bennies.

"Well . . . I guess we could always go over there later this afternoon."

I saw her freeze for a moment before responding. "Oh, I really don't think we'll have enough time to drive all the way to Adamstown. Maybe next visit." She turned around to face the counter and began mincing an onion.

All right, I thought. *This is it.* "Then first thing tomorrow morning we're going down to Renningers antique market. You can drop me at the bus stop on your way back home."

The mincing noises stopped, and I watched her shoulders slump. "Well, Dana, the thing is—I don't think I can manage that."

I was determined to play dumb for as long as it took to elicit a confession. "Sure you can. It's—what?—five miles down the road. Not even. You'll be home in time to make lunch for the boys."

"That's not what I meant." She turned to face me, tears streaming down her face. I sat there, feeling like an utter shit for forcing her to confront her deepest fear—until I realized that the onion was most likely responsible for her tears, and the sooner she conquered agoraphobia, the better.

"I mean, I could definitely make it to Renningers," she continued. "But the drive back here from the bus stop?" She shook her head slowly from side to side. "Impossible."

It all came out then: the terror that gripped her every time she backed the car out of the garage, the indefinitely postponed trips to the doctor and the dentist and the post office and the mall.

"I'm fine as long as someone's with me," she explained. "And of course now that Angus can drive, he's always begging to take the wheel. Which has been making things progressively worse since he got his learner's permit. The last time I went someplace on my own was . . . jeez. June. The semiannual plant sale at Home Depot."

"But—wait a sec. I'm confused. You wouldn't have been on your own if we'd gone to Willy Joe's yesterday. There would have been five of us in the car."

"Oh, that. It wasn't the driving I was worried about—for once. It was Cal's triglycerides. The doctor read him the riot act after his physical last week."

The doorbell interrupted us: UPS with a delivery from Land's End, just as Cal had presaged the day before. Elinor Ann slit the box open with a knife at the kitchen table. "I'm pathetic," she said with a sigh, pulling out a half dozen pairs of socks.

"Listen," I said. "I don't know how to handle this any better than you, but it seems to me you're going to have to force yourself into driving alone."

"I *can't*!"

"Can't what?"

We'd had our backs to the door, so neither of us had noticed when the boys entered the kitchen. Now we turned to face dual expressions of fear and concern.

"She can't make her potpie recipe without onions," I explained— rather brilliantly on such short notice, I thought. "But just look at her eyes! She's torturing herself!"

Satisfied, they proceeded to the bread box, removed the remains of last night's pies, and headed toward the door.

"We're Wii bowling," Angus said.

Eddie paused on his way out and returned to the table. "Your potpie'd be just as good without onions, Mom." He hugged Elinor Ann, and I experienced one of those rare moments when I understood why humans propagate their own species.

"Okay, you're on," she said once the boys had raced each other to the top of the stairs, pounding her fist on the table for emphasis. "I can make it back alone from the bus stop tomorrow. I hope."

The door to the master bedroom cracked open when I tiptoed to the bathroom at seven the next morning, but it was Cal who poked his head out.

"Where's Elinor Ann?" I said.

"Shoot, she's been down in the kitchen since—I dunno, before daybreak. Told me the potpie wasn't sitting well, but it's pretty obvious that weren't it."

"She admitted as much yesterday." I told him about our planned excursion to Renningers. "If she can drive herself home—well, at least it's progress."

"I'll say. I sure do appreciate this, Dana."

"It's going to be okay." Briefly I considered giving him a reassuring hug, but we'd never had that kind of relationship. Also, he wasn't wearing a shirt.

"I sure hope you're right."

I sure hope I am, too, I thought, dragging my overnight bag down the stairs, where I almost tripped over Eddie. He was leaning against the balustrade on the bottom step, semicomatose. *"Fiiiinally,"* he groaned when I took a seat by his side.

"What are you doing up?"

"Saying goodbye. Took you long enough to get ready."

"It's my prerogative as a female. We're entitled to take forever."

"No kidding." He paused and glanced toward the kitchen door before saying, "Aunt Dana?"

"Yes?"

"Is Mom . . . okay?"

"What makes you think she isn't?"

"Angus and I were up late playing computer games. Really late. Like, four in the morning. And then right after we turned out the light, I heard her go downstairs."

"Oh, that. It was nothing. She had indigestion from the potpie."

"But she always makes potpies. They never make her sick."

"Well, your dad just told me this one did."

I watched relief replace the apprehension on his face, but only for a moment.

"Aunt Dana?"

"Yes?"

"You'd tell me if my mom was gonna, like, die, right?"

"Is that what you're worried about? Believe me, Eddie—if your mother was sick, I'd be moving into your guest room, *not* taking the 11:14 back to New York City."

Finally Eddie relaxed, hugged me goodbye, and retreated upstairs to sleep off his gaming hangover. I used my sleeve to blot my suddenly moist eyes before joining Elinor Ann in the kitchen.

She was pacing between the stove and the refrigerator, gnawing on a thumbnail and hyperventilating.

"Ready to go?" I said.

In response, she leaned over the sink and threw up.

"God, I wish I could blame the potpie for that," she whimpered, flicking the switch on the disposal.

CHAPTER NINE

THE CAT IN THE HAT COMES BACK

By the time we pulled into Renningers' parking lot, Elinor Ann had run through nearly half a roll of paper towels mopping the sweat from her palms. "Thank god you remembered to bring these," she said, tearing off another sheet. "If my hands had slipped on the steering wheel—"

"But they didn't," I interrupted. "And you didn't crash the car, and we didn't die, and nothing bad's going to happen on your way home, either."

She winced at my mention of her pending solo trip. "I'd really rather not talk about that right now." She parked, and we entered the low building that housed the antique dealers: two narrow aisles of jam-packed booths that connected at one end to a larger structure occupied by a farmers' market. I turned left toward the market, but before I could take a single step, Elinor Ann's hand clamped onto my shoulder.

"Where do you think you're going?"

"The Plain & Fancy Donut Shop, where else?" We always kicked off our visits to Renningers with their Long Johns, éclair-shaped sugar bombs roughly four times the size of a normal doughnut. In the unlikely event I make it to heaven, I expect to see Long Johns sharing space on the buffet table alongside the more traditional fare of manna and ambrosia.

"Don't make me eat anything today," she pleaded. "I'll just barf again on my way home from the bus station."

Her expression was so mournful, all I could do was envelop her in a hug. "It's going to be okay," I said, stroking up and down her spine. I could feel her whole body trembling. Over her shoulder, the sleazy antique firearms dealer whose booth we always took pains to avoid leered at us unabashedly.

"Have a super day . . . ladies," he said, in a tone reminiscent of the late Barry White, after we'd let go of one another and passed by the front of his display case.

"What's with him?" Elinor Ann whispered.

"I think he mistook our exchange for girl-on-girl action."

She rolled her eyes. "No wonder I'd rather stay home."

"Well, you've come this far. Let's find the crazy woman with the four-foot-long braids—she ought to have vintage dish towels."

Elinor Ann picked up eight towels, and I expanded my collection of amateur dog paintings with an astoundingly awful portrait of a German shepherd that appeared to have both eyes on the same side of its head, and then it was time to face the inevitable.

"I'm sure you can manage this," I said.

"I'm glad one of us thinks so."

"Of course I do. Why, I'll bet you could even handle a detour to the convenience store on our way to the bus stop."

She groaned. "I should have known. Your precious *New York Times*."

"Hey—you can't deprive me of my Saturday crossword. I've already been denied my Long John."

She made a show of consulting her watch. "We still have a few minutes. I'm sure that creepy gun dealer would be delighted to provide you with *his* Long John."

"A joke! There's hope!"

"Shut up."

I refused to let Elinor Ann wait with me for the bus to arrive from Reading. "Keep your momentum going," I instructed. "And call me the instant you get home. The bus isn't due for fifteen minutes; I'll still be sitting right here."

She sighed. "I know this is stupid."

"No, it isn't."

"Yes, it is. If I can manage to get back and forth to work every day, you'd think I'd be able to drive the five miles home."

"Well, sure—that's the logical way to look at it. But you're crazy, remember?"

Finally she managed a smile. "I knew I could count on you for moral support."

I gave her a parting squeeze, then stood and waved and prayed—even though I don't usually go in for that sort of thing—until the car was out of sight.

"She has to get better," I beseeched the vaguely face-shaped image embedded in an overhead cloud formation. I'd been praying to sort-of-faces in clouds ever since I was a kid, preferring a visible embodiment of my alleged creator over the amorphous "force of nature" that many agnostics espouse.

"Please let Elinor Ann get home safely," I added. "And while you're at it, maybe you could just . . . cure her?"

I sighed and sat down on the curb. The next few minutes would be harrowing for both of us. Thank Cloud I had the newspaper to pass the time.

I was all the way up to the Metro section, more than enough time for her to cover the distance between Fair Street and the Burkholder homestead, when the bus rounded the corner. What the hell was going on?

Nothing, I answered myself. *She's probably so happy she made it back, she forgot to call. Or one of the boys woke up and distracted her with a breakfast order. Or she stopped to chat with the old lady next door.*

Or she's stranded on the side of the road in a state of coronary arrest.

I reached into the little side pouch of my purse where I always keep my cell phone, but it was empty. With growing anxiety, I rooted through the entire bag, but to no avail. Even though I knew I hadn't put it in my duffel, I checked that next and confirmed the obvious. Had it slipped out onto Elinor Ann's car seat? Had I laid it down while paying for the dog portrait?

I cursed under my breath. Of course I hadn't. I could see the phone in my mind's eye, still attached to its charger, which was plugged into the socket next to the bureau in the Burkholders' guest room.

Which was fine. Elinor Ann was home, and she was fine. She'd taken the first step. And she'd take another step on Monday, just as soon as I convinced her to drive to the post office and send me my damn phone, which I was a *stupid, stupid idiot* for leaving behind.

But there was nothing I could do about that now, so I might as well get on the damn bus and solve the crossword.

Since it was just under a half hour's ride from Kutztown to Wescosville, and since the devious Saturday puzzle often took longer than a Sunday, I always challenged myself to complete it before the doors of the bus opened for the next influx of passengers. For the past several years, I'd achieved my goal even before the bus made the turn off Route 222, but as soon as I opened the Arts section and located the puzzle, I knew today's ride would be a race against time. The byline on top of the grid read "W. W. W. Moody."

To put it succinctly, I was his bitch. This was a man—I was convinced he was a pudgy, middle-aged mathematician—who knew exactly how to phrase his clues to elicit maximum confusion ("Number?" for NOVO-CAINE); who packed his grid with misleading letter patterns (ONTV?

Ohhh—"On TV"); who rarely included a theme to ease the plight of the solver. His diabolic constructions usually appeared on Saturdays, and my finished product would invariably be riddled with corrected squares, the pen marks getting darker and thicker each time a letter was changed, then changed again.

I could hardly wait for the bus to get moving.

I had read nearly half the Across clues before I was sure enough of an answer to ink in three squares: "Bill supporting science education" was definitely NYE, as in "Bill Nye, the Science Guy."

"Catawampus"? "Complects"? "Cassowary"? *Crap!*

"Lola locale," 33-Down, was surely COPA. What a sadist that W. W. W. Moody was. Not only was he causing me to feel like a complete moron, but now Barry Manilow was singing his lungs out inside my cranium.

"Shop securer"? "Saganaki selections"? "Strep source"? *Shit!!*

Eventually the Saganaki selections turned out to be FETAS and the source of the dreaded strep was revealed as a DRSERROR—doctor's error. . . .

Ahhh. "Shop securer" was C CLAMP, and "Catawampus," AWRY. But what the hell was a "rudra veena," and what could its successor possibly be?

SITAR. *Satan!!!*

The hiss of bus brakes served as my two-minute warning. We were about to turn off into the parking lot of the Charcoal, a former restaurant that had forsaken its burgers for buses a few years earlier. I glimpsed its faded, free-standing sign out my window before fixing my gaze on the last empty area of the puzzle, a gaping white hole in the upper-right corner of the grid.

The Acrosses were killing me. The clue for number 8, "Like 19-D," was useless, since 19-Down was TORAH. The answer could be anything, as long as it started with a *B*—I was sure BENEFIT was correct for "Capitalize."

"Charcoal!" the driver announced.

The doors to the bus whooshed open, and passengers began to board. I tuned out everything but the grid while I stared intently at the "Down" clues emanating from 8-Across.

Wait a second. "Capitalize" wasn't BENEFIT; it was MAKE HAY!

The bus lurched into motion, causing my pen to slash a jagged diagonal line through the puzzle before I could complete the fill. "Loan request" . . . Of *course*! CARRY ME. And "Battle line" was IMHIT—I'm hit! And that pesky "Like 19-D," meaning the Torah?

MOSAIC.

Bastard.

Finally I laid down my pen, the smell of burned brain cells flooding my nostrils, and checked my watch. Twenty-five, twenty-six minutes—a mortifying time for a Saturday puzzle, but respectable for a W. W. W. Moody.

"Impressive," said a voice from the aisle seat opposite mine. I glanced up into a pair of gray-green eyes.

Or maybe they were more green than gray.

"Fancy meeting you here," Scruffy said, with just the tiniest hint of a smirk in his tone.

I was momentarily struck dumb by the one-two punch of cuteness and coincidence.

But only momentarily. "This is . . . wow. Unexpected. Hey—sorry you missed that first bus on Thanksgiving."

"So was I." His eyes darted to my completed crossword, which shared the page that day with the theater listings and assorted ads for Broadway shows. "So, how long did it take you?"

"Oh god—forever," I said, before remembering how he'd struggled last Thursday. If it had taken me twenty-five or -six minutes to solve this puzzle, it must have consumed the better part of Scruffy's morning. Declining to share my solving time, I pointed to the *Times* poking out of his backpack. "Have you finished it yet?"

"No. Well, actually"—he pointed toward my newspaper—"I'm him."

I focused on the display ad he seemed to have indicated and immediately became confused.

"You're . . . the Cat in the Hat?"

He laughed and extended his hand, tapping a finger squarely on the puzzle's byline before he offered it to me. "Billy Moody."

Billy. As in William. As in . . .

No. Way.

"You're lying," I said, simultaneously shaking my head and his hand and hoping he wouldn't notice the slight tremor in my grip. "W. W. W. Moody is a frumpy academic with a slide rule and a pocket protector."

"That's not a bad guess. Quite a few constructors are mathematicians. But I'm telling you the truth." He reached into his back pocket for his wallet and extracted his driver's license. "See?"

"This is simply not possible," I said, blinking at it in disbelief. But there was his face, right next to the words, "Moody, William."

And there was his thumb, partially obscuring his date of birth—which was probably for the best.

He grinned. "Believe me now?"

"I . . . guess I have to." *Oh my god,* I thought. *Elinor Ann is going to die when she hears about this.*

"Good. I'm glad that's settled."

Oh my god, I thought. *Elinor Ann.*

"Uh, listen," I said. "I know we've only just met, and I hate to ask, but I have this sort of emergency, and I left my cell phone in Kutztown. . . ."

He pulled his from a shirt pocket. "Of course you can borrow mine. But the least you can do is tell me your name first."

"Oh! Sorry. Dana Mayo."

"Yo! Amanda!"

"Huh?"

"It's your anagrammed name."

God, this guy was a nerd. But so cute. So ridiculously, fatally cute.

"Unless you're prone to making regular guttural noises," he added.

"Excuse me?"

"Then it could be Moan A Day," he explained.

I would ponder the implications of that after I completed my call.

As soon as I heard her voice, I knew Elinor Ann's trip had not gone as planned.

"Where *are* you?" she said.

"Where are *you*?"

She sighed. "Home. Finally."

"How'd you get there?"

She sighed louder. "I walked."

"You *walked*?! Why didn't you ask Cal to come and get you?"

"I tried to call, but he was out in the garage doing—I don't know. Man things. And you know how the boys are on weekends. They could sleep through the Rapture."

"But—"

"I was fine at first," she said. "I turned off Noble Street onto 737, and I was sure I was going to make it. But you know that stretch where the road opens up to two lanes, right before you get onto 222? Well, right then this huge FedEx truck passed me—I swear he almost took the door handle off—and it just—I don't know. Spooked me. Eventually I got out and walked the four miles home, which was almost as bad as driving would have been."

Route 737 was a narrow, twisty death trap with virtually no shoulder and a steady stream of traffic. "You could have been killed!"

"You don't know the half of it. When I was almost to the house, the creepy gun dealer from Renningers pulled over and offered me a lift."

"Oh god. You know, that would be hilarious if you weren't, uh—"

"Crazy. I know."

"So what do we do now?"

"Beats me."

"What'd you tell Cal?"

"That I had a flat. Which I did, once I let the air out of the tire. He and Angus are down there changing it now."

"Damn. You really are crazy."

"I know. Oh, Dana, *why* didn't you answer your phone?"

"I couldn't. It's still in your guest room."

"Ohhhh."

I tried to think of something positive to say, but no reassuring words were forthcoming. I was at a loss to suggest what her next move should be. Elinor Ann had always held psychiatry and its practitioners in low regard, and I couldn't imagine her taking so much as a vitamin, let alone Prozac. And she'd just failed miserably at her attempt to tough it out. "So . . . what now?"

"Stay busy until Monday, then hope I can still drive to work, I guess. I'll have the shipping department send your phone out then." She paused. "Wait a minute. There's something I don't understand. If your phone is upstairs in the guest room, then how are you talking to me?"

I looked over at Billy Moody, who was doing a lousy job of pretending to read the Business section while he eavesdropped on my conversation. "Uh—are you planning to take the boys back to that . . . kennel?" I said to Elinor Ann.

"What kennel?"

"I really do think they're ready for a dog. And that one we saw yesterday was so cute. . . . What was his name again?"

"Whose name?"

"*That's* right," I said. "Scruffy! How could I forget?"

"What Scruffy? What are you talking about? Are you—"

Finally my implication sank in, and she fell silent.

But only momentarily. "You have *got* to be kidding me. He's on the *bus*?"

"I'll say!"

"He lent you his phone, didn't he? You have *got* to call me the instant you get home."

"Fair enough. We'll discuss it then."

"Don't even take off your coat. Dana?"

"Yes?"

"I guess I should thank you."

"For what?"

"For helping me take my mind off my problem. And Dana?"

"Mmm?"

"If you give Scruffy your phone number, you are going straight to hell."

"Okay, then! Talk to you soon!"

Billy Moody was regarding me with a bemused look that seemed to convey, "I know you were just referring to me as a dog named Scruffy" when I snapped the phone closed and handed it back to him. I had an awful suspicion that my face was turning the shade of a stop sign.

"Are you hot?" he said.

Of course not, I silently responded. *I'm always this color. My blood pressure is three thousand over eight hundred and forty.*

"A little," I said instead. "So tell me—were you the kind of kid who peed in your baby sister's cereal, or did you wait until adulthood to become the devil incarnate?"

"Hey—you finished the puzzle."

"Barely. How do you come up with this stuff?"

"I usually start with words containing unusual letter patterns and build from there. Which is a little different from most constructors, who come up with a clue set first."

"A clue set?" God, this kid was adorable, even if he did happen to be a sadist who spewed unintelligible jargon.

"You know—those long clues that appear in most puzzles and have some sort of common bond. Remember the one we both did in the bus station last Thursday?"

Ahh. The turkeys. "I get it."

"I stink at coming up with themes. I'm strictly a grid guy. In fact, that's my email address. Gridmeister . . . at rocketmail, in case you were wondering."

This was the moment I was supposed to turn a hose on our burgeoning flirtation with a pointed comment along the lines of, *My boyfriend uses rocketmail, too!* Instead, I said, "Is that some kind of a hint?"

He smiled. "Maybe you could send me a clue set sometime."

Hmm. Maybe I could.

I counted the letters in an endless array of phrases—none of which could exceed the fifteen-letter width of a daily puzzle—all the way back to Ninth Street. I had just made the serendipitous discovery that both the opening lines "Call me Ishmael" and "Who is John Galt" contained thirteen letters (according to Billy Moody, symmetry was crucial) when the cab pulled up in front of my building.

Vivian yanked open the car door the instant it came to a stop. "What took you so long? Your cat's fine, by the way. I fed him this morning."

"Thanks." *Then again, maybe* Atlas Shrugged *isn't sufficiently well-known to merit inclusion. . . .*

"Dana, are you listening to me?"

"Uh-huh." *Dickens will never work—just think how long it takes Pip to introduce himself in* Great Expectations. . . .

"Then what did I just tell you?"

Wait a minute! A Christmas Carol! *Marley was dead! One, two . . .*

"Dana!"

Thirteen!!!

"Dana!!!"

"Oh. Sorry. What were you saying?"

"I said your damn cat is fine—and *you're welcome*. Oh—and I dropped off a few pieces of costume jewelry when I went up there earlier—mostly Trifari, early sixties."

Not for the first time, I questioned the prudence of giving a spare key to my employer, even if she was the most convenient choice for pet care.

"I was thinking you could work them into a few new Hannahs," she said.

"Sure."

"By Tuesday."

"That's only three days from now!"

"Fine, fine—a week from Tuesday." She cocked her head to get a better look at the dog portrait poking out from the top of my open duffel bag. "That's not one of yours, is it?"

"No."

"Thank god."

I went upstairs and let myself into the apartment, where I was nearly blinded by a glittering mountain of garishness heaped nearly half a foot high on my kitchen table. Puny, intently batting around a faux-pearl earring only slightly smaller than a manhole cover, barely acknowledged my return. After concluding he couldn't possibly fit the thing inside his mouth, let alone swallow it, I dropped my luggage and went to have a closer look at Vivian's haul.

I held up a lucite brooch in the shape of a cicada. Imbedded inside it were actual cicadas. I shuddered and backed away from the table. The jewelry could wait until I unpacked, found space on my bedroom wall for the dog portrait, and googled the phrase "agoraphobia cure."

No sooner had I hung the picture—underneath a painting of a cocker spaniel that appeared to have three legs and next to a mastiff that bore an uncanny resemblance to Ernest Borgnine—when inspiration struck. I removed the German shepherd from the wall, returned to the kitchen, and found the mate to Puny's earring, as well as a gold-and-pearl contraption that could have served as full-frontal body armor but was more likely a necklace. Propping the portrait against the mound of jewelry on the kitchen table, I positioned both pieces on the appropriate areas of the dog.

Perfect.

And I had just the model to pull off the look, right down on Seventh Street.

"I'll call it 'Pearls Before Swine,'" I murmured, reaching for the telephone.

But it rang before I could pick up the receiver.

"Hello?"

Click.

Swell, I thought. *It's not bad enough I've just flirted the entire width of New Jersey, but now Ray Devine checks in the instant I decide to call my boyfriend.* What did he get out of these calls? And did I really want to spend another second of my life wondering?

Maybe it was time to put an end to them and move on.

By the time I'd returned the German shepherd to its position on my bedroom wall, righteous indignation had kicked in. Of course it was time to move on. I'd scrupulously avoided all contact with Ray for two decades, but clearly a more decisive approach was called for. I had a relationship to nurture. Portraits of pigs to paint. A best friend to counsel. Crosswords to construct.

I sat on the bed and punched in Ray's number. I was about to give up after the sixth ring, when his voice came on the line.

"Hello?"

"Why do you keep calling me?" I said. "Don't you think this has gone on long enough?"

"Who is this?"

CHAPTER TEN

A WAKE-UP CALL

"Just kidding," Ray said, effectively saving my life, not to mention my pride and self-esteem. Who would have thought "just kidding" could do all that? "How the hell are you, Dana?"

"I'm all right. And you don't have to tell me how you're doing—I already know you're healthy, wealthy, and wise."

He chuckled. God, it was good to hear his voice. "I'm still breathing—guess one out of three ain't bad. A photographer buddy of mine hooked me up with that ad. God, it's good to hear your voice."

Without even realizing it, I found myself splayed on the bed, eyes half-closed like a nodding junkie, twenty-one and stupid again, squandering my time on someone else's husband.

Only he wasn't Rhea's husband anymore. Renée Devine had told me so at the open house in Bay Ridge.

Then again, she'd also told me Ray was dead. "So, how's your . . . wife?" I'd never quite gotten the hang of saying her name out loud to him.

"Happily married. Not to me, though."

"I'm sorry. When did you split up?"

"Oh, about an hour after the last time I saw you."

I snapped out of my stupor and sat rigid on the bed while he explained what had happened: how Rhea had been convinced of our affair; how she'd followed him to the bar the afternoon I'd broken up with him; how she'd refused to believe it was over, opting instead to decamp to her parents' house in Canarsie, Renée in tow, never to return.

"But—why didn't you *tell* me?"

"You told me not to call you, remember?"

"Yeah, but—"

"Look, Dana. Of course I wanted to tell you. I can't count the number of times I almost picked up the phone over the past twenty years."

"What are you talking about? By my calculation, you've picked up the phone somewhere between four and five hundred times over the past twenty years."

"Now I don't know what you're talking about."

"All those hang-up calls!"

"What hang-up calls?"

I felt a whooshing noise inside my head, which I attributed to the collapse of the castles in the air I'd started building half a lifetime ago. "Are you serious? You really never called me?"

"I really never have."

I stared dumbfounded at my wall of dog portraits while I digested his statement. "Woof! Woof!" they seemed to be saying. "You've scaled new pinnacles of delusion. Woof!"

Ray finally broke the silence. "Here's the thing, Dana. By the time I got home that night, I had to admit you were right. You didn't need to be wasting your time sneaking around with a guy like me. And just because Rhea took off—well, that didn't necessarily turn me into the right guy for you."

I didn't need to hear him explain why. Even back then, I'd never been able to wholeheartedly embrace the fantasy of a father-aged husband and a sister-aged stepdaughter. "But . . . you came out of it okay?"

"I always get by somehow. Listen—whatever you do, don't blame yourself. If my marriage had been any good in the first place, you and I never would have happened."

"I guess you're right."

"I know I am."

I was glad one of us did. Suddenly I realized I'd reverted to my reclining position on the bed. His voice had a sandpapery quality to it, no doubt caused by years of tobacco and alcohol abuse, that had always mesmerized me. That hadn't changed.

But it should have by now. Ray was ancient history. And, as he'd just confirmed, we'd had no contact with each other for more than twenty years. I sat up straight, determined to end the conversation on a friendly—but not *too* friendly—note.

"So, how are you doing?" he said. "Still painting?"

"I am."

"Got a guy?"

"I do."

"He treating you okay?"

"He is."

"Then I'm glad you asked me to pretend you were dead all these years. But it's really great to hear from you."

"You, too."

"Maybe we'll get together one of these days."

"Maybe we will."

"Well, until then . . . take care of yourself, Dana."

"You, too."

I sat there with the telephone in my hand, unsure whether to laugh, cry, or consume high-calorie foods devoid of nutritional value. Before I could return the phone to its cradle, it rang again.

"Did you forget something?" I asked Ray, only it wasn't Ray calling this time. An anguished wail came through the receiver, followed by heartfelt sobbing.

"Hi, Lark," I said with a sigh.

"How did—you know—it was me?" she managed to get out.

Because I was you, I silently responded. *And I'm well aware that there's nothing like a holiday weekend for wreaking havoc on an extramarital affair.* "Were you supposed to be seeing Sandro tonight?" I asked her, triggering a fresh spate of tears.

"I waited all weekend," she sniffed. "I had Lean Cuisine for Thanksgiving dinner. But I didn't even mind, because . . . Oh, Dana, he *promised* he'd get away this afternoon, and that was *hours* ago. He only just now called to cancel."

He was never going to get away, I thought but didn't say. *He's probably eating turkey sandwiches with his in-laws this very second.* "I'm sure he tried," I said. "But—and I know you don't want to hear this—families always take precedence at times like this."

"I know. I'm just so disappointed, that's all."

"I know. But—Lark? I hate to have to say this, but you'd better get used to it. Unless you meet somebody else—"

"Oh, Dana. I *can't.* Besides, Sandro promised to make it up to me. He's taking me out to dinner tomorrow night!"

That was quick, I thought to myself. *She's already figured out a way to let him off the hook.*

"Then you can have your Thanksgiving dinner a few days late," I said, too addled from my conversation with Ray to do anything but humor her. And what would be the point of telling her the truth? I knew from experience she wasn't ready to hear it. "I'm sure Sandro's sorry about this afternoon."

"Oh, he was. He told me he was devastated." She'd stopped crying, and I was determined to keep it that way.

"So . . . do you think you'll be okay for the rest of the evening?"

"I guess. . . . I have to pick out my outfit for tomorrow's dinner. Oh—that reminds me. The gallery's holiday party is the Friday after next, and I'm allowed to bring a Plus One. I was hoping you'd go with me."

"I don't know, Lark." It had been quite a while since I'd worked there.

"Please, Dana?"

Then again, the gallery threw a hell of a party. During the years I'd attended, I'd been consistently impressed by the sheer volume of interesting, attractive people—well, men—in attendance.

That was when I had an idea. "Is Sandro going?"

"Yes, but he has to bring his—you know. *Her.*"

Perfect, I thought. *If Sandro is there with his wife, then I'm going to make sure Sandro's girlfriend is the belle of the ball.* "You know, I'd love to be your Plus One, but I don't have anything to wear."

"Oh, I know. Me, neither."

Good. She'd taken the bait. "You really ought to check out the vintage clothing shop downstairs from my apartment. The owner just got in a slew of fifties cocktail dresses." Including an electric-blue satin Jean Desses number that would keep the spotlight fixed firmly on Lark all evening.

"Isn't that store kind of expensive?"

"I'm sure Vivian would give you a discount."

"Do you really think so?"

"I do." *Especially if I throw in a Hannah to sweeten the deal.* "Why don't we meet there next Tuesday during your lunch break?"

She didn't answer.

"Lark?"

"Oh, I'm sorry, Dana. Sandro just texted me from his bathroom to tell me he misses me!"

"Then I guess you want to text him back," I said, rolling my eyes. "I'll see you at the shop, okay?"

Dead silence. I could picture her face, illuminated by the glow of her cell phone, as she composed a heartfelt response that Sandro would barely have time to glance at.

Yeesh, I thought after hanging up. *Young girls can be so gullible.*

And so could grown women. I winced, thinking about how Ray's hang-up calls had been such a comfort to me over the years.

But if he wasn't the one calling, who was?

On a hunch, I punched in the first nine digits of my number, but instead of the final digit of three, I pressed two. A screeching noise on the other end of the line told me I'd reached someone's fax machine. I tried again, this time changing the three to a four.

"Lichi Garden. May I take your order?"

I sighed and returned the handset to its cradle. Maybe those hang-up calls hadn't been for me after all. Maybe they'd been for General Tso.

At least one thing was clear: None of them had come from Ray Devine.

"He has to be lying," Elinor Ann said, once she'd castigated me for the Billy Moody bus peccadillo, which I'd insisted was no such thing, then listened in gasping amazement after I changed the subject and shared the details of my conversation with Ray. "He had to be the one making those calls."

"He sounded pretty truthful to me," I said, once I'd chastised her for not discussing her agoraphobia with Cal, which she'd insisted she'd take care of any second, then elicited a promise to call after she arrived safely at work on Monday morning.

"Of course Ray sounded truthful. He's an accomplished liar. Look how long he was able to convince Rhea nothing was going on between the two of you."

"That's just it. He didn't convince her. She followed him, remember?"

"I guess." She hesitated. "Dana, you're not going to do anything . . . stupid, are you?"

I'd already given the matter some serious consideration. On the one hand, meeting Ray in person could provide some form of closure. And it didn't seem nearly as risky as it once might have been. No matter how robust he might appear on a billboard, Ray Devine was still in his sixties, and no amount of Photoshopping could change that fact.

On the other hand, he hadn't sounded all that enthusiastic about getting together. Why would he? Two decades had elapsed, and according to him, no time had been spent dialing my telephone number during either of them.

I sighed. "We didn't make any definite plans."

"Well, that's a relief. There's just one thing I can't figure out. If Ray wasn't the one making those calls, who was?"

"I just told you—people trying to order in Chinese."

"Oh, come on. That many people couldn't possibly be that clumsy. You're going to have to come up with a better explanation than that."

I pondered the question on the way to Hank's that evening, mentally running through a list of the men I'd dated after breaking it off with Ray. Could it have been the actor?

Too narcissistic.

The bartender?

Too easily distracted.

The copywriter?

Too—

Hmm. Actually, quite a contender.

My half brother had warned me about his type—adver-groupies, he called them—years earlier. "They're obsessed with the golden age of Madison Avenue in all its three-martini glory," Tom-Tom explained. "Dad is like a messiah to them. If one of your dates ever asks if your father's the 'Mayo' in Mayo, Masters, and Moore, do yourself a favor. Lie to him."

I remembered wishing I'd heeded his advice when Bert, the copywriter, asked that very question on our first date.

"Oh my god," he said. " 'Shaving's for Sissies'! 'The Lady Will Have a Pabst'! 'You Won't Believe Your Thighs'!"

I winced a little at his recitation of the last slogan, which had always struck me as an awfully sexist way to sell panty hose, even if it had sold quite a few pairs of them. "Yeah, those are all Dad's."

"His agency did the launch for California Airways, right?"

Speaking of sexist. "I was pretty young at the time." Six, if memory served. All I could recall was that the stewardesses were called Cali Girls, and they were all blond, and they wore bright yellow micro-minidresses, and my mother seemed to have some kind of grudge against them.

"I studied that campaign at Pratt! 'The Right Way to the Left Coast'!"

"Well, it was, until a brunette sued them for illegal hiring practices," I said, suddenly remembering how much I'd always disliked the name Bert. The airline had managed to survive hair integration, but not the oil crisis of the mid-seventies. It folded shortly thereafter.

Bert managed to survive four more dates, at which point his incessant references to advertising royalty and repeated suggestions to take a three-day jaunt down to my parents' in Florida sufficiently creeped me out. I'd only been seeing him to get over Ray, anyway. Which was bad, but not as bad as pursuing someone because you had a crush on her father.

Now I wondered: Could Bert Sugarman really be the mystery caller? It seemed even less likely than my Lichi Garden theory.

But he *had* gotten in touch a few years after I dumped him, "just to see how I was doing." Was he still wondering?

If so, it would be a bigger letdown than discovering your parents were Santa Claus.

Even though I was carrying only a small purse, my baggage threatened to derail my reunion with Hank. He was waiting for me on the brownstone's stoop, sipping from a can of beer, when I approached.

"Want one?" he said, tilting his head toward the six-pack by his side.

"The lady will have a Pabst."

"Huh?"

Stop it! I screamed at myself inside my head.

"Never mind." I reached the top step, put my arms around him, and breathed in his wonderful Hank smell, telling myself that everything was going to be just fine.

"You sure are a sight for sore eyes," he said, leaning in to kiss me.

Hmm, I thought, kissing him back. *Sight for sore eyes . . . Ah. Too bad. Sixteen letters . . .*

Stop it!!

"So, what'd you do all weekend?" I asked him.

"Been workin' like a mule, that's what. I must've hauled half a ton of drywall up to the second floor yesterday." He turned to meet my eyes. "How 'bout you? Everything okay?"

"Why wouldn't it be?"

"Called you a couple times today. The cell phone went right to voice mail. Then when I tried your apartment, the line was busy. Thought there might be some kind of problem."

"Not at all." Unless of course, flirting with barely post-collegiate boys and reliving one's past with her elderly ex, rather than focusing on one's age-appropriate boyfriend, constituted a problem. "I accidentally left my cell at Elinor Ann's," I explained, reaching for a beer. All of a sudden I was parched.

I awoke the following morning to the sound of heavy breathing. Dinner was staring at me intently, his head resting on Hank's vacated side of the bed. He was unbearably cute, as long as I inhaled shallowly through my mouth. His breath smelled like month-old salad.

"Hold that pose," I said, groping for my bag on the nightstand. I extracted my camera and took a close-up. It came out a little dark, but would be fine for my purposes. "Do you think you could give me a profile?"

He obliged by trotting to the window, resting his hooves on the low sill, and looking skyward—a porcine Joan of Arc. A single manhole-sized earring and a few strands of faux pearls would be all I needed to create a breakthrough Hannah. "That's going to turn out great," I told him.

In fact, everything looked like it was going to turn out great. After I'd doused my jitters with beer, Ray, Billy, and Bert, the copywriter, had retreated to the back burner of my mind, and I was finally able to focus on Hank, who looked particularly desirable that evening. A hint of five o'clock shadow had made his eyes appear bluer than usual, and all that drywall hauling had his biceps straining the sleeves of his T-shirt. I'd scooted closer to him on the stoop, but before I could slip my arm around his waist, he stood and offered his hand.

"So, how 'bout I order in some food for us?" he said. "What sounds good to you?"

I wasn't sure about a main course, but I could think of an appetizer that would really hit the spot. "Can we discuss that in, say, forty-five minutes?"

He grinned. "I reckon I could manage to hold out." Then he pulled me to my feet and led me inside, down the long hallway and into the little room off the kitchen. We never did get around to ordering in.

Now I was hungry enough to browse through Dinner's slop bucket. "Where's your dad?" I asked him, which apparently sounds exactly like "How about an apple?" to a pig, because he tore through the door and into the kitchen. I pulled on my clothes and followed him, but there was no sign of Hank.

I opened the canvas flap leading to the front hallway and set off to find him. *It's funny,* I thought, wandering through the downstairs rooms. *The place doesn't look much different, and I've been coming here for nearly a month.*

But hadn't Hank told me he'd hauled yesterday's drywall delivery up to the second floor? Maybe that was where the metamorphosis was taking place. I went up the stairs and poked my head inside the first doorway I came to.

Surrounded by tools and an electric switch plate, he was leaning against the far wall of the room, engrossed in a volume entitled . . .

The Time-Life Big Book of Easy Household Repairs?!!

He looked up, met my gaze, and slammed the book shut in the manner of a sixth grader caught perusing his mother's copy of the *Kama Sutra*.

"What's that?" I asked, even though I knew perfectly well what it was: the kind of manual a suburban father might refer to in the event of a recalcitrant dimmer switch. I also knew what it wasn't: a volume that belonged in the hands of a master electrician. Master electricians were supposed to be capable of rewiring the ceiling of Grand Central Station on expertise alone. With one hand tied behind their backs. Blindfolded.

"What—this?" Hank said.

"Is that what I think it is?"

"Aw, heck, this here book's the greatest. The wiring system in this place is so out of date, I needed an old diagram to get to the bottom of the problem." He opened the volume to reveal a drawing so basic that the plate screws had little arrows pointing to them with the words "plate screw" printed at the other end.

"I guess. . . ."

He rose to his feet and put his arms around me. "Forgot to say good morning." I kissed him, and he kissed me back; after a few minutes, I managed to lose sufficient interest in the home repair manual to relegate it to the file cabinet in my mind earmarked for nagging doubts. There it took up residence with folders labeled MYSTERIOUS HANG-UP CALLS; PROPRIETY OF FLIRTING WITH YOUTHFUL CROSSWORD CONSTRUCTORS; LEGALITY OF POSING AS AN OCTOGENARIAN PAINTER FROM MAINE, and others far too numerous to mention.

"Told you he was a con man," Elinor Ann said, once I'd arrived home from a late brunch with Hank at Fred and Ethyl's and told her what I'd seen.

"Well, it's *possible* he needed to refer to a vintage diagram," I replied, in a tone so dubious, a toddler would have questioned my sincerity.

"Tell you what. Cal's pretty handy—let me ask him if he'd ever have to consult a book like that to replace a light switch." She covered the phone while she called down to the basement, where he was no doubt rebuilding a carburetor or repairing wrought iron with a blowtorch.

"What's he saying?" I asked after a few seconds.

"Nothing—yet. He's laughing too hard to answer the question. Dana? I hate to ask you this, but . . . are you absolutely certain Hank Wheeler is who he says he is?"

I sighed and flopped on the only corner of my bed not covered with sections of the Sunday *Times*. "I'm not sure about anything anymore, but I hope he is. Especially after last night. And I felt so comfortable at brunch just now, and he's always so attentive, and—"

"Dana, can you hang on a sec? Just while I get Eddie some glue for a school project."

"Sure." I reached for the magazine to see who'd constructed this week's puzzle—not Billy Moody—then turned to the Styles section. An article about the resurgence of bourbon on the first page . . . animal-print bracelets on three . . . Christmas windows in Midtown . . . a vast slew of people younger than me getting married or engaged . . .

"Okay, I'm back!" Elinor Ann announced.

I didn't respond. I'd become transfixed by a photograph of two men. They'd exchanged vows at a ceremony in Great Neck the previous weekend.

"Dana?"

The groom on the right was Bert Sugarman.

I was never, ever going to unearth the identity of my mystery caller.

CHAPTER ELEVEN

THERE GOES THE NEIGHBORHOOD

"Oh my god." Vivian was pacing back and forth in front of the portrait I'd just brought down to the shop—the first Hannah to feature a live subject.

"Oh my *god*." I couldn't tell if she was horrified or struck nearly dumb by genius. Her expression was inscrutable, much like Dinner's in the painting.

"Oh. My. God." Finally she turned to face me. "We are going to make *so much fucking money!*"

As happy as I was to hear it, I was a little annoyed by her use of the word "we." I was the one doing all the work—especially now that the blowsy woman with the Galerie Naifs business card was doing all the buying. If I could just learn her identity, I could pose as a dealer based in Maine. . . .

"How many more do you think you can bang out by the weekend?" Vivian wanted to know. "If I call Graciela and tell her Hannah's struck out in a bold new direction, she'll probably come running over here on Saturday."

I decided to play dumb. "Graciela who?" All I needed was a last name to cut out the middleman.

"You know—the Comme des Garçons addict."

Crap.

She shrugged. "I don't know where the fuck she's putting them all."

I had a pretty good idea where she was putting them all: into the homes of clients, at double or triple or octuple what Vivian was charging her. Unfortunately, I'd already thought to google the phrase "Galerie Naïfs" and been confronted with a mind-boggling 779,000 results—779,129, to be precise.

"Why are you still here?" Vivian said. "That pig isn't going to paint himself, is he? Oh—and be sure to put that faux-sapphire necklace in the next one."

"Not so fast," I said. "You know those cocktail dresses that came in a couple of weeks back?"

"What about them?"

"Do you still have the blue satin Jean Desses?"

"Are you kidding? That dress is so fucking tiny, *I* can't even fit into the damn thing. Thank god it only set me back a hundred—the guy running the estate sale had no idea how to price couture. And it does class up the inventory to have a museum-quality piece like that. . . ." She frowned. "Why do you ask?"

As if on cue, the bell over the front door jingled and Lark walked in. "Here I am!"

"So *that's* why. I'll go get it," Vivian said, adding in a low voice, "Don't forget—I have a key to your apartment. If you tell your friend over there what I paid for the dress, I'll kill your cat."

But not even Vivian could hide her admiration once a beaming Lark emerged from the dressing room. "Holy shit. I *hate* you, bitch."

Lark giggled and spun around, causing the chiffon underskirt to billow, cloudlike, around her waist. The sleeveless bodice, a masterpiece of overstitched pleating, hugged her torso perfectly. "Sandro will love this!"

Sandro will hate that, I thought, smiling in satisfaction. *Forget my*

Twenty-Men-in-New-York theory—there'll be three times that many guys in the gallery Friday night, and they'll all be lined up to meet her. Let's hope one of them manages to make a favorable impression while Sandro sits fuming on the sidelines with his wife.

Lark went off to inspect herself in the three-way mirror, and I turned to Vivian. *How much?* I mouthed.

In response, she held up ten fingers, then made fists before flashing two more. I raised my eyebrows in disbelief, but she just shrugged.

Sighing, I tilted my head in the direction of Dinner's portrait, which got her down to seven fingers. "Are you *kidding*?" I telegraphed with my expression. Vivian folded her arms and met my eyes, defiant.

"I feel like a princess!" Lark called from the back of the store.

She looked like one. *What the hell,* I thought, gesturing again at the portrait and holding up two fingers of my own.

Vivian's eyes narrowed as she leaned across her desk to whisper in my ear. "Who the hell is this chick—your long-lost daughter or something?"

More like my long-lost self, I silently responded. And if it was going to take two Hannahs to get Sandro out of Lark's life, well, that would be cheap compared to what the alternative would cost her. "Do we have a deal?" I whispered back, just before Lark rejoined us.

"You know, that dress looks so good on you, I'm only going to charge you a hundred bucks for it," Vivian told her. Lark erupted into shrieks and skipped off to the dressing room while Vivian and I glared at each other behind her back.

The message light on the answering machine was blinking when I returned to the apartment.

"Hey—it's Ray, uh, noon on Tuesday. I'm in your neighborhood—had an idea about buying you lunch. Oh well. Maybe next time. Take care of yourself, Dana."

"Well, that was quick," Elinor Ann said, approximately three seconds after I'd replayed the message for the dozenth time. "Just under forty-eight hours. Still think he's not your hang-up caller?"

"It's *possible* he was in the area."

"Oh, sure. Refresh my memory. How many stops did you tell me it was between your subway station and his in Brooklyn?"

"Nineteen."

"So it isn't exactly like the guy wandered a few blocks out of his way, is it?"

"Good point." Was one phone call really all it took to summon Ray Devine to the East Village? More important, would he try it again, and what would I do—wear—say—if he did? "Where are you, anyway?" I asked my friend.

"In the car, on my way home from work. It's the first Tuesday of the month."

Of course—it was smelting day. The plant took advantage of reduced energy rates by starting the process at three in the morning.

Perfect timing, I thought. This was the opportunity I'd been waiting for ever since researching Elinor Ann's condition the Sunday after Thanksgiving.

"Are you on Route 22?" I said.

"Just coming up on Krumsville."

"Then do me a favor. Get off at the exit."

"Are you nuts? What makes you think I can do that?"

"It'll just be for a second. Then you can get right back onto the on-ramp."

"Oh, I get it. Force the patient to confront her phobia in small, manageable doses."

It was called exposure therapy, and it was the only treatment I'd found on the Web that seemed logical. It was also the only treatment that didn't want to sell me a series of self-actualization tapes at breathtaking prices. "Are you getting off?"

She didn't answer, but I could hear the *ding-ding* of the turn signal on her car's dashboard. I held my breath and listened to what seemed like an hour of silence before I heard the signal ding again. We exhaled in unison.

"How do you feel?" I asked her.

"Terrified." She was breathing heavily, but at least she was breathing. "Which is why I've never had the guts to try this on my own before."

"You know about exposure therapy?"

"You're not the only person with an Internet connection, you know. Don't you think I've googled agoraphobia by now?"

"Is that the only word you googled?"

"What are you talking about? That's what's wrong with me, isn't it?"

"I'm not so sure. According to my findings, you've got panic disorder."

"Well, that's a load off my mind. Tell me—what the hell's the difference?"

The difference was, Elinor Ann was lucky. Her condition was more easily treatable. All she had to do was keep making herself panic until she got used to it—or sick of it—and learned how to control it. At least, that was how easy the article I'd read made it sound.

"This isn't nearly as serious as agoraphobia," I told her. "Something triggered it. And if you ask me, it's Angus. As soon as he got his learner's permit, you got panic disorder."

"How come?"

"Because he doesn't need you as much as he used to."

"That's what *you* think. If it weren't for me, he'd starve to death under a mountain of dirty laundry." She paused. "But I guess that's . . . plausible."

"I know it is."

She sighed. "I suppose this means I have to get off at the Krumsville exit again tomorrow, doesn't it?"

"I think that would be a good idea."

"For how long?"

"Until you get better."

"Terrific." I heard her turn signal again; she was just a few miles from home now. "Dana?"

"Yes?"

"Thanks. But . . . Dana?"

"Yes?"

"If you were trying to get me off the subject of Ray Devine, you could have just asked me about the weather."

I replayed Ray's message once more before retrieving Vivian's costume jewelry from a box at the foot of my bed. The necklace she'd requested for the next Hannah had become hopelessly enmeshed with a drop earring as long as an earthworm, and far less attractive.

But the faux sapphires were actually quite pretty—teardrop-shaped and arranged to cascade down to a single, much larger stone that would end cunningly in cleavage range. *Dinner will look fetching in these,* I thought, *especially if I set the painting up like a formal portrait. . . . Maybe use that oval canvas I picked up at Utrecht last week . . .*

The phone rang.

I jumped, and the necklace went flying, hitting the wall and disappearing behind the headboard. I looked at my watch: a quarter to two. Had Ray been hanging around all this time?

"Hello?"

"Why, what in the world is the matter, honey chile? You sound plumb scared to death!"

Land sakes, I thought. *My mother just addressed me as honey chile.*

"I'm fine," I responded. "Just, uh . . . wasn't expecting to hear from anyone at this time of day."

"Well, I can't imagine why not! I'm calling about the guest list for your father's birthday, of course."

Of course. It was less than four months away. The caterers must be up in arms. "I tried to get hold of Tom-Tom a few weeks ago," I told her. "He was out of town—how about I try again tonight?"

"That's my girl!"

"How's Dad doing, anyway?"

"Just fine and dandy! Your uncle Jim and aunt Connie drove down from Saint Augustine this morning." My mother was referring to his old business partner, Jim Masters, and his glamorous wife, a former model whom I'd never caught in the act of ingesting solid food—unless ice cubes could be construed as food. Uncle Jimmy had been the first person to ever give me a twenty-dollar bill. I was in nursery school at the time. "How long are they staying?"

"Why, I don't rightly know. The Commodore's fixing to take us all down to *Twofers* in a little while."

Ah, the boat. Dad always referred to it as his very expensive bar—which was certainly accurate. It had barely left its mooring slip since he'd purchased it seven years ago.

"Are you actually going out on the ocean?"

"Good heavens, no! Connie's just had her hair done! But it's a lovely day for margaritas on the deck."

"I'm sure it is." Unless a hurricane watch was in effect, it was invariably a lovely day for margaritas on the deck.

"Besides, Jimmy showed up with a box of Cuban cigars, and I just had to put my foot down," she continued. "You can't imagine how long the smell of smoke lingers in the living room curtains."

Not for the first time, I marveled at my father's ability to party. He probably hadn't missed a cocktail hour or turned down a good cigar in eighty years, and he didn't look a day over—well, ninety, but still.

"Sounds like fun," I said, although just the thought of overindulging in tequila under a blazing Florida sun was enough to make my temples throb. "Give everyone my best—I'll get back to you as soon as I get hold of Tom-Tom."

"Splendid. Now, you're *sure* everything's okay, young lady?"

"Of course I'm sure."

"Woof! Woof!" the dog portraits seemed to admonish me after I hung up. "That's what you get for not screening your calls."

I left my half brother a message, then prepared to go spelunking under my bed for the necklace. But last Sunday's *Times Magazine* on the nightstand, still open to the completed crossword, caught my eye. I hadn't yet tackled the diagramless puzzle on the preceding page. What would be the harm in postponing my next Hannah for just a tiny bit longer?

I flopped on the bed and grabbed a pencil. Pens were fine for the regular crossword, but too much could go wrong in a diagramless, even if they did tell you which square to start in. Surveying the empty grid, I recalled a comment Hank had made as he watched me cruise through yesterday's puzzle. "Heck," he'd said. "If I had to do one of them things, it'd look exactly the same an hour later—all blank squares."

Blank squares. Hmm.

What if one were to construct a crossword where the word "blank" was represented by . . .

Fill in the [blank]! Point [blank] range! [Blank] verse!

Oh my god. Beach [blank]et Bingo! Pigs in a [blank]et! [Blank]ety-[blank]!

The possibilities were myriad. I grabbed a sheet of paper and began to compile a list—or rather, a clue set, as Billy had called it.

Within the hour, I had more than a dozen blank-themed phrases. Surely that was enough to get the ball rolling. I typed the list into an email, added a short note, addressed it to Gridmeister, and just before I hit Send, I did something highly uncharacteristic. I thought about the consequences of my actions.

On the one hand, having a crossword puzzle appear in the *Times* would be an unparalleled thrill. On the other, reestablishing contact with Billy Moody could turn out to be a major lapse in judgment. Adorable boys who engaged in flirtatious banter with women old enough to be their aunts could inflict serious damage on one's primary relationship.

But it was *such* a good idea for a puzzle. . . .

"What the blank," I said, sending my clue set into cyberspace with a decisive click.

I finally got around to retrieving the necklace, positioned the oval canvas on my easel, and applied a coat of gesso to its surface. The process took a bit longer than usual, since every three seconds or so I retreated to the bedroom to check the computer for email activity. No response from Billy Moody was forthcoming, but Amazon was brimming with gift suggestions for everyone on my Christmas list.

I printed out a full-frontal headshot of Dinner for reference and immediately realized I had a problem. Pigs' necks were not designed to wear certain items of jewelry. Such as necklaces. The sapphire pendant that would land in the vicinity of human cleavage would dig into Dinner's Adam's apple—if he had one, and if the necklace managed to make it all the way around his neck in the first place, which was unlikely.

Ah. But if I concealed the ends of it behind his ears, the necklace would drape beguilingly, with the pendant falling at midforehead—if that was the correct anatomical term for it. . . .

The phone rang. This time I managed to hold on to the sapphires.

"Hello?"

"Oh dear," Tom-Tom said. "Whoever you were hoping to hear from, it obviously wasn't me."

"Don't be silly! How are you? How was London?"

"I'll tell you all about it over dinner. Le Veau d'Or? Seven thirty?"

I called Hank to let him know I wouldn't be around that evening. We hadn't made definite plans, but we were at that point in the relationship where one would call the other late in the day, and we'd wind up getting together more often than not.

It sounded as if a 747 were idling inside the brownstone when he answered the phone. "It's Dana!" I hollered.

After a moment the noise began to recede. I heard the front door slam shut; he must have gone out to the stoop. "Sorry about the racket," he said. "I got the floor guy here sanding down the front parlor."

The floor guy? I thought, eyeing the pine planks beneath my feet. I'd gone over to the hardware store on Avenue B, rented a sander, and refinished them myself one weekend shortly after moving in. Granted, it was probably the single most grueling experience of my young adulthood, but I lacked a man's upper-body strength. Besides, I didn't drive around town in a truck with the words BROWNSTONE RENOVATION SPECIALISTS painted on the side of it.

"He's pretty near done for the day," Hank said. "How 'bout you come on by in an hour or so?"

"Tonight's not good." I explained about Tom-Tom, and Hank made me promise to come over the following evening, and then he reminisced about the blow job I'd given him the night before, reeling off a string of highly complimentary adjectives, and after a few minutes I came to the conclusion that a person would have to be crazy to sand his own floors if he could afford to pay somebody else to do the job for him.

———

I spotted my half brother's mane of snow-white hair as soon as I walked into Le Veau d'Or. He was leaning against the bar, engaged in a heated argument with an inebriated elderly couple. *"Finally,"* he said when I reached his side. "Can you please tell these charming but misinformed bibliophiles that it was Harold Robbins, and not Sidney Sheldon, who wrote *The Love Machine*?"

"I always thought it was Jacqueline Susann."

"Of *course*!" all three of them shrieked in unison, drawing stares from the conservative clientele. Tom-Tom raised his gin and tonic in a toast.

"To Jackie!"

"To Jackie!" we chorused. My brother was nothing if not festive. In that regard, he reminded me of our father, but in all other matters there was no resemblance. Dad, for example, would never dress up as the opera diva Beverly Sills on Halloween and lip-synch arias all night with the help of an MP3 player hidden in the bodice of his gown. And Tom-Tom, for his part, would never consider going duck hunting with Lee Iacocca.

He offered me his arm and led me to his regular banquette in the back of the restaurant. A waiter scurried over with his usual bottle of Brouilly, and the two of us sat there, smiling and sizing each other up, until the wine was poured and we were alone.

"You've lost weight." He hadn't.

"Liar. Love the stones." He reached across the table and fingered the faux sapphires. Vivian had already closed up shop by the time I left the apartment; she'd never know I'd taken them out for a night on the town.

I laid my hand over his. "I have to ask you something before we move on to more . . . pleasant topics."

He groaned. "Why do I know this is going to involve certain residents of the Sunshine State?"

"Sorry. Mom's planning a hundredth birthday party for Dad. And she thinks it would be nice to have all his children in attendance."

He sighed and retrieved a datebook from his Hermès man-purse.

"April first . . . Damn. I'm free. Oh, what the hell—tell Lucinda I'm looking forward to it."

"She'll be delighted."

"That makes one of us. So, what's the happy couple up to these days?"

"The usual. They were about to have margaritas on *Twofers* when I spoke to Mom."

Tom-Tom shook his head slowly from side to side, but I noticed he was suppressing a smile. "Honestly. What a thing to do to Aunt Lizzie."

Dad's older sister. She was long gone by the time I arrived on the scene. "What about her?"

"She had a stroke. Never did quite get her speech back—she sounded like somebody with bad dentures. A lot of sibilant esses."

"That's a shame."

"Not really. Once she learned how to drink left-handed, she was pretty much back in action. Whenever she came to visit, we'd set her up on the couch with a Chivas and soda, and whenever her glass got low, she'd shake her cubes at Dad and say, 'Twoferssss, Tommy!'"

"That's terrible!"

"I know. You always felt like a real shit when you laughed." He shrugged. "We're not the Cleavers, sweetie."

"I always wondered how that boat got its name."

"Mystery solved." He took a deep pull from his wineglass, then looked me in the eyes. "So . . . who is he?"

"Who's who?"

"The person you were hoping to hear from instead of your devoted brother this afternoon."

I felt my face flush. "It's not important."

"You're not having trouble with that new beau of yours, are you?"

"Of course not. This is a somewhat . . . older problem."

Tom-Tom leaned back in his chair, studying my expression. "Oh no," he finally said.

"Oh no, what?"

He sighed and laid his hand over mine. "Why in the *world* do you persist in flogging that dead horse known as Ray Devine?"

"It's not like that! It's—"

"Honestly, Dana. Reparenting is one thing when you're in your twenties, but after all these years . . ."

"Reparenting, Dr. Freud?"

"What would you call it? It's a perfectly reasonable way of dealing with an absentee father. I did the same thing myself with a charming, ruggedly handsome antiquities dealer back in the early sixties, when *I* was the one who'd just fallen off the turnip truck. I owe my entire career to Percy."

"Yeah, but—"

"I know what you're about to say, and dear Percy's treatment of me could hardly be categorized as parental, either. That's not the point. Between me and your Mr. Devine, you wisely formed relationships with protective, experienced older men who could lavish you with the attention you deserved."

"It sounds like a book: *Dana Has Two Daddies.*"

"Exactly! Ray Daddy and Gay Daddy!"

I raised an eyebrow. "Gay Daddy?"

"It takes a village, sweetie."

I pondered the ramifications of my half brother's theory during the cab ride home. I couldn't help but regard his logic as skewed. My relationship with Ray was simply too sexually charged to be labeled Ersatz Paternal.

But Ray Daddy *did* have that unconditional love thing down pat: My conversation was scintillating, my witticisms inspired guffaws, my paintings were invariably deemed masterpieces. I could do no wrong.

I thought back to my lunch date with Lark and the expression on her face when she talked about Sandro. I knew it well. Maybe you had to be that young, and your boyfriend had to be that old, to experience that kind of love. Had I been wasting the last two decades trying to recapture the kind of relationship I'd simply outgrown?

Hmm. Ray Daddy. Maybe Tom-Tom was onto something.

For his part, Gay Daddy had been an exemplary sort-of-father as well—always ready with a few hundred dollars to cover a rent shortfall or treat me to an unaffordable, yet perfectly cut, pair of jeans. And he'd made sure I ate a decent meal—generally the sole meunière at Le Veau d'Or—at least twice a month. And who could forget that unfortunate incident back in my college days, for which he'd provided expert criminal defense?

Hmm. Maybe Tom-Tom was right. Whenever I'd needed somebody to take care of me, one of my daddies had always come through. Thanks to them, I had finally been able to parlay that support into a healthy, mature relationship with Hank Wheeler.

Naturally these thoughts didn't stop me from racing to the computer to check for email from Billy Moody the instant I'd unlocked the door to my apartment.

There was nothing from Gridmeister, but Elinor Ann had been in touch twice. I opened the first message, which had a subject heading of "Forgot to tell you":

Just packed up your phone. Will try to get it out tomorrow.

That was good news. We'd only been able to converse a mere two or three times daily since I'd left it behind. Her second message bore the heading "Krumsville":

Have to start getting off at that exit both to and from work.
Came home to find Angus laundering his football gear all by
himself.

I hit Reply, typed in the words, "I'm proud of both of you," and sent it off to Kutztown.

I was just about to settle in with a game—or twenty—of computer Scrabble when I heard the *ping* that signaled incoming email.

It was from Gridmeister.

He thought I was a genius.

At least, that was what it said in the subject line: "You're a genius."

I could hardly wait to read the rest of it:

> Fantastic theme for a Thursday-ish puzzle ... unless it's been done before, but I don't recall one that utilized blank squares. Let me do a little digging in the database to see what I can find.
>
> Even if it has been done, you still qualify as a genius—I look forward to a long and fruitful collaboration (and perhaps dinner, at your convenience?).
>
> Keep 'em coming!
>
> W.W.W.

Wow, I thought. *Somewhere in the five boroughs—probably two or three stops into Brooklyn on the L line of the BMT—Billy Moody is sitting at his computer . . . calling me a genius!*

I opened up an email, typed, "You just made my night," and clicked Send.

He immediately responded with, "I could do even better in person."

Okay, I thought. *Enough. Any more back-and-forth would most definitely constitute flirtatious banter. And you already have a boyfriend.*

The Brownstone Whisperer. Who hires floor guys. And consults diagrams to install switch plates, irregardless of the words painted on the side of his truck. Was I fooling myself into thinking I'd found the right guy?

I shrugged. Maybe there was no such thing as the right guy.

I was seconds away from launching my Scrabble program when yet another *ping* froze my hand midway to the keyboard.

"Where do you live, anyway?" Billy wanted to know.

"9th St. near 2nd Ave."

"No way! 3rd between C/D!"

Okay, I thought. *I am not answering that email. I am not—*

Ping!

Okay, I thought. *This is absolutely the last email I'm reading tonight:*

Want to meet at the halfway point and have a beer? Like . . . right now?

CHAPTER TWELVE

TWO ACROSS, SIX DOWN

I quickly nixed Billy's initial suggestion, which entailed my walking east and his walking west until converging at one of the bars along Seventh Street. The way I had it figured, we might make contact right in front of Hank's truck—or Hank himself, if he happened to be sitting on the front stoop. Instead, I proposed walking down my side of Avenue A and meeting him on the corner of Third.

It was a long walk, psychologically speaking. By the time I reached Saint Mark's Place, I'd convinced myself there was nothing wrong with having one measly beer with someone who could reasonably pass for a colleague. By Seventh, I was a duplicitous harlot with her foot pressed firmly on the accelerator to hell. At Sixth, I didn't care—I was too busy picturing Billy's compelling profile and springy, dirty-blond ringlets. And on it went: cradle robber; budding crossword superstar; pervert; adventurer.

I'd forgotten about the paucity of drinking establishments along the stretch south of Fourth. A large housing project, devoid of storefronts, spread for blocks on the far side of the avenue. On my side, what looked like a promising bar turned out to be a vacuum cleaner repair shop.

Billy was standing in its recessed doorway. "Nothing on tap here, that's for sure." He shrugged. "Want to try Houston Street?"

We wandered east until we came to an off-puttingly slick-looking place that seemed poised to become the next hot spot, judging from the stanchions and velvet rope set in front of the entrance. But no clipboard-wielding bouncer was manning the door, and no assembled throng clamored for admission.

"I'm thirsty," he said. "Let's give it a shot."

We stepped into what was quite possibly the most romantic setting on the island of Manhattan. Little marble-topped tables, set with groupings of votive candles, were scattered across the floor, separated by potted palms that afforded protection from prying eyes. *Swell,* I thought, wondering if God had decided to put me on some sort of trial for loyalty to my boyfriend. If He had, at least He'd chosen extremely flattering lighting for His courtroom.

Only a couple of the tables were occupied by patrons. A lone bartender sat fiddling with his cell phone at the far end of a glamorously backlit bar.

"You serving?" Billy said.

"Sure am. It's our first night—we're having a soft opening before Saturday's premiere party." He looked out over the room. "It's a little softer than we anticipated, though. What'll it be?"

Of course I should order a beer. Beer was casual. Beer only got one so drunk. Beer turned a potential date into Just Hanging Out.

But I didn't want a beer.

"Stoli and tonic," Billy said.

"Dewar's rocks."

The bartender hesitated and turned to my potential date. "Listen, I hate to do this to you, buddy, but can I see some ID?"

I knew right then and there that I would never, *ever* tell Elinor Ann about this part of the evening.

Billy probably turned red, but it was hard to tell in the dim lighting. Besides, I was studiously avoiding looking at him by feigning fascination with the liqueur selection behind the bar. He reached for his wallet and presented his license. "Jeez, dude. I'm twenty-five."

Twenty. Five.

Oh well. At least Tom-Tom can't accuse me of reparenting with this *one,* I thought to myself.

We collected our drinks and settled into a burgundy velvet love seat at a corner table. I didn't dare touch my drink; my pulse was pumping so furiously that I was sure my wrists were visibly throbbing. Instead, I kept my hands in my lap and stared at Billy Moody's ridiculously handsome face, which looked even better in the chiaroscuro of candlelight than the fluorescent glare of the Bieber bus. God, he was sexy.

"I gotta tell you, I started setting up a grid right after I got your email," he said. "I've already got some killer fill words."

"Fill words?"

"You know—all the words in the grid that aren't related to the theme. I've got 'guayabera' in the southwest."

"The southwest?" I said, too embarrassed to reveal my ignorance by saying, "Guayabera?" God, his eyelashes were long.

"The lower-left-hand corner," he explained. "Constructors refer to the different sections of their grids directionally."

"Interesting." Oh, right—a guayabera was a shirt. My brain seemed to be on strike. *The hell with my throbbing wrists,* I thought, reaching for my glass. *If I don't get some scotch into my system, I'm liable to have a coronary episode. Unless the alcohol* causes *a coronary . . . God, he has beautiful hands.*

Billy lifted his drink and offered it in a toast. "To crossword domination. And new friends."

I clinked glasses and said a silent prayer that somewhere behind that glamorously backlit bar lurked a CPR kit.

Our eyes locked over the rims of our drinks and stayed that way after we'd returned our glasses to the table. "So, Miss Mayo."

"So, Mr. Moody."

"Before we continue this conversation, there's something I really need to do." He sidled closer, turned my face toward his, and kissed me.

Of course I kissed him back. My entire body had lost its musculature, and I became flooded with pure desire, physically incapable of pulling away. Not that I wanted to pull away. Either the bartender turned on the music or my own imagination decided to provide a soundtrack as Billie Holiday began to croon "You're My Thrill."

Was he ever. The kiss was so heated and seemed to go on for so long that when we finally stopped, I was surprised to discover the ice in my drink hadn't melted.

"What was that for?" I said.

"I thought it would decrease the tension."

"Oh yeah, that really did the trick. I'm not in the least bit tense now."

He chuckled. "Sorry. I've been wanting to do that since Port Authority."

"Yeah, but . . . why? You get that I'm a lot—uh, I'm somewhat more mature than you, right?" *And I have a boyfriend,* I meant to add, but somehow I managed to forget that part.

"What can I tell you? Girls my age aren't all that fascinating—at least, not the ones I've been meeting. The cute ones would all want to be lined up behind that velvet rope outside when this place opens on Saturday night. And the nerds are . . . well, nerdy."

"Oh, come on. They can't all be that bad. *I'm* a nerd."

He grinned. "I know. So am I."

Uh-oh, I thought. *He's sidling over again. What's taking him so long? God, he has gorgeous skin.*

Just before he kissed me, he turned his head to whisper in my ear.

"Don't worry. This isn't Oedipal. My mom had me really late in life."

"You're a cougar!" Elinor Ann said when we spoke the next morning.

"Don't be ridiculous. Cougars are at least fifty."

"Not necessarily. *Good Morning America* had one on who was in her mid-forties. I don't have to point out how soon you'll be reaching that milestone, do I? Less than two years!"

"I thought you didn't have to point that out."

"Did you tell him exactly *how* much older than him you are?"

Our get-together had not, in my view, been an occasion for precise accounting. "I didn't quite get around to it."

"What a shock. And what about Hank?"

What, indeed. I'd been overwhelmed with remorse seconds after kissing Billy goodbye—again—on the corner of Third and Avenue A. I checked my watch: just after midnight. Maybe Hank would still be awake, or at least amenable to being awakened. I could go over there and pretend the last couple of hours had never happened, which would be the wisest decision I could make that night. *What* had I been thinking?

Oh, right. I hadn't been thinking. My brain had been otherwise engaged. And Billy Moody kissed as expertly as he constructed crossword puzzles.

I reached into my purse and cursed out loud when I remembered my cell phone was still in transit from Kutztown.

It's not the end of the world, I told myself. *They still have pay phones on street corners, don't they?*

The one on Fourth Street had been covered in some kind of sticky, noxious-smelling substance. I moved on to Fifth, where I found the metal box with its array of buttons, but not the receiver or its connecting cord. The only evidence that a phone had sat on the corner of Sixth was a rusting metal spike poking out from the sidewalk.

Finally, just past Saint Mark's, I hit pay dirt. I grabbed the receiver and started to punch in the first digit of Hank's number, only to discover that the buttons had all been Krazy Glued into the pushed-down position. Defeated, I turned down Ninth Street for home.

I unlocked my door and came face-to-face with the half-finished painting of Dinner.

"What are you looking at?" I asked him, stifling a pang of guilt.

I awakened late the following morning to the sound of Vivian's broomstick pounding on the floorboards. Never had I so fervently wished she'd climb onto it and ride far, far away. I reached across Puny and fumbled for the phone.

"I still need a day to finish that painting," I told her.

"What the fuck is taking so long?"

"I had some . . . complications last night. I'll bring it downstairs tomorrow morning, right after you open."

Complications, I thought to myself after hanging up. Such a useful euphemism for doing the wrong thing.

I finally managed to summon a modicum of professionalism and approached my canvas. It was actually a relief to focus on something other than Billy Moody. I settled into a comfortable flow, completing the background and fine-tuning Dinner's expression, until I was interrupted by the harsh buzz of the intercom. I glanced at the clock on the microwave: ten minutes to three. Not bad. I'd been working for nearly four hours.

"Hello?"

"Package for Mayo!"

My phone! I flew down the stairs and thanked the postman more effusively than an actress accepting an Academy Award.

Once downstairs, I realized I was starving. The last solid food I'd ingested had been last night's sole meunière. I had a twenty in my jeans pocket, but no coat. But it was only a hundred feet or so to the deli on the corner. . . .

There was just one problem. I'd have to pass in front of Vivian's storefront to get there, and I was most definitely not in the mood to be harangued for slackerism.

I crept halfway down the stoop and bobbed my head around the corner like a SWAT team member clearing a crack house. Perfect: Vivian had her back to me; she was fussing with a mannequin. I dashed to the corner, got a sandwich, and repeated the process in reverse, feeling even more ridiculous on my second pass by the shop.

When I returned to the apartment, I ripped open Elinor Ann's package to discover not just my cell phone, but a framed copy of the photograph I'd asked for during my Thanksgiving visit. How like her to take care of it right away.

But wait a second. If she'd taken care of it right away, did that mean she'd managed to get to a store, to have the picture scanned, and then perhaps another store, to purchase its frame?

"I wish," she said. "But I'm not cured just yet. I had Eddie copy the picture on the scanner we got them last Christmas."

I should have known.

"What about the frame?"

"I bought it at Renningers last Saturday when you went off to find the bathroom."

"Why, you little sneak. But I really appreciate your sending it. *And* finally getting my phone back."

"Are you kidding? I wanted you to have it back almost as badly as you did. And I guess I should thank you, too."

"For what?"

"On my way to work this morning, I got off and on at the Krumsville exit again. It was a little less scary this time."

"That's fanstastic!" I dropped a chunk of tuna from my sandwich into Puny's bowl, then wandered over to the computer to check my email. "Maybe tomorrow morning you could manage a detour. How about a mile down the road and back?"

"Hmm. I don't know about that. . . . Well, maybe if you were on the phone with me for moral support. Would I be waking you if I called around seven thirty?"

I didn't respond. I was transfixed by my in-box, which contained a message from Billy Moody with the words "Preliminary grid" in the subject line.

"Dana? Are you still there?"

"Huh?"

"Oh no. You just got an email from that adolescent, didn't you?"

> Hey, Dana—Here's what I've come up with so far. Not bad for a first pass.
>
> I've still got some tweaking to do, especially in the northeast, but I couldn't wait to write to you.
>
> Can't wait to see you again, either.
>
> W.W.W.
>
> P.S. You are so hot.

Raging lust was rendering me so discombobulated, it took a couple of attempts before my reflexes allowed me to successfully click open the attachment. Finally the grid appeared on the screen.

He'd worked his usual alchemy. "[blank]ety [blank]" was cleverly positioned in the center of the puzzle so the other themed entries could end or begin there. I located "guayabera," as promised, not to mention "Boyz II Men" and "qwerty"—all appropriately challenging for a Thursday puzzle. But what was a "Sandl"? Oh, of course—Savings and Loan . . .

I hit Reply.

> What do you mean, "preliminary"? This is flat-out magnificent!

"So are you," I said to the screen, hitting Send before I could succumb to the temptation of a postscript.

I returned to my portrait of Dinner, which was almost completed. I'd saved the faux-sapphire necklace-turned-headdress for last so it would achieve maximum pop on the canvas. Beginning with a dab of ultramarine blue, I mixed in a little viridian green, but before I could lighten the color, I heard the *ping* of temptation.

You are not *going to read that email until this painting is finished,* I told myself, stabbing my palette knife into a can of titanium white.

You are not *going to read that email until the outline of this necklace is sketched in.* I checked the clock, which read 4:59.

You are not *going to read that email until five o'clock.*

> Dana—I'm as big a sucker for flattery as the next guy, but the grid has a ways to go before it's magnificent. I've got a couple of really annoying fill words in there—namely, VENI and ETUI. There's absolutely no way to clue the former except "Part of Caesar's boast," since anything utilizing "I came" might have a hard time passing the Breakfast Test (the premise there being that the solver is sitting in the kitchen, working on the puzzle over breakfast, and there are certain words or phrases that he or she doesn't want to see at that hour. Explains why "The _____ mightier than the sword" is our fallback for—well, you know).
>
> As for ETUI—ptui! There are only so many variations on "Needle case." That one's got to go.
>
> W.W.W.
>
> P.S. This grid wouldn't still be preliminary if you weren't such a distraction.

Rather than indulge in an extended fantasy about how, specifically, Billy Moody was distracting himself with me, I reopened the grid and scrutinized the troubled northeast. ETUI, I had to admit, was one of those mundane clues that turned up almost weekly—and no wonder, given its array of useful vowels.

Now, PTUI, on the other hand, would make for a lively substitute, if one could get away with the letter change. . . .

I set about composing a response as the sapphire-colored paint swatch hardened on my palette:

> I see you've got MEET as your Down and MING the Across in that ETUI area. If you changed the former to KEPT, you'd have KING going across and your ETUI would no longer provoke a "ptui!"; it would be PTUI.
>
> As for VENI . . . maybe you could go with "Caesarian section"? Unless you're morally opposed to puns, of course.

I sent it off immediately to prevent myself from making an imprudent comment about his closing remark. Then I wisely put the computer to sleep so I could gain enough momentum to complete the portrait.

A few hours later I stepped back from the canvas to survey the finished product. Dinner was a high priestess in his regal pose—not so much Joan of Arc this time around as Joan Crawford, albeit with less-pronounced cheekbones. The riotously bright Lilly Pulitzer scarf I'd draped in the background flattened out the image, the blues in its pattern competing with the sapphires for dominance. Vivian would be delighted.

But after all that hard work, I decided Vivian could wait until tomorrow while I treated myself to a quick peek at my in-box:

> Yo! Amanda!
> I actually arrived at the same conclusion regarding ETUI/ PTUI shortly after sending the last email. Your having made an

identical tweak merely confirms my initial suspicion that this is going to be a legendary collaboration.

And as for "Caesarian section"? . . .

!!!!!!!!!

Veni.

W.W.W.

P.S. You know I'm in love with you, right?

Of course he was joking, but that didn't stop a tsunami of exhilaration from washing over me, one that had nothing whatsoever to do with my newly discovered flair for clueing. I flopped on the bed and considered my next move. The way I saw it, I had two options: I could further roil the waters by responding in kind, or I could ignore Billy's provocative postscript and wax rhapsodic over what was sure to be our first published puzzle.

Or I could wait. Pretend I hadn't read the email. Go down to Seventh Street, where Hank was expecting me, to have dinner and earth-shattering sex—preferably in reverse order.

A ghost answered the door. Hank was covered in a fine coating of white dust. Immediately I regretted wearing my black turtleneck.

"Aw, heck," he said. "I wish you'd called to let me know you were on your way. I been sanding them fancy strips of plaster up by the dining room ceiling all day. I'd hate to ruin your sweater."

"Don't worry—it's washable," I said, even though it wasn't, and even though I couldn't help but wonder why a contractor didn't know those fancy strips of plaster were called crown moldings.

But at least he was performing the task of a contractor. I peeled my sweater over my head and tossed it in the direction of the banister, then slipped my hands underneath his shirt.

"Whoa! What's the rush? Give me a minute to clean myself up."

"I don't feel like waiting."

He hugged back but then pulled away to meet my gaze. "Are you sure you're all right? You seem . . ." His eyes traveled from my face down to my camisole, which I'd chosen especially for the occasion. It was made of some sort of stretchy white lace material that neither concealed the breasts of its wearer nor provided protection from the winter chill. As a garment, it failed miserably. As incentive, it seemed to be just the ticket.

He ran his hands down the sides of it. "Mmm . . . I *like* this."

Finally.

We passed through the hallway to the bedroom, where we discovered his ungainly house pet splayed across the mattress, snoring contentedly. Hank returned to the kitchen to retrieve an apple, waved it in front of Dinner's snout until he awakened, then rolled it out the door.

Alone at last.

"Missed you last night," he murmured, unzipping my jeans.

"Missed you, too," I replied, which technically wasn't a lie. I'd missed him terribly on my way home.

Pig or no pig, the bed was awfully crowded that night. Hank was taller than Ray Devine, but shorter than Billy Moody. Heavier than Billy, but a little thinner than Ray, with a completely different approach to oral stimulation . . .

Which begged the question: How would Billy . . . ?

Focus!!!

I finally managed to climax, but I couldn't be entirely sure who was responsible for bringing me to it.

I would have drifted off, but Dinner was head-butting the bedroom door with single-minded determination. Besides, I couldn't go to sleep until I rinsed off the plaster dust that had accumulated on various parts of my anatomy.

"You hungry?" Hank said. "How 'bout I call for some Thai and we jump in the shower real quick?"

He was shaving when the delivery guy rang the doorbell. I threw on one of his sweatshirts, turning it into a bulky minidress, and ran to pay for the food. After refastening the padlock, I sniffed. There was an overpowering smell of pine in the entrance hall, and obviously it wasn't coming from the drunken noodles. I slid open one of the pocket doors leading to the parlor and the smell intensified. There, in the middle of the room—on a beautifully refinished parquet floor—stood a massive tree.

I heard Hank approach from behind. "Shoot," he said. "Wanted to surprise you. Christmas'll be here before you know it. I was kinda hoping we could spend it together this year."

I immediately recalled one of Vivian's many adages on the subject of men: "If they want you for Christmas, they want you for life."

I had to admit, it was a titillating prospect.

There was just one problem with the convivial scene I was already picturing in my mind: tradition. I always, *always* spent the holiday with Tom-Tom. Elinor Ann had a houseful; her two spinster aunts faithfully made the pilgrimage from nearby Shartlesville every December. And Dad's middle-child, Jeffer, had a standing invitation to visit my parents' in Florida, wife and teenage boys in tow.

"I don't know about that," I said. "I've been going to my half brother's on the Upper East Side for the past twenty years. I'd hate to disappoint him."

Hank put his arms around me and nuzzled the back of my neck. "Then bring him," he said. "It's high time I met your people."

CHAPTER THIRTEEN

MISTER EXCITEMENT

"Oh boy," Elinor Ann said when I called on my way home from Hank's the following day. "Christmas with the boyfriend. That's big."

"I guess it is."

"So why don't you sound excited?"

Hmm. Why didn't I sound excited?

Because Hank was happy to see me every time I showed up on his doorstep. And conversation came easy, and our silences were comfortable, and when I wasn't with him, I missed him. Which wasn't necessarily exciting, but it felt pretty good—really good.

"I'm beginning to think excitement is overrated," I told Elinor Ann.

"Wow, Dana."

"Wow, what?"

"I never dreamed I'd be saying this, but I think you're in a serious relationship."

"I am, aren't I?"

"Well, you would be if you could manage to steer clear of that teenager."

But I had steered clear of Billy Moody, aside from the occasional grid-related email, ever since our ill-fated evening out, and I intended to keep it that way. Things were going well with Hank—Christmas well. I was spending almost every night at the brownstone now; in fact, we'd already made plans to get together again after work.

Plans I realized I had to cancel when I checked my messages later that afternoon—specifically the email from Lark with the words "Holiday Party" in the subject line:

> Sandro's arranged a limousine for us! I'll pick you up at 5:00 sharp!

Swell, I thought, recalling gallery parties from the past: an army of ectomorphic caterers circulating endless flutes of champagne, which our well-heeled clients would sip politely while our artists overindulged, until one of them—a few years back it had been Sandro—had to be escorted to the curb and into a cab.

But tonight Sandro would be with his wife, and Lark would be the center of attention.

But what was I going to wear? I'd been so busy planning her outfit, I'd given no thought to my own.

I opened my closet and grabbed my fallback dressy ensemble: a pair of black, wide-legged trousers and a creamy satin blouse. I was just tying the shirttails in a knot around my waist when I realized I'd worn the exact same thing the last time I'd attended the gallery party. Come to think of it, so had the caterers.

But what did it matter? No one would be looking at me this evening—unless they wanted their champagne flute topped off. The night belonged to the Girl in the Blue Satin Dress.

I'd gone outside to wait for her when a comically elongated limo, stretching nearly the length of the block, pulled up to the stoop. Its back door swung open, but before Lark's feet touched the pavement, Vivian materialized in front of her.

"*Slingbacks?* Are you fucking *kidding* me?"

"Well, I—"

"What size shoe do you wear?"

"Six and a half. But—"

Vivian grabbed her arm and marched her into the shop as I followed close behind. "I'm thinking the Valentino peek-toe pumps, but try the silver kitten heels while you're at it," she said, pointing to the shoe rack built into the rear wall. Lark dutifully scampered off.

"You are *not* charging my friend another dime for that pair of shoes," I whispered once she was out of earshot.

Vivian rolled her eyes. "Fine. One more Hannah and we'll call it even."

"Forget it. No more Hannahs."

Lark reappeared before Vivian could react. She took a few paces back and forth in the pumps, then went off to try the kitten heels.

"Everyone at the party tonight is going to ask her where she got that dress," I said. "She'll tell them. That's payment enough, Vivian."

"Oh, you think so, do you?"

I shrugged. "Of course, she could always wear those slingbacks she came in with. . . ." I turned to watch Lark approaching in the silver kitten heels.

So did Vivian. "Those are the ones," she announced, reaching into a desk drawer and scooping up a stack of business cards. "And if you're willing to hand these out to the women who'll want to know where you bought your outfit, the shoes are on me."

Lark threw her arms around her benefactor. "You're the sweetest person I've ever met!"

I gave Vivian a nudge after Lark had gone into the bathroom to retouch her makeup. "Admit it. You *are* sweet."

"I'm a lot of things, but we both know sweet isn't one of them." Vivian frowned. "What is it about that girl, anyway? You're giving me two Hannahs for her dress, and here I am throwing in the footwear."

"She's us, before life intervened," I said.

Vivian shook her head. "I was never that young. I was older than her on the day I was born. So . . . who's the guy she's getting all dolled up for?"

"A creep."

"Married?"

"Naturally."

Vivian sighed. "I take it back. I *was* that young once." She returned to her desk and rummaged through the top drawer until Lark emerged from the bathroom in fresh lipstick.

"I guess I'm ready."

"Not quite." Vivian held up a glittering bracelet that made Lark gasp.

"Are those real diamonds?"

"What do you think?" Vivian replied, fastening it around her wrist. "Just keep one thing in mind: This bracelet is a loan. If you lose it, I'll track you down and stab you to death with those kitten heels you've got on."

"How sweet of you," I murmured, smirking, as Vivian ushered us out the door.

"Go fuck yourself," she murmured back.

Lark was trembling with anticipation by the time we pulled up in front of the gallery. "Oh, Dana, I can't believe this night is finally here!"

"I know exactly how you feel."

Did I ever. Apparently, so did Vivian. I tried to remember how I used to pass the time between my Thursday afternoon dates: Working. Talking to Elinor Ann. Wishing I'd hear from Ray.

Mostly in vain.

I turned to face Lark. "Listen—I know this party is a big deal for you, but . . . don't you think you deserve a real boyfriend?"

"What do you mean? Sandro is my real boyfriend."

No, he isn't, I thought but didn't say. *A real boyfriend answers the phone when you call him. Yours can only text you from his bathroom. And you'll spend this entire evening on opposite sides of the room, pretending to ignore each other.*

And somehow, you'll find a way to convince yourself it's all worth it.

The chauffeur swung open the door, and Lark clutched my hand. "This is so exciting!"

Excitement's overrated, I thought, wishing I were back at the brownstone with my real boyfriend.

The party was well under way by the time we arrived, but the noise level dropped perceptibly when Lark removed her coat and turned to face the room in a swirl of satin and chiffon. The owner of the gallery approached her with open arms. "You're exquisite!" he gushed, kissing her on both cheeks before handing me his empty champagne glass.

"Hi, Lucien," I said, handing it back to him.

"My goodness. Is that you, Dana? I thought you were one of my caterers."

He sauntered off before I could confirm my identity.

I surveyed the crowd while Lark accepted compliments from a steady stream of admirers. All eyes were on her.

All eyes but Sandro's. I spotted him in a corner next to one of his triptychs, his gaze fixed firmly on his wife: a statuesque Italian with a prominent nose, bright yellow hair extensions, and the perkiest breasts I'd ever seen on a woman in her fifties. Her husband's face was a furious shade of magenta.

Lark plucked two flutes of champagne off a passing tray. "Do you think Sandro knows I'm here?"

I looked back to the corner. His color had risen; his eyes were still riveted to his wife.

"I think he's aware."

"I'm going to the ladies' room. Maybe he'll follow me back there."

She made her way through the horde, and I braced myself for an onslaught of refill requests. But salvation arrived in the guise of my former coworker. We'd been inseparable during my years at the gallery.

"Rodney Ambrose," I said, embracing his tiny frame. "Skinny as ever."

"Look who's talking," he drawled, hugging back. Over his shoulder, I watched Sandro excuse himself and disappear down the hall leading to the restrooms.

Rodney took a step back and looked me up and down. "I hate to admit it, but life after Lucien seems to be agreeing with you. Even though I'm never going to forgive you for abandoning me."

"I didn't realize you were still working here."

But I couldn't say I was surprised. The artwork Rodney produced in his off-hours had limited appeal. He was a photo-realist who painstakingly re-created the covers of romance novels, replacing the original model's face with that of his alter ego, Ambrosia.

He squeezed my hand. "God, I've missed you, Dana. I can't even keep track of how many assistants we've run through since you left."

"Sorry to hear it."

"You know how it is. They manage to get one of their pieces into a group show at some god-forsaken outpost in Gowanus or Dumbo, and the next thing you know, they're the toast of the demimonde."

"Don't worry, Rodney. Your day will come."

"So, how about you? Sell any paintings lately?"

I didn't have time to answer before I felt a tug on my sleeve. I turned to face an agitated Lark, our coats draped over her arm. "Come on, Dana. We have to leave. *Right now.*" She tugged harder, and I followed, giving

Rodney the universal "call me" sign just before he was engulfed by the crowd.

We made it to the sidewalk before her tears began to flow in earnest. "I've ruined everything," she whimpered, letting out a high-pitched wail.

I took her by the elbow and steered her down the block to the corner. "Tell me what happened. What did Sandro say to you?"

"Oh, Dana. He said I looked like a slu—a slu—"

"A slut? Seriously?"

In response, she wrapped her coat more tightly around the offending outfit.

"Lark, everyone at that party was dazzled the minute you walked in. You looked like a real-life Cinderella tonight." *And if you could only have managed to stick around a little longer, you might have finally met your prince,* I thought, scanning the traffic streaming up Tenth Avenue.

"Then why did Sandro—?"

"He was jealous, pure and simple," I answered before leaping halfway into the left lane to flag down an approaching taxi.

"Do you really think so?"

"Of course he was jealous," I said, wincing at the realization I'd bartered two Hannahs for a dress Lark had worn in public for mere minutes. Damn that Sandro Montevecchi.

"Are you positive?"

"What else could it be?"

She pondered the question for a moment, then sighed happily. "Then I was right to leave the party. I'll apologize, and he'll calm down, and then everything will be okay."

Sure it will, I thought. *For Sandro.*

Lark unfastened the diamond bracelet and handed it to me before getting into the cab. "Tell Vivian thanks again!"

Yeesh, I thought, watching her wave goodbye from the rear window.

At least when I'd squandered my future on a married man, I'd done it with a nice guy.

I looked at my watch and was sure it had stopped. Could it really be only half past six?

Of course it could. I'd barely had time to finish my glass of champagne.

I pulled out my phone and called Hank on my way to the L train stop on Fourteenth Street.

"Don't tell me that party's over already," he said when he picked up.

"Oh, it's over, all right."

"Does that mean you're coming down?"

"As soon as I change clothes."

The first thing I did when I arrived home was secrete Vivian's bracelet in the toe of a sock, which I buried in the bottom of my hamper. I couldn't bear the thought of going downstairs and telling her how the evening had played out; the diamonds would be safe until morning. I added my party outfit to the top of the pile, then turned on the computer.

Gridmeister was at it again:

> I'm bored. You up for some excitement?

"No more excitement," I said, dispatching his email to the trash and grabbing my keys.

CHAPTER FOURTEEN

A HOT DOG MAKES ME LOSE CONTROL

The happy prospect of spending the holiday with my brother and Hank further strengthened my resolve to avoid Billy in the week leading up to Christmas. And I nearly managed to pull it off—but not without a great deal of typing. A few days after the gallery party, a final grid arrived in my in-box, along with a note: "Let's get together and clue this thing."

"I don't think that's such a good idea," I wrote back.

"What did I do?"

"Wreaked havoc on my equilibrium."

"You have no idea how pumped I am to hear that."

And so on. This guy was making my insides melt, even though his use of the word "pumped" did render me just the tiniest bit queasy. People in my peer group tended to use the word as a verb, not an adjective.

Eventually I convinced Billy to let me compose the initial set of clues remotely, but just this once. According to him, crossword construction software was required to produce puzzles in the proper format. "But don't worry," he wrote. "I'll burn a copy of the program and give it to you when we get together to go over the finished product."

"And you *agreed*?" Elinor Ann said the evening before the rendezvous was to take place.

"I hadn't planned on it. But then I realized that seeing Billy would be the perfect Christmas present for Hank."

"Is that so? Tell me—how does one go about wrapping such a generous gift?"

"You didn't let me finish. If I sit down with Billy and tell him I have a boyfriend, he'll back off. Hank will never have to know anything happened, and then everything will be fine."

"*If* you tell Billy about Hank."

"Of course I will."

"I don't know, Dana. . . . Can't you just tell him in an email?"

I'd considered that option but ultimately decided it was best to have the conversation face-to-face. "I'm the one who messed up here. He had no idea Hank even existed. Besides, I'm hoping to salvage our friendship. If it weren't for Billy Moody, I'd never realize my dream of having a puzzle in the *New York Times*."

"That's only been a dream of yours for—what? Two weeks?"

"More like three. But that doesn't make it any less of a dream."

"If you say so."

Elinor Ann had problems of her own. Angus had broken his wrist during the first basketball game of the season, when the Tulpehocken Trojans had defeated the Kutztown Cougars.

"So now the only Cougar I know is you," she said. "Plus my eager errand boy isn't allowed to drive until the cast comes off."

"Will he be okay?" I asked, relieved she hadn't thought to throw in a Trojan joke while she was at it.

"I expect so. The doctor said it was a clean break."

"Will you be okay?"

She sighed. "Now that I'm forced to go to the grocery store on my own—well, let's just say I had to take a saw to the deep freeze the other night to liberate the last bag of frozen peas."

"I think you're looking at this the wrong way. If Angus can't drive, he's less independent. He needs you again."

"Hmm. I hadn't thought of it like that."

"Maybe grocery shopping won't be as scary as you anticipate. Don't you think tomorrow's as good a time as any to find out?"

"I guess so. On one condition."

But I was way ahead of her. "You've got yourself a deal. You go shopping, and I'll come clean to Billy."

I chose Katz's Delicatessen for our meeting, since its cavernous, cacophonous room and lack of table service struck me as an appropriately unromantic setting in which to conduct our business. And the moment that business was concluded, I'd follow through on my promise and bring up the real issue at hand.

But I'd forgotten how skilled Billy was at derailing my good intentions. When I spotted him outside Katz's, my pulse rate soared. I don't know how he managed it, but we were kissing before we'd even exchanged hellos. I braced my hands against his chest in an attempt to distance myself, but somehow they found their way around his neck, and in no time we were grinding away like bonobos.

We were eventually interrupted by a stentorian blast from the horn of a passing dump truck. "Nail her, buddy!" the driver hollered, loudly enough to be heard the entire length of Houston Street.

The incident, while mortifying, had the desired effect of bringing me to my senses. "Maybe we should go inside," I said.

"Great. I'm starving."

I wasn't. As soon as the smell of food hit me, I realized I had no appetite. A patron walked by carrying a pastrami sandwich the height of a seven-layer cake, and a wave of nausea—or was it panic?—swept over me.

Ah. But I could order a knish. A nice, bland, relatively compact knish. We approached the counter, where Billy caught the eye of a server.

"I'll have a knish," he said.

Great, I thought. I wasn't about to order the same thing. What else on the menu was smallish?

"I'll take a hot dog."

What the hell had I ordered that for? There was no genteel way for a woman to ingest a hot dog. Now I was about to sit directly across from Billy Moody and go down on a six-inch length of meat.

We picked up drinks and made our way to a table, where I turned my head and took a surreptitious bite of my lunch. What the hell had I done that for? Now I was going to have hot dog breath when Billy kissed me again. *If* he kissed me again. God, I hoped he was going to kiss me again.

No, I didn't. I had to stay focused. I took a big swig from my bottle of Dr. Brown's Cel-Ray, hoping its medicinal taste would jolt me back to reality.

Billy pulled the puzzle and two pages of clues from his backpack and spread them out on the table. "I think we're all set here. Just wanted you to look it over one last time before I send it off."

I'd looked it over on the computer so many times in the past week that I could practically recite the clues from memory, but I dutifully scanned the pages. "Seems fine to me. So . . . what happens now?"

He shrugged. "I send it in and we wait."

"For how long?"

"For as long as it takes to hear back."

"But—that's torture!"

He grinned. "Maybe you'll learn a lesson from it."

"Such as . . . ?"

"It's not nice to keep a person waiting for too long."

We sat there, smiling at each other and allowing the sexual tension to ratchet up a few more notches.

Which was not what was supposed to be happening. Our business had nearly concluded. It was almost time for the big reveal. There was just one more matter to discuss.

"Did you bring that disc with the crossword construction program?"

Billy mock-hit his forehead with the butt of his hand. "Son of a gun. Slipped my mind."

Suuuure it did, I thought.

"Do you have a few minutes?" he said. "We could go over to my place, and I'll burn it for you right now."

I shot him a bemused look. "Are you sure you forgot, or is this how word nerds lure women to their lairs?"

"Why don't we just call it a happy accident and leave it at that?"

Why not, indeed. If I did go over there, perhaps the post-collegiate dorm room I imagined he called home would have an adverse effect on my libido. And wouldn't it be better to tell him about Hank in private?

Of course it wouldn't. But once I told him, I had a feeling I was never going to see Billy again. And the closer I got to that moment, the longer I wanted to put it off.

"Okay." I took a final slug of Cel-Ray and got to my feet. "Let's go."

The apartment was remarkably nice, a real one-bedroom on the third floor of a walk-up with no evidence of roommates. Instead of the beer-can pyramids and dirty-sock funk I'd expected, there was a grown-up's leather sectional. Framed, matted copies of his published puzzles hung in an eye-level frieze around the living room. And all of the lamps had shades.

"This is . . . surprising," I said, ogling his midcentury modern coffee table and sisal area rug.

"You expected a basketball hoop and assorted swimsuit calendars, didn't you?"

"Well . . . what do you do, anyway? Besides crosswords."

He groaned. "Tutor rich prep school brats." He cocked his head toward the blinking answering machine on his desk. "That thing's probably full of frantic messages from neurotic moms who want to arrange extra flash-card sessions before the next SATs. The only reason I put in a landline is so I don't have to talk to them until they've calmed down."

"I see. So if I called you, I'd get a machine?"

He slipped his hands into the back pockets of my jeans and pressed me against the wall. "If you called me, you'd get my undivided attention."

He tasted like knishes, which meant I surely tasted like hot dogs, but neither of us seemed to mind. In fact, I wouldn't have minded kissing Billy Moody for the rest of the year, and the year after that . . .

Until something brushed up against my ankle and I shrieked.

"Relax," he said, scooping up—Puny? "This is Biddy."

"No, it isn't." I opened my wallet and extracted a photograph. "It's Puny."

"Yow. Maybe they're brothers. I got mine off Craigslist from some nutcase whose new landlord didn't allow pets." He looked at the picture, then at Biddy, and back to the picture. "You know, when you and I move in together, we'll never be able to tell which one is which."

"Oh, right—move in together!" I laughed, even though the thought of having Billy Moody around all the time wasn't so much funny as dangerously enticing. Plus I'd wind up with a much nicer coffee table.

"Don't mock me," he said, dropping the cat and pulling me onto the couch in one fluid gesture. "It's not that preposterous an idea. Tell you what—let's pretend for a little while. Give us a chance to see what it'd be like."

I should not *be kissing this boy,* I thought, kissing this boy. *This is wildly inappropriate. Not to mention wrong. Not to mention Hank, who really does deserve to be mentioned . . . just as soon as we stop . . .*

The phone rang—not his cell, but the landline.

"Ignore it," he muttered, tugging on my shirt button.

I followed his advice until the beep sounded and a woman's voice came through the speaker.

"Biiiiilllly," she said in a breathy tone that would be ideally suited for a career in the phone-sex industry. "Billy *Moooody*. Pick up. We have pussy issues to discuss."

I leapt from the couch. *"Pussy* issues?" I said, rebuttoning my shirt—which should never have been unbuttoned in the first place.

He leapt from the couch. "It's not what it sounds like."

"Are you free tonight?" the woman on the answering machine continued. "I was thinking I could come over after dinner, around ten. Let me know!"

I was almost to the door by the time she hung up, but he somehow managed to grab hold of my wrist. Briefly I considered screaming my head off until the cops arrived, but if there *did* turn out to be a perfectly reasonable explanation, well—there went my shot at a crossword in the *New York Times*.

I shook free of his grasp and drew myself up to my full height of five feet, nine and seven-sixteenths inches. "I had no idea rich prep school brats had such youthful-sounding mothers."

"They don't." He rolled his eyes. "That was the nutcase whose new landlord doesn't allow pets."

Ohhh. So *that* was what she'd meant by pussy issues.

"And she's not just nuts," he went on. "She's annoying, too. The cat's full name is Widdle Iddy Biddy Kiddy. But when she told me she wanted visitation rights, I went along with it." He shrugged. "Figured she'd eventually get sick of coming all the way across town to see him. And, well . . . she was kind of cute."

"Ahhh. So you slept with her."

His face flushed. "Hey—it's not like I'm proud of myself. It happened months ago. *One time.* I've been dodging Maya ever since."

I tried to calculate how young a woman would have to be to have a trendy name like Maya, ultimately concluding she must have been born within a year or so of 2006.

But that wasn't important. This was my golden opportunity to finally set the record straight. "It's probably for the best that she called. Because—because I really shouldn't be here. Because—because I—because I have a boyfriend."

There. I'd said it. Phew.

He broke into a wide grin. "Why, you little strumpet."

This was hardly the reaction I'd anticipated. He was supposed to give me a look of pained disgust, at which point I'd mollify him by explaining that I'd found him so irresistible I couldn't help myself, and then we'd resolve to embark on a new relationship that would be all business and no pleasure—at least, not the kind of pleasure that had permeated our last two assignations.

"So, when do I get to meet this guy?" Billy said, still grinning and edging toward me.

"*Meet* him? Uh, how about never?"

"Oh, c'mon. I have to make sure he's good enough for you, don't I?"

"Can't you just . . . take my word for it?" I said weakly, wondering what had become of all that resolve I'd left my apartment with. He was now standing so close, I could feel his breath on my face. Then I couldn't, because he was kissing me again and I was kissing him back, which wasn't at all what one would expect to happen mere seconds after one confesses to having a boyfriend.

"*Good* enough for you?" Elinor Ann said. "If you ask me, you're the one who's not good enough for Hank!"

"That's quite a change of heart. Do you recall insisting he was a con man for the past couple of months?"

"Well, he's officially off probation. Dana, I thought Hank was—you know. The One."

"Same here."

"So, what does that make Billy Moody? The Two?"

I sighed. *Elinor Ann's right,* I thought to myself. *I am Goldilocks in reverse. Unless a guy is too young or too old, he's never just right.*

"Look, I told him about Hank, didn't I?" I finally said. "And I know I shouldn't have kissed him. From now on I'm going to limit my communication with Billy to email only. If I don't see him, nothing can happen, right?"

"That's exactly what I was hoping you'd say."

I was about to get off the phone when I heard a *ping*.

Elinor Ann heard it, too. "That's him, isn't it?"

I opened the email and whimpered involuntarily.

"What's it say?"

" 'Forgot to burn you a disc of the crossword software,' " I read aloud. " 'I'll give it to you next time we get together.' "

Elinor Ann let out a snort. "For your sake and Hank's, I hope that second sentence refers to the disc."

At least I made good on my promise, I thought to myself while attempting to wrap the more traditional gift I'd bought for Hank, a rugged black leather jacket that simply refused to be folded into submission. I'd intended to have the presents ready well in advance of Christmas Day, but now that I was due on Seventh Street in an hour, the pressure was on. Just the thought of my boyfriend and my half brother attempting small talk in my absence was turning me into a hopeless bumbler.

Perhaps I should warm up with Tom-Tom's exquisite antique opera glasses. Finding an appropriate present for him invariably posed a challenge: What did one purchase for a millionaire whose hobby was shopping? But he'd love the tiny binoculars, with their inlaid-pearl handles and silk-lined case. Vivian had bartered hard for them. They'd cost me one and one-third Hannahs.

Hank's present had cost me approximately one and one-third of my net worth. Wrapping it would be nothing compared to paying for it, which I calculated would take until March.

But that was as it should be. Guilt was expensive.

I finally determined that the most efficient way to package Hank's jacket would be to roll it up lengthwise in wrapping paper and tie ribbons around each end, like an oversized firecracker. After laying the paper on the floor and shooing Puny off it three times, I had it in position when the phone rang.

"Hello?"

"Meeeerrrrrry Christmas!" my mother squealed. There was a ferocious racket in the background. It sounded like . . .

Bon Jovi?

"We got the grandkids a karaoke machine!" she announced. "That's your nephew, Jeffer Junior. Listen." She held the phone so the music swelled for a moment before she returned to the receiver. "He's a cowboy!"

"I can hear that."

"And he's wanted!" she added.

"Dead or alive?" I said.

"*Dead or aliiiive!*" she trilled.

Every so often my mother could be undeniably endearing. I laughed and flopped on the couch. Puny, of course, flopped on the wrapping paper.

"I wasn't sure if you'd be home," she continued. "I thought you might be out in Pennsylvania with your Edith Ann."

"Elinor Ann," I corrected. Mom invariably confused my friend's name with that of the Lily Tomlin character from the 1960s. "I'm leaving in a few minutes to have Christmas with Hank." And Tom-Tom, but, of course, she didn't have to know that.

"Ahhh. Your young man. Sounds like it's getting downright serious."

"We'll see. How's Dad?"

"Couldn't be better! I'd put him on the phone, but he's gone off to the bedroom to freshen up. He just brought the house down with a rousing performance of 'My Way'!"

I couldn't help but question the appropriateness of a ninety-nine-year-old singing about the end being near and facing the final curtain. "Are you sure that was the best choice of song?"

"You know the Commodore. He loves his Sinatra!"

Then again, Dad would never have managed to hit those high notes on "Stayin' Alive."

I got off the phone, rolled up Hank's jacket, and put on some makeup. Just before I prepared to walk out the door, the phone rang again. But I was in a hurry.

I did, however, have enough time to listen to whoever was calling leave a message.

Click.

Especially if the caller didn't leave one.

My timing was flawless. When I arrived at the brownstone, Tom-Tom was unloading gift after gift from the trunk of a black town car.

"What'd you do?" I said when I reached his side. "Buy out Barneys?"

"What'd *you* do?" he said, eyeing Hank's bulky present. "Buy me a corpse?"

"Damn. How is it you always guess what I got you before you even unwrap it?"

We emptied the trunk, and the town car drove off just as Hank opened the door. I heard Tom-Tom gasp under his breath.

"That's *him*?"

"Who else would it be?"

"Why didn't you *tell* me?"

"Tell you what?"

"How criminally handsome he is."

Hank did look handsome in his blue cashmere sweater and faded jeans. He bounded down the steps and offered his hand to Tom-Tom.

"Let me help y'all with those," he said, picking up roughly twice his weight in presents. "Sure is nice to finally meet you."

"I assure you, Mr. Wheeler, the pleasure is all mine."

"Your boyfriend's charming," Tom-Tom whispered during the house tour, after the gifts had been placed under the tree. "Too bad he can't stop staring at me."

His comment was all I needed to hear to know Hank had passed muster. My half brother always signaled his approval of my boyfriends by insisting they were gay. My shoulders dropped about six inches. Everything was going to be fine.

Things got even better when we entered the kitchen and Dinner emerged from the butler's pantry. I handed Tom-Tom an apple, and by the time it disappeared, he was smitten. "I *want* one of these."

"Well, I'll tell you," Hank said, "keeping pigs ain't exactly legal round these parts."

"Then I want one even more. You know, Hank, I'm having a devil of a time pinpointing your accent. Where are you from, anyway?"

"Eastern Tennessee. Little bit south of Knoxville."

Tennessee? I thought. *What happened to Las Vegas?*

My cell phone rang before I could raise the question. I had a strong hunch about the identity of the caller. Best not to answer it.

On the other hand, spending Christmas with one's boyfriend could be considered the adult equivalent of going steady. Maybe if Billy knew I was at Hank's, he'd finally back off.

"Hello?"

"The Bieber bus is lonely without you."

"Uh . . . I think you've got the wrong number."

"Oh, *I* get it. You're with that guy you were telling me about, aren't you?"

"This is four-three-*seven*-three."

He chuckled. "Tell him his competition wishes him a merry Christmas. It's the last one he'll be spending with my girl."

"Happy holidays to you, too, sir." I flipped the phone shut and willed myself not to get all gooey at Billy's use of the term "my girl."

My half brother gave me a quizzical look. "Are you feeling all right?"

"Of course. Why wouldn't I be?"

"Your face is all red. You look as if you've been imbibing eggnog since the crack of dawn."

"I guess it's the heat. It must be a thousand degrees in here with that oven blasting!" I could only hope that Tom-Tom, on the opposite side of the room, couldn't feel the frigid air seeping in from Dinner's pet door. I shrugged off my cardigan for emphasis and prayed I wouldn't start shivering.

Hank glanced at the timer on the stove. "Tell you what. That roast's got a good half hour to go—how 'bout we go on back to the parlor and open up some presents?"

I would have agreed to open up a vein, as long as it detracted attention from my conflicted state. Besides, one of Hank's offerings had caught my eye when I'd added my packages to the pile: a compact box, just the right size for a small item of jewelry.

"Excellent idea."

Not that I was ready for a ring—at least, not a diamond. Not yet. And I hardly deserved one after my recent lapses in judgment. But an opal would be nice. An opal would make the statement, "I genuinely care about you, but I'm not so cocky as to assume you'd agree to marry me seven and a half weeks after our first date."

The four of us made our way down the hallway, but just before we reached the parlor, a thunderous crash sent Dinner scurrying back to the safety of the kitchen. We crowded into the door frame to discover the toppled tree, which had missed shattering the bay window by mere inches.

"Aw, heck," Hank said. "I just knew building my own tree stand was gonna turn out to be a lousy idea."

CHAPTER FIFTEEN

MAKE MINE A DOUBLE

The gifts were spared, but Hank's reputation wasn't.

"He's a fraud," Tom-Tom whispered after Hank had gone to the kitchen to find a broom for sweeping up the broken ornaments.

I sighed. "That's what Elinor Ann keeps telling me." No doubt Cal was capable of building a Christmas tree stand that would keep a conifer upright in the face of gale-force winds.

"I'm not sure exactly what he's up to, but I'm confident that most contractors know their way around a toolbox."

"He doesn't seem to have much experience with electrical wiring, either," I confided, recalling the switch-plate incident of the previous month.

Tom-Tom hoisted the tree and propped it in a corner. "On the other hand, he did a fabulous job refinishing this floor."

"He sure did." My half brother had been presented with enough damning evidence for one afternoon. He did not need to know about the floor guy who'd been brought in to do the actual refinishing—or the fact that Hank seemed to be a native of both Las Vegas and Eastern Tennessee. "So . . . what do you think I should do?"

"Oh, sweetie. With my track record, I'm the last person you should turn to for advice. I will say one thing, though. He's terribly attractive."

"Yeah, there's that."

"And he does seem utterly devoted to you."

"There's that, too."

"And . . . I like the guy."

"Yeah. Me, too."

I liked him even better when I opened the compact box, suitable for a small item of jewelry, and discovered an antique sterling silver key ring.

"I know you got your own place and all, but I want you to feel welcome anytime," Hank said, handing me a key to the brownstone. "Well, least as long as I'm here."

Tom-Tom laid a hand over his heart. "That is *so sweet*."

"Hey—that's my line," I said, giving my boyfriend a hug.

"I mean it, Dana," Hank whispered. "I really like having you around." Over his shoulder, my half brother was silently mouthing something, but I couldn't quite make out what. Two words, beginning with the letter *B* . . .

I raised my eyebrows, and he repeated the phrase more slowly:

Background check.

"I sure do like that brother of yours," Hank said after the gifts had all been opened, the roast had been eaten, and Tom-Tom had departed for the Upper East Side. "It was real nice of him to get me all them presents." He'd received a couple of tickets to the opening night party for the Outsider Art Fair next month ("contingent on your escorting my half sister"), a pair of Ray-Ban Wayfarers ("flattering on everyone"), and a very good bottle of champagne ("no one should ring in the new year with swill").

"He's always been generous." I myself had been gifted with enough cashmere to keep the entire population of Siberia warm all winter. "But your present was my favorite."

"Yours was mine."

This was the moment when we were supposed to embrace and begin wending our way down the hallway to the little room off the kitchen. But it was also the optimal occasion for posing the question that had been nagging at me for the past four hours.

"Hank . . . can I ask you something?"

"Course you can."

"Well . . . when my brother asked where you were from, you told him Tennessee."

"Shooks."

"Shucks?" What was that supposed to mean? Shucks, my cover is blown? Shucks, I can't keep my stories straight?

"No, Shooks—Shooks, Tennessee. Little bitty town that don't even show up on most maps. Wheelers have been living there since pretty near forever."

"Then how come you told me last month you were from Las Vegas?"

He laughed, but just before he did, a fleeting expression crossed his face that might have conveyed panic. Then again, it might have conveyed indigestion, since Tom-Tom had brought an unbearably rich blackout cake for dessert.

"Aw, that. My daddy was a horse trainer. He met some folks from that Circus Circus casino, and when I was round about thirteen, he packed up the family and moved us out west."

Suuuuure he did, I silently responded. *What did your mother do? Sing backup for Wayne Newton?*

Hank stood and offered his hand. "Getting kind of late. What do you say we turn in?"

That would be the simplest thing to do—smile sweetly and forget about all the things I'd been hearing lately that didn't quite add up. And I was just about to comply—until I looked over his shoulder and saw the Christmas tree leaning against the wall, broken ornaments hanging from its branches.

"In a second. There's something I've been meaning to discuss with you."

"Like what?"

"Like . . . well, sometimes I get the feeling you're not being completely honest with me."

He frowned. "I got no idea what you're talking about."

Then stop staring at your shoelaces and look me in the eye, I thought but didn't say. I took a deep breath. "I'm talking about that tree stand you built, for starters. It just seems strange to me that it—you know." I tilted my head toward the corner.

"I'm a contractor, Dana. Never said nothing about being no carpenter."

Or a floor guy. Or any of the skilled professions listed on the side of your truck, for that matter. "I guess I just figured contractors were—you know. Handy."

He grinned and returned to the couch, slipping his arm around my shoulders. "I can be real handy when I put my mind to it. Come here—let me prove it to you."

"Hank, I'm serious. One minute you say you're from Las Vegas and the next, Tennessee. What am I supposed to believe?"

"Believe that." He pointed to the box on the coffee table that held both the key chain and the key to the brownstone. "I want the two of us to be together, Dana."

"Are you sure?"

"Course I'm sure."

I'd been sure, too. Sure enough to tell Billy about him, even though my confession had hardly been as aboveboard as I'd intended. I thought back to our meeting at Katz's deli last week. Not only had we kissed; I'd wound up at his apartment—where I'd kissed him some more before finally doing the right thing. And would I have done the right thing if we hadn't been interrupted by Maya's phone call?

Maybe I should cut Hank some slack. He was hardly the only person in the room who wasn't being completely honest.

"I'm sorry," I said.

"For what?"

I wasn't about to go into detail. I rose from the couch and started for the door. Hank got up and followed me, down the hallway and into the little room off the kitchen.

And everything was fine—until the following morning, when curiosity lured me into the front parlor for a closer inspection of Hank's tree stand.

At first I thought he must have tossed the bulk of it into the Dumpster out front. The only part that remained was a three-foot square block of thick plywood, a bent nail protruding from its surface.

Wait a second, I thought, lifting the board. Was this the entire tree stand? Had Hank simply placed the plywood against the base of the trunk, pegged in a single nail, and expected it to keep a Christmas tree erect for the duration of the holiday?

"There you are." Hank stood in the doorway holding two mugs of coffee. "I was wondering where you'd gone off to."

In response, I brandished the plank. "What the hell is this supposed to be?"

"A tree stand—what's it look like?"

"A Dadaist sculpture by Marcel Duchamp."

"Huh?"

"Did you honestly believe this would work?"

"Well, sure. It worked for a couple of days, didn't it?"

I just stood there for a moment, trying to come up with a plausible explanation for all the discrepancies I'd shrugged off for the past two months. "Hank, are you . . . a squatter?" I finally said.

"What? Hell no! If I didn't have a client, how could I be shelling out all this cash on plumbers and roofers and refrigerators and stuff?"

"I have no idea," I said, brushing past him and heading for the back room.

"Where are you going?"

"Home."

"Dana . . ."

I didn't respond. I marched into the bedroom and stuffed my clothes into my backpack. I needed time to sort things out, and this was the last place I intended to do it.

Hank was waiting for me by the front door when I was ready to leave, my Christmas present dangling from his finger. "I wish you'd stay."

I noticed he'd attached the brownstone's key to the silver ring. "Are you sure you want me to have that?"

He reached over and dropped the key chain into my coat pocket. "Dana, we're doing good here. Let's not mess it up now."

Dinner emerged from the back hallway and looked up at me with an expression nearly as mournful as his master's. *You're not making this any easier,* I thought, returning his gaze.

"I don't want to mess anything up. But if you're not going to be honest with me—"

"That's what I been. Look, Dana—contractors . . . contract. That's the job. I hire guys and tell 'em what to do." He smiled, shaking his head from side to side. "Wish I could hire you. Then I could tell you to stick around."

I have to admit, I was tempted. It would have been so easy to go back to the bedroom and not reemerge until Monday morning. But if Hank really was the perfect boyfriend, then how come I found myself kissing Billy Moody every time the opportunity presented itself?

I hugged him, and he hugged back. "I just want to take a breather," I said. "At least give me a chance to miss you, okay?"

"Does that mean you'll come over for New Year's Eve?"

"We'll see."

"Oh, come on, Dana. That's a whole week from now. Isn't that long enough for you to miss me?"

I leaned against the wall, thinking it over. Usually I spent New Year's home alone, avoiding the drunks who flocked to my neighborhood leaving broken glass and vomit in their wake. I'd been looking forward to spending it at the brownstone. And I couldn't imagine having a whole week pass by without missing Hank.

"You're on," I said. "We'll talk things over then."

"I'll be waiting." He kissed me on the cheek and opened the front door.

I walked down the stoop in a daze. What had possessed me to flee the premises just as the relationship seemed to be getting serious? Was it nothing more than garden-variety fear of commitment?

No, it was Hank. And his tree stand, and his floor guy, and his ever-changing autobiography.

Or was it Billy?

I shook my head. Billy hadn't influenced my decision. He wasn't even around this week. He was in Allentown, spending the holiday at his parents'. Right now he was probably out with his old high school gang, doing something youthful. Like snowboarding. Or ecstasy.

He'd still managed to intrude on my Christmas with Hank the previous evening. Shortly after hearing the words "Circus Circus," I was off and running with another theme for a puzzle. Could doubled word phrases—tautonyms, I believed they were called—be combined with another word to form a new phrase, such as "buddy buddy system"?

Damn. Sixteen letters.

Ah, but "Sing Sing praises" was fifteen!

"You okay?" Hank had asked me, his hand poised over my belt buckle.

"I'm sorry. I was a million miles away." In Walla Walla. Or Bora Bora.

Or, to be completely honest, Circus Circus. No matter how hard I tried, I just couldn't manage to buy another one of Hank's stories.

I sighed. Billy was off the hook. Hank wasn't.

I arrived at my building and reached into my pocket for my house keys, but I pulled out my Christmas present instead.

Maybe I'm being too hard on Hank, I thought to myself, eyeing the key chain. After all, this gift was hugely significant. It meant he wanted me around. All the time. Giving me a key to the brownstone had been a major declaration of affection. It meant so much more than if he'd given me . . .

Bling bling. Ten letters.

I'd barely hung up my coat when I heard pounding from below. I reached for the phone.

"I'll be right down," I told Vivian.

"No, you won't. I'll be right up."

I slammed down the receiver and groaned. She wasn't likely to arrive empty-handed. What would I be required to work into my canvases this time?

Hats, as it turned out. An enormous box of them.

"I can't sell these goddamn things to save my life," Vivian said as she shoved the open carton across the threshold. "I was thinking if you put a few of them on that pig, it might generate interest."

I wasn't so sure. Women tended to purchase clothing that transformed them into something other than swine. But the hats were actually quite charming—little felt-and-feather concoctions in a full spectrum of colors that probably dated to the late 1940s.

"I'm thinking window display," she said. "Hang the paintings with invisible wire and line up a row of mannequin heads in front of them."

I was thinking grid—a large grid, maybe four canvases by four, each about a foot square. If I gave them all a decorative border and they were hung close together, the grouping would resemble a patchwork quilt. "I can work with these."

"Of course you can. So start working already." She waved a hand at the box of hats before heading for the door.

"Wait a second," I said. "There's something different about you."

"I have no idea what you're talking about."

She stood there scowling while I scrutinized her appearance. At last I figured out what had changed: I could see her entire left hand.

"What happened to your engagement ring?"

Vivian rolled her eyes. "That fucking Chad, that's what happened. He's in Baja. He's . . . *fishing*." She made the word sound like a felony, punishable by twenty years behind bars in the company of amorous, weight-lifting lifers.

"I take it you're not a fan?"

She looked at me as if I were pointing an Uzi directly at her forehead.

"Guess not. Sorry to hear you guys broke up."

"I'm not. You should have seen the performance of his hedge fund last quarter. *All* the numbers were in parentheses." She yanked open the door and stalked out.

I watched her go, suppressing a smile. "At least I'm not that bad," I said to Puny, filling his bowl and reaching for my coat. Time for a run to Utrecht on Fourth Avenue to replenish my canvas supply.

The intercom buzzed as I was locking up; Vivian must have forgotten to tell me something. But when I walked down the stairs, there was a different blonde waiting on the other side of the front door.

"I'm engaged!" Lark shrieked, presenting her . . .

Right hand?

I opened the door and let her hug me while she jumped up and down. "That's . . . great," I finally said. "But I think you're wearing that ring on the wrong finger."

Her face fell. "Oh, Dana. I know. But Sandro said seeing me at the gallery party made him realize he didn't want to wait any longer."

I'll bet, I thought. *Once he saw the attention you attracted, he knew it was just a matter of time before another guy made his move.*

"He told me I could switch hands as soon as his divorce is final," she said, breaking into a beatific smile.

You poor, young, dumb girl, I thought but didn't say.

She held out the ring for inspection. The diamond was similar in size to Vivian's, but Sandro, never one to stint on glitz, had outdone Chad by flanking the stone with square-cut rubies. "So? What do you think, Dana?"

I think you should pawn it and spend the proceeds on therapy and a master's degree. "It's . . . singular."

"Isn't it? I was in the neighborhood, and I just had to show it to you."

For someone who lived all the way up on West 108th Street, Lark was in my neighborhood with astonishing frequency. "I'm glad you stopped by. I'd invite you in, but I've got to pick up some art supplies."

"Can I go with you?" She sighed. "Sandro's busy all day. His son's visiting from Santa Barbara."

"Why not?" *Sandro is always going to be busy,* I thought, wishing I could tell her this but knowing she'd never listen. *You'll waste years of your life, and eventually you'll move on.*

We turned up Second Avenue, where a billboard of Ray Devine smiled down at us from a tenement wall.

And I ought to know, I silently added.

I finally arrived back home, tiptoeing so Vivian wouldn't find out I had yet to start my latest Hannah. I cut the twine holding the canvases together and vowed not to focus on anything but work for the remainder of the afternoon.

Just as soon as I checked my email.

There were a few forwarded jokes and a request from eBay to leave feedback on the vintage Pyrex nesting bowls I'd purchased for Elinor Ann's Christmas present, but nothing from Billy Moody. Which was unusual. He'd been relentlessly in touch ever since our lunch at Katz's, whether to solicit my opinion on a section of a grid or to ask if I wanted to get together—a query I always deflected with some variation on "not a good idea." Had I finally gotten through to him?

If so, I should be delighted, or at least relieved—not sinking into despair and debating the wisdom of sending him a partial clue set based on tautonyms.

I rummaged through Vivian's box, pulled out a maroon cloche with a mini-veil and a rakish spray of pheasant feathers, and reached for my palette. There was no point in furthering a dialogue with Billy Moody. The odds were firmly stacked against anything but a tawdry affair, one that would induce cringing and remorse—and more cougar jokes from Elinor Ann—for years thereafter.

I managed to prime exactly one canvas before convincing myself that my tautonym theme was simply too compelling not to share.

But Billy had beaten me to the keyboard. His email was waiting in my in-box, with a subject line of "Miss me?"

> Sitting here stuffed with pie and dutifully wearing this year's ugly Christmas sweater from Grandma. (She's outdone herself. There's a big jolly snowman on the front of this one.) My three-year-old nephew is screaming so loud that I'm tempted to feed him a peanut and put him permanently out of his misery. Give me a light at the end of the tunnel. Have dinner with me when I get home tomorrow.
>
> W.W.W.
>
> P.S. In a blatant attempt to influence your decision, I got you a Christmas present.

Even though I knew better, I highlighted his postscript and hit Reply.

> Would said gift happen to be an ugly Christmas sweater? What
> color?

He was still at his laptop:

> I have no idea. I've got red-green color blindness. And that's not
> what I got you. Say yes.
> W.W.W.

His affliction inspired me to respond one more time:

> Color blind? No wonder you're misreading my signals. Those
> are red lights, not green ones, I've been giving you.
>
> P.S. I have to admit, I'm curious about that gift. A first edition of
> *Anne of Red Gables* or *The Green Badge of Courage*? A CD by Red
> Day or the Green Hot Chili Peppers?

My email probably hadn't even reached its destination when inspiration struck. By the time he wrote back, "Are you thinking what I'm thinking?" I had a tidy list of potential phrases for a clue set:

> Little Green Riding Hood; Red Thumb; Green-letter day; Red-
> eyed monster; Better Dead than Green; The Red, Red Grass of
> Home . . .

I didn't even bother with the pretense of returning to my easel. I just sat there until I heard the *ping* signaling his reply.

Little Green Riding Hood is 21 letters. I think we've got
a Sunday puzzle on our hands. If you don't meet me for a
brainstorming dinner, I'll be walking around with green-rimmed
eyes for the rest of the week.

W.W.W.

Of course I knew I should say no. And, as I'm sure we both knew, any brainstorming could be accomplished on our respective computers.

But Hank and I were on hiatus.

Or were Hank and I on hiatus because I'd known it was just a matter of time before Billy turned up?

The way I looked at it, there was only one way to find out.

Not dinner. Quite honestly, I don't trust myself to spend that
much time with you.

But I will agree to *one drink*. Meet me tomorrow night at 9
in front of the bar just north of 13th on Avenue B.

I'd never patronized the establishment, but it looked appropriately low-key from the outside. Its main selling point was its relative remoteness from my apartment—and Hank's brownstone. Northeast was the least likely direction in which he would wander if out for an evening stroll.

And on this particular evening, only a masochist would be out wandering. The temperature had plummeted to the low teens and the wind had buffeted my hair into Southern-beauty-queen dimensions by the time I arrived at my destination.

Billy was out front with his head down, shifting his weight from foot to foot with his back to the entrance, when I walked up and tapped him on the shoulder. He jumped roughly twelve feet, then turned to face me.

"Yow! You nearly gave me a heart attack!"

"Weren't you expecting me?"

"Well, yeah, but—uh, have you ever been to this place before?"

"No. Why?"

"I didn't think so. It's, uh . . ." He began to smile and looked into my eyes. "I'll explain in a minute. Hey, Dana." He leaned me against the wall and kissed me, and instantly I forgot about my hair and the suitability of the bar and the arctic chill and kissed him back.

I would have happily spent the next hour or so risking frostbite, but the door swung open and two patrons exited the premises.

"Breeders," one of them hissed when they passed by.

"Ohhh," I said to Billy.

He chuckled. "Yeah. Oh."

"I didn't realize it was that kind of bar."

"I didn't think so." He picked up a shopping bag that I surmised held my Christmas present, took my hand, and started up the avenue. "There's a place right around the corner on Fourteenth. It'll be full of old geezers, but they won't object to having us there."

He was right. None of the customers even looked up when we walked in, presumably because they were too loaded to lift their heads.

Billy hesitated after closing the front door. "Hope the ambience isn't too . . . louche for you."

"Are you kidding? It's perfect."

Ray and I had never rendezvoused at this particular establishment, but I felt right at home. All the dives in Manhattan seemed to have identical feng shui. I'd been immediately transported back in time the instant I spotted the scuffed, red and black linoleum floor tiles and breathed in the familiar combination of ancient beer and wet wool.

There were a few battered booths in the back of the room. I slid into one, taking the side that faced away from the action—if guzzling boiler-makers could be construed as action. Billy slid in next to me after he returned from the bar with our drinks and immediately resumed kissing me.

I'd expected this, and I had a plan to shut him down after a minute or so—ten, tops—but my brain just couldn't seem to manage to send the correct signals to my body. Man, this kid was talented.

He was the one who ultimately backed away. "Are you sure that guy you were telling me about is your boyfriend? Because you're kind of acting like you like me, Dana."

Like, schmike, I thought. *Let's hop a red-eye to Rio.*

But now was no time for dangerous fantasy. Did I really want to throw Hank over for a kid?

"Yeah, I like you. Obviously. But you're just not . . . tenable."

"And this boyfriend guy is?"

"He's the right age, and he's devoted, and he isn't too young for me, and he's decent, and we were both born in the same decade, and he has a pet pig."

"Whoa. Why didn't you tell me he had a pig? That explains everything."

He put his arms around me and was nuzzling my neck before I could think of a single preventative action. "I'm an old soul," he murmured in my ear.

"And kissing you is as addictive as opiates," I said, *finally* backing away. "But I'm serious. This guy's good for me. I mean it." Why was I so unwilling to say "this guy"'s name? Hank. Hank Hank Hank Hank Hank.

"I guess you spent Christmas with him, huh?"

"I did. And he met my big brother."

"Oh. In-law stuff. Okay."

"Okay what?"

"I'll back off."

I was much too sad to hear him say it, but I commanded myself to feel relieved.

And I was, in a way. But oh, how I wished we had never stopped kissing.

"On one condition," he added.

I raised my eyebrows.

"We continue to collaborate."

"I was hoping you'd say that."

"Oh—and one other thing," he said, reaching across the booth to retrieve the paper bag he'd been carrying. "You have to let me give you your present."

I'd been dying of curiosity from the moment I'd laid eyes on the bag, but Billy had managed to make me forget all about it over the course of half a drink. Now, as he pulled out a flat rectangular package, I began to speculate anew: Was it a picture? A mirror? One of his framed puzzles? That would be a bit gauche, actually.

I untied the ribbon and fumbled with the tape on the wrapping paper. "This was really sweet of you," I said, hoping the contents inside were nice, just not *too* nice.

Then again, what could compete with the key to the brownstone?

"It's kinda strange," he said. "I saw that in the window of this antique shop in Allentown, and I just—I don't know, thought it would appeal to you. Don't ask me why, though."

I pulled the last piece of tape off the paper. It was a picture; I was looking at the back of a framed canvas. I turned it around and gasped, nearly dropping it from shock.

"Oh my god," I said. "How did you know?"

"Know what?"

I redirected my gaze to the portrait in my hands: a spectacularly one-dimensional, very badly wrought beagle.

CHAPTER SIXTEEN

PLAN C

"He must have seen that German shepherd painting you brought home at Thanksgiving," Elinor Ann said.

"That's just it. He didn't see it. Before I got on the bus, I slid it down the inside of my duffel bag, which I never opened in his presence—and *no*, I didn't use the bathroom during the ride, and you've got a lot of nerve suggesting he'd go through my luggage!"

"I didn't say a thing about him snooping!"

"But you were thinking it, weren't you?"

"Well, kind of," she admitted. "But what other explanation could there possibly be?"

According to Billy Moody, innate compatibility. I was so transfixed by his Christmas gift that he had to wave his hand in front of my face to get me to look up.

"I have over a dozen dog primitives hanging on my bedroom wall," I said once he got my attention.

"No way."

"This is . . . astonishing. What made you buy it?"

He shrugged. "I don't know. It just . . . looked like you."

I gave the painting a quizzical glance. The beagle was so flattened, it appeared to have been run over by a tank. And its ears had been embellished with purple smudges to create a shadow effect, which one should never attempt unless one is Francis Bacon. "Gee. Thanks a lot," I said.

"That's not what I meant. For whatever reason, it seemed like the kind of thing you'd appreciate. And based on what you just told me, that's true." He grinned and edged closer. "Maybe it's proof."

"Of what?"

"Of how instinctively well I understand you. You know, I'd really like to see those other dog paintings sometime."

"What a surprise."

"As a matter of fact, I'm free all evening."

I pushed up my sleeve and carefully inspected my watch. "You don't have a very good memory, do you? I seem to recall your saying something about backing off less than five minutes ago."

"Changed my mind." He kissed me again. "Come on. Let's go over to your place."

It would be so easy to say yes, to take this beautiful boy home for a test drive. And if I were still Billy's age, I wouldn't have thought twice about it.

But I hadn't been his age in a chillingly long time. "You know how I'm going to answer that." I stood and reached across the table for my jacket.

Billy reached for his. "Tell you what—New Year's Eve is just a couple of days away. How about then?"

"I have plans."

"I had a feeling you were going to say that." He kissed me for what I swore would be the last time that night—no, ever. "Well, you know how to reach me if your plans fall through."

———

If I were a more religious person, I might have concluded it was God's decree that Billy and I get together when my New Year's plans fell through.

Hank called the morning of December 31. "We got a problem," he said.

Panic set in immediately. Had he seen me kissing Billy in front of the gay bar? If so, what was he doing out on the coldest night of the year—and, more important, would I be able to convince him I had a doppelgänger who lived somewhere in the vicinity of Thirteenth Street and Avenue B?

"It's Dinner," he said. I covered the receiver to mask my sigh of relief—and then the meaning of his words sank in.

"What's the matter?"

"He ain't eating. He wouldn't touch his apple last night. I got up early to give him breakfast, but he wouldn't have nothing to do with that, neither."

"Maybe he's just . . . going through a finicky phase?"

"That ain't how it works," Hank explained. "Pigs don't not eat. Pigs eat till they explode, long as you keep feedin' 'em."

I had a roommate like that sophomore year. "So what do you do now?"

"He's probably got pneumonia—it's real common in winter. I hate to have to cancel our plans tonight, but I'm heading down to Mullica Hill, New Jersey. That's the closest vet I've found who can work on livestock."

It sounded strange to hear Hank refer to his pet as livestock. By now I'd come to regard Dinner as a morbidly obese puppy. "Do you need me to help you get him in the truck? I can be there in ten minutes."

"It's real sweet of you to offer, but I can walk him in. And I really got to leave right away. The sooner he's medicated, the better. I sure am sorry about messing up New Year's."

He must be telling me the truth, I thought. *It's been nearly a week since we've seen each other. Or is this yet another lie?*

I shrugged. For the time being, all I could do was believe him.

"Just make sure Dinner gets better," I said.

"We been through this before. I reckon he'll come out of it in a day or so."

"That's a relief. So . . . I guess we'll just have to celebrate the new year when the two of you get back home."

"Sounds good. And thanks for understanding. I'll miss you, Dana."

"It won't be long."

Just long enough for thoughts of Billy Moody to gambol unchecked through the treacherous fields of my subconscious, I silently added before hanging up.

Not that I had any intention of getting in touch with Billy Moody. Of course I didn't. I would spend my evening painting. What a creative, self-sufficient—dare I say feminist?—way to start the new year.

"You are *not* getting in touch with Billy Moody," Elinor Ann said.

"Of course I'm not!" Even though I *had* come up with several brilliant clues for our color-blind-themed puzzle, and it was probably imperative he receive them immediately. "What makes you think I would do such a thing?"

She just laughed. "So, what are you doing instead?"

"Staying in. You?"

"Going out."

"That's fantastic!"

"Not really. I've got a chauffeur. Eddie's soccer coach and his wife are having an open house over in Macungie, and Cal thought it sounded like fun."

"I still think you should consider it a positive step. You know—going somewhere new, expanding your circles . . ."

"I guess. Plus I decided this was as good a time as any to test out my new coping strategy."

"Which is . . . ?"

"Act As If. I read about it on the Internet. If I Act As If I'm not suffering from panic disorder, then I can leave the house—which proves I don't have panic disorder, which is what I'll tell myself the next time I have to leave the house."

"Ingenious." Briefly I wondered if the strategy would work with Billy Moody. If I could just manage to Act As If I found him physically repulsive . . .

I would be headlining on Broadway, acclaimed as the greatest actress of my generation.

"Let's just hope it's the cure I've been searching for." She paused. "So, Dana?"

"Mmm?"

"I hate to ask, but . . . what about Dinner? Think he's really sick?"

"That's an awfully elaborate excuse to get out of a date, wouldn't you say?"

"Well, sure, but I was just thinking—well, what if Hank has to have an end-of-calendar-year session with his parole officer or something?"

"Will you *stop*? Hank's *not* a criminal. I'm sure he'll be home tomorrow—*with* his medicated pig."

Besides, parole officers don't work on national holidays, do they? I thought to myself after we'd said goodbye.

I rummaged halfheartedly through Vivian's assortment of hats, ultimately pulling out a plum-colored mini-porkpie with rhinestone trim. I'd been working at a blistering pace over the past week. One more canvas and my sixteen-painting grid would be complete.

But speaking of grids, maybe I should just fire off a quick email to Billy with those last-minute clues I'd thought of.

No, you shouldn't, I admonished myself, securing the canvas in place on my easel.

My brain became engaged in an excruciatingly boring debate for the next hour or so, with a back-and-forth consisting of two words:

Billy.

No.

Billy.

No.

Billy, Billy, Billy.

No, no, no.

Obviously the only way to get any work accomplished was to email him and be done with it. Besides, the puzzle would be even better with the addition of one more grid-spanning, twenty-one-letter clue, and "The Green-Nosed Reindeer" filled the bill perfectly. And if Billy happened to ask why I was still home at eleven o'clock on New Year's Eve, well, I simply wouldn't answer him. Let him assume I'd dashed it off mere seconds before leaving the house at one minute past the hour.

His response landed in my in-box so quickly, I could be excused for surmising he really was as devoted to me as he alleged.

Until I saw the words "Automated Response" in the subject line and read the email:

> I am out of town until January 6, with only sporadic access to the Internet. I will respond to your email as soon as possible, and in the meantime, Happy New Year and thank you for your patience.
>
> W.W.W.

Huh?!

I sat at my desk, rereading the message several billion times before concluding that his sudden departure was attributable to one of two scenarios:

In the first, he had been summoned to Allentown—but not to ring in the new year. His flurry of emails over Christmas proved he had virtually unlimited access to the Internet at his parents' house. Therefore, a family member—perhaps the grandmother given to knitting hideous snowman sweaters—was on deathwatch.

But how would Billy—or anyone else, for that matter—know the exact date of her impending demise? And wasn't January 6, Epiphany, the traditional end to the Christmas season across America?

That was when I had my own epiphany.

One of his clients—no doubt the trophy wife of a Wall Street megastar—had cajoled him into tutoring her nubile twin daughters at their Aspen chalet when her husband ceded his seat on the family Cessna in favor of remaining in town to pursue a hostile takeover of Exxon Mobil.

The nerve of some people. The unbridled nerve.

I picked up my paintbrush with renewed fervor and approached the canvas as if my life depended on it. Which, of course, it did. If I didn't stay busy, images of Billy Moody schussing down slopes flanked by golden-haired sylphs—not to mention their well-preserved MILF— would eat away at my brain until there was nothing left but a smoldering nub of hostility.

I worked methodically, roughing out the porkpie hat and pig silhouette as noise from the street escalated in advance of midnight. It was strange Hank hadn't yet called with a progress report. I'd tried his cell phone hours earlier, but it had gone straight to voice mail.

"You have to get better," I said, addressing the beady eyes staring back at me from the center of the canvas. Maybe for this portrait I'd put a thermometer in Dinner's mouth to memorialize the emergency. The old-fashioned kind, with mercury inside . . .

The phone rang—*finally*—and I lunged for the receiver.

"How is he?"

Click.

I looked at the clock: twenty to midnight. My mystery caller was early this year. He usually waited until a quarter of.

I had barely hung up when it rang again.

"Who the *fuck* is this?"

"It's me," Hank shouted over the roar of what sounded like the Indy 500. "Sorry I'm calling so late. I only just now found a 7-Eleven with a pay phone and a clerk who was willing to give me a mess of quarters."

What year was this—1962? And since when did the state of New Jersey suffer from a dearth of convenience stores?

"I cut out so fast this morning, I didn't have time to juice my cell," he explained. "Forgot the charger, too."

"I see," I said, instead of, "How does a veterinarian manage to run a business without a functioning telephone?" which had been the first response that had sprung to mind. "Uh, did you call earlier? Like, two minutes ago?"

"Sure didn't. Is . . . everything okay up there?"

"Of course. What about down there?"

"It's pneumonia, all right. The doc wants to keep him overnight, but said he ought to be good to go by tomorrow. So I checked into a Motel 6, grabbed a nap, got me something to eat, and I been trying to find me a phone ever since."

"I'm glad you did," I said, instead of, "How does a motel chain manage to retain their clientele without in-room telephones?" Why was I finding it so hard to believe he was telling the truth? If I broke with tradition and made a resolution for the coming year, perhaps it should address my overly suspicious nature. "And thank god about Dinner."

"I'll say. He's—"

A recording came on requesting a deposit of sixty-five cents to continue the call.

"Shoot. I'm a nickel short."

"What's the number?"

"Ain't one. It's scratched out. Listen, Dana—happy New Year, okay? I'm freezing out here in this here parking lot. I'll call you tomorrow when I get back to town. And I l—"

The phone went dead.

"I l—?" What was that supposed to mean? "I listened to the radio on the drive down"? "I lunched with the president"? "I left my heart in San Francisco"?

"I love you"?

Whatever the sentence, it would be at least twelve hours before I'd hear the end of it.

By now only minutes remained of December 31. It was time to compose my annual New Year's statement of purpose.

It was a ritual I'd picked up from my father, who, in a rare reference to spirituality, described it as an offering. "It's not a resolution. It's a kick you give yourself in the ass," he'd explained. "And don't worry, kid. God ain't listening. You don't go to hell if you blow it."

This year I knew exactly what declaration I wanted to make. I'd been thinking about the wording all evening while I worked on Dinner's portrait. Now I addressed the canvas in front of me, uttering the sentence aloud:

"Allow me to develop my talent without obstacles."

It was a fine wish for the coming year; one I'd be wise to heed. In the half a lifetime between college and the present, I'd squandered an awful lot of time dating the wrong men and entering letters into the little white squares of crossword grids.

Then again, Billy genuinely seemed to believe I had a flair for puzzle themes. I had no reason to doubt his judgment. Besides, he was so incredibly . . .

"Without obstacles," I reiterated, bonking myself on the head with the end of my paintbrush for emphasis.

Just then, a frenzy of noisemakers and shrieks erupted on the street.

Puny, who had been lolling on the counter keeping me company, leapt from his perch in terror, scattering my can of brushes and upending my palette facedown on the floor in his haste to find safety under the bed.

I turned over the palette to discover a riotous Rorschach of color. At first glance, the image looked like a vengeful old crone—Hannah, perhaps.

Of all the nights my best friend decides to battle panic disorder, it had to be this one, I thought, grabbing a sponge and a roll of paper towels. I immediately felt guilty when the phone rang a few minutes later. If that was Elinor Ann on the line, she hadn't lasted very long at the open house in Macungie.

"Hello?"

"What the hell are you doing home? I was expecting to leave a message."

All of a sudden, December 31 didn't seem nearly as lonely as I'd made it out to be.

"Long story," I said. "And I could ask you the same question."

"You know I hate New Year's."

"Oh, right. 'Amateur night,' you always called it."

"Good memory."

I could hear the clink of ice cubes in the background. "Still drinking Jim Beam?"

"I stand corrected. Great memory. So . . . what are you up to?"

"I'm on my hands and knees, scrubbing the kitchen floor."

Ray chuckled. "Guess there are worse ways to see in the new year."

Okay, I thought. *He's got to be the mystery caller. He obviously heard the anxiety in my voice when I picked up just before midnight and checked back to make sure I was all right.*

"So, where's this boyfriend of yours, anyway?" he wanted to know, further confirming my suspicions. "Aren't the two of you supposed to be out on the town on a night like this?"

I sighed. "Something like that."

"I'm sorry. You thought I was him on the line, didn't you?"

"Not at all!"

Well, maybe a little. It would have been nice if Hank had asked for more quarters at the 7-Eleven so he could complete his tantalizing sentence.

"I'm glad it's you," I said, and I was. Genuinely. Truly. Honestly.

But I'd really hoped the caller would be Billy, even though of course I was supposed to have hoped for Hank. Hank Hank Hank Hank Hank.

"You two didn't get into a fight, did you?"

"No. He had a medical emergency."

"Nothing life-threatening, I hope."

"Oh, he's not the one who got sick. His pig came down with pneumonia."

Ray immediately started laughing his head off. I guess I couldn't blame him. No doubt he was expecting a woeful tale of a shattered femur, or angioplasty—at the very least, a concussion. Instead, he got indisposed swine.

"I'm sorry," he finally gasped. "I know it's not funny, but—"

But it was. Several minutes elapsed while I sat there, letting him get it out of his system and willing myself not to join in. I was not about to be complicit in turning my boyfriend into an object of ridicule—even if he didn't know how to wire a switch plate. Or sand floors. Or build a Christmas tree stand that actually supported a Christmas tree.

Finally Ray calmed down. "You know, Dana—if you'd told me you were on your own tonight, I would've packed up my bottle and brought it into town. Too bad it's so late."

"Yeah."

"And so many stops on the R train."

"No kidding. Nineteen."

"How the hell did you know that?"

Oh dear, I thought. *The last thing Ray needs to discover is how the hell I know that.* It had been nearly two months since Renée's open house, but I still cringed every time I spotted a pair of pale pink Uggs, which occurred regularly enough to make me wonder if karma had declared a vendetta against me. "I counted the stops on a subway map once. Back when we were . . . you know."

"I'm flattered."

"You should be."

"And I'm sorry I laughed about your boyfriend's pig."

"You should be. He's really very endearing." I didn't dare refer to Dinner by name for fear of setting Ray off again. "And he's turned out to be a wonderful muse for me. I'm working on a portrait of him right now—part of a sixteen-canvas series. He's modeling a collection of vintage hats."

"That sounds promising. Send me some pictures?"

"I'd love to." He gave me his email address, and I finger-painted it in porkpie-hat plum onto a blank area of my canvas.

"Do it tonight, okay? It's been too long since I've seen your work."

"I've already got thumbnails on my computer. I'll send some right after we get off the phone."

"Well, in that case . . ."

"See you next year?"

"Hell no. It's half past midnight. See you this year."

I went over to my computer, located the Hannah file, and selected a half dozen of my favorite portraits. But as soon as I launched my email program and discovered one new message in my in-box, it became clear that Ray was going to have to wait just a little while longer to see them. "So much for 'sporadic access to the Internet,'" I muttered under my breath.

But the words in the subject line were profoundly confusing.

Greetings from Fort Lauderdale!

CHAPTER SEVENTEEN

CUSH AND BOOTS

"Fort *Lauderdale*?!" Elinor Ann said when I called as early as post-New-Year's etiquette would allow the following morning. "What in the world is he doing down there?"

According to the email, taking a busman's holiday:

> Dana—Green-nosed reindeer is a definite go! Adds a nice yuletide element to the red/green theme (and Xmas falls on a Sunday next year . . .).
>
> Got a call the other day from a constructor buddy who runs an annual crossword cruise. A couple of the guys he'd lined up to judge the tournament that serves as its main event came down with the flu, and he was desperate for replacements. So here I am, surrounded by sea, sun, and sky, and from 11 a.m. tomorrow until just before dusk I'll be stuck inside a windowless meeting room full of nerds hunched over puzzles. More of the same the next day. And the day after.
>
> Needless to say, wish you were here.
> W.W.W.

"People actually do that?" Elinor Ann said. "Pay good money for a tropical getaway and stay inside all day long?"

"Apparently crossword people do."

It had taken several exchanges with Billy before I was able to sort out the details. "They solve a series of puzzles varying in size and difficulty," I explained. "They're awarded extra points if they finish before the time limit, have points deducted for incorrect letters—that's where the judges come in."

"I suppose that sounds like a rip-roaring good time to you."

The idea of spending three nights in a stateroom with Billy Moody certainly did, but I wasn't about to mention that. "The tournament part, sure. But flying back and forth to Florida during Christmas week and spending the entire day below deck? Not exactly."

"Maybe there's hope for you after all."

There was one other salient point I neglected to bring up. A different crossword tournament—*the* crossword tournament, according to Billy—was held every February right across the Brooklyn Bridge. And, according to Billy, I absolutely had to compete in it this year.

But that was a conversation for another time—like the day before the tournament was to take place.

"Speaking of hope, what about you?" I said. "How was Macungie?"

"Surprisingly not bad. Of course, Cal was right by my side the whole time, but I Acted As If I were just like everybody else and—well, I was. And then this morning I drove into town and back, just to see if I could manage it."

"And?"

"Well, I didn't throw up. Or pass out. I guess you could call that progress."

"Of course it's progress!"

She sighed. "I just hope I can keep up my momentum. Angus's cast comes off in a couple of days, and he can't wait to get back behind the wheel."

"Don't forget. . . ."

"I know, I know. The boys still need their mother."

I'd spent the bulk of our call in front of my easel, trying to determine whether Dinner's final portrait in the plum porkpie hat required any finishing touches. It did. I'd forgotten to put the commemorative thermometer in his mouth. After a quick image search on the Web, I painted in the glass tube and thin silver line of mercury and stepped back. The canvas was complete, and so was the series.

I went into the living room and upended the coffee table onto the couch, which I shoved against a wall. I had just enough floor space to lay out all sixteen canvases. For the next hour or so, I played with the arrangement, making sure the brightest colors were evenly distributed and the portraits done in profile were looking directly at my favorite head-on poses.

Only one painting remained in its original position, in the upper-left-hand corner of the grid: the one I'd promised to Ray Devine.

He'd called back minutes after I'd sent the jpegs the night before.

"I want one."

I'd been hoping to hear those exact words. "You do?"

"Dana, I—I love them. They're so clever and colorful and witty and . . . you. They're so you. I'm so proud of you."

Despite my solitary state, this was shaping up to be the best New Year's in recent memory. Ray had a good eye, and his opinion had mattered to me since the first day we'd worked together at Prints on Prince.

But back then, Ray's review would have made my day—no, my year. And as happy as I was to have his approval, I already had my own. I knew the work was good.

Hmm, I thought to myself. *Can I finally be growing up?*

"You know, you'd better not break up with that boyfriend of yours," Ray added.

"Huh?"

"That pig is your Helga."

"Huh. I guess he is. So . . . which one do you want?"

"Which one do you think I want?"

My eyes fixed on the canvas featuring the leopard skin pillbox hat. Bob Dylan was Ray's favorite musician; in fact, he'd provided most of the soundtrack to our affair. "Let me guess. The one that reminds you of a certain song from *Blonde on Blonde*?"

He laughed. "Like I always say—best album old Bob ever put out."

"I remember. The painting's yours."

I went to get my camera and took several shots of the final layout. Then I rummaged under the sink for enough shopping bags to carry all sixteen canvases downstairs. Vivian would be clamoring for them as soon as she opened the store tomorrow.

By the time I was done, I heard my stomach growl, and no wonder—it was nearly two o'clock. Maybe I should run down to the falafel place on Second Avenue and pick up a baba ganoush.

On second thought, Hank had told me the vet expected to release Dinner after his overnight stay. Maybe I should run down to the falafel place, pick up two baba ganouches, and surprise him when they returned from Mullica Hill.

That was exactly what I'd do. It had been a long week. I'd missed Hank and my nights at the brownstone.

I thought back to the list I'd been compiling in my head on the day we met. Hank had all the qualities I'd been looking for in a man: Funny. Kind. Devoted. Smart, but not necessarily book smart.

Billy had those qualities as well. But Billy was a kid—albeit a book-smart kid. The age difference hadn't mattered to me when I'd been with Ray, but that was only because I'd been too young to know better. The way I saw things now, it was difficult enough to make a serious commitment to someone. Why complicate the situation even further?

I nodded to myself, taking one final look at the paintings. It was time to start living like a grown-up. What better day to begin?

I grabbed the key and my purse and went out to greet the new year.

I could tell from the chain holding the double front doors shut that he hadn't arrived home yet. The padlock was on the outside. I opened its hasp, stepped into the foyer, and pulled the chain around. So much for surprising him. He'd know I was in the house as soon as he noticed the position of the lock.

But I was the one who turned out to be surprised when I heard the sound of hooves approaching from the back hallway.

"What are you doing here?" I said.

Dinner regarded me impassively, gave the bag containing the baba ganoush an enthusiastic sniff, then turned and retreated to the kitchen.

There was no sign of Hank in there, nor was there any evidence of a recent trip to the vet. The counter was free of pill bottles, as were the cabinets, and, though I was no expert, Dinner appeared to be in perfect health. His appetite had certainly revived; when I reached into the bowl of apples and tossed him one, it disappeared in an instant.

I wandered back to the foyer and poked my head inside the parlor. No overnight bag, no medication. Just a rapidly desiccating tree, still leaning in the corner where Tom-Tom had propped it on Christmas Day.

I decided to continue my inspection upstairs, where I was relieved to discover new signs of renovation. The switch-plate challenge had at last been met: Each room had new ones screwed into place, and when I flipped the toggle in what was to be the master bedroom, a bare bulb hanging from the ceiling illuminated the murk.

But the real revelation came when I opened the door to the adjoining bathroom, which had undergone such a luxurious transformation that it now rivaled the kitchen for sheer opulence. Walls had been knocked out to create a space just a tad smaller than Carnegie Hall. The original claw-foot tub was now reglazed in a matte white finish, which contrasted nicely with an ultramodern corner shower sporting six water jets on each of its marble walls. But the true masterpiece was the floor. Hundreds— maybe thousands—of pieces of pastel beach glass had been arranged there in meandering curves, then sealed with sand-colored grout. Hank had been busier than I realized.

Or not. I thought back to the words he'd spoken the last time we'd seen each other: "Contractors contract."

I scanned the room until I spotted a business card stuck into a corner of the mirror that hung over a pedestal sink. ART UNDERFOOT, it read. TILEWORK BY TIMOTHY.

Another floor guy. I should have known.

Before I could investigate the provenance of the shower and refurbished tub, I heard pounding at the front door. He was back.

"Do *not* confront him right away," I instructed myself on my way downstairs. "Give him a chance to explain why his pig is home and he isn't."

I fumbled with the lock, then threw open the door.

"Sure am glad you decided to drop by," Hank said, grinning at me. In one hand he held his truck keys and a knapsack; in the other, a garment bag. "I been driving around looking for a parking space ever since I dropped off Dinner." He walked inside, dropped his luggage, and wrapped his arms around me. "Boy, am I glad to see you. I sure missed you, Dana."

I was *such* an asshole.

As if that wasn't sufficient, I was an asshole who couldn't leave well enough alone.

"What's in the garment bag?"

"What, this? Just my tuxedo."

I drew back. "I had no idea a trip to the vet was such a dressy occasion."

He laughed, but I could have sworn I saw his shoulders tense before he responded. "Aw, heck. That thing's been hanging in the back of the truck for months now. Didn't want to get plaster dust all over it, but now that the hall closet's got a door, I reckoned it'd be safe to bring inside." He gestured toward the closet, which indeed had a new door—no doubt installed by a door guy.

Clearly it was time to take a page from Elinor Ann's playbook if I wanted to salvage this relationship. It was time to Act As If everything was fine instead of wondering what possible sequence of events would require a general contractor to don formalwear on New Year's Eve.

After he'd hung the garment bag on the closet pole, I smiled and tilted my head toward the hallway. "I picked up lunch on my way down. You hungry?"

"Starving."

We went into the kitchen, where I spotted his cell phone charger sitting empty on the far end of the counter. So he *had* forgotten to take it with him on his trip to New Jersey. At least some percentage of what came out of his mouth was the truth.

"I was worried about you last night," I said as he was unwrapping the sandwiches.

"Why's that?"

"It was awfully late when you called. I was beginning to wonder if you'd been in an accident."

"Yeah, I sure am sorry about that. I was so beat when I finally checked in to the motel, I just plumb forgot to do anything but shut my eyes. By the time I woke up, I was so hungry—well, same deal." He pulled his phone out of the knapsack and placed it in the charger. "Not that there's gonna be a next time, but if there is, I promise to stay in better touch."

"Good." I took a deep breath. "Uh . . . Hank?"

"Yeah?"

"What was it you were saying last night when our call got cut off?"

"Last night?" His eyebrows knitted together while he tried to remember. "Oh, that. You didn't hear me?"

"No," I said, instead of what I really wanted to say, which was *"No!!!"*

A sly smile crossed his face. "You mean right after I wished you a happy new year?"

"Yes," I said, instead of what I really wanted to say, which was *"Yes!!!"*

"Oh, not a whole heck of a lot. Just . . . I love you."

"You do?"

He leaned over to kiss me while my brain pinged around my cranium like a ball inside a pachinko machine. "Course I do. Can't you tell?"

Hank Wheeler loved me! This highly attractive man with impressive (albeit temporary) housing and a lucrative (albeit potentially imaginary) career and undeniable (albeit grammatically incorrect) charm was in love . . . with me!

And how convenient that he already owned a tuxedo for our inevitable foray down the aisle!

My appetite had vanished, and apparently Hank's had, too, because we proceeded directly to the bedroom. Hours later, we polished off one extremely soggy baba ganoush sandwich (I had foolishly left mine too close to the edge of the counter, and Dinner's clutches) and Tom-Tom's bottle of champagne before going back to bed, where I slept the untroubled slumber of the delusional.

It was not until the following morning, when curiosity compelled me to open the door to the hall closet and pull down the zipper on the garment bag, that I realized precisely how delusional I was.

Hank had been honest, up to a point. There was indeed a tuxedo inside the bag.

But attached to its lapel was a boutonnière that was only just beginning to wilt.

"Maybe he had to go to a funeral," Elinor Ann said.

"Yeah, but don't the flowers generally wind up on the coffin, as opposed to the lapels of the guests?"

"Then where do you think he was last night?"

I'd been trying to figure that out all the way home. "I can only come up with one possible scenario."

"A wedding," we said in unison.

"But why wouldn't he have invited you?" She hesitated. "Dana, you don't think Hank's the one who—"

"The one who got married?"

"I hate to say it, but . . ."

The thought had crossed my mind, but based on his recent behavior, it didn't make sense. "Not unless he felt obligated to help some illegal immigrant get her Green Card." Or unless he was a pathological liar who got some sort of perverse kick out of telling women he loved them just before marrying someone else.

"Do you think Hank would get involved in a scheme like that?"

"I have no idea. Oh, Elinor Ann, *what* was he doing in a tuxedo in New Jersey on New Year's Eve?"

"I think you're asking the wrong person. I hate to say this, but I think you're just going to have to confront him about this."

But I didn't want to confront Hank. Not on the day we'd finally put an end to our hiatus. Not right after he'd told me he loved me.

But what oh *what* had he been up to?

"Looks like I have no choice," I conceded. "I'll just have to ask him point-blank what's going on. And who knows? Maybe there's a perfectly logical explanation for all of this."

But I couldn't fathom what that explanation could possibly be, and I was hardly in a hurry to hear it. Maybe I'd wait a week or so—a month, max—and garner a few more declarations of love before ruining everything, not least of all my future.

The phone rang so quickly after we ended our conversation, I assumed Elinor Ann was calling back. "Now what?" I said upon picking up.

"Mercy me! Can't a mother call to wish her daughter a happy new year?"

"Of course she can! Same to you!"

"Did you spend it with that gentleman friend of yours?"

"I'd planned to, but something came up."

"Oh dear."

"An illness in his family—nothing serious, as it turned out." *At least, not as far as Dinner is concerned,* I thought, wincing at my own gullibility. "How's everything?"

"Well, to tell you the truth, I'm a little worried about the Commodore."

Now it was my turn to say oh dear.

"It's just . . . Well, he keeps going on and on about God lately."

This was indeed cause for alarm. Tom Mayo had always been a hard-core realist. "There's no god; there's only nature," he was given to saying. "Human nature. We're on our own, kid."

I didn't want to pose the next question, but seeing as how my father was exactly ninety-nine and three-quarters—plus one day, I felt it was called for. "You don't think he's preparing to . . ."

"Good heavens, no! It's dementia I'm worried about. Why, Cush Keating's husband's convinced she's a spy. He makes her taste all his food before he'll take a single bite."

None of my mother's childhood friends had normal names. There was Cush, and Git, and Mim, and Tig. They called her Boots, though I'd never been given a satisfactory answer as to why, nor had I ever seen her in any footwear other than heels and golf cleats. "Did you speak to Cush about Dad's, uh, newfound faith?"

"Of course not! She'd be worried sick about me! And so far he hasn't been showing any other signs of . . . slippage. He knows who the president is."

"Then maybe there's nothing to worry about."

"I certainly hope not. If your father gets religion . . . well, there are an awful lot of sins I'll miss like the dickens."

After I hung up, I thought of calling Tom-Tom to discuss my mother's concerns, but I didn't see any reason to alarm him as well. Besides, wasn't it fairly common for the elderly to take stock of their lives? A spiritual conversion seemed reasonable, given the amount of time Dad had left. There was nothing demented about it.

I hoped.

I wandered over to the window. Vivian was out front, draping a black velvet cape around the mannequin she placed outside the store to signal it was open for business. The first thing she was going to get from me was her unwieldy box of vintage hats, which had been taking up way too much space in my kitchen for the past several weeks.

I dragged the box down the front stoop, and together we pushed it through the shop door. "Does this mean you're finally done?" she said.

"It does."

"So where the hell are the Hannahs already?"

"Give me five minutes. I think you'll be pleased with the result."

"After all this time, I'd better be." She reached for the phone.

Her smile grew broader with each canvas she pulled from the bags. "Fabulous," she declared them. "I'm going to leave them up until February. They're just what this place needs to draw customers on the slowest month of the year. Smart idea, turning them into a set like this—I bet Graciela will snap up the whole series!"

"That won't be possible." I pointed at the portrait I'd promised to Ray. "The leopard skin pillbox is already spoken for."

"What the fuck do you mean, 'spoken for'?"

"Sorry, but that's the way it is."

She fumed for the next hour while the two of us hung the canvases according to my layout. "I can't imagine what you were thinking. How you can break up a grouping like this is beyond me. Can't you just grab another hat and bang out a replacement?"

Of course I could. But I was getting awfully tired of Vivian's demands. "I'll have to mull that over and get back to you."

"*Fine.* But you'd better mull fast if you want to keep working for me."

Come to think of it, I was getting awfully tired of her threats as well—not to mention the fifty percent commission she was about to receive after just one quick phone call to Graciela.

She placed the last of the paintings on its hook and nudged it level. "At least that's over with. Now, before you leave, go into the dressing room. There's a Victorian wedding dress in there, and I need to get a photo for the Web site."

Swell, I thought. I'd heard the word "wedding" enough to last all year, and it was only the second of January.

The ivory satin gown had something like a thousand close-set buttons running up the back of its bodice, but I knew better than to enlist Vivian's help with them when her mood was this dark. Instead, I stepped into the dress backward and started fastening it from the bottom up. I'd swivel it around when I reached the armpits and trust she'd have calmed down when the time came to close the final, unreachable top buttons.

I had barely begun when the bell on the front entrance jangled and a yelp pierced the quiet.

"They're spectacular! My dear, I'm over the moon!"

Graciela. I figured she'd been on the receiving end of Vivian's call.

"I knew you'd adore them. I think they're Hannah's best work ever."

Temporarily trapped, I stood in the dressing room and listened to my patron's jewelry rattle while she paced back and forth in front of the paintings. "They're certainly her most cohesive. I'm sure you realize I've simply got to have the entire series."

Uh-oh, I thought. *If Vivian agrees to sell her all sixteen canvases, a very*

*pissed-off half-dressed bride is going to have to go out there and put a stop
to it.*

But to her credit, and my amazement, Vivian stood firm. "Well, here's
the thing. My stupid little fag of an assistant mistakenly sold one this
morning—but don't worry. I've already called my picker up in Maine.
He said he'd go by Hannah's place tomorrow with more canvases and a
ton of Cool Ranch Doritos and sweet-talk her into painting a replacement."

"Do you think she'll agree to such a request?"

"I'm sure of it."

So am I, I thought. *But first, Vivian's going to have to apologize for calling me her stupid little fag of an assistant.*

"I'd really love to pick them up next weekend," Graciela said.

"I think we might just be able to pull that off."

So much for leaving the series up all month, I thought. *And Vivian had
better be prepared to rethink her commission if she expects to get a new painting before Labor Day.*

"You realize this is a breakthrough series for Hannah," Vivian continued. "A milestone, really . . ."

Graciela heaved a theatrical sigh. "How much?"

"Twenty-five thousand."

Inside the dressing room, I gasped. But my reaction wasn't due to the
figure Vivian had quoted—not that it wasn't gasp-worthy. I had just
managed to turn the dress around and wriggle my arms through the
sleeves, and the sight of myself in the most perfect wedding dress in the
history of matrimony had taken my breath away.

I had to have that dress.

And Vivian had to have one more Hannah.

How convenient.

CHAPTER EIGHTEEN

CLEANUP ON AISLE THREE

"Whatever happened to 'Marriage is an outdated institution'?" Elinor Ann wanted to know when I called, bubbling over with particulars of ecru satin and flattering drapery that tapered to a train in the back.

"I know, I know. I always swore I wouldn't be brainwashed by the wedding industry. But . . ."

But then I'd gone into Vivian's dressing room and wound up in a parallel universe, wondering if Hank would agree to walk down the aisle to Sam Cooke's "Nothing Can Change This Love" and picturing Dinner as our flower bearer, girdled in a gossamer pink tutu and carrying a wicker basket of gardenias in his mouth.

"Well, at least your boyfriend has something to wear to the nuptials," Elinor Ann said. "Unless he got married in the tuxedo last weekend, of course."

I'd been expecting her to raise the issue. I'd been trying to raise it myself, with Hank, but so far I'd been unable to come up with a conversational gambit that didn't involve the word "snooping."

"I'm sure he has a perfectly reasonable explanation for whatever he was doing in New Jersey last weekend."

"Yikes, Dana. That must be some dress."

Was it ever. The gown had transformed me into a pre-Raphaelite portrait by Rossetti, a vision I barely recognized. Its high neck and long, fitted sleeves gave me a regal bearing, one I accentuated by fishing a hair clip out of my purse to create a quick up-do of messy, yet artfully cascading, curls. As soon as Graciela exited the shop, I grabbed a nosegay of dried flowers from the vase sitting on the dressing-room table, then parted the velvet curtains.

"Holy crap," Vivian said when I walked toward her. "You just doubled my asking price." She reached for her camera, but I extended my newly elegant arm across the desk to stop her.

"Not so fast."

She issued the sigh of the long-suffering. "Now you want a piece of the action? After all that money I just made for you?"

"That's not what I meant." I turned toward the mirror to catch another intoxicating glimpse of the new *moi*. "I was thinking we could work out some kind of . . . barter arrangement."

Her eyes widened. "Since when are you in the market for a wedding gown?"

"I'm not." As far as Vivian knew, I'd been chronically single since the day we'd met, and I saw no reason to enlighten her. Hank had visited my apartment on only a couple of occasions; there was so much more room at the brownstone, and Dinner was a more high-maintenance pet than Puny. "But a dress like this comes along once in a lifetime. I'd just like to be ready when—if—I meet the right guy."

She pointed in the direction of the hat series. "You know, if you wanted to make it easy on yourself, I'd swap you for that painting in the upper-left-hand corner."

"Like I told you, it's spoken for."

"*Fine.* Then the dress is going to cost you three Hannahs."

I would have readily agreed to double that number, but I forced myself to look aggrieved as I nodded my acquiescence and returned to the dressing room. It seemed like a waste of time to unfasten all those tiny buttons. As soon as I got the gown upstairs, I was just going to put it back on and twirl around and around until it was time to meet Hank for dinner.

"Don't forget—I need the replacement for the leopard pillbox first," Vivian called after me as I walked out, the dress draped over my arm.

"No problem. I'll have it for you early next week."

But early next week would turn out to be too late. On my way home from the brownstone the following afternoon, I encountered a blank wall where the paintings had hung. Graciela had shown up right after Vivian opened the store, packed up her fifteen canvases, and driven off with them.

"What'd she do that for?" I said. "I thought she was willing to wait for the replacement."

Vivian shrugged and handed me the portrait I'd promised to Ray Devine. "Do you want your half of the twenty-five grand or what?"

I entered my apartment in a state of extreme giddiness. The five-figure sum was by far the largest payday I'd ever had. Vivian had postdated the check ("You'll wipe out my operating budget if you cash it before Graciela's clears"), but I didn't mind. For the next five days, I'd have a visual reminder that my creativity paid the bills.

There was only one problem. My creativity was paying Vivian's bills as well, and I was becoming increasingly rankled by our fifty-fifty split.

Then again, what if Elinor Ann's assertion was true? What if I *was* committing fraud by posing as Hannah—punishable-by-jail fraud? Maybe having Vivian serve as an intermediary between me and my patron provided me with a useful measure of protection.

Even so, the twelve thousand five hundred dollars she'd just pocketed struck me as an insanely high price to pay for it.

I slid the check into the edge of my bedroom mirror, topped off Puny's bowl, then turned on the computer.

Billy Moody was back on dry land:

> Hey, Dana—sitting in FLL waiting to board my flight to
> LGA and wondering if you could do me a favor. I've never
> constructed a Sunday puzzle before, so I thought I should find
> out if I was up to the job before tackling our red/green theme.
> The crossword cruisers were such an early-to-bed bunch, I
> finally had time to finish it. Would you mind test-solving it for
> me? I'm so locked into Saturday mode that I need to make sure
> the clueing is appropriately easyish.
>   If you're willing to help me out, I'll buy you dinner.
>   W.W.W.
>
> P.S. Even if you aren't, I'll buy you dinner.

Of course I was honored. Of course I'd solve it. But dinner?

I raised my eyes from the computer screen and beheld the satin gown hanging on the outside of my closet door, then hit Reply.

> Are you kidding? Being asked to test-solve a prepublication
> W.W.W. Moody makes me feel like crossword royalty. Send away.
>   The only drawback to helping you out is that some Sunday
> down the road I'm going to open up the Magazine section and
> curse when I realize I've already solved the puzzle. So instead of
> dinner, how about buying me brunch on the day it runs? You
> know—broad daylight, hustle and bustle, *waaay* less romantic . . .

There. I'd done it: I had finally sent a clear message that my relationship with Billy should be based on words, not deeds—especially not The

Dirty Deed. And proven, perhaps, that I was worthy of that wedding dress.

But was Hank worthy of me?

Until the mystery of the boutonnière was solved, there was no way to answer the question.

Despite my ongoing suspicions, the events of the previous evening had brought us closer, in a way I hadn't anticipated.

I'd arrived at the brownstone to discover him applying primer to a new set of balusters on the foyer staircase, although "set" was hardly the right term for them, nor was the adjective "new." Each of the twenty or so antique posts was shaped differently, one with ornate curves and a ball top, another with a square base and fluted column, and so on.

"That looks *so cool*."

Hank smiled. "I reckon it does. Wasn't sure what I was going to come up with when I yanked out those old broken-down ones, but the client told me he wanted color and whimsy. In fact, he just about went ape last week when I sent pictures of the bathroom floor. So I figured I'd keep it up."

"These are whimsical, all right," I said, secretly rejoicing that he'd defined the word correctly. "What about the color part?"

"Ain't thought that far ahead yet."

"Mind if I give it a shot?"

His face brightened. "Would you?"

I examined a few of the balusters. Giving them the full Hannah treatment might be a little too raucous, especially if the client intended to hang art on the foyer walls. But if I toned the palette down to pastels . . .

"How about I try one and you decide after that?"

He came down the stairs and put his arms around my waist. "I don't need to wait—I seen your paintings. That's good enough for me."

I tried to remember what had been on my easel during his most recent visit to Ninth Street. Handbags, probably. It had been right after Vivian scored a slew of Judith Leiber evening clutches at a New Jersey estate sale. "Are you sure?"

"You're hired. It'll be real nice having you around during the day."

Hmm. It would be nice. And illuminating as well, since I'd finally discover exactly how much of the brownstone renovation was actually being carried out by Hank. "What do you think a reasonable budget would be for something like this?"

He laughed. "Name your price. Some people are only happy when they're blowing too much money, and this guy's the biggest spender I ever had."

I counted the balusters from the bottom step up, arriving at a total of twenty-two. "Do you think a hundred apiece is too much?"

"What the heck—make it two."

I did a quick mental calculation. "Forty-four hundred dollars? For a paint job? Are you serious?"

"Shoot, that's nothing to this guy. He paid at least three times as much for the bathroom floor."

"Forty-four hundred dollars? For a paint job? Are you serious?" Elinor Ann said when I called to tell her about my new commission. "Dana, are you absolutely sure you're going to receive this money?"

"I don't see why I wouldn't." After all, the Timothy of "Tilework by Timothy" had completed his work in the bathroom. He wouldn't have done the job for free, would he? "The brownstone's really come a long way over the past few months. I wish you could see it."

"Right. As if *that's* ever going to happen."

She had a point. Elinor Ann had been to visit me a grand total of once, shortly after I'd moved into my apartment. She'd decided New York City was too dirty and expensive and crowded to ever return.

Now I had to wonder: Was her reaction a harbinger of her panic disorder? I'd invited her back repeatedly, but she'd always had an excuse to remain at home.

"How's the driving coming?" I asked her. "Are you still Acting As If?"

She sighed. "I'm trying. But now that Angus's cast is off, I'm back in the passenger seat more often than not."

"Just make sure you take a trip on your own every day," I said. "Even if it's only a mile or two down the road. Inure yourself."

"Oh, don't worry. I'm inuring."

I heard a *ping* coming from my computer and went into the bedroom to check my in-box. Billy's Sunday puzzle had at last arrived. I opened the attached document, sent it to the printer, and rushed back to the kitchen so Elinor Ann wouldn't hear the whir of the machine.

I was too late. "What's that sound?"

"Oh, nothing."

"Oh no. Why do I get the feeling this has something to do with your youthful friend?"

As soon as I glanced at the printout, I groaned. Many of the boxes in the grid had been shaded so that gray, somewhat lopsided plus-sign shapes were scattered across the page. When it came to crosswords, I was a purist. The only thing I hated more than shaded boxes was the addition of circles to individual squares.

I skimmed the clues and groaned louder. There was, come to think of it, one thing I found even more heinous than circles: cross-referenced clues. This puzzle was loaded with them.

16-Across: With 7-Down, clue for 13-Across.

53-Across: With 44-Down, clue for 39-Across.

Swell.

Cross-referencing clashed with my solving style. I liked to start at the first clue and sweep my way diagonally across the page. But in this puzzle, the only way to figure out the words that made up the themed clues would be to solve the surrounding fill.

To my relief, Billy had made those clues extremely easy. In no time I discovered that 16-Across was GAME SHOW, and 7-Down was PHRASE, which made the themed clue in 13-Across CIRCLE GETS THE SQUARE. And the combined clues for 39-Across, STIEGLITZ and PALETTE, meant that answer was BLACK AND WHITE.

Aha. Crossword terminology. And each of the paired clues for the themed entries comprised . . . crossed words; hence the gray shading.

Clever.

> Never thought I'd say this, but your puzzle just proved there is justification after all for cross-referenced clues. Diabolically brilliant, as usual, and the inclusion of interesting fill words like "McJob" and "Bichon Poo" will only serve to burnish your reputation.
>
> If anything, some of the clues for the fill might be just a little *too* gimme-ish. How about "7th Avenue venue, briefly" (as opposed to "Controversial flavor enhancer") for MSG? Or "Lost '70s cause" (as opposed to "Pitcher's stat") for ERA? Still gettable, but a bit meatier than your current fallbacks. Happy to supply more suggestions if you're amenable.
>
> I have a feeling you'll be buying me that brunch in a matter of weeks!

I figured it couldn't hurt to remind him—or myself—about the brunch, and the new ground rules for our relationship. But even if Billy were to suggest an impromptu liaison, I'd be much too busy to consider it. Between Hank's balusters and my three-Hannah debt to Vivian, I'd be painting late into the evening.

She'd asked me to work with several colorful pairs of Acme cowboy boots dating from the 1950s for the next series, which ruled out Dinner as my model. The boots, however, would make wonderful vases. I decided to run over to the Korean market on First Avenue and pick up a few bouquets for inspiration.

By the time I returned home, the message light on the answering machine was blinking.

"Hi, sweetie. It's your big brother. I'm looking into flights for Dad's birthday and had a quick question about your schedule that week. Oh well. No need to call back—we can discuss it next Thursday night. See you then!"

Next Thursday?

I looked at the calendar hanging over the stove. Of course—the Outsider Art Fair. Tom-Tom had given Hank that pair of tickets to its opening night party as a Christmas gift.

"We ain't never going to find your brother in this crowd," Hank said once we'd made our way past the scrum at the entrance to the art show. I could hardly disagree. It seemed every New Yorker with a penchant for theatrical makeup and complicated hairstyles had squeezed into the catacombs-like space. One hapless dealer, set up near the endless line for the coat check, stood with his arms spread in front of his tabletop display of eerie, head-shaped urns in a valiant attempt to prevent them from becoming a pile of worthless shards. When a chubby downtown doyenne in Madame Butterfly whiteface bumped into the table, he let out a terrified shriek.

"Maybe there'll be more room around the corner," I said, craning my neck for a glimpse of Tom-Tom's shock of white hair.

The crowd was sparser in the second aisle, but only marginally—the difference between, say, a five thirty northbound 6 train and a five forty-five. Full-body contact with strangers was the rule, not the exception. Despite the overwhelming heat, I was relieved to have the protection of the shearling coat I'd just treated myself to, courtesy of Graciela's largesse.

Miraculously, Hank managed to commandeer an empty stretch of wall. Exhausted and damp, I leaned against him and pulled out my cell phone.

"I hope you're not at the show yet," my half brother said when he picked up. "Oh dear. You are, aren't you? I can hear the clamor of the arrivistes."

"Why didn't you warn me it would be so packed?"

"I thought I had. But don't worry. It invariably thins out after a couple of hours."

"A couple of *hours*?" Hank and I exchanged glances. "Tom-Tom? I don't think we'll be able to hold out that long."

"Don't worry—I'm on my way. My driver just turned left onto Fifth in front of the Pierre—try to enjoy yourselves until I can meet up with you."

"Tell your driver to run the yellow lights."

"I already have, sweetie."

Hank eyed me warily while I returned my phone to my purse. "It won't be a couple of hours," I told him. "More like twenty minutes, I'd say."

"That's a relief. Guess we might as well try to see us some art while we wait."

As usual, there was some wheat amidst the chaff. A spectral portrait of a woman in an empty, moonlit room made me long for more discretionary income. And one of my favorite crazed geniuses, A. G. Rizzoli, had a booth dedicated to his meticulous drawings of imaginary palaces. As we made our way from booth to booth, I kept my hand on the back of Hank's jacket and let him lead the way through the crush.

When he rounded the third corner, he stopped dead. "Would you look at those," he said, pulling me around to his side and pointing to the end of the aisle. "They look just like Dinner!"

The woman in front of him—a PETA activist, judging from her

rubber messenger bag—turned to give him a withering glance. "You're *sick*," she hissed.

But I was the one who felt sick all of a sudden. There was a reason the paintings looked like Dinner, of course. They were Dinner.

The press of people seemed to be thickest in front of the display, which was topped with three-foot-high red letters spelling out "HAN-NAH." Below them, all fifteen portraits from the hat series were lined up in rows of five, and dozens of my other canvases hung on the adjacent walls.

Suddenly, the din of the crowd was replaced with a buzzing noise inside my head.

But Graciela's voice penetrated the drone.

". . . And she's positively *mad* for Cool Ranch Doritos!" I heard her say, just before I burst into uncontrollable peals of laughter.

Hank seemed to sense something was wrong, as opposed to hilarious. He put his arm around my waist and began to steer a path against the incoming tide—which parted readily when confronted with a cackling madwoman, mascara-blackened tears streaming down her face.

When we finally made it past the show's entrance and out to the elevator, its doors opened to reveal my half brother.

"What in the world happened to you?" he said, whipping out one of his Irish linen handkerchiefs and dabbing at my eyes. By now my laughing jag was subsiding, but I couldn't seem to form a sentence.

Hank laid a hand on Tom-Tom's arm. "Give us a few minutes," he said. "We'll be in there." He tilted his head in the direction of a door marked STAIRS, and we proceeded toward it, while my baffled brother pressed his handkerchief into my hand before joining the line of people waiting to enter the exhibit.

We had the landing to ourselves. We sat down on the top step, and Hank waited while I cleaned myself up as best I could. By the time I finished, Tom-Tom's handkerchief was soggy and gray.

"Mind telling me what was so funny back there?"

"Nothing. That's just this . . . psychological tic I have. I guess you could call it a coping mechanism for dealing with shock."

His concerned expression gave way to one of relief. "That's good. I mean—that's bad, but it's better than what I was thinking. I was thinking you might be, well . . . pregnant or something."

"Pregnant? Of course I'm not pregnant! I'm—I'm Hannah."

"Who?"

"The artist. Who paints pigs. And is positively mad for Cool Ranch Doritos."

"No kidding? You're her? That really *was* Dinner?"

I nodded.

Now it was his turn to laugh. "Damn! You're about to be famous!"

"Well, here's the thing. It isn't quite that simple. Hannah's supposed to be an eighty-two-year-old resident of Maine who lives in a tar paper shack and eats squirrels she traps in the woods."

He raised an eyebrow. "How'd that happen?"

"The woman I work for thought it would—I don't know—add cachet, I suppose."

Hank rubbed his temples, taking it all in. "Looks like she was onto something. That booth sure was packed. So . . . what's the problem?"

"I'm worried our subterfuge might be construed as . . . fraud."

"Fraud? Heck, that ain't fraud. From what I seen, them paintings were the best thing in the whole show."

"Thanks, but in case you haven't noticed, I'm hardly eighty-two."

"That don't matter. If you say you're Hannah, you're Hannah, right?"

"Yeah, but—"

He stopped me with a look. "Dana, this here's America. You can be anybody you want, long as you ain't killin' people or blowin' stuff up. And . . . I ought to know." He reached for his wallet and pulled out a driver's license, but not his current one. This one had been issued in

Tennessee—quite a while ago, judging by the picture of a much younger Hank in its corner.

He held out his hand. "Nice to meet you . . . Hannah."

I absentmindedly shook it while continuing to inspect the license. "Nice to meet you, too. . . ."

Jefferson Davis Calhoun?!!

CHAPTER NINETEEN

DOUBLE JEOPARDY

"You can keep calling me Hank," he said while I sat gaping at the license, my emotions ping-ponging between confusion and outrage. "I been him going on eleven years now."

I looked into his eyes. "So . . . who *are* you?"

He met my gaze and shrugged. "Who are you? Dana Mayo? Or this Hannah lady?"

"But—"

But wait a second. This was different. Whatever Hank—no, J.D.—no, Hank—was involved in, I had a feeling it was a more serious transgression than painting under a *nom de pinceau*.

But what, exactly, *was* he involved in? Identity theft? Apparently. But what had necessitated the name change? Was he on the lam? If so, from what? Murder? Kidnapping?

Oh god. I *so* should have followed through with Tom-Tom's suggestion at Christmas and conducted a background check.

I backed up as far as the wall would allow and handed Hank the license. "You need to explain what this is all about. Immediately."

"That's just what I'm planning on doing. But let me tell you right off the bat—there ain't no stain on the name Calhoun. We're just poor folks, that's all. Never did have nothing. When my daddy died, all he left me was his truck."

"The panel truck?"

He nodded. "Used to be his daddy's. Soon as I got it, I started doing odd jobs here and there—painting, moving . . . whatever paid cash."

"I don't see what this has to do with—"

"I'm gettin' to it. One day a guy hired me to clear out one of them self-storage units. Turns out when folks don't pay their bill for a couple of months, whatever they got in there gets sold off to the highest bidder."

"I thought about going to one of those auctions a while back. But then I heard you don't get to look inside the units before you bid."

"You sure don't. I always figured you'd get stuck with a bunch of broken-down junk. But this guy I was working for decided he'd take a shot anyway. He laid out forty bucks and wound up with some fancy Art Deco bedroom set, and a whole mess of other old stuff, and he took it on over to the antique mall outside Knoxville and made himself a whole mess of money."

"So you decided to do the same thing."

"You bet I did. And I'll tell you what—I wound up with more broken-down junk than you ever saw in your whole life. Don't matter how busted a bike is, folks can't seem to get rid of it. Or old newspapers. Or beat-up rugs full of holes. Once in a while I might make a buck or two off a set of tires or a baby crib, but it was rough going, that's for sure. And then one day I got lucky."

Finally, I thought. By now my fingernails had left burgundy-colored half-moons in the palms of my hands.

"I kept showing up, and after a while I started to get pretty chummy with the auctioneer. One day he tells me about this old guy whose brother'd died up in New York City. Guy drove north, packed up the brother's apartment, hauled everything down to Tennessee, and put it all into a storage unit earlier that year. Now that guy was dead, too. With no kin."

At last I understood where his story was going. "And the brother's name was Hank Wheeler."

"Sure was."

To hear Hank tell it, anybody would have recycled the name.

"First box I opened was nothing but a bunch of old paperwork. I'll tell you, I sure wasn't happy to see that. But I dug around a little and found a folder full of tax returns. The last year this guy filed, he made over two hundred grand. Well, I near about fell over when I saw that. And when I looked at what line of work he was in and read 'contractor,' I thought, heck—I could do that."

My mind immediately returned to the switch-plate incident. "Guess it turned out to be a little more involved than you expected, huh?"

"Not really. I knew the job was more than slapping on paint and hammering nails. But Wheeler hired folks to do the hard stuff for him. There was piles of invoices from all sorts of specialists—plasterers, stained-glass restorers, you name it—and every last one of 'em charged a fortune. Not that old Hank minded. Turns out every time they'd send him a bill, he'd just turn around and charge his clients even more for the work they done."

"Twenty percent more," I said.

"How'd you know that?"

"My brother." I remembered Tom-Tom railing against the practice—called ten and ten, for ten percent overhead and ten percent profit—when he'd had renovations done on his town house a few years back. No wonder Hank had encouraged me to double the price on those balusters.

"Ain't that the sweetest deal you ever heard of? I couldn't hardly believe what I was lookin' at."

I couldn't hardly believe what I was hearing. "But—I don't get it. If the real Hank Wheeler was dead, wouldn't his clients and all those crafts-men have heard about it?"

"They knew all about it. That's why I had 'Hank Wheeler and Son' painted on the side of the truck."

"Ohhhh. And *Son*."

"After that, I was all set. Made some calls and moved on up a week later. Hank Wheeler did some real fine work in this town. Folks couldn't wait to hire Junior."

Damn, I thought to myself. *New Yorkers are so gullible when it comes to . . . brownstone whisperers. And I ought to know.*

The door to the stairwell squeaked open, and Tom-Tom cautiously poked his head inside. "Is it safe to come in yet?"

"Be my guest. I'm fine." I held up a sodden lump of cloth. "Your handkerchief wasn't so lucky."

He waved a hand in dismissal and extracted a pillbox from his jacket pocket. "Have a Valium. God knows you look like you could use one. In fact—have two." He shook a couple of tablets into my palm, and I gulped one down, putting the other in my change purse for safekeeping. The way the evening was going, I had a feeling it would come in handy.

Tom-Tom took a seat and peered into my eyes. "That was quite the exit you made. Are you sure you're feeling all right?"

My brain was so overloaded with new information about my boyfriend, it took a few seconds before I could recall the circumstances. "Oh, that. Uh—did you happen to notice the pig portraits in there?"

"How could I not? The mob around them was so dense, I could hardly squeeze past. I found them charming, actually—don't you think they looked just like Dinner? And what a story about the artist." He placed one hand over his heart, intoning, "A geriatric star is born."

Hank chuckled. "That's a fine way to talk about your kid sister."

"I beg your pardon?"

"She's the one painting 'em."

Tom-Tom let out a yelp. "They're *yours*? You're—?"

My brother's laugh has always been distinctive. When people first hear it, they often wonder aloud what happened to his beard and red suit. Robust ho-ho-hos echoed in the stairwell for the next few minutes.

"What in the *world* were you smoking to come up with a story like that?" he finally said.

"I didn't come up with it. Vivian did."

"The bitch who sells the vintage clothing?"

I nodded. "Graciela—the dealer you just saw in there—came into the store one day, and Vivian just . . . went to town. Next thing I knew, I was Hannah."

"Extraordinary. And I'm impressed. The paintings really are quite charming."

"I appreciate your saying so. But is what I'm doing . . . legal?"

Tom-Tom rose to his feet. "I'm famished. Let's discuss it over paella."

Normally I loved going to dinner at El Quixote, but that evening I would have preferred to be stretched out on my bed digesting Hank's revelation, not jammed into a banquette digesting paella. I laid out the details of my arrangement with Vivian while Tom-Tom listened intently.

"A fifty percent commission is unconscionable," he declared. "Although it *does* provide you with an added layer of protection."

"Protection?" The forkful of rice I'd just taken turned to Styrofoam in my mouth. "So I am committing a crime?"

"That's a bit of a gray area. The paintings are all the work of a single artist, so thankfully forgery's not an issue. It's just that the artist has very little in common with her official biography." He shook his head slowly from side to side. "Honestly, that Graciela woman is a real rube. The first thing any reputable dealer would have done is establish provenance."

"How would they do that?" I asked, just as Hank was requesting a definition of the word.

"Provenance is a way of authenticating a work of art," Tom-Tom explained. "Which can be accomplished using a variety of methods. With

212 • **JANET GOSS**

the type of artists I tend to represent—long-dead ones—one would need to have a professional appraisal done by an expert if there was any question about a painting's lineage."

"I get it," Hank said. "But Hannah ain't dead. What happens then?"

"For a living artist, a personal encounter could suffice, and allegedly this New England picker Vivian dreamed up has regular contact with her. As long as your partner in crime sticks to her story—and why wouldn't she, for half the take?—I can't imagine your secret would be exposed."

Hank squeezed my arm. "See? You got nothing to worry about."

"Of course," Tom-Tom continued, "should some intrepid dealer decide to make a trip to Maine in order to ferret out Hannah . . ."

He stopped midsentence and slapped his forehead with the butt of his hand. "That's it!"

"What's it?" Hank and I chorused.

"Some intrepid dealer"—he pointed at his head with both index fingers—"just decided to feign a trip to Maine. Two Hannah sightings is twice the protection, especially when one of them comes from a professional with more than forty years in the business."

I was touched by Tom-Tom's willingness to get involved, but I wasn't convinced he was the right person for the job. His affluent clients were the type who purchased Rembrandts, not folk art. And if his machinations on my behalf were discovered, they wouldn't be buying any art from him ever again. "Don't you think you're taking an awfully big risk with your reputation? What if something . . . happened?"

"Then I'd retire. Air travel's become so abysmal of late, I've been considering it, anyway. God, I miss the Concorde." He covered my hand with his. "Honestly, Dana, Vivian's taking advantage of you this way makes me so livid, I consider it my brotherly duty to stick my neck out. Give me your next couple of canvases and let me reach out to that gallery owner."

"Take him up on it," Hank said. "You'll double your money."

"But I can't cut off Vivian entirely. If I stop giving her paintings to sell, she'll expose me to Graciela in a heartbeat."

"Then at the very least, reduce her supply curve," Tom-Tom instructed. "Now, what can you tell me about Hannah that only someone with an intimate knowledge of her work would be aware of?"

I pondered the question while Hank poured another round of sangria. "I've got it. You know the hat series Graciela had on display? It was originally a grid of sixteen paintings. She's one short."

"Is she aware of this?"

"She was pretty disgruntled about not getting the entire set."

"Do you still have it?"

"It's in my apartment."

Tom-Tom clapped his hands in delight.

"Not so fast," I cautioned. "I promised it to an old friend of mine." Judging from the expression on his face, my half brother knew immediately which old friend I was referring to. "And don't try to talk me into giving it to you, because that's not going to happen."

"Then I hope you're prepared to make a damn good copy."

"That was some night," Hank said after we'd said our goodbyes to Tom-Tom and settled into the backseat of an eastbound cab. "I sure am glad your brother decided to help you out."

"I don't know. I'd never forgive myself if he got into trouble over this."

He draped an arm across my shoulders. "I wouldn't worry about him. That boy sure can talk. And there's nothin' folks like better than a good story."

Yeah, and I'm one of those folks, I thought, wincing at how readily I'd absorbed tales of Hank's bucolic childhood—in the fertile crescent of Las Vegas, of all places—and blithely relegated his lack of contracting skills to the back burner of my mind. How much of what came out of his mouth was the truth?

And couldn't he at least have revealed his true identity before telling me he loved me? Or was that a lie, too?

Oh god. Elinor Ann was going to have a field day.

I had a million questions, but as the cab made a right onto Second Avenue, I realized I didn't have the stamina for a lengthy cross-examination. I leaned forward and tapped on the plastic divider to get the driver's attention. "It's going to be two stops tonight," I called out. "I need you to drop me off at Ninth Street."

I felt Hank's body stiffen. "What's wrong? I mean, I got a pretty good idea what's wrong, but please give me a chance to explain why I done what I done, Dana. I didn't hardly get started when your brother showed up in that stairwell tonight."

Maybe I was overreacting. Maybe he could explain. But Mr. Jefferson Davis Calhoun was just going to have to cool his heels until I got some rest.

"I promise I'll give you all the time you need," I told him. "But right now I'm too overwhelmed to take in any more information."

"I reckon I can't blame you. But you'll call me after you get up?"

"I'll see you after I get up. I've got all those balusters to paint, don't I?" I forced a smile.

Finally he relaxed and leaned over to kiss me good night. "You don't know how happy I am to hear you say that."

Staggering up my front stoop, I knew I'd made the right decision. Everything could be put on hold until tomorrow.

Well, almost everything.

As soon as I unlocked the door to my apartment, I strode to the bedroom and removed the Victorian wedding gown from its featured spot on the front of my closet door. The last thing I needed to see upon opening my eyes in the morning was this trenchant reminder of my steadfast gullibility. I hung it on the inside rod and shut the door tight.

There. Now all I had to do was crawl into bed with that extra Valium Tom-Tom had so thoughtfully provided.

On second thought, perhaps it would be wise to put Elinor Ann on notice that an extended phone conversation was in her immediate future. It was just after eleven, much too late to call, so I turned on the computer and sent off an email. Then, even though I knew I shouldn't, I gave my in-box a quick once-over.

Billy Moody had finally had time to go over the alternative clues I'd supplied for his Sunday behemoth.

> Great job—loved (and used) about 80% of your suggestions, as you'll discover when you open the attached final puzzle. "Pieholes" for TRAPS was particularly inspired.
>
> I'll wait for you to look it over one last time before I send it off. Really appreciate both your time and your inimitable way with clues.
>
> Can't thank you enough (but I'd love to try).
> W.W.W.

I clicked open the attachment, but as soon as the grid appeared on my monitor, I decided it was one more thing best dealt with in the light of day.

> Glad you're glad, even though you're as adept a cluemeister as you are a gridmeister, and you know it. I'll give this my undivided attention in the morning, after I've recovered from the most harrowing evening in recent memory.

My phone—the cell, not the landline—rang seconds later. Of course I knew who was calling. Of course I knew not to answer it. I flipped open the phone and held it to my ear.

"Why don't you come on over and tell your uncle Billy all about it?"

CHAPTER TWENTY

MAKE ROOM FOR DADDY

"I'm not going anywhere," I told him.

"That's okay. I make house calls."

I should have known better than to email him. Billy was adorable and attentive and uncomplicated. And if I let him come over, I wouldn't give Hannah or Hank or Jefferson Davis Calhoun another thought for the rest of the night—which was obviously what I wanted, because of course I'd known better than to email him.

"Good," he said.

"What is?"

"You haven't uttered a word for the past two minutes. That means you're struggling with your conscience. Give in."

God knows I wanted to. Just the sound of his breathing through the receiver was making certain parts of my body misbehave. "That wouldn't be fair to anybody," I said. "Least of all you."

"I don't mind. Go ahead—use me."

The second Valium I'd taken was beginning to kick in, which wasn't at all conducive to shoring up one's resolve.

"To be honest, I can't think of anything I'd rather do right now than use you. But I'm trying to be a grown-up here." For once.

"Being a grown-up is overrated. Let me come over and remind you how much fun it is to be an adolescent."

"Stop," I whimpered, my mountain of resolve quickly crumbling to molehill proportions. "It's been a rough day. I really need you to back off."

"Then at least tell me what was so harrowing about your evening."

"I'd rather not get into that over the phone."

"Then it's settled. I'll be right over."

He'd already hung up by the time I shrieked, "You *can't*!"

Oh crap. Billy Moody would be right over.

But wait a second. He couldn't be right over. He didn't know where I lived.

Oh crap. Yes he did. I'd given him my coordinates of Ninth and Second in our first spate of email exchanges.

But wait a second. My apartment was a few doors down from the corner. He'd never figure out which building was mine.

Oh crap. Yes he would. Because on that fateful night we'd met for one drink, I'd mentioned I worked for the owner of the vintage clothing shop *right downstairs from my apartment*.

Get a grip, I told myself. *Just because Billy knows how to find you doesn't mean you have to let him in—or even see him. Just turn off the light in the front room, get ready for bed, and by the time he shows up, the Valium will have lulled you off to safety.*

I went into the bathroom and brushed my teeth, then put on a little loose powder and lip stain because . . .

Ah. Because you never knew when there might be a fire, and no woman would want to find herself out on the street in the middle of the night looking her worst, would she?

My cell phone rang just as I was getting into bed, but, according to plan, I let the call go straight to voice mail. I fluffed my pillows, switched off the light, and closed my eyes.

But only until enough time had elapsed for me to retrieve the message.

"I know you're up there," Billy said. "And if you don't come down and talk to me in the next two minutes, I'm going to give you my best Stanley Kowalski impression until you do."

He wouldn't. He *couldn't*. He—

"Daaanaaaaa!"

Oh crap.

"Daaaaaanaaaaaaa!!!"

I jumped into a pair of jeans and raced down the stairs to discover Billy leaning against the mailboxes in the outside foyer. Grinning, he mouthed, *What took you so long?*

I unlocked the front door and opened it just wide enough for us to converse without having to shout through the glass. But he was too fast for me. Instantly my back was against the door of my super's apartment, and Billy was kissing me and kissing me and kissing me. . . .

Until the super's mangy little mongrel started yapping frantically and hurling its body against the other side of the door. We froze, eyes locked.

"You are *not* invited upstairs," I said.

"Then come outside and sit with me on the stoop for a while. Tell me about this harrowing evening of yours."

The last thing in the world I wanted to do was discuss my harrowing evening. "Honestly, it's not important. Besides, it's twenty degrees out there." I'd run downstairs too fast to grab a jacket.

He opened his and cocooned me inside it, and my brain turned to pudding while I let him guide me out the door. We settled on the top step with me sitting between his legs, both of us snug in his coat. "See? Nice and warm."

Warm, my ass. It was hot as hell out there.

He squeezed me tighter. "Comfortable?"

My thighs were already going numb from the cold stone and my nose was beginning to run, but I'd have happily spent eternity nestled between Billy's legs.

Which was not at *all* what I was supposed to be thinking.

I leaned forward and half turned to face him. "Why are you doing this?"

"I think we have something. Call it chemistry if you like."

That we did. I'd felt his chemistry rubbing up against my leg back in the hallway, and it was showing no signs of abating.

"Yeah, but—why me?"

"I don't know. . . . You *get* me. It's like we're on the same wavelength. I mean, look at how many of those clues you wrote wound up in my puzzle."

"I'm sure there are plenty of like-minded people at that crossword tournament you were telling me about. Including women born in the same decade as you." Many of whom no doubt clamored, groupie-style, for the attention of W. W. W. Moody.

He laughed. "You'll change your mind when you compete this year and see the crowd."

"I don't believe you. I bet you're the Leif Garrett of the crossword set."

"Who's Leif Garrett?"

"*See?* I *am* too old for you!"

"I'm kidding! His first name is a really common fill word. After a while you get sick of clueing it 'Explorer Ericson.' Which reminds me— you're in for a surprise tomorrow."

"What kind of surprise?"

"You'll see, Miss Mayo."

The phone woke me the next morning. As I fumbled for it, I was astonished to discover the clock read eleven thirty.

"Congratulations," Ray Devine said when I picked up. "You're famous."

"Huh?"

"I'm sorry—were you sleeping?"

"Well, yeah, but I shouldn't have been. Uh, what did you just say?"

"Guess you haven't seen the paper yet. You're famous."

Both my pulse and my temples began to throb as I swung my legs onto the floor. "Hang on a second," I said, nearly trampling Puny in my haste to open the front door and retrieve the *Times* from the doormat, where my early-rising upstairs neighbor always dropped it.

"Second Arts section," Ray said.

I located it and yanked it from the stack, scattering the other sections across the kitchen floor. There, just below the fold, was a shot of Graciela's booth. NEO-FAUVES, TRAMP ART, AND A NEW GRANDMA MOSES AT THE OUTSIDER ART FAIR, the headline read.

"Oh shit."

He chuckled. "I'll wait while you read it."

I scanned the article until I located the name "Hannah." The salient aspects of her background were all there: Maine, tar paper shack, Cool Ranch Doritos.

"I can't believe you never told me about this, Dana."

"I guess I was just . . . hoping it would magically go away. Believe me—it wasn't my idea."

"Sounds like a hell of a story. I can't wait to hear all about it—*and* get that painting you promised me."

His painting. I still had to create the replacement for Tom-Tom. "As it turns out, I'm going to need a little time before I can hand it over. Do you think you could give me, say, one more week?"

"Of course I can. How about we get together next Friday night? I'll take you out for a long-overdue dinner."

"Oh no you won't! If we're finally going to see each other after all this time, then I want the reunion to take place in exactly the type of dive bar we used to frequent back in the day."

"Tradition—I like that." He paused. "But you know, that might turn out to be impossible. I'm not sure there are any dive bars left in this town."

Ray had a point. Gentrification had wiped out Shandon's up on Twenty-Third Street, George's on East Seventh, far too many Blarney Stones to count . . .

Ah. But there was one lone survivor. Billy had taken me there last week.

"I know just the spot," I said. "South side of Fourteenth, just east of Avenue B. I guarantee you'll feel right at home."

"Then it's a date."

"Eight o'clock?"

"Can't wait."

"Well, it's been twenty-one years," I reminded him. "One more week shouldn't make that much of a difference."

"Yeah, but—you know something? It does. I've missed you so much, Dana."

"I've missed you, too."

I hung up the phone, remembering the last time we'd seen each other, when I'd somehow managed to break it off with him. So much had changed since . . .

Since I'd been Lark and he'd been Sandro, I thought with a shudder. Thank god I occasionally did the right thing. Maybe I should try it more often.

My hip joints were stiff from the hour or so I'd sat on the stoop with Billy, alternately kissing and bantering. No wonder I'd slept so late. It was high time I started putting together the supplies I'd need for painting the balusters that day—what was left of it. At the rate I was going, I wouldn't get to Hank's until midafternoon.

My gaze alighted on the newspaper. The second Arts section, still open to the article about Hannah, rested on top of the pile.

What the hell, I thought. *I guess there's time for the puzzle.*

I located the page with the crossword and glanced at the grid's upper-right corner. "Puzzle by W. W. W. Moody," the byline read. So that was what Billy had meant when he'd told me I had a surprise in store.

As usual, he was merciless. "So much for 'You *get* me,'" I muttered as I scanned his evil clues, desperate for even a three-letter word to enter into the squares. I finally managed to crack the southwest quadrant, then slowly filled in the rest, counterclockwise, until I circled back to 1-Across: DIETER'S DIRECTIVE. *Hmmm.* Blank-blank-L-D-T-blank-blank-M . . .

Of course.

HOLD THE MAYO.

Very funny, Mr. Moody.

By the time I'd solved the puzzle, it was nearly one o'clock. I picked up the phone to let Hank know I was on my way.

"Boy, am I glad you finally called," he said.

"What's wrong? I told you I'd be coming over, didn't I?"

"Yeah, but after what I told you at that art show, I thought maybe I seen the last of you. Dana, I don't want that to happen."

"Neither do I," I replied, and I meant it. Despite my recent behavior to the contrary, the boyfriend position was still his to lose. In the long run, Hank was Day In, Day Out. Billy Moody was a debauched Spring Break Week in Daytona. And if Hank could manage to explain the discrepancies in his autobiography to my satisfaction, then I felt sure I could manage to stay away from the undertow.

"I'll be over in half an hour," I said.

"That sounds good. We'll talk then."

Would we ever. I'd be the one asking all the questions.

"Tell me about Las Vegas." I was sitting on the stairs, brushing pale lilac-colored acrylic into the recesses of a fluted support column. "Did you really grow up there?"

"All through high school," Hank responded from the top step of a ladder, where he was stripping decades' worth of paint from the crown moldings—or "fancy strips of plaster," as he was given to calling them. "Like I told you, my daddy trained horses for casino acts. Least he did until my grandma took ill and called us back to Tennessee."

"I'm surprised you retained such a strong—uh, rural way of speaking."

He grinned. "I ain't never gonna lose my accent. It's good business, plain and simple. Like my daddy always said, 'Folks is likely to remember a country bumpkin from Sin City.'"

"I imagine they would be. So, tell me—does the country bumpkin really work for a celebrated Spanish chef?"

"He sure does. This guy's the best client I ever had. He don't come around, he don't run no tabs, and we're living for free." He looked down at me and smiled. "And he's gonna love that staircase."

"Thanks. Let's hope so."

"So . . . Hannah, huh?"

I should have known I wouldn't be asking *all* the questions. I felt my face flush.

"You don't need to explain," Hank said. "That story's a real money-maker. Look, Dana, it's like I told you last night—you can be anybody you say you are."

"I guess we both can."

"Now, is there anything else you been wanting to ask me?"

"No . . . Oh. Just one more question: Were you and Dinner really in Mullica Hill, New Jersey, on New Year's Eve?"

He shifted his gaze from my eyes to his knees. "Well, not exactly. I was there."

"But Dinner was here, pneumonia-free?"

He nodded.

"Would this have anything to do with the tuxedo you were carrying when you got home the next day?"

He nodded again, looking decidedly sheepish. "I was at a wedding."

My pulse kicked into high gear. "Wearing a tuxedo? Were you the one who was getting married?"

"What? Hell no! I was the guy who was giving away the bride."

"He has a *daughter*?!!" Elinor Ann said, once I'd finally managed to return home on the pretense of feeding the cat and picking up additional art supplies. I needed a few hours on my own to assimilate Hank's latest revelation.

"I should have realized it was a possibility. And I definitely should have known there'd be an ex-wife kicking around somewhere. He's never once left the toilet seat up."

"Where exactly is the former Mrs. Wheeler?" she wanted to know.

"Still in Tennessee. Apparently they were just a couple of crazy kids who never had no business gettin' hitched. It all sounded pretty amicable—the divorce, the custody arrangement. . . . He claims he wants me to meet this girl."

"Then why didn't he invite you to the wedding?"

I'd been wondering the same thing—especially since Hank had been so insistent about spending New Year's together. "He didn't find out about it until the last minute. Apparently the happy couple was all set to elope before the groom's parents got wind of it. They pulled the ceremony together in a matter of days."

"I still don't see why you couldn't have gone with him."

Nor did I. But we'd been on hiatus the preceding week as a result of his half-truths and sins of omission, and a daughter was the biggest omission of all.

"He said something about not wanting to spring too much on me at once," I told Elinor Ann. "I can only assume he thought I'd find it odd when everyone at the ceremony addressed him as J.D. Calhoun."

"That would have been odd, all right. How old is this daughter, anyway?"

I'd been afraid she was going to ask me that. "Twenty-five."

"Really?!"

"Don't say it."

"Too bad she just got married."

"*Don't*, Elinor Ann."

"She's the perfect age for Billy Moody!"

"I thought I asked you not to say that."

I was just about to reread the review of the art fair when the phone rang again.

"Hello?"

"Glory be! You're finally home!"

"Hi, Mom." I could hear ferocious banging noises in the background. "Is everything okay down there?"

"Everything's just peachy!"

"Then why does it sound as if Noah is building his ark in your living room?"

"Oh, that. Just some . . . temporary unpleasantness. I'm having the wall-to-wall carpeting replaced. You're father's up in arms about it, but I told him I'd die of mortification if the sixty people coming to his birthday party saw the sorry conditions we've been living in."

"Typical Dad, huh?"

"You know the Commodore."

When I was a kid, my father would resole the same pair of shoes six times, but he never failed to trade in his car for the latest model every September. He hated to spend money on necessities—although one could hardly categorize new wall-to-wall as a necessity when ninety percent of it would be obscured by my mother's extensive collection of Oriental area rugs. "How's Dad feeling?"

"Fit as a fiddle! He's downstairs at the chickee hut playing gin rummy with some of the neighbors."

"Is he . . . still talking about God?"

"Mercifully, that seems to have passed. The other day he invoked his name to damn the Internal Revenue Service to hell, but that's certainly nothing unusual."

"Not at all." I covered the receiver to mask a sigh of relief. "So everything's back to normal?"

"It will be once this dreadful carpet is out of my living room. Now, I wanted to ask if you've booked your flights yet."

"I've been meaning to get on that. This weekend, I promise."

"And I've been thinking. You certainly seem to be spending a great deal of time with this young man of yours. Do you think it would be appropriate for us to extend a birthday invitation to him?"

Not if he neglected to extend one to me for his daughter's wedding. "I don't know about that. That's an awful lot of . . . pressure for a first meeting with the parents."

"Then I'll leave the decision up to you."

"Great—another decision," I muttered after I got off the phone and sat down to check my email. Lately I seemed to be incapable of making them. In fact, when my mother had referred to "this young man of yours," my initial reaction had been to wonder how she knew about Billy Moody.

And now here he was, lying in wait in my in-box:

> Been thinking about last night all day. Any chance I can come
> over there and 1-Across this evening?
> W.W.W.

I was about to respond with a simple no when I realized I could respond in kind. He'd provided me with the perfect riposte in this morning's crossword. I went into the kitchen to retrieve the puzzle, located the phrase I had in mind, hit Reply, and typed "16-Down" into the body of the email.

I expected he'd know immediately what the fill read:

WHEN PIGS FLY.

Within minutes, my phone rang.

"Touché," Billy said.

"You left yourself wide open."

"I guess I did. And speaking of wide open, that's an accurate description of my schedule. Let me take you to dinner."

"Uh—no."

"But you had a good time with me last night, didn't you?"

"I'm changing the subject now. Your puzzle this morning was brutal."

"Glad you enjoyed it. Of course, you were my inspiration."

"I suppose having one's name appear in a constructor's crossword fill is the word-nerd equivalent of flowers and candy."

"I'll give you those, too, if you let me take you to dinner."

"*Stop.*"

Our conversation had rendered me so discombobulated, I found myself wandering from room to room in a fugue state after it ended.

God, Billy was sexy.

But Hank was sexy, too, and so much more appropriate.

But Billy hadn't concealed his true identity for the past three months.

But Hank wouldn't be in his forties when I was eligible for Social Security.

But Billy didn't have a kid.

But Hank wasn't one.

But Billy didn't use double modifiers.

But Hank—

"Enough!" I shouted, loudly enough to send Puny scurrying under the bed. I could equivocate indefinitely. What I really needed was a third party to decide my future. Some kind of judge, whose decision would be final and binding.

Elinor Ann? No. She'd already made it clear how she felt about Billy. And about Hank, for that matter, and his never-ending cavalcade of new revelations.

I went into the kitchen and came face-to-face with the portrait of Dinner in his leopard skin pillbox hat.

Of course. Ray Devine could be my Solomon.

I'd lay out my dilemma when we got together for drinks. He'd loved me once; I was sure of it. He'd still want what was best for me, wouldn't he?

All of a sudden, Friday couldn't come soon enough.

Apparently Ray had lost his sense of urgency when the day finally arrived. I'd been sitting with a book of Saturday crosswords at the bar, nursing a scotch and water down to nothing but ice cubes and consulting my watch incessantly for the past forty-two minutes and fourteen seconds, when I reached for my cell.

I let his phone ring twelve times before giving up and calling Elinor Ann.

"Maybe there's a problem with the subway," she said. "Didn't you tell me he's way out in Brooklyn?"

"Nineteen stops on the R train." A hirsute patron with homemade—or prisonmade—tattoos spelling out an expletive on the fingers of his left hand arose from his stool near the end of the bar and took a seat by my side. "Buy you another?" he slurred.

You just had *to pick a dive bar for the big reunion,* I thought to myself.

"I'm set, thanks."

The hirsute man ignored my response and signaled the bartender to bring another round. "Set for what?" Elinor Ann asked.

"Imminent peril."

Another drink materialized before me. I managed a pallid smile and clinked glasses with my benefactor, then returned to my phone call. "You know, Ray was never late when we used to get together. Maybe he changed his mind."

"Somehow I doubt that."

"So . . . what are you up to?"

"Cleaning up after supper. Oh! Guess what we had?"

Hirsute Man's arm was sliding dangerously close to my strike zone. "Uh—why don't you just tell me what you had?"

"Salmon. *With* fresh dill I picked up after work at the farmers' market!"

"You went all by yourself? That's fantastic!"

"Hooray!" Hirsute Man raised his beer in solidarity.

"How did you manage to do it?" I asked my friend.

"Well, I noticed something. Whenever I thought about having to go out alone, the anxiety gave me so much nervous energy that I'd just sit there and—well, vibrate, I guess you could say. So I thought if I could do something to get all that tension out of my system, maybe I'd be too tired to panic."

"And it worked?"

"Just before I left the plant, I went into my office and did twenty squat thrusts. Then I did fifty jumping jacks. I was drenched with sweat when I walked out of there—our foreman told me I looked like I was coming down with the flu—but I stayed calm enough to make it all the way to the market."

"Jumping jacks," I said. There was no way I was going to use the words "squat" or "thrust" in the presence of my new admirer. "What a solution. Who would have thought?"

My comment inspired Hirsute Man to break into a rousing rendition of "Jumpin' Jack Flash."

"Oh my god," Elinor Ann said. "That wasn't Ray, was it?"

"God, no. Listen—I am *so* proud of you." Hirsute Man was wrapping up the chorus. I had to shut him down before the inevitable air guitar solo. "Oh—and I have good news, too! The doctor gave me a new prescription today. This time she's one hundred percent sure it will *finally* get rid of my yeast infection!"

Hirsute Man excused himself and went over to peruse the titles on the jukebox.

"Dana, what in the *world* are you talking about?"

"Nothing."

"Are you okay?"

I sighed. "Not exactly."

Where the hell was Ray Devine?

CHAPTER TWENTY-ONE

I GUESS I'M LOSING MY MIND

completed two more crosswords and drained the drink Hirsute Man had provided before scrounging around in my purse for something to write on. All I could find was the stub from my guest pass to last week's Outsider Art Fair, but at least the back of it was blank.

Ray, I wrote, *Hope nothing serious has happened (even though something serious better have happened for you to stand me up). Call when/if you get this—D.*

I caught the eye of the bartender. "What do I owe you?"

"Four and a quarter."

I handed him a ten, along with the note. "If a good-looking older man comes in tonight, would you make sure he gets this?"

"I'll keep it in the register. If he shows up, he'll get it."

"But—don't you need more of a description?"

"Don't worry. I'll know him."

"But—"

"Take a look around, lady—you see any good-lookin' men in this dump?"

A bitter wind hampered my progress home, buffeting the portrait of Dinner I'd carefully wrapped for Ray. End-of-week revelers crowded the sidewalks, darkening my mood even further. How dare they enjoy themselves in the face of my humiliation?

I unlocked my apartment door and raced to the nightstand. The red light was blinking on the answering machine. I had one new message.

From my dentist's office, reminding me of my Tuesday cleaning at ten forty-five.

I had one sleeve of my coat off when the phone rang. "Thank god," I said, lunging for it.

"What *happened*?"

Click.

"I'm sure Ray didn't intend to stand you up," Elinor Ann said. "Maybe that was him on his cell, but he's stuck in the subway and the call couldn't get through."

"Then his hang-up wouldn't have gotten through, either."

"Oh. Good point."

I'd logged on to the MTA's Web site just after she answered her phone. "Hang on a second," I said, accessing the link for current service status. Every subway line was running smoothly, with the exception of the R. "Oh my god! The Transit Authority's reporting major delays on his train line!"

"Yay!"

"I know! Yay!"

"I mean, that's a shame, of course, but—"

"I know exactly what you mean."

"Yay!" we chorused.

"You realize we're not being very nice," Elinor Ann said.

"Are you kidding? We're assholes. Yay, anyway."

"See? I told you there'd be a perfectly logical explanation. I wonder what happened to the train."

"I'm way ahead of you," I replied, typing in the address for News Four

Online. " 'One Dead in Canal Street Shooting—R Service Suspended—Passengers Stranded Underground,' " I read aloud from the headline.

"Oh, jeez. I hope Ray's not the one who got shot. Then we really would be a-holes."

"Don't worry. They're saying it's gang related. He's probably stuck between stations." And would be for hours. Meaning I was on my own tonight.

"Well, the important thing is that he's okay. I'm sure he'll get in touch with you as soon as he can."

"He'd better."

"You could see him tomorrow."

"I guess."

"So . . . what are you going to do tonight?"

"No idea."

"Oh, come on, Dana. It's been—what? Twenty-one years? You can manage to hold out for another twenty-four hours, can't you?"

"Looks like I have no choice."

While I appreciated Elinor Ann's attempt to put things in perspective—especially since I knew she was far from enthused about my reunion with Ray—my dark mood refused to dissipate. I'd been so looking forward to finally spending time with him, to telling him about Hank and Billy, to having him unravel all my romantic entanglements. But mainly I just wanted to tell him how much he'd meant to me when I was young and scared and far from certain I could survive in this town. If Ray hadn't loved me, I might not have believed in myself long enough to stick around. Who knows what would have become of me?

Oh, *why* had I waited twenty-one years to see him? And why couldn't the Chinatown gangs have declared a truce for just one night?

I hung up my coat and assessed the situation. If I had the evening to myself, it wouldn't be a bad idea to finish the painting sitting on my easel—the last of the bartered Hannahs owed to Vivian. The freesias in the cowboy boot were already beginning to wilt.

But I didn't want to paint. I wanted to be sitting in a dive bar with Ray.

I really should eat something. Lunch had been hours ago, and I felt the effect of my two scotches.

But I didn't want to eat—unless Ray was my dinner partner.

Hank was probably free. He hadn't mentioned any plans when I'd left the brownstone that morning.

But I didn't want to see Hank. Not until I saw Ray.

Well, at least I could leave Ray a message.

But when I dialed his number, the phone just rang and rang.

I crawled into bed with Puny and *Remembrance of Things Past*, which had proven to be a surefire cure for insomnia. In fact, I'd started it well over a year ago and only just made it to page seventeen.

The Proust must have worked, because when the telephone jarred me awake, sunlight was streaming through the bedroom window.

"Hello?"

"Is this Dana Mayo?"

The voice sounded familiar, but I couldn't quite place it. "Who is this?"

"Uh—it's Renée Devine."

"Uh . . ."

"Uh . . . listen. There's no good way to tell you this. My father's dead."

"What?"

"My father—Ray. He's dead."

This couldn't be happening. I had to be having a dream—or more accurately, a nightmare. But there was Puny, and there was Proust, and here I was, sitting on the side of my bed with my feet on the floor and a telephone in my hand.

"Are you still there?" A note of impatience had crept into Renée's tone.

I couldn't think of anything to say. The only words that came to mind were *Oh no. Oh no. Oh no.*

But hold on a minute. This wasn't the first time Renée had told me her father was dead. "How do I know you're—"

"He had a heart attack. Yesterday morning. He managed to call 911, but . . ." She caught her breath. "I just saw in his datebook that he was supposed to meet you in the city last night."

"He was, but—"

But what? I knew she'd never believe me if I told her we'd only recently reestablished contact; that I hadn't seen Ray in more than two decades.

"Anyway," Renée continued, "I just thought—you know, that you should . . . know."

Oh no. Oh no. Oh no. "But—"

"Listen—I knew that was you at my open house last year. I recognized you as soon as you walked in. The only reason I'm calling is because I think Dad would have wanted you to know what happened, okay?"

I could hardly blame her for trying to end the conversation as quickly as possible. And, of course, seeing my name in his datebook couldn't have made her happy. "Your father was a wonderful man," I finally managed. "And I'm very, very sorry for your loss. For . . . everything."

She hung up.

I tried to stand, but my legs started to buckle, and I sat back down on the mattress, too shocked to cry or scream or—thank god—laugh, and too numb to do anything but let the words *Oh no, oh no, oh no* echo inside my head.

I had to reach Elinor Ann.

"Aunt Dana!" Eddie said when I called the house. "You're a day too early. My birthday isn't until tomorrow."

Oh god. His birthday. I'd forgotten all about it. "I know. I was planning on calling you then. But I need to talk to your mother right now." *Right* now. Immediately. Get. Her. To. The. Phone.

"She and Dad went out."

"Any idea where?" *Please, please, please let it be someplace near a cell phone tower.*

"Well, if you promise not to tell Mom . . ."

"I promise." *I promise, I promise, I promise. Only please, please, please stop torturing me and tell me where she is.*

"I'm pretty sure they went to Phillipsburg. Guess why?"

Oh god. Now I had to guess. "Eddie, I have absolutely no idea what they're doing in New Jersey. Just tell me, okay?"

"Okay. Don't say anything to Mom, but . . . Well, you know how long I've wanted a bulldog, right?"

Yes, you little sadist. Ray Devine is dead. The hell with bulldogs. The hell with everything. "Of course I do. Practically forever."

"Since I was like, four, right? So, I saw her and Dad whispering to each other a couple of days ago, and I checked the history on her browser that night—Aunt Dana, you can*not* tell her that or I will get into *so* much trouble—and she'd been on the home page of a bulldog breeder in Phillipsburg!"

"That's fantastic!" I was going to keel over and expire, right in the middle of this conversation. "Listen, Eddie—I promise not to say anything, but only if you send tons of pictures when you get him, okay?"

"And you'll come out and see him, right?"

"Of course I will. But I've really got to get hold of your mother now—don't worry, I swear I won't say a word—so I'll call back on your birthday tomorrow, okay?"

"Okay. Talk to you then."

———

The instant I heard Elinor Ann's voice, the tears came. Streams of tears, with so many more behind them, I could have wound up crying forever.

"Dana, what in the world happened?"

Between sobs, I somehow got out the words "Ray" and "is" and "dead."

"Oh no. That's—oh no. Oh, Dana. But—why would a gang member want to kill Ray?"

I was so perplexed I stopped crying. "What are you talking about?"

"The shooting on the subway last night. What are *you* talking about?"

I'd forgotten all about that, as well as everything else in the universe. "That's not how it happened. He had a heart attack—yesterday morning."

"Oh, Dana. That's terrible." She paused. "How'd you find out?"

"Renée Devine just called and told me."

"She did? Oh my god. What did she say to you?"

"Nothing worth repeating, other than her father was dead."

I could overhear Elinor Ann giving Cal a quick summary of our conversation. The phone connection began to crackle ominously.

"Dana, listen—I am so, so sorry. And I hate to tell you this, but I forgot to charge my cell last night, and Cal left his home with the boys. If we get cut off, do you think you'll be okay until we get back to Kutztown?"

I didn't have time to respond before the line went dead.

All right, I told myself. *At least she knows. She'll call you back as soon as she can. You just have to hang on until she does.* I'd finally stopped sobbing, but tears continued to roll down my face.

I needed to do something. Commemorate Ray in some way, even if it set me off all over again.

Of course.

I went over to the CD rack and searched the titles until I found the disc with the song I was looking for—the one he'd played for me on our first official date, two days after he'd declared his love for me and made everything shockingly, deliriously perfect.

"There's a bar on the corner of Twenty-Fifth and Third," he'd said. "I'll meet you there at four."

"Which corner?"

He'd laughed. "I guarantee you'll figure that out."

I'd laughed, too, when I walked up Third Avenue the following afternoon and spotted the bar with the words "Sepret Tables" written on its awning. I'd entered the dark, nearly deserted room and come up behind Ray, who was bent over the jukebox.

"Sepret?"

He'd turned around and kissed me for a long time—maybe an hour, maybe five minutes. "I know you love a good typo."

Pulling some coins out of his pocket, he'd fed all the quarters into the Rock-Ola's coin slot. "So, which song should we play for our first dance?"

I'd scanned the titles. "Wow. It looks like every single one of these is by Frank Sinatra."

"It's a Mafia joint," he'd whispered in my ear. "But don't worry. The bartender and I go way back." He'd punched a couple of buttons on the jukebox. "Not every song's by Sinatra," he'd said, wrapping his arms around me as dreamy doo-wop harmony began to fill the room.

> *I guess I'm losing my mind*
> *I looked around and found*
> *You were gone*

"The silky-smooth sounds of the Satinettes," he'd murmured while we swayed back and forth. I had never, ever been so completely, swooningly in love, or so supremely happy.

I guess I'm losing my mind
I think of you from dusk
Until dawn

I guess you really do have to be that young to be that in love, I thought as I listened to the song a few more times before setting it on continuous play and turning down the volume. Then I did something I had never before even contemplated. I knelt down by the bed and pulled out the box of journals I'd been amassing for years, at least since my high school days.

I made it a point never to reread them. The thought of having to face incontrovertible proof of my naïveté was simply too cringe inducing. In fact, I mainly kept the volumes around as suicide insurance: If I ever felt the desire to end it all, I always figured by the time I burned all those journals, I'd have come to my senses and saved my own life.

But this was a singular moment for reminiscing. I scanned through the spiral notebooks until I found the first mention of Ray, just after I'd started my job at Prints on Prince:

I am wild about him. But he's married. And I think at least 40 (!). And has beautiful blues eyes & I love his body & he's really cool & smart & knows about art & has a manner with women. I know he likes me & sometimes we exchange looks but I can't see him fooling around on Rhea. I would just die to be with him, though. Does he want to be with me? I guess maybe, but he'd never do it. Why would he? I am not that great. He's probably just being nice to me because I am the new girl at work.

Yeesh. No wonder I avoided revisiting my past in print. And thank god I'd become a painter; clearly, writing was not my strong suit. I flipped forward to the days just before the affair officially began, when we were still in our kissing-in-bars-for-hours phase:

He said the killer part about it all is that he knows how great we would be together. I just stressed how Up To Him that decision was and that I am ready & waiting & don't care about anyone or anything but him. And we kissed & kissed & kissed. Oh god, I love Ray Devine so much! I know he sees me as the escape hatch to his life, but I don't care. As long as he sees me, I never will.

I was actually beginning to find my twenty-one-year-old self rather endearing. Insanely immature, and about to make an epic mistake, but sweeter, and much more innocent, than I ever remembered being at the time.

I continued to relive our history until days before the end came:

I just don't understand why we have to be so Out Of Time. Was I destined to fall in love with Ray Devine, or do I have some hidden psychological quirk that makes me only fall in love with someone in his situation? And by that I don't just mean "married." He is so much older and has known so many different women, but he still seems/claims to love me more. Or does he just have a corresponding hidden psychological quirk that complements mine? I refuse to believe that's all this is.

I'll always refuse to believe it, even though we both should have known better than to get involved, I thought to myself. *Especially Ray.*

At least one of us must really be in love. I'm pretty sure we are both really in love. He tells me there is nothing like this in the world, that not being together is the hardest thing he's ever heard of. I told him I wished I could fall in love with someone else and let him off the hook, but he says he wants to stay on the hook.

I put the book away before I got to the breakup and the anguished, mournful passages I still remembered writing. I was already living that part of it all over again, right here in the present.

I must have cried myself back to sleep, because the next thing I knew, a couple of hours had passed and someone was frantically pushing the button on my intercom.

It was probably Vivian, wondering where her final Hannah was. *Forget it,* I thought, pulling a pillow over my head and closing my eyes.

Until someone began pounding on my front door a few minutes later.

"Dana! Let me in! *Dana!*"

My eyes shot open.

I leapt out of bed and rushed to undo the lock.

Elinor Ann staggered inside and threw her arms around my neck, gasping and trembling.

CHAPTER TWENTY-TWO

THE SALVATION ARMY

stood there, propping Elinor Ann up, while she caught her breath. "Are you all right?" I asked.

"I will be. It's just—the drive took a little more out of me than I'd expected." She unclasped her hands from my neck and took a few shaky steps into the living room. "I know we have a lot to talk about, but can you hang on for just a second?"

Before I could respond, she leapt skyward and began to perform a vigorous set of jumping jacks. "Sorry," she panted. "I—just—have to—calm—myself—down."

Finally she dropped her arms and took in her surroundings. "Wow. I never thought I'd be back in your apartment again."

"Me, neither. But are you sure this was a good idea? You seem pretty—"

"Panicky. I know. I was positive I'd be okay making the trip, but I'd forgotten how overwhelming New York City is. There are *so* many people on the streets. And it's so far from Kutztown."

"Is that the reason you came to visit me only the one time?"

"Hmm. I guess it is. I guess I've been prone to panic disorder for longer than I realized."

"At least you're fighting it. You made it here, didn't you? And god, I'm so glad you did."

"Honestly, it wasn't my idea. It was Cal's. As soon as I explained to him what you were going through, he blew right past the Phillipsburg exit on Route 78 and told me we were on our way to Ninth Street."

Cal's idea. Bless him.

She wandered into the kitchen, then poked her head in the bathroom door. "This place looks a lot smaller than I remember."

"I have twenty years' worth of additional junk."

"I guess that's it."

She examined the half-finished Hannah on the easel, went into the back room to stroke Puny, who was sprawled across my unmade bed, then stopped at the bureau. She picked up the photograph of us taken at her wedding. "Sometimes I wish we could go back to being us then, don't you?"

I'd been wishing it all day long. "Ray would still be alive."

"And I wouldn't be crazy."

"Yeah, but you're not—you're in the big bad city and you're still breathing."

"Yeah. I am." She smiled in relief.

"I can't thank Cal enough for bringing you."

"He didn't think twice about it—well, at least not until he saw the backup at the Holland Tunnel. But he insisted on coming. He said it was the right thing to do."

"Where is Cal, anyway?"

"Circling the block."

"That figures. It's really hard to find parking in this neighborhood on a Saturday afternoon."

"Oh, he's not looking for a space. He told me he'd just drive around until we're done visiting. He's worried someone will steal the hubcaps off the truck if he comes inside."

I had to laugh, even though it felt alien to do so.

"Oh, Dana." Elinor Ann came over and hugged me again, and this time I couldn't hold it in any longer. The tears came back full force. I stood there, shoulders heaving, while Cal circled and circled the block.

"I've never seen you like this," she finally said.

"I've never seen me like this, either." I'd probably shed more tears in the past few hours than I had in the past twenty years.

"Dana, I—I don't get it. It's been more than two decades since you and Ray . . ."

"I know. But I always knew he was out there. I always thought we'd see each other one more time." I sighed. "So much for closure."

She sat on the bed and beckoned for me to join her, which I did.

"I'm sure it hurts, knowing how close you came to meeting up with him again. But all that—the two of you—happened a long time ago. You've already survived without Ray for half your life."

"I know."

But now he was gone forever, and I hadn't even seen him, or talked things over with him, or said goodbye, and there wasn't a thing I could do to change it.

"And Dana? I'm not trying to upset you, or say anything bad about Ray, but do you remember the reasons you gave for breaking up with him?"

Of course I remembered. "The age difference, Rhea, Renée . . ."

But right now I would give anything to undo those twenty-one years of self-imposed separation. I should have been selfish. I should have let Ray move in with me, even though I'd been certain that by Year Two, I'd have been standing right here in my bedroom screaming, "Get out of here! You ruined my life!"

And he would have, too. My parents never would have accepted a boyfriend who was nearly as old as my own mother. My friends—well, maybe not Elinor Ann, but the rest of them—would have drifted away, uncomfortable in our presence, bewildered by my choice.

But at that moment I was convinced it would have been worth it—all the mess, all the fallout and rage and recriminations—just to have that first perfect year with him.

"Oh, Elinor Ann, how could he die on me? He was supposed to show up one more time and prove that what we had was real."

"Of course it was real."

She went into the bathroom and returned with a cool washcloth. "Put this over your eyes. It'll help with the puffiness."

"Thanks, Mom."

"Aren't you supposed to be seeing Hank tonight?"

"He told me to come by anytime."

"Maybe that's not such a good idea."

I agreed, but the alternative—listening to the Satinettes and reading ancient journal entries—was simply too depressing to consider. "I think I should try. I think I need to get out of here."

"Then I think so, too. Are you going to let him know about . . . what happened?"

Good question. "Maybe I'll wait a couple of days. I want to be able to tell him without breaking down."

I saw Elinor Ann sneak a look at her watch, so I looked at mine, which was resting on the nightstand. It was just after three.

"You don't have to leave yet, do you?" She couldn't. I wasn't ready to be on my own—or to face Hank and pretend everything was fine.

"I'm sorry. I wish I could stay a little longer, but I'm starting to feel bad for Cal. I hate to think how many times he's been around the block by now."

Just then I had an idea. "Do you think he could drop me at Hank's on your way to the tunnel?"

"I can't imagine he'd mind."

"And maybe you could stop in for a minute and meet him? I'm sure he'd love to show you guys around the brownstone." And I was sure my anguish would be less obvious with the distraction of out-of-town visitors.

"Meet Hank? Oh, I don't know. . . . Yes. Yes, I do. Of course I want to meet Hank. If I can make it all the way to New York City, well, then I can stick around long enough to see this boyfriend I've been hearing so much about."

Now it was my turn to hug her. "I'll call him."

"Make the next two rights, then a left onto Saint Mark's Place," I directed Cal, once we'd climbed into the truck and convinced him his hubcaps would be safe for the next hour or so.

"You got it," he said, giving his wife's knee a squeeze. "You okay?"

Elinor Ann, sitting between us, nodded. She did seem okay, if a bit overwhelmed—like a refugee from a third world country on her first visit to an American supermarket, slack-jawed at the abundance and variety unfolding before her. She kept up a steady stream of patter as we turned up Third, down Tenth, and onto Second.

"A restaurant that serves nothing but mac and cheese? How is that even possible?

"That man is selling handbags right in front of that handbag store. That hardly seems fair.

"A dollar a minute, just to have somebody rub your feet?"

"Here's Saint Mark's," I said to Cal, who made the turn.

"Oh my god, you guys—look at that guy with the tattoos. He has *real horns* growing out of his forehead."

Cal chuckled. "Saint Mark's Place ain't changed much, that's for sure."

Elinor Ann and I turned our heads to stare at him. "You've . . . been here before?" I said.

"Not since rumspringa. Bunch of us piled into my buddy's 'sixty-two Impala one night and had ourselves a time."

I flashed on an image of a teenaged Cal, newly free of his plain clothes and Amish ways, whooping it up a million miles from Lebanon County.

I'd never loved the two of them more than I did at that moment.

Cal maneuvered into a spot across from Tompkins Square Park just north of Sixth Street. As we rounded the corner of Seventh, he stopped cold at the sight of Hank's panel truck. "Man, would you look at that beauty." He read the words painted on its side and met my eyes. "This belongs to your Hank?"

I nodded.

"Heck, Dana. Marry the guy."

Hank was waiting in the doorway when we approached the brownstone. "Glad y'all could make it," he said. "Feels like I know you folks already, what with all I been hearing from my girl here. Come on in—I'll give you the grand tour."

We followed him single file through the corridor leading to the kitchen. Elinor Ann formed an "okay" sign with her hand behind her back, where only I could see it. I leaned forward, whispering, "Told you you'd like him."

"I know you said he was attractive, but . . . no wonder you don't care about his carpentry skills," she whispered back.

Persuading her to meet him had been a wise decision. Seeing Hank through Elinor Ann's eyes was helping to remind me how lucky I was to have him. And if he wasn't Ray, well—nobody could ever be Ray Devine again, any more than I could be twenty-one and so obsessively, deliriously in love.

I lingered for a moment in the corridor and took a deep, stabilizing breath. Everything was going to be okay. Eventually.

I heard Elinor Ann let out a yelp when she entered the kitchen. "It's like something out of *The Jetsons*!"

"I'll say." Cal had been wide-eyed, taking in every detail along the route. "Tell me, Hank—how you stripping the paint off those moldings in the front hallway?"

He laughed. "Damn slow, that's how."

"I bet. Looks like you got about thirty coats on there. You want to be using Magic Strip—takes six, seven layers off in one shot."

"Thanks for the tip."

"Check this out," I said, pushing the button that caused the bamboo panel over the sink to disappear into the ceiling.

"A backyard? I didn't know they existed in New York City!" Elinor Ann was clearly delighted with the tour so far—and with Dinner, who had remained steadfastly by her side since we'd entered the house.

Cal let out a low whistle. "You must need some serious juice to hoist something that size. What kind of electrical setup you got?"

"Come on down to the basement and I'll show you."

"You're on."

Elinor Ann and I sat down at the kitchen counter. "I take back ninety percent of what I've been saying about that guy," she told me. "I mean, I still think he's a fraud, but . . ."

"I understand. You didn't expect to find him quite so personable, did you? Or so good-looking. I saw you checking out his . . . attributes."

Her face flushed. "I can't believe how shallow that makes me sound, but I have to admit, there's some truth to what you're saying. It's more than that, though. Hank's nice. And it's obvious he really cares about you." She peered into my eyes. "So . . . you're feeling a little better?"

"I am right now. You saved my life today, you know."

"Are you kidding? You saved mine. I really think I made some major progress coming here today."

Before I could respond, she glanced at the clock on the stove and gasped. "The boys! I forgot all about them! They were expecting us home hours ago!"

I handed her the receiver from the wall phone and listened while she explained to Angus that they'd been unexpectedly delayed.

"We won't be any later than nine o'clock. . . . Well, I'm sorry about that, but we'll get pizza tomorrow night. . . . Oh, boo hoo. I'm sure the two of you can manage to survive on Hot Pockets and ice cream until we get back."

"I'm liking this new, assertive Elinor Ann," I said after she hung up.

"Me, too. And by the way, I think Cal's right."

"About what?"

"Maybe you *should* marry this guy."

We heard footsteps coming up the basement stairs. "That system down there is a work of art," Cal announced. "This place's got more power than Three Mile Island."

Hank chuckled. "Think you could spare your husband for the next couple of months, Elinor Ann? I could use a good man like him on the job."

My friend and I exchanged glances. "Looks like these two are in loooove," I said.

Cal turned crimson. "Uh . . . how are the upstairs rooms coming along?"

"They're getting there. I still got a whole heck of a lot to do, but if you folks feel like poking around . . ."

"Let's go!" Cal started for the hallway.

"Look at him," Elinor Ann said, beaming. "He's in hog heaven— literally." She bent down to pat Dinner, and the four of us went to join her husband in the front hallway.

Hank pulled me aside before I could follow our guests upstairs.

"You don't look so hot. You feeling okay?"

So much for waiting a few days to tell him. "I . . . heard some sad news this morning. An old friend passed away."

"Boyfriend?"

I nodded, not trusting my voice.

He put his hands on my shoulders. "That's okay. I get it."

"You do?"

"Ain't neither of us kids. We both got pasts."

A loud "Damn!" echoed from above. "Sounds like Cal discovered the master bathroom," I said, forcing a smile.

I remained downstairs, taking a seat on the bottom step with Dinner at my feet, while Hank went up to continue the tour. I should have known he'd pick up on my distress. And I should have given him more credit for understanding. Of course I was allowed to be sad. Of course we both had pasts.

I just hoped he wouldn't ask me any more questions after my friends went home to Pennsylvania. I wanted to keep Ray all to myself for a little while longer.

God, why couldn't he have lived for just one more day? I blinked hard, refusing to succumb to another spate of tears.

Dinner issued a sigh and half rose, laying his head on my knees and looking at me with an expression I could interpret only as empathy.

"Who's hungry?" Hank said after we'd reconvened at the bottom of the stairs.

I was surprised to discover I was. Maybe getting my appetite back could be construed as further progress, along with managing to remain dry-eyed since leaving my apartment.

"I guess it would make sense to eat something before we get on the road," Elinor Ann said. "But I want to go someplace really New York-ey. Really Greenwich Village-y . . . just not too far away, okay?"

I knew Hank was thinking of the same destination when I told her I knew the perfect restaurant. "Fred and Ethyl's—it's right around the corner."

"They got a Saturday night special that'll blow you away," he added. "Fried chicken and corn bread."

Cal reached for the jacket he'd hung on the newel post. "You just said the magic words."

Fred and Ethyl were at their Village-iest, singing an off-key duet along with the oldies station, when we walked in the door.

"Hiya, kids," Ethyl said. "Plenty of room at the big table." Fred passed her a basket of corn bread through the long, rectangular window in the wall separating the dining area from the kitchen, where just his head was visible. Most of his face was obscured by the ladle he held like a microphone.

Ethyl deposited the basket and a pile of napkins in front of us. "Beers all around?"

We nodded, and she disappeared through the swinging doors.

I'd been concerned about the fate of Eddie's birthday present since Elinor Ann had called home. This seemed like as good a time as any to bring it up—without betraying his confidence, of course. It was the least I could do after calling the kid a sadist. "So, what were you guys doing in Phillipsburg, anyway?"

"Oh, that." Elinor Ann looked sideways at Cal, then back at me. "We were on our way to pick up a bulldog. Now that Eddie's turning twelve, we decided he's old enough to take on the responsibility."

"That's fantastic! He's going to be *so* excited."

"He better be," Cal mumbled, his mouth full of corn bread. "Those puppies aren't cheap; that's for sure."

"But—won't it be too late to get him tonight?" If they arrived home empty-handed, Eddie might never forgive his aunt Dana for causing their change of plans.

Ethyl set a heaping platter of chicken down on the table, along with twin mountains of green beans and mashed potatoes, while Fred began to sing "Crimson and Clover."

"We worked it all out with the breeder when we stopped to gas up in Clinton," Cal mumbled, his mouth full of chicken. "She said it'd be fine if we came on over there tomorrow. That way Eddie can pick out his own puppy."

"I hate to admit it, but I'm having second thoughts," Elinor Ann added. "Dinner makes a great argument for getting a pig."

"That's chicken you're eating, hon," Ethyl said. "Pork chops is tomorrow night." She returned to the kitchen while Elinor Ann suppressed a giggle.

"Oh, you guys—I can't believe I'm sitting here in New York City!"

I couldn't believe it, either. The cautious expression I remembered from our November visit had vanished, and seeing her exuberant reaction to the brownstone and the neighborhood—not to mention Hank—filled me with hope.

But oh, how I wished she'd come to town for any other reason.

The check arrived and both men pounced. While they argued over it, Elinor Ann leaned closer to me.

"So you think you'll be okay tonight?"

"Yeah, I do, thanks to you guys. I'm so glad you—"

The song on the radio changed and in a heartbeat, so did my resolve. I buried my face in my napkin, releasing a fresh torrent of tears, the moment Fred picked up his ladle.

I guess I'm losing my mind. . . .

Elinor Ann immediately hoisted me to my feet and hustled me off to the bathroom.

The two of us could barely squeeze into the tiny space. I had just perched on the edge of the toilet seat when there was a hard rap on the door.

"Occupied!" Elinor Ann called out.

"Open up, missy!"

She cracked the door and Ethyl's arm, a shot glass of whiskey in her hand, appeared. "Drink up, girlie. It'll do you a world of good. And don't you worry—I told that son of a bitch if he ever makes you cry again, he's banned from this place for life."

"Wow," Elinor Ann said after Ethyl left. "New Yorkers are a lot nicer than I expected . . . in their own way."

I drained the shot and dabbed at my eyes with toilet paper. "Poor Hank." I could only shake my head at the absurdity of the situation.

"I'm sure we can manage to convince her this isn't his fault."

I felt the warmth of the alcohol spread from the pit of my stomach to my fingertips. Ethyl had been right—it was helping. And we'd been in the bathroom for at least three minutes, so the song would be over by now. I got up, and we performed an elaborate pas de deux so I could reach the sink and splash water onto my face.

"Ready?" Elinor Ann said, turning the lock on the doorknob.

"Close enough."

Ethyl was glaring at Hank, dark eyes blazing, when we returned to the table. "He's not the reason I was crying," I told her.

"You sure?"

"I swear."

"Well, that's a relief. I always thought you two kids made a real cute couple." She shot Hank one more look. "But only if girlie here is telling me the truth. I'll be watching you, sonny boy." She swept the cash off the table, and the four of us reached for our coats.

The cold air helped, and so did Hank's protective arm around my waist. "Don't worry," he whispered. "I ain't letting go of you."

We arrived at the pickup truck and waited while Cal circled the vehicle for a quick hubcap check. "Looks like they're all here." He reached over to shake Hank's hand. "Real nice to meet you." He hesitated, then leaned over and engulfed me in a bear hug. "I sure am sorry about what happened, Dana. But that's a good man you got there. Take care of him—and yourself."

"I will. Thanks for coming to my rescue."

Elinor Ann hugged Hank, then turned to face me. "Are you sure you're going to be all right?"

"Of course I am, now that I've seen you. God, I'm glad you came." I appraised her expression. "But what about you? I know it's only half past six, but it's a long way back to Kutztown."

She thought for a minute before responding. "You know something? I'll be fine—I'm sure of it."

I gave her a nudge. "Oh, come on, Elinor Ann. Don't you want to show off your new coping tactic? I'm sure the boys would love to see it."

She grinned. "Well, okay, but only if you join me."

"Deal."

The two of us shrugged off our jackets and tossed them into the bed of Cal's pickup. Then, to the amazement of our respective men and assorted passersby, we dropped to the sidewalk and performed a symmetric set of squat thrusts, right there on Avenue A, just north of Sixth Street.

CHAPTER TWENTY-THREE

NUDE ASCENDING A STAIRCASE

Hank was quiet on the walk home—too quiet, as the cowboys in Westerns say, just before the Indians arrive to ambush their encampment and have their way with the womenfolk.

Now you've done it, I thought to myself. Obviously my outburst in the restaurant had alienated him—not to mention put him on probation with Ethyl. I wanted to apologize, or explain, or implore him to forget what he'd seen, but instead I trudged along beside him, too nervous and too drained to know what to say.

But everything changed as soon as we were inside the brownstone. Instantly my back was up against the wall and Hank was kissing me, fumbling with my belt buckle with one hand and undoing his with the other.

"Wait—what?"

"Shhh." He rubbed against me and began to ease my pants past my hips. His dick felt like granite.

"But why . . . ?"

"Best thing for death is life. Let me take care of you."

I wasn't about to argue, especially since I agreed with him. Bone-rattling, whiplash-inducing sex was exactly what I needed. I managed to free one leg from my jeans and wrapped it around him while he pounded me into a welcome state of oblivion.

It went on like that all night. He carried me over to the stairs, then down the hall to the kitchen, and eventually into bed, letting up just long enough for us to catch our breath or gulp water straight from the faucet.

The sky was just beginning to turn gray when I dozed off—or passed out, I wasn't sure which. When I came to, the clock read four and Hank was lying next to me.

"You all rested up?"

I nodded.

"Good." He rolled on top of me, pinning my wrists with his hands. "'Cause I ain't done yet."

This was a whole new Hank Wheeler. He'd never been so tireless, or shown such single-minded intensity. Even Dinner, who usually had to be barred from the bedroom prior to foreplay, had taken refuge in his kennel when we'd burst into the kitchen, clothes scattering in our wake. "You're my girl now," Hank said as my head banged against the rails of his brass bed. "That's the only thing you need to be thinking about."

I loved it. I couldn't get enough of him. All my focus was on his body, and the sex, and the moment, and I would have eagerly kept going until I was dead.

Which I nearly was, by the time I staggered home early Monday morning on weakened knees.

"Wow," Elinor Ann said. "I guess he's not the jealous type."

"Or he is, and was on a mission to prove he's king of the jungle."

"So . . . did it work?"

"*Vive le roi,*" I said. "I'm only just now getting full feeling back in my feet." I thought back to the night before and shivered. "Hank was the perfect boyfriend this weekend," I told her. "Not every guy would have been so—I guess you could say, sympathetic, even though that was the farthest thing from a mercy fuck I've ever experienced."

"Well—I'm glad, then. Uh, can we talk about something else now?"

"Of course. I'm sorry. You know, I'll never be able to stop thanking you for coming to see me. How was it getting home?"

She laughed. "I was asleep before we got across the Bayonne Bridge. And it's a good thing, too—I've been cleaning up dog wee-wee around the clock ever since Eddie and Cal brought Lurch home from Phillips-burg."

"Lurch? I love it. How'd you come up with that?"

"Once you've seen him walk, you'll realize it's the only name for this . . . creature."

"I'm looking forward to it."

"So are we. God, I'm glad you finally called, Dana. I was really beginning to worry."

"What are you talking about? I called as soon as I heard the message you left Sunday morning."

"Oh, come on. 'I'm fine—can't talk—bye'? You call that a conversation?"

"I just told you—I was . . . busy."

"Apparently." She paused. "So . . . are you feeling a little less sad about Ray?"

"Yeah. I am. It's like Hank said—the best thing for death is life."

"I like that. And I really am relieved that he turned out to be so . . . understanding, if that's the right word for it."

It was the right word. Just before I left the brownstone that morning, Hank had walked me to the front door, then looked down at his feet. "So was that guy, like, the love of your life?"

I saw no point in lying to him. He'd been an eyewitness to my melt-down in the restaurant. He already knew the answer. "I guess you could say that."

He leaned in to kiss me goodbye. "Well, maybe you could have two of them."

Or three, based on the contents of my in-box, which featured four messages from Billy Moody.

"What are you doing?" read the subject line from Friday. "Where are you?" had come in Saturday afternoon, followed a few hours later by, "Hope everything is okay." Finally, on Sunday, he wanted to know, "Was it something I said?"

"No," I replied aloud to the computer screen. "It was something Hank did—repeatedly."

I'd allay Billy's fears, but first I had to look over the photos Eddie had sent at my request. Lurch was adorable—mostly white, with a few well-placed brown spots, including one over his right eye.

"Cutest. Bulldog. Ever," I wrote back. "Can't wait to meet him in person."

By the time I'd sent off the email, my in-box was fuller by two. Billy again, and . . . what was this?

> Dear Crossword Tournament Contestant:
>
> Just a brief note to let you know we received your entry fee and look forward to seeing you in Brooklyn at the end of the month. If you have any questions, please feel free to write back, or visit our Web site.

I hit Forward and addressed it to Gridmeister, replacing the subject line with "Is this your doing?"

My cell phone rang so quickly, I simply held it to my ear and said, "Well? Is it?"

"I had to come up with some way to repay you for rewriting all those clues for my Sunday puzzle, didn't I? Which, by the way, was accepted."

"Uh, that's great. Congratulations. But what about—"

"So where should we go to celebrate?"

"Billy, haven't I made myself clear by now?"

"Oh, come on. Valentine's Day is the day after tomorrow."

I was well aware of that. I'd spotted a large pink envelope amidst the stack of mail I'd pulled from my box before going upstairs. My mother never failed to send a card, always signing it, *Love, ? + ?* Which was thoughtful, if a bit depressing when I found myself alone for the holiday.

"Billy, I am not going anywhere with you on Valentine's Day."

"I figured you were going to say that." He sighed. "Guess you spent the weekend with my competition, huh? The least you could have done is check your email, you know. I was genuinely concerned about you."

"I'm okay. That's sweet, though."

"I can be a lot sweeter than that if you give me half a chance."

"Good*bye*, Billy."

"See you in Brooklyn, Dana."

I hadn't planned to be home longer than the time it took to feed the cat and pick up a change of clothes. All my painting supplies were at the brownstone, and I'd decided to give Hannah a rest for a week or two while I finished the baluster project.

But the stack of mail was larger than I'd anticipated, even though the bulk of the correspondence looked to be from my dear friends at corporations like Verizon and Con Edison.

Maybe I'd start with Mom's Valentine's card. I extracted it from the pile, but before I opened it, I happened to glance at the postmark.

The letter had come from Brooklyn, not Florida.

Oh god. Ray must have mailed it the day before he died.

I walked into my bedroom, staring at my name on the envelope in his familiar hand, and flopped on the bed next to Puny.

It was a simple card, with just the word *you* on the front of it, rendered in elaborate, flowery cursive. Inside, the word reappeared on five lines, growing larger with each repetition: *you, you, you, you, you*.

He'd signed it at the bottom, *Luv, Eggs*.

Luv, Eggs?

Of course.

I flashed back to a long-ago conversation held just before another Valentine's Day, between Ninth Street and a pay phone somewhere in Bay Ridge, Brooklyn.

"I found you the perfect card," Ray had said, causing a rush of phero-mones to swirl through my system, which was what happened every time he let me know I'd been on his mind.

"I can't wait to get it." He'd gone into a store! And picked out a card!! For me!!!

"But you know, Dana, that could be incriminating, your having a Valentine's card with my name on it."

"So sign it X," I had told him.

He'd hesitated while I listened to the static of our bad connection.

"Sign it . . . *eggs*? What would I want to do that for?"

I'd burst out laughing, and so had he, once I'd explained what I'd really said. Three days later the card arrived, depicting an old Chevy with the windows steamed up and rivulets of water running down them. He'd been right—it was perfect. I'd never known passion actually did cause car windows to fog up until I'd spent all those hours kissing Ray good night while we sat in his beat-up VW wagon, idling in front of my building.

And of course he'd signed it, *Luv, Eggs*.

For the first time since Renée's awful phone call, I was able to smile. He'd remembered. He really had been thinking of me, at least some of the time, during all those years apart. Maybe he really had loved me.

Not maybe—of course he had. I was holding the proof in my hands.

At that moment, I knew I would somehow come to terms with never seeing Ray again, just as I knew I would never, ever part with that Valentine's card.

But I hadn't managed to do it yet, as Tom-Tom's call soon made clear.

The phone rang just as I was getting ready to leave. "Okay, we're all set," he said.

"For what?"

"I've lined up our flights for the Thomas Mayo, Senior, birthday extravaganza. And I hope you don't mind, but I thought we deserved a little decompression time after the festivities."

"So you booked us a suite at the Shores."

"You're psychic."

"No, I'm your half sister. When have you ever visited the Estates at Waterway Village without reserving a suite at the Shores?"

"Hmm. Never. Oh dear. I had no idea I was so set in my ways. Now I'm going to have to take up . . . capoeira, or some such life-altering activity."

I tried to picture Tom-Tom swooping and kicking to the rhythmic strains of a berimbau. The image failed to materialize. "You know, I hear capoeira is pretty strenuous."

"Fine—mah-jongg. Now, on an unrelated note, I hope you've had time to get to that replacement Hannah that Graciela's been panting for."

I hadn't. But it didn't matter anymore. I looked over at the canvas, still wrapped in the brown paper I'd used to transport it to the dive bar for my date with Ray, and took a deep breath.

"As it turns out, you can have the original," I said in a shaky voice.

My tone made Tom-Tom pause before he spoke. "Oh, sweetie. When did he die?"

"Friday." I took another deep breath, determined to get through the conversation without crying. "But how did you know . . . ?"

"He never would have stood you up. Not after all this time."

But he had stood me up. Permanently.

I needed to get back to the brownstone immediately.

I gave Ray's Valentine a prominent position on the bulletin board over my desk, then walked out the front door—and straight into Vivian.

"Where the hell have you been?"

"Elsewhere." I didn't owe her an explanation. And the last thing I wanted to do was waste time talking to her when Hank Wheeler was just two blocks away, ready to take care of me.

"I'm still waiting on that third painting, you know."

"Yeah—about that. It seems Hannah's come down with a bad case of pneumonia." Let Vivian wait. I needed a break—from her especially, but also from the canvases, and my apartment, and anything else that had the potential to upset me.

"Pneumonia? What are you talking about? You *owe* me!"

"Well, you're just going to have to sit tight. I'm working on a project right now that takes precedence."

"It *can't!*"

I almost laughed out loud. "What are you going to do about it?"

And why had it taken me so long to realize that the answer to my question was, "Not a damn thing"? Vivian was at my mercy. If I wanted to give Hannah a case of pneumonia so I could spend time with my boyfriend, well, then, that was what was going to happen.

"Don't worry—she'll probably recover," I called over my shoulder on the way to Seventh Street.

Hank and I soon settled into a routine: balusters, paint stripping, takeout, and sex. Mostly the latter. Valentine's Day came and went, marked by a bouquet of pale pink roses and very little hoopla, which was just the way I wanted it. By that point I didn't need proof of his devotion. I just needed him to stick around until I regained my equilibrium.

After about a week, he regarded me from his perch on the ladder to where I sat near the top of the staircase, finishing up the second-to-last baluster. He smiled.

"There you are."

"Huh?"

"You're back."

Huh. I guess I was back. I was still thinking about Ray, but that was nothing new. I'd been thinking about Ray for twenty-one years. But lately the pain wasn't quite so searing. He'd died a day too soon—well, decades too soon—and that was sad, but that was what had happened, and I couldn't change it.

"I'm glad you're feeling better, Dana."

"I am feeling better. I guess you fixed me."

He grinned. "I'm real sorry you needed fixing, but I can't say I minded putting in the labor."

Naturally, I couldn't leave well enough alone. I borrowed Hank's laptop one afternoon to clandestinely visit the crossword tournament's Web site.

The rules were byzantine. Each word in the grid received a score, with points deducted for errors, for a solving total. Perfect puzzles received bonus points, which were also allocated for each minute a crossword was completed in advance of the time allotted—which differed, based on difficulty and size.

Most daunting of all, I discovered there were six puzzles to complete over the course of Saturday, with a seventh to solve at the ungodly hour of nine o'clock Sunday morning.

This was supposed to be fun? I hadn't been forced to use my brain cells that early since I'd taken the SATs. Maybe I didn't need to match wits against hundreds of other contestants.

Or maybe I was scared. Maybe I didn't want to compete and discover how bad I was at one of the things I did best.

Or maybe I was scared for a different reason. I'd sent an email to Billy, asking if people went into training for this sort of thing.

"Some do," he'd replied. "I know one guy who solves a hundred puzzles a day for the two months leading up to this weekend."

> Are you serious? You could train for a decathlon in less time than it takes to solve a hundred puzzles a day. And why do they have to schedule that final puzzle so early on Sunday morning, anyway?
> D.

> If you're worried about getting to Brooklyn in time for puzzle #7, you don't have to be. I've booked a room right upstairs for Saturday night, and it's got a nice, comfy, king-sized bed in it.
> W.W.W.

Swell, I thought, dispatching the message to the junk folder before I was tempted to respond. Not only were my brain cells going to be put to the test this weekend—so were my morals.

Then Hank made an announcement that further complicated my situation.

"Spoke to my daughter this morning. Looks like I finally convinced her to come up to the city and visit her old man."

"That's great. I've been looking forward to meeting her. When are you expecting her?"

"She's driving up with her new husband for the weekend."

"This weekend?"

"There some kind of a problem?"

"No . . . Well, there's this crossword tournament they hold every year out in Brooklyn. I was thinking about competing in it."

"No kidding? You got to go, Dana. I never seen anybody do crosswords as fast as you. You'll win the grand prize!"

I laughed. "I seriously doubt that. Some of the contestants sound awfully . . . driven. What day are they coming?"

"She reckons they'll leave Mullica Hill right after work on Friday and get in around seven o'clock."

Maybe my situation wasn't as complicated as I'd feared. According to the schedule posted on the tournament's Web site, that evening was given over to game night, which was optional, and registration, which I could put off until Saturday morning. "That's a relief. At least I'll get a chance to meet her."

But as it turned out, the meeting was anything but a relief, and if I'd thought my situation was complicated before, it was nothing compared to how complicated it would become once I encountered Mrs. Jolene Calhoun Butz.

CHAPTER TWENTY-FOUR

IN THE BELLY OF THE BEAST

"What could possibly have been so terrible that you had to run out of there?" Elinor Ann wanted to know as I hustled down Houston Street on my way to Second Avenue and the F train stop. All of a sudden I couldn't wait to participate in game night.

"Oh my god. You would not believe—"

But nobody would believe how much could go so dreadfully wrong in just under twenty minutes.

As soon as Jolene entered the brownstone, she fixed her eyes on my newly completed baluster set and grimaced. "I hope that's the next thing you're going to renovate, Daddy." She hugged him, and he looked over her shoulder at me, visibly mortified.

"Actually, that's . . . here to stay," he told her. "This here's my girl—Dana, Jolene."

"Real nice to meet you, ma'am."

I shouldn't condemn her based on her taste. She'd grown up differently than I—in the land of be-jeweled and be-riveted denim, as her outfit made clear.

And I had grown up in Snobville, as my hideously judgmental

attitude made clear. What did it matter if our sensibilities were misaligned? We both cared for Hank, didn't we? She seemed pretty, with her father's dark hair and blue eyes, but it was hard to tell through makeup nearly as thick as the coats of paint on the crown moldings above our heads.

But enough of that. "Welcome to New York City." I smiled and shook her hand. Everything would work out fine, if I could just behave myself— for once.

The front door swung open, and Jolene's husband tromped in with two duffel bags. He dropped them with a thud and pointed at the staircase. "Who's movin' into this place? Some fag?"

My potential stepdaughter dissolved into giggles as Hank introduced me to Gordon "Call Me Gordo" Butz.

"Well, I can hardly see how Hank's responsible," Elinor Ann said. "It's not like he raised the girl. Didn't his ex-wife get custody? And didn't you tell me he only met this husband of hers at the wedding?"

"I did. And I know this isn't his fault. But I just couldn't stand to be in that house another second."

We showed them through the corridor and into the kitchen, where I'd made tea. I opened the refrigerator and added a six-pack to the table, thinking it might come in handy.

"So. Mullica Hill, New Jersey," I said. "I think I drove through it on my way to the shore once. What do you guys do down there?"

"I guess you could call us farmers." Jolene pointed to her husband. "His family's owned a complex of greenhouses for near about a hundred years. They grow herbs for the food industry."

An herb farm. How bucolic. This was more like it.

"Won't be much longer, though," Gordo said, popping open a beer. "Developers have been putting up condos like crazy round there. We're just holding out for a sweet price." He let out a whoop. "Then it's off to NASCAR Nation, baby!"

Surely there was *some* way to find common ground.

"So, now that you're in town, what would you like to see?" I asked.

Jolene frowned. "I can't think of anything. . . ."

"The Empire State Building? The Metropolitan Museum?" I prompted.

At last her face lit up. "I know! Trump Tower!"

Hank was avoiding eye contact with me. I didn't know whether to be relieved or insulted. He was obviously delighted to see his daughter, and what father wouldn't be? It was only right, as was my intention to accommodate our guests with as much hospitality as I could muster. "Anybody hungry?" I said.

"You bet." Gordo reached for a second beer.

"There's a real good restaurant we like just around the corner," Hank said.

"Restaurant?" Gordo's tone made it clear he was opposed to the suggestion. *Oh god,* I thought. *Please don't expect me to cook.*

Jolene smiled indulgently at her husband. "He just hates tipping them waitresses."

"I don't believe in gratuities. Besides, it's Friday night. For me, that's two Big Macs, large fries, and a hot apple pie. You got a McDonald's round here?"

"I think there's one over on Second Avenue," I said.

Gordo got to his feet. "Let's me and you go over there, Hank. This neighborhood's no place for any wife of mine to be walking around."

"This area seems kind of . . . ethnic," Jolene explained. "He don't believe in the mixing of the races."

Oh no no no.

"I always say that's why the track's got two sides—a white one and a wrong one!" Gordo roared at his own joke, and I reached for my jacket.

"I'm terribly sorry I won't be able to stay for dinner," I said. "But I'm already late—I'm supposed to be out in Brooklyn at a crossword tournament." Finally Hank met my gaze. He nodded, as if to say, *Vaya con Dios*.

Gordo let out a grunt. "Crosswords. Talk about a waste of time."

"So the guy doesn't solve crossword puzzles," Elinor Ann said. "Not everyone does, you know."

"I know." I sighed. "Hank doesn't." And he used double modifiers, and his daughter had married a redneck, and Hank wasn't even his real name, I thought, sinking into despair. All of a sudden I couldn't fathom how we'd managed to get along for the past three months.

"Dana, calm down. I'm sure you guys can work this out."

"I'm not. That meeting was a disaster—I hope I never have to see those two again as long as I live. And the last thing I want is for Hank to feel that he has to choose between his daughter and me."

"Oh, Dana. I really, really wish you were on your way back to Ninth Street right now."

I should have known Elinor Ann would try to talk me out of going to Brooklyn this evening, I thought after boarding a southbound train. And maybe she was right. Maybe this foray was a bad idea. But I couldn't stay at Hank's. Nor did I want to go home, where memories of that disastrous encounter would crowd out all other thoughts for the duration of the evening.

Hank understood. "I'm sorry," he said after he'd walked me to the front door. "I don't blame you for wanting to get out of here."

I hugged him. "No, I'm sorry. But—"

"No need to be." He laughed. "Wish I was going to Brooklyn with you."

"Just enjoy your visit with Jolene. She seems very sweet. I'll call you when I get home tonight."

"Good luck—even though I think I'm gonna need it more than you."

———

Twenty-five minutes later I walked into an alternate universe—one where most of the natives wore glasses and had scant concern for their personal appearance.

The hotel lobby was packed with animated geniuses. Some of them had helped themselves to puzzles stacked on a center table, then plopped down right there on the floor to begin the solving process.

Immediate panic set in. These people were driven. These people were hard-core. As I made my way toward a rear hallway with a sign reading REGISTRATION, I overheard snippets of conversation:

"It was gorgeous. Three rows of stacked fifteens at the top and bottom of the grid."

"So after I bingoed, I played 'azalea' on a triple-word score—with the *Z* on a double letter."

My people.

I joined the end of the line in front of a box labeled *H* THROUGH *M*. My fellow contestants seemed almost preternaturally friendly, smiling and chatting and patiently waiting their turn. After I'd reached the front, where I was handed a name tag and a yellow folder, I turned around and found myself face-to-face with Billy.

"There you are. Wasn't sure you'd show tonight."

"Neither was I."

"Listen—all the judges have to help out with game night, but stick around. At least we could have a nightcap and share a cab home." He smiled and trailed his fingers down my arm while I struggled to maintain my composure.

"We'll see." I joined the throng streaming toward the grand ballroom, but Billy called after me. "Dana?"

I turned and raised my eyebrows.

"You look really cute tonight."

So much for composure, I thought, grinning like an idiot all the way to my destination.

Inside, hundreds of eager participants sat at mile-long tables running the length of the enormous room. I took a seat near the back and listened as a guy who bore a strong resemblance to Phil Rizzuto explained the rules.

"We're going to be presenting a series of thirty word games. . . ."

Thirty?

Surely such a prolonged mental challenge would deplete brain cells best conserved for the actual competition. I slipped out a side door and headed directly to the bar.

It was nearly empty, except for a table full of boisterous drinkers who looked as though they were having way more fun than the crowd in the ballroom, and a gay couple seated at the corner of the square-shaped bar. I slid onto a stool perpendicular to theirs and discreetly observed the revelers, just as a girl wearing a purple coat with marabou trim around the collar erupted with a high-pitched peal of laughter.

"They call themselves the Brain Cell Killers," the shorter, blonder of the two men said. "I don't know how they manage to make it through Saturday."

"Let alone Sunday," the taller, balder one added.

I shot them a look of pure gratitude. "Thank you for talking to me and saving my life."

The shorter one reached his arm across the corner of the bar. "I'm Kevin. He's Patrick. And don't worry—we'll look after you. We decided we adored you the minute you walked in."

"Dana," I said, shaking hands. "But what made you decide . . . ?"

"You're not wearing mom jeans," Kevin said.

"Or gingham." Patrick shuddered. "*Where* do these people *shop*, anyway?" He took a sip from his glass of red wine. "I take it you're a rookie."

"Well, I will be, if I can bring myself to come back here tomorrow."

"Don't worry—you'll do fine. Just watch out for the Five," Patrick said.

Kevin took note of my confusion. "The fifth puzzle," he clarified. "It's by far the hardest. Although the Three can trip you up, too."

"But not like the Five." Patrick took another sip. "God, remember last year's? Worst puzzle I've seen in nine years of competing."

"Some people were lucky to score twenty points on it, and that was only because they knew to put an *S* in any square where the clue implied a plural." Kevin rolled his eyes. "Of course, the constructor was W. W. W. Moody."

"Billy didn't tell me he had a puzzle in last year's tournament," I said, causing both men to regard me with renewed fascination.

"You know him?" Kevin half rose in his seat. "Bartender—another drink for our new best friend here."

"Both of us would kill to fuck him," Patrick confided. "Would you happen to know if he's . . . ?"

"Sorry. Straight."

They leaned forward in unison. "Would you mind telling us how you know that?"

"Yes. Yes, I would mind."

Patrick nudged Kevin. "I *love* this girl."

Their line of questioning had gone on long enough, I decided, changing the subject to the puzzles. "I get that the Five is the hardest one, but why should I fear the Three?"

"There's invariably a word that seems right, but it'll have a misleading clue that might make you enter a wrong letter—like 'lie' for 'pie,' or 'scrabble' for 'scramble.'" Kevin waved his hand. "There goes your perfect-puzzle bonus."

An hour or so flew by while I was schooled on the fine points of the A, B, and C rankings, the nerve-wracking digital-countdown clock that loomed in a corner of the ballroom, and other matters of no interest whatsoever to the vast majority of the population.

Finally Kevin turned and looked out the bar's window to the lobby. "Oh god. Game night's letting out. Hurry! Order another round before they swarm!"

I laid a twenty on the bar. "Thanks, but I'm good."

And I was going to stay good, and get out of there before Billy Moody showed up. I'd had enough excitement for one night.

Besides, I had a feeling I needed all the sleep I could get before tomorrow.

"Come find us between puzzles," Patrick called after me as I was walking out. "We'll be outside—the ashtray on the right."

I made my way to the Borough Hall subway station, where I boarded a Manhattan-bound 4 train and opened the yellow folder I'd been handed at registration. A welcoming letter, a schedule of events, and the rules I'd seen on the tournament Web site filled the right pocket, along with the word counts of each puzzle and a list of constructors—Billy among them. The names appeared in alphabetical order, so there was no way to tell who was responsible for which puzzle, but they read like a who's who of crossword titans.

I reached into the left pocket, which contained a roster of all preregistered contestants, divided by geographical region. *Wow,* I thought, leafing through the pages. People had come all the way from Oslo and Winnipeg and Caracas for this event. Based on the number of names per sheet, I'd be competing against roughly six hundred others.

And what careers they had. There were slews of computer programmers, an army of teachers, attorneys galore; even a hip-hop impresario. I turned to the section for New York City, which ran nearly four pages long, and found my name. Billy had chosen to list my occupation as "Muse."

It was official. I was doing this, no matter what the outcome.

I called Hank as soon as I got home. "I'm sorry for running out on you like that."

"Heck, Dana, I'm glad you did. We shouldn't both of us had to suffer." He let out a sigh. "Guess you figured out why I didn't invite you to that wedding, huh? I had a bad feeling about that guy. Turns out I was right."

"I wish you'd said something earlier. I'd have understood. I mean, Gordo's not your kid."

"No, but he's married to my kid. That's plenty bad enough."

"You know, maybe if you had a talk with Jolene—"

"Ain't nothing I can say. She's grown. She made her choice. All's I can do now is hope that as time goes by, she gets a whole lot more smarter."

More smarter, I silently repeated, slowly shaking my head.

We lapsed into silence. Apparently Hank didn't want to tell me how the rest of the evening had gone any more than I wanted to hear about it.

"So . . . where are they now?" I asked.

"The back bedroom. Reckon they're in there watching television."

"Where are you sleeping?"

"The couch in the front parlor."

"Do you want to spend the night here instead?"

Finally he managed a laugh. "Scared to. Old Gordo might decide he's doing me a favor and tear out your staircase while I'm gone."

"I'm glad you called him," Elinor Ann said as I made my way to the Union Square subway at a quarter to ten the next morning. "It was the right thing to do. Now, please do yourself a favor and keep up the good behavior."

"Will you stop worrying?"

"I promise, just as soon as this tournament is over and I hear you've managed to stay away from Billy Moody."

My new best friends weren't at their designated ashtray when I approached the hotel, so I returned to the grand ballroom and took a seat at the end of a table toward the back. I consulted my watch: twenty-five minutes before Puzzle One was scheduled to begin. Maybe I'd make a quick trip to the ladies' room to run cold water on my wrists. As I stood to leave, a man strolled by wearing a wedding dress, the fabric of which had been turned into a satin crossword puzzle with the aid of a felt-tipped pen.

I spotted Billy in the center of the lobby when I passed through. He was surrounded; a rock star among mortals.

Perfect, I thought. *He'll be far too busy with his groupies this weekend to have any time for me.*

But when I exited the ladies' room, I found him waiting outside the door.

"What happened to you last night?"

"I decided to be smart and get some sleep."

"Good. Then I can keep you up late tonight."

"Billy, can you just—give it a rest? I'm nervous enough as it is."

"Don't be. You're going to do just fine."

And I was fine, as soon as I flipped over Puzzle One a few minutes later. Kevin had assured me it would be easy—"like a Monday"—and when I finished in five minutes and looked up to discover row after row of heads still bent over their papers, my spirits rose. *Maybe I won't do so badly after all,* I thought.

Until I entered the lobby and encountered a multitude of my fellow solvers, most of whose conversation consisted of phrases such as "Two minutes" and "Three minutes."

Oh crap.

"Don't panic," Kevin said when I found him at the ashtray. The abbreviated length of his cigarette made it obvious he'd finished well ahead of me. "Those elite solvers can whip through a Sunday puzzle in the time it takes you to finish a Tuesday. You can't let them psych you out."

"I'll try not to. Where's Patrick?" I said, just before he burst out the door with an agonized *"Fuck!"*

"Jook. I can't *believe* I wrote 'jook' instead of 'jock.' What the *fuck* is a jook?"

I quickly determined that the ashtray was an excellent spot for allaying— or confirming—one's deepest fears. By the time I'd completed the Two puzzle with a twelve-minute time bonus, I rushed to the gathering and called out, "Alioto?" How was I supposed to know who the mayor of San Francisco had been in the 1970s?

"You got it—I lived in the Haight back then," an elderly man wearing a crossword-patterned tie responded, setting off a smattering of groans among the contestants.

"You're doing great," Kevin said just before we went in to confront the hazardous Three. "Just don't forget to cross-check your fill on this one."

I was glad I'd heeded his advice when I walked out nineteen minutes later—and into the great J-bar kerfuffle.

"There's no such thing as a J-bar," Kevin was insisting as I approached. *Of course there is,* I thought. It was a bar, shaped like the letter *J,* used to transport skiers up mountains. Granted, the T-bar was much more common, especially as a fill word, but . . .

"Then how do you justify 'toke' instead of 'joke' for 'It might get a giggle'?" another smoker parried.

"*You* know." Kevin held two fingers to his lips in the manner of pot-heads everywhere, setting off gales of laughter—and more than a few impassioned expletives.

"Nice try," said a bespectacled man with salt-and-pepper hair and a judge's yellow name tag around his neck.

I exhaled for the first time all morning.

I couldn't eat during the lunch break, choosing instead to wander up and down nearby Fulton Street in a futile endeavor to clear my head. When I got back to the hotel, the smokers welcomed me as if they'd paid ransom for my safe return. By now we were family. I would have willingly donated a kidney—or, more appropriately, a lung—to any one of them.

Speculation began to brew as we gathered up our folders and went inside to begin the afternoon round.

"Scuttlebutt has it the Five's a Moody."

"That's impossible. He did the Five last year."

"Well, his name's on the list of constructors. . . ."

But Billy wasn't responsible for the dreaded fifth puzzle. Not that it wasn't challenging. I stared blankly at the clues for several minutes, refusing to look at the countdown clock, before I cracked the northeast corner. Kevin had been right. It was hard.

But not all that much harder than a typical Saturday puzzle. I filled in the last of the squares with two minutes remaining on the clock and a strong hankering for a cocktail—or twenty.

Billy had been hovering on my side of the room, collecting papers from contestants, for the duration of the tournament, but he always retreated to the judges' chambers to score puzzles in between rounds. Finally, when I finished the Six—which wasn't by him, either—with a respectable time bonus, he dashed over to retrieve it.

"Don't disappear on me tonight," he whispered. "You hurt my feelings yesterday."

"We'll see."

With a sly smile, he leaned in closer. "By the way, I checked into my room just after lunch—2611, in case you felt like stopping by."

I walked out of the ballroom, reeling off sets of random numbers in my head in a desperate attempt to addle my memory. No good could come from retaining the information I'd just been given.

———————

By the time I reached the bar, I was woozy from lack of nourishment.

"Dana! Over here!" The smokers had commandeered a large round table just inside the door. I ordered a burger and a double Dewar's and gave myself permission to relax.

Not everyone was able to do so. Patrick, seated next to me, was rocking back and forth with a dazed expression. "Jook," he muttered every ten minutes or so. "Fucking jook."

Since vice tends to beget vice, I wasn't surprised to discover that the smokers were an enthusiastic band of imbibers. In fact, I was dangerously close to blotto when Billy turned up around nine thirty.

"Where you been?" I slurred, wondering how there could be two of him standing before me.

"Judges' dinner. By the way, congratulations."

"For what?"

"Didn't you see the rankings?"

"They're posted?"

"You're in ninety-ninth place. Told you you'd do great."

"Ninety-ninth?!"

This called for a drink!

I celebrated long into the night with my tobacco-loving brethren, all the while keeping an eye on Billy, who was doing likewise with me. As I'd expected, he was in great demand, but eventually he made his way over to the bar, where I was settling my tab.

"Come on upstairs," he said.

"I don't think so."

"Not to my room—there's a constructors' party up on the fourteenth floor. Got some people I'd like you to meet."

"But I'm not a constructor."

"Themes and clues," he said, taking hold of my elbow and ushering me toward the exit. "That's close enough." As we passed the smokers' table, Kevin stuck out his tongue to mimic a panting dog.

After we'd entered what Billy referred to as "the palindromic room 1441," I found myself in the company of what was quite possibly the highest concentration of brainpower—and beer bottles—on the planet. Most of the name tags I was able to make out bore the appellations of legends. What was I doing in their exalted company?

"Should've known Moody'd be the only one who could get a date for this soirée," said a goateed leprechaun whose puzzle had appeared in last Sunday's paper.

"This is Dana," Billy announced. "Be nice to her—she's a rookie. Dana, I'd like you to meet—let's see—Wendy LaBron . . . and that's Hank Blob . . . our host, Spider C. Fop. . . ."

It took a moment before I was able to cut through my alcohol-induced fog and figure out what he was doing: anagramming the names of each constructor, right there on the spot.

If I'd thought I was out of my league in the ballroom, that was nothing compared to this. I meekly accepted a beer, even though I was already drunk enough to know I'd wake up feeling as if I'd participated in a prison riot. Oh, *when* would I learn that Benedictine never, *ever* made an appropriate chaser for multiple double Dewar's on the rocks?

I took polite sips from my bottle of microbrew while a hot debate raged over the merits of the day's Five puzzle.

"The fill was lively, but the difficulty was hardly on a par with last year's Moody," said—well, Wendy LaBron, as he'd been dubbed for the evening.

"You flatter me," Billy countered. "Mine was a cakewalk compared to the one you provided a few years back."

I finally managed to drain my bottle. "Listen," I said. "It's been a genuine honor to meet you all, but I've got that Seven puzzle to solve to-morrow morning. I'd better be on my way."

"Already?" Spider C. Fop looked insulted. "You just got here!"

"Sorry. The nine a.m. start time would be tough enough without the hangover I'm anticipating." I shrugged on my jacket and rose from my seat at the foot of the bed.

Billy got up, too. "I'll walk you downstairs and put you in a cab."

But once we were inside the elevator, he pushed the button for twenty-six, not L.

CHAPTER TWENTY-FIVE

JUDAS PRIEST

"Hey!" I reached out to jab the button for the lobby, but Billy grabbed my wrist and pulled me up against him. I couldn't tell him to stop; that I had no intention of going to his room, because he was kissing me and whatever willpower I'd had was gone, vanquished by alcohol and exhaustion and euphoria.

"Don't say no, Dana," he pleaded when the doors opened onto the twenty-sixth floor. "I've been waiting such a long, long time for this."

He was irresistible. There was no way I could stand inside that elevator and travel twenty-six stories away from him.

Not until later, and that was such a long, long time from now.

We stumbled into the hallway, kissing and crashing into the walls of the corridor leading to room 2611, even though of course it was wrong and of course I should have been anywhere in the world but there. He fumbled with his key card, and finally we were inside and on the bed, moaning out loud with relief. The room was in shadows, with only the lights of the distant city glowing faintly outside the windows.

"That was torture," he said, peeling off my jacket and easing me back against the pillows.

"What was?"

"All day. Last night. Watching you out of the corner of my eye when all I wanted to do was this." He ran his hands all over me, his whole body pressed tight against mine.

I reached up under his shirt and let my fingertips buzz along the surface of his skin. Maybe I'd regret this—of course I'd regret this—but not right now. If losing Ray Devine had taught me anything, it was to stay in the moment and go after what I wanted, before it was gone forever. And god, I wanted Billy Moody, and this was the moment.

But this would have to be the only moment. "Billy," I said, "this is . . . just for tonight. You understand that, don't you?"

"I'm not going to turn you down, but—no. I don't." His smile flashed in the half-light. "I think you're the one who doesn't understand."

"Billy . . ."

"Tell me about this boyfriend of yours. Tell me why he's so much better than me." He had his hand halfway down the front of my jeans, and it was about to get soaked.

"He's . . . sexy," I slurred, shuddering when I felt his fingers. "And he . . . loves me."

"Well, other people could love you, too, you know."

Wow, I thought. *I've been in this room—what? Four minutes?—and he's already made me come.*

Twice.

Then the strangest thing happened. I experienced déjà vu—which, coincidentally, had been the fill for 1-Across in that day's Three puzzle.

"Listen, Dana," Billy said. "I know I'm probably about to screw up your life, but I just can't help it."

There. That was it. My transgression-in-waiting had just been sanctioned from beyond the grave. Ray had spoken those exact words to me, just before he'd kissed me for the first time and made me fall in love forever.

Then again, I probably could have justified the regime of Kim Jong-il at that heated moment. Billy and I undressed each other in slow motion, hands shaking with anticipation. Finally he was poised high above me, my legs wrapped around him, every molecule of my body screaming, *Now, now, now.*

He hovered over me, making me wait. "What's your boyfriend's name?"

"Hank." A wave the size of several oceans came crashing down on me.

"What is it?"

"Hank." *Oh Jesus.*

"What is it?"

"Oh, Billy." Billy Billy Billy.

I hadn't intended to spend the night, but by the time we'd finally had enough of each other, sunlight was filtering through a gap in the curtains and someone was banging loudly on the door.

"Shit! Who's that?" I dove for his flannel shirt at the foot of the bed.

"Don't panic—I ordered room service."

"When did you find the time to do that?"

"Right after I checked in. Filled out the card and hung it on the door-knob." He tugged on his jeans and went to let in the waiter.

There were two of everything on the overloaded tray—plates of bacon and eggs, coffee cups, racks of toast. I would have taken offense if I hadn't been so hungry.

"Don't you think all this is a bit . . . presumptuous?"

Billy let his pants fall to his ankles and grinned. "Power of positive thinking."

I hadn't stood a chance last night.

He came back to bed and stayed there until our breakfast was cold.

The spray from a hot shower finally enabled me to redirect my focus to something other than Billy Moody. What had I done last night—not to mention three times this morning?

And what was I supposed to do next?

There was no question of our physical compatibility.

But I had that with Hank, too.

Billy seemed convinced we belonged together, and not just in bed.

As did Hank.

But Billy and I had . . . some sort of bond. A mental connection that was beginning to make me wonder if he could read my mind.

"You know, I was just thinking—'multiple orgasms' is fifteen letters," he said as I was going in to shower.

"I was just thinking, too. 'Indefatigable' is thirteen," I replied, quickly pulling the bathroom door shut so he wouldn't make me late for the final puzzle.

I turned off the water and reached for a towel. Maybe Billy was right. Maybe we really did have something here.

By the time I was in the elevator, a queasy feeling was growing in the pit of my stomach, and it wasn't attributable to the cold scrambled eggs I'd just devoured. What had I been thinking, befriending two gay men at this tournament? They'd take one look at Billy's shirt, which I was wearing with its too-long tails tied in a knot above yesterday's jeans, and know exactly where I'd wound up last night.

Kevin sauntered over as I was ordering another cup of coffee at the bar. He looked me up and down with a smirk and tugged on one of the flannel tails.

"Nice outfit . . . Daisy Mae."

Patrick—or "Jook," as he'd changed his name tag to read—was right behind him. He peered closely at my face. "You're *glowing*," he said. "I *loathe* you."

"You guys . . ."

They burst out laughing.

"Oh, honey," Kevin said. "I know you're in ninety-ninth place, but you walked away with the trophy this weekend. You'd better be prepared to tell us everything after the Seven puzzle."

They went outside for a last-minute cigarette, and I made my way to the ballroom.

The bride in the crossword-patterned gown I'd spotted on Saturday had upped the ante for the final round. Today he was Janet Leigh from *Psycho*. The butt of a dagger sprouted from his head, and a metal ring around his neck supported the weight of a bloody black-and-white-gridded shower curtain.

"Isn't it hard to solve with that thing on?" I said.

In response, he pushed his hands through two hidden slits in the curtain. "It's all in the planning, baby."

I reclaimed my seat from yesterday and listened to the chatter around me. Speculation was running rampant as to whether Billy had constructed our upcoming puzzle.

"No way. He's much too hard for the general public."

"And his puzzles almost always run on Saturdays. I bet you he did the fifteen-by-fifteen for the championship final."

"Oh man. Can you imagine trying to solve a Moody on that stage, in front of six hundred people?"

I pulled out my phone, thinking I'd check my messages. On second thought, maybe that wasn't such a good idea. Elinor Ann would be wondering how yesterday had gone, and, more urgently, where I'd been last night. And Hank—

A pang of guilt hit me hard. He didn't deserve my betrayal, no matter how irresistible Billy was, or how attuned to each other we might be.

I sighed. Would I ever learn to think before I—

Just then Billy squeezed my shoulder as he passed by my chair on his way to the front of the room. I watched him join the cluster of judges, losing my train of thought as I recalled all the things we'd done last night. All I wanted to do was take him home and do them all over again. And again. Forever.

Oh god, I thought. *Billy's right. He is the man I'm supposed to be with.*

It took a whopping five minutes before I found out how spectacularly wrong I could be.

The public address system was activated, and the announcement everyone had been dreading came through the speakers. "The seventh and final puzzle of this year's tournament is by W. W. W. Moody."

Immediately a chorus of lament filled the air. Billy defensively covered his face with his hands, grinning furiously. He was flat-out adorable. Maybe he could ask the front desk for a late checkout and . . .

The judges fanned out to distribute the puzzles, with Billy making a beeline for my row. As he laid the sheet of paper before me, he leaned in and whispered, "Just take as long as you did the first time."

Just—what?

But he was gone, down at the other end of the table.

It wasn't until I flipped over the page and came face-to-face with shaded boxes of crossed words that I understood the meaning of Billy's statement.

That son of a bitch.

My initial impulse was to get up and walk out of there, effectively incurring a score of zero for my final puzzle. But then I thought about Billy's instructions: To take the same amount of time as I'd taken when I test-solved this very puzzle.

But I hadn't timed myself. Had I completed it in my usual twenty minutes or so, or had the Moody factor lengthened my solving time?

The only way to be completely fair was—well, there wasn't a way. Billy had seen to that.

That son of a bitch.

Even though it had been years since I'd needed a full half hour to solve a Sunday-sized crossword, I finally determined that was how long this one would have to take. Nobody in this ballroom should be penalized because I'd been given an unfair advantage—even though I'd never asked for it, and I would have given anything not to have it.

I'd been so overjoyed, and so inspired, by the prospect of finishing in the top hundred. How could Billy have done this? And why would he have thought I'd be willing to cheat?

Oh. Maybe because I was a cheat. What better word to describe me after what I'd done last night?

Traitor. That was an even better word. So was bitch. So was slut.

It took me about fifteen minutes to fill in all the squares, mainly because a number of my rewritten clues had been rewritten yet again, but also because every minute or two I'd stop cold, overwhelmed with anger and hurt. And remorse. Couldn't forget remorse.

Billy had wisely opted to work the other side of the room. I could see his blond head bobbing between tables as he retrieved papers. I kept one eye on him and one on the digital countdown clock, wishing it would hurry up and tick off thirty minutes so I could finally refer to this entire, horrible episode in the past tense.

At last I walked through the revolving doors of the hotel, where a cluster of smokers lay in wait next to their preferred ashtray.

"Where do you think *you're* going?" Patrick said, blocking my path. "We're expecting a full accounting of your evening, young lady."

"I . . . can't. I have to get home right now."

Kevin took note of my morose expression and nudged his friend. "Let her go." He turned to me. "We'll see you next year, right?"

"I—I don't know." All I knew was I had to get out of there before Billy came looking for me. "I'm sorry." I raced down the street toward the subway before any of us could exchange email addresses, or even good-byes.

A train pulled into the station, and I sank into a seat. I'd be safely at home soon. I just had to hang on for twenty more minutes.

But when I got to Ninth Street, I discovered a limo idling in front of my building—one that looked suspiciously similar to the one Sandro had arranged the night of the gallery party. I hadn't even pulled out my house keys before Lark flung open its door and came flying toward me, shrieking in excitement. "We did it! We got married!"

Terrific.

Sandro emerged from the backseat, a sleazy grin on his face and a bottle of Veuve Clicquot in his hand. "Please," he said, handing me the bottle. "We celebrate, no?"

"Uh, no," I replied. "I really can't right now."

Lark latched onto my arm with both hands. "Please, Dana? We've been waiting for over an hour—I was scared to ring your doorbell again in case you were sleeping. Can't we please, *please* just come upstairs for one tiny little glass?"

Sandro chuckled and gave his bride a look that was so patronizing, I wanted to bash him over the head with his own champagne bottle. "Please, Dana. I beg of you—my bride, she insist."

His accent was about as authentically Italian as a can of SpaghettiOs. I happened to know the guy had grown up in Bensonhurst; the gallery director had confided in me after downing too many glasses of chablis during an art opening the previous year.

But Lark's pleading expression finally got to me. "Well, I guess one glass won't hurt." I unlocked the front door and trudged upstairs. Sandro scooped up his conquest and carried her, giggling and squealing, over my threshold.

"When did all this . . . happen?" I asked once we were settled in and we'd raised our glasses in a toast.

"I surprise her," Sandro said, taking in the humble environment with a pitying smirk. "The divorce, it become final last week. So I come to the home of my beautiful maiden last night, and I swoop her off her feet!"

Lark beamed and refilled my glass before I could stop her. "Don't you just love the way he talks?"

Sandro got up and asked if he might visit my *gabinetto*. I pointed in its direction, realizing with a sinking heart that I'd hand-washed half the contents of my underwear drawer the night before last. Bras and panties were strung across the length of the bathtub. The guy was in for a real treat.

Lark came over and hugged me, refusing to let go for what seemed like a week. "I'm sorry we caught you at a bad time. But I just had to come over and share this moment with my mentor!"

Some mentor, I thought. *All I've ever done is humor this poor girl. And now look what she's gotten herself into.*

Then again, maybe it wasn't too late to start being a mentor. At least I should try.

"Lark," I said, "you'll keep in touch with me, won't you?"

"What do you mean? Of course I will."

"And if anything—you know—happens with Sandro, I want you to promise you'll let me know about it right away."

She blinked. "What are you talking about?"

"Well, if things don't work out . . ."

"Of course they'll work out! We're married now."

"Well, sure, but Sandro was married when he met you. . . ."

I watched anger replace the confusion in her eyes. "Sandro would never cheat on me."

Sandro's been in my gabinetto *for so long, I think he already has,* I silently responded. "I'm sure you're right, but just in case he does . . ."

"He *won't.*" She sprang to her feet and stomped over to the bathroom door. "Come on, darling. We're leaving."

"So soon?" he called. "Uh . . . just give me the one minute, my dearest."

Yuck, I thought to myself, making a mental note to burn half the contents of my underwear drawer the instant my guests departed. Could this day get any worse?

Finally I heard the hinges creak, and Sandro returned to the living room. Lark grabbed her coat, thrust her husband's jacket into his hands, and pulled him outside, slamming the front door behind her.

Swell, I thought, shaking my head. *Now even my biggest admirer can't stand me.*

But who could blame her? I couldn't stand myself, either.

The results for the crossword tournament were posted on its Web site by the time they left. I'd finished one hundred and thirtieth, which landed me in eighth place among the rookies. Under ordinary circumstances I would have been elated, but now all I felt was rage.

And guilt. Bucket loads and bucket loads of guilt.

Hank had promised to call as soon as Gordo and Jolene took off for Mullica Hill, but the light on the answering machine wasn't blinking, and the only messages on my cell were from an increasingly concerned Elinor Ann. Of course, I'd have to tell him what had happened—her, too—but at least I had a little time to figure out how to go about it.

I flopped on the bed, staring at the bulletin board on the opposite wall and the Valentine's card signed, *Luv, Eggs.* I sighed. Maybe I should have been as dumb as Lark and married Ray. For all I knew, he might still be alive. My whole life would have turned out differently. And then I'd never have made such an awful, selfish mistake with such an awful, selfish man. No—boy. No—bastard.

Despite my revulsion, I flashed on an image of Billy from the night before, poised above me, and I stopped breathing for a minute.

I shook my head in disgust. Some mentor I was. Lark was well rid of me.

The phone rang, and I consulted my watch: It was half past two. Billy was probably still out in Brooklyn, where the final championship round had just concluded, so it was safe to pick up.

If talking to Hank could be construed as safe.

"Hello?"

Click.

I gaped at the receiver in disbelief before hurling it across the room, where it shattered into pieces just above the bulletin board. Ray's Valentine's card tilted forward, then tumbled facedown onto the floor.

Great. Now even he had given up on me.

The phone rang again as I was tacking the card back into place, but of course, there was no way to answer it now. I rooted around in my purse for my cell while the answering machine picked up.

"Hey, darlin'—just wanted to let you know the coast is clear. Jolene and her redneck got out of here about five minutes ago. Oh—and I just went on that crossword Web site to see how you did, and boy, am I impressed. I sure am proud of you, Dana. Can't wait to see you."

"That's what you think," I said to the machine before pulling a pillow over my head and curling into the fetal position.

CHAPTER TWENTY-SIX

TRUTH AND CONSEQUENCES

"You have to tell Hank," Tom-Tom said over dinner that night.

"I know." I sighed. "That's what Elinor Ann said, too." Actually, she'd said, "Oh, Dana, do you really have to tell him?" then quickly reversed her position. I'd had the same conversation with myself, ultimately concluding it was the only decent thing to do. I'd had enough of lying and cheating—and my own duplicitous nature—for one lifetime.

My half brother had come all the way down to the Village once I'd alerted him I had an emergency—and about what had precipitated it. This effectively allowed me to postpone my confession until the following day. I'd told Hank I had no choice but to meet with Tom-Tom that evening; he needed to pick up the Hannah he'd promised to Graciela in advance of their Monday appointment.

Another lie. What was one more at this point?

Tom-Tom reached across the table and squeezed my hand. "You don't know what people are capable of until you put them to the test, sweetie. Honestly, I never expected Dad would be so sanguine when I informed him his namesake was a flaming fairy. Maybe Hank will surprise you."

Before I could respond, my cell phone rang. I pulled it out, checked the name on the screen, then returned it to my purse.

"The youth?"

I nodded. "For at least the sixth time today."

"Well, they are indefatigable at that age."

"No kidding. Thirteen letters."

"I beg your pardon?"

"Never mind."

"I really think you're being overly pessimistic about Hank, Dana. Don't forget—he wasn't entirely forthcoming with you, either. You didn't even know his real name until—when? A matter of days ago?"

"True." For a moment, his words gave me hope—until I remembered what had taken place in Brooklyn. "But he didn't fuck a beautiful twenty-five-year-old boy."

"Oh, sweetie. If Hank were fucking beautiful twenty-five-year-old boys, then you'd *really* have cause for concern. Now, have a little faith, and finish your manicotti."

Thank god for Gay Daddy, I thought, walking back to Ninth Street. Then again, maybe if my actual daddy had been more involved in my upbringing, Tom-Tom could have just been my big brother. And Ray Daddy could have just been my coworker. And . . .

No. Ray had been worth it. Even though we had no future and it could never have lasted, my only regret would have been not going through with it. When someone you love that much loves you back, all you can say is yes.

I got home and listened to the messages on my cell phone, deleting the three from Billy the instant I heard his voice.

The fourth was from Hank.

"Hey, genius—just hoping you got a second wind after dinner, but I guess you're still with your brother. Well, you know where to find me. I'll be up for at least another hour or so."

And I'd be up all night, rehearsing what to say to him tomorrow.

I did my best to keep myself busy the following morning, getting a good jump on the final Hannah I owed Vivian. But by one o'clock, I couldn't stand the suspense any longer—or the plaintive mea culpas Billy kept repeating every time I checked my voice mail. I called Hank to let him know I was on my way over.

When I arrived, the brownstone was a hotbed of activity. Plasterers were fanned out on both floors.

"I didn't realize it would be so . . . frenetic around here," I said.

"It's got to be. Pretty much all the surfaces are done, 'cept the walls."

I looked into the parlor and up the stairs. Hank was right. The house had really come together over the past few weeks, so gradually I hadn't realized it until now. All the floors were sanded and stained; the partitions upstairs had long been demolished to re-create the original layout; the bathrooms were glitzy showplaces.

Hank leaned in to kiss me. I kissed him back, but then I pulled away. "Listen—I have . . . something I need to tell you."

He assessed my expression, which I could only assume was doleful. "This got anything to do with Jolene and Gordo?"

"Not at all." Now I felt even worse, if that was possible. His first instinct had been to shoulder the blame for whatever bad news he was about to receive. "Your family's not the problem—I am."

His brows knitted together. "Guess we better talk out back." He turned and started down the corridor to the little room off the kitchen.

Stay calm, I instructed myself. *Remember what Dad always says: When under pressure, always answer a question with a question.*

When we got inside, Hank shut the door and turned to face me. "This is about that guy you were with last weekend, isn't it?"

"How'd you know?" I said, before realizing that the question I should have answered his question with was, "What guy?"

But it was too late.

"I didn't know," he said, averting his eyes. "I do now."

"Hank, I—I made a terrible mistake. I wish I could undo it. I wish . . ."

But what else was there to say? No words could justify my behavior.

He looked at his feet, shaking his head slowly from side to side. "I don't know, Dana. Last month you're crying over a dead boyfriend. Now you got a live one, too. Anybody else I should know about?"

"It isn't like that. I'm not—"

Yes it was. Yes I was.

Then he did something I could never have anticipated. Still refusing to meet my eyes, he began to unbutton my shirt.

"What are you doing?"

"Show me what he did to you."

"What?"

"Show me. How did it start?"

Despite my trepidation, I was becoming dizzy with arousal. "He . . . put my legs around his waist. . . ."

"Like this?"

It went on for hours, just as it had with Billy. But this was different. This was hostile sex. For which I had no one to blame but myself, of course.

Although "blame" was hardly the correct word. More than once I found myself biting on the quilt to stifle a scream—of pleasure, not terror. I really was shameless. If Hank thought he was punishing me, my responses made it obvious he'd failed in his mission.

Or was he trying to show me what I'd be missing out on from this day forward?

"I do love you, you know," I said, once it was over—even though it had become glaringly obvious to me I didn't know the meaning of the word.

"Yeah, well." He was still looking anywhere but into my eyes.

"Hank, is this—it? Did I ruin everything?"

He shrugged and reached for his clothes. "You're going to have to give me some time to figure that one out."

"Well . . . you know how to get hold of me," I said, slipping on my jeans.

"Yeah, well . . ." He opened the bedroom door. "Guess everybody else does, too."

Ouch.

I walked into the kitchen, where Dinner regarded me solemnly from his kennel, then through the corridor and out the front door, past a sea of smirking workmen.

"I suppose it could have been worse," Elinor Ann said as I made my way home up Avenue A. "He could have just thrown you out."

"I think he just did. But first he had to—"

What was that all about, anyway?

"I guess he had to mark his territory," I surmised. "You know—the way dogs have to pee all over their neighborhood."

"Please—whatever you do, don't mention pee."

"Still?"

"The vet said Lurch should be house-trained any day now, as long as we stick to the walking schedule." She hesitated. "Dana? Maybe this would be a good weekend for you to come visit. You know—see the puppy, get away from all . . . that. Them."

"I don't know. If Hank decides he's ready to talk, maybe I should be in town."

I turned the corner onto Ninth Street and jumped when I found myself looking into the eyes of the meanest woman I'd ever seen. She was the subject of a formal portrait—a very old one, based on the weathered, ornate frame—that had been set out with the trash for tomorrow morning's pickup.

"Elinor Ann, you wouldn't believe what I just found." I described the photograph.

"Who would throw out an ancestor? That's terrible. Bad karma, too."

"If this was your ancestor, you've probably got worse things to worry about than incurring the wrath of a dead woman. Like how to pay for your nose job, for starters." I picked up the portrait. "I'm taking her home with me."

"Why? She sounds creepy."

"She is, but . . . maybe I can do something with her."

Or with the frame, I concluded after I'd been in my apartment for about ten minutes. The woman's steely gaze was undeniably unsettling, as if she were saying, "I know what you did, you unscrupulous miscreant. See you in hell."

I turned the picture around so it faced the wall and went to check my email. As I'd expected, there was one from Billy, with "Please, please read this" in the subject line:

> Dana—I don't even know where to begin, other than to tell you how sorry I am, but you've probably heard my messages by now and already know that.
>
> The thing is, I didn't know my—our—puzzle was going to be in the tournament at all. Not until after I'd paid your entry fee. Turns out the one they'd planned to use had a repeated word in the grid, and no amount of tweaking could get rid of either one of them. When they asked if they could use mine—ours—as a last-minute substitute, I agreed, never dreaming you'd be battling for a spot in the top hundred.
>
> And I apologize if that sounds like I wrote you off in advance, but some of those hard-core competitors can coast through one of my Saturday puzzles in minutes. I had you pegged for a respectable top-third finish.

Which is still no excuse for not telling you until Sunday morning.

But if I'd told you earlier, I might have missed out on Saturday night.

Come to think of it, I don't regret what I did at all. You were so, so worth it.

Come to think of it, yes, I do. Because now I'll never get the chance to be with you again.

But if you could just forgive me for being such a selfish, thoughtless asshole, that would at least be something.

Love (and I'm not just saying that),

Billy

Despite my anger and remorse, I couldn't help but go a little gooey when I got to the part about Saturday night. Billy's shirt—the one I'd borrowed on Sunday to conceal the sweater I'd been wearing Saturday—still hung from the bedpost. I picked it up and breathed in his scent.

Maybe, seeing as how I'd already screwed things up so disastrously with Hank . . .

Maybe I should pick up a damn paintbrush and get back to work.

But before I did, maybe I'd put Billy out of his misery.

Message received. Apology accepted. And you're not the only party who's at fault here. (Or, truth be told, thought Saturday night was so, so worth it.)

But now I really need you to back off. I paid a very high price for the transgression.

Sincerely,

Dana

I read it over, deleted the sentence referring to Saturday night, hit Send, and went into the kitchen to finish the final Hannah.

"Well, halle-fucking-lujah," Vivian said when I walked in with the painting Tuesday afternoon. "Thought I'd be dead by the time you turned up with that thing." She was surrounded by cardboard boxes.

"What's all this?"

"My picker down in Tampa hit the eighties mother lode." She slit open one of the cartons and pulled out a hideous sequined jacket in a zebra print, fashioned from thousands of glittering paillettes. "Bob Mackie. How Alexis Carrington can you get?"

"Are your customers actually going to . . . purchase this stuff?"

"The decade's having a bit of a moment in the clubs these days. And of course the drag queens will pounce on anything they can squeeze into."

I gave the jacket another look, and an idea began to germinate. "Do you mind if I borrow that for a little while?"

"Knock yourself out."

"And how about some necklaces? Is any of that sixties costume jewelry still around?"

In response, she opened a drawer of the flat file used to store accessories. "I definitely overestimated the market for this crap. Pile it on. The pig will look fabulous in that getup."

But it wouldn't be the pig this time.

I went upstairs and laid the portrait of the evil ancestor on the bed, where I positioned the jacket and necklaces on top of her. It was high time she received a makeover.

Work was a godsend. Having something to focus on besides Hank's lengthening silence allowed me to maintain my stasis, and re-creating all those paillettes in paint required it. Under a watchful glare and a heart-ache that throbbed all day, I worked nonstop to transform the somber portrait into a riotous hybrid of two centuries.

When I finished, I stepped back and smiled for the first time since Sunday. If anything, the woman's expression was rendered even more malevolent by the addition of zebra print and the colorful strands of beads that cascaded down her neck.

She just needed one finishing touch.

I picked up a pair of coral-colored starburst earrings and, after making two tiny incisions in the surface of the photograph, affixed them directly to my subject's ears.

Perfect. Now I was done.

As soon as I spotted the mannequin outside Vivian's shop on Friday morning, I took the piece downstairs.

Initially, her expression rivaled the portrait's for sheer peevishness. "What the hell is going on here? Where's the damn pig?"

"On sabbatical."

She drew closer to inspect the surface of the photograph. "Actually, this is pretty clever. I love what you did with the earrings—and the Mackie jacket really pops. Guess this is a whole new direction for Hannah."

"That's not a Hannah," I said. "It's a Dana."

"But—"

"Sorry to break the news like this, but Hannah passed away last week. Complications from pneumonia."

"You can't do that! It's like—it's like throwing away a fortune!"

"I see it differently. You'll save a fortune not having to hire an attorney to defend you against a fraud indictment." Tom-Tom had done some additional research on the matter. As he'd informed me during our recent dinner, Vivian and I, as well as Graciela, were very much liable if Hannah's true identity was ever exposed.

But it was more than fear of prosecution that had caused me to lay Hannah to rest.

"I've finally decided to lead a completely honest existence. Which means I'm no longer willing to paint under an alias." *Or lie to another boyfriend,* I thought. *Or derail my future in some new, unprecedented manner.* I tilted my head in the direction of the canvas. "Take it or leave it."

She paced back and forth for a minute or so, eyeing the portrait and cursing under her breath. "What the hell," she finally said. "Let me put it in the window this weekend and see how it goes over. We'll stick with our usual fifty-fifty split, of course."

"Sixty-forty."

"What?"

"Whoever buys the painting is likely to spring for the jacket as well. That's pure profit for you."

"All right, *fine.* Sixty-forty."

"Unless it sells by the end of the weekend. Then we'll know we're onto something, and I'd say that entitles me to seventy-thirty." Before she could unleash a fresh torrent of venom, I added, "I'm sure the volume will make it worth your while."

"Sixty-five percent, and you're lucky I'm in a good mood. And speaking of volume, where do you expect to find a steady supply of old portraits?"

"I have an idea about that."

When the 7:42 Bieber bus pulled into Kutztown that evening, Elinor Ann was waiting in the parking lot. I'd called right after my meeting with Vivian to let her know we had some major antiquing to do that weekend.

"You're skinny," she said after hugging me.

"I'm aware." I'd lost nearly five pounds since my confrontation with Hank. I looked over at her idling car. "Where's Cal?"

"At home." She paused. "*With* the boys." She stood there, beaming, while the meaning of her statement sank in.

"That's fantastic! Was it the jumping jacks?"

"Not this time." She rolled her eyes. "It was Lurch."

During the drive home, she explained how her miraculous cure had come to pass.

"Cal had to go see one of our suppliers in Harrisburg a couple of days ago. He was already running late, and he couldn't find his cell. Turns out Angus has a new girlfriend, and he'd borrowed the phone for some late-night pillow talk. Well, Cal was mad enough about that, but when they turned the bedroom upside down and couldn't find the phone—you can imagine. By that point the boys had to get to the school bus stop, so Cal stormed off in the truck with my cell, and it was time for me to take the dog out."

"That reminds me—how's the house-training going?"

"It's—don't ask. So anyway, Lurch, uh, assumed the position, and right after he was done and I was scooping up his, uh, deposit, I heard the faint strains of Iron Butterfly coming from inside the dog."

"What? Why?"

She shot me a meaningful glance. "'In-A-Gadda-Da-Vida' happens to be Cal's ringtone."

"Oh no."

"Oh yes. Well, by then the bus had already picked up the boys, and Cal was westbound on Route 22, so what choice did I have? I didn't have time for jumping jacks. All I could do was grab Lurch and rush him to the vet. And ever since then"—she shrugged, smiling—"I've been making myself go out at least once a day ever since, no matter what."

"I can't wait to meet this dog. He's my hero."

"Well, your hero just cost me twenty-two hundred dollars in surgical fees, but I think maybe it was worth it."

"I bet that's cheaper than a shrink would have been."

"That's what I keep telling myself. Besides, all that exercise was giving me shin splints."

We led a charmed life that weekend. On Saturday morning, Elinor Ann and I rose at dawn to go scour the outdoor markets and antique shops of Adamstown.

I'd already picked up three portraits when we spotted an aging biker-type leaning against his run-down truck in the parking lot of the Clock Tower Antique Mall. Propped against a tire was an oval-framed photograph of an exceedingly prim, white-haired matriarch with a neck like a giraffe—perfect for adorning with necklaces.

"How much?" I asked.

"Twenty-five."

"Is that your best price?"

"What the hell. Make it fifteen."

As I opened my wallet, the man said, "Got a lot more like her in the truck if you're interested in that sort of thing."

Did he ever. More than a dozen portraits were stacked inside, and most of them met my needs perfectly.

"To tell you the god's honest truth, I can't hardly get rid of these things," he confided. "I clean out houses for a living, and damn near every one of 'em's got a bunch of dead relatives hanging on the walls. Ugly dead relatives."

We quickly exchanged cash and email addresses before loading up the trunk of Elinor Ann's car.

"You know, Angus is always looking to make a few extra dollars," she said on the way back home. "I'm sure he'd be willing to come out here every month or so to make pickups for you."

"That sounds great. Now, how much is it going to run me to have you ship them out from the plant?"

"Don't be silly."

That night, Lurch, who was as adorable as promised—even with a huge plastic cone on his head to prevent him from chewing on his stitches—slept at the foot of my bed. Which was no substitute for Hank sleeping next to me, but it was probably the best action I was going to get for a while.

All weekend, I checked my cell incessantly for messages, but none of consequence appeared.

"Aunt Dana?" Eddie said while we were at Willy Joe's, having a late lunch before Elinor Ann took me to the bus. "How come you keep messing around with your phone?"

"Oh, I'm just hoping to hear from a friend of mine. We had a fight."

"About what?"

But how to answer the question? "My loose morals," was concise, but obviously age-inappropriate. "I . . . did something that made him mad."

Angus let out a grunt. *"Men."* I smiled, wishing he weren't at that age where a hug in public from one's aunt constituted a severe breach of etiquette.

"Don't worry, Aunt Dana," Eddie said. "You're too nice to stay mad at."

"Eddie's right," Elinor Ann said while we waited in her car for the bus to appear. "I'm sure Hank will get over this. You just have to give him time."

"How much time?"

"I'm not Nostradamus, in case you haven't noticed. But when Cal and I came to the city and I saw you two together, it was obvious he cares about you. Four good months shouldn't be undone by one unfortunate . . . lapse in judgment."

But Hank not only knew about my lapse in judgment; I'd spent Tuesday afternoon showing him exactly what had transpired for the duration of it. "I guess all I can do is . . . nothing. And hope he eventually comes around."

"Or not," Elinor Ann said.

I raised an eyebrow. "What do you mean?"

"Maybe it's time to move on from Hank and meet someone new."

"What are you talking about? Didn't you tell me it was time for me to be sharing my life with someone when I was here at Thanksgiving?"

"I was, but then I realized something. Maybe you're just not ready yet. People mature at different speeds. I got married and had kids—I had to do it faster than you. And I hate to admit this, but maybe I'm a little . . . jealous of you."

"Elinor Ann, *nobody* should be jealous of me. Especially lately."

"Well, you never got panic disorder."

"True."

"And you get to paint for a living. And you don't have to pay for two college educations. And for all you know, you might meet the man of your dreams next Thursday." She shrugged. "You can't force yourself to settle down. Maybe being a grown-up is overrated."

I smiled, shaking my head. "That's exactly what Billy Moody said to me a couple of weeks ago."

"Well, maybe he's right."

I peered at her suspiciously. "Who are you? And what have you done with Elinor Ann?"

"Oh, stop. Listen, Dana—I hope things work out with Hank. I really do. But if that doesn't happen—well, I have a feeling you're going to be okay."

"God, I hope so." The bus rounded the corner, and I reached for my overnight bag and two portraits—enough to keep me occupied until the shipment arrived from the plant—and hugged her goodbye.

"Think positive," she said. "And for god's sake—eat something once in a while."

By the time I returned home to discover an unblinking red light on the answering machine, despair forced me to take action.

I was going to go over to the brownstone first thing in the morning and plead with Hank to forgive me. He hadn't been unfaithful. If one of us was going to have to throw him- or herself on the mercy of the other, he was the obvious choice for throwee.

I noticed with satisfaction that the ancestor painting was no longer displayed in the window of Vivian's shop when I went out the following day. Good—my initial attempt to live an honest life had apparently been a success. Now all I had to do was hope my luck would hold.

Hank's truck was nowhere to be found on Seventh Street, but that was hardly unusual. He could just as easily be parked on Sixth, or Avenue A. Besides, even if he wasn't home, I refused to be dissuaded. I'd brought my key, and I was prepared to go inside and wait for as long as it took for him to return. At least Dinner would be happy to see me.

But instead of the familiar padlock, I discovered a pair of ornate brass doorknobs had been installed in my absence.

I rang the bell, my heart pounding despite my determination.

After a few minutes, an elderly, elegant blond woman dressed in a red velveteen pantsuit opened the door.

"Can I help you?"

"Oh—uh, is Hank around?"

"You mean the contractor? He cleared the last of his things out of here over the weekend. I'm the decorator."

"The . . . decorator?" I stood there like some sort of jilted fish, my mouth opening and closing in wordless disbelief.

"Yes, dear. He went off to—I forget where he said he was going, but if you've got a minute, I'm sure I have one of his business cards around here somewhere."

"That's okay." I slowly turned and began to navigate the front stoop, praying my legs would hold out until I made it back to the safety of home.

"I'm sure you can track him down on the Internet," she called after me. "It's Wheeler. W—H—E—E . . ."

CHAPTER TWENTY-SEVEN

A SIGHT FOR SORE EYES

A couple of weeks passed, the time feeling like both an eternity and an instant, marked by working, musing, self-recrimination, and sad, sad music. I became a nocturnal creature, sleeping late into the afternoon after painting until dawn. It was a good way to stay out of sight, where I belonged.

"You're really starting to worry me, Dana," Elinor Ann said. "Maybe you should just call the guy."

"Hank has both my numbers. Obviously he doesn't want to talk to me."

"Maybe he just needs a little push."

"All evidence points to the contrary." Just the memory of walking down the brownstone's steps under the watchful eye of the decorator was enough to make my stomach hurt.

"Are you eating?"

"Trying." All I could manage was tea and English muffins, like a sick person—which was exactly what I was. Not to mention heartbroken. And guilt-ridden. I'd lost almost ten pounds by now, but Elinor Ann didn't need to know that.

"Well," she said, "at least the paintings are selling."

That they were. One afternoon I was awakened by Vivian's broomstick, followed by a phone call when I failed to materialize.

"You *have* to come downstairs."

"I don't have to do anything."

"Come on—it's good news. Incredible news."

"We're a Best Bet!" she announced, brandishing a copy of *New York Magazine*, when curiosity lured me into the shop an hour later.

Oh, "we" are, are we? I silently responded.

Even so, my mood did lift a bit when I saw the picture of my longnecked matriarch next to an enthusiastic blurb with the headline, FASHION VICTIMS.

> Dana Mayo's clever pastiches of ancestor portraits and vintage froufrou are just the thing to add zing to your walk-in closet—or studio apartment. Better still, you can pick up both the artwork and the outfit that inspired it at Chase, Manhattan on East Ninth Street.

"That is somewhat exciting," I conceded.

And the perfect offering to take with me on my trip to Florida at the end of the month. Dad had made it clear he didn't want birthday presents, but he'd be delighted if I were to present him with proof of my productivity. Perhaps I'd go on down to Gem Spa on Saint Mark's and buy him a copy—along with one for myself.

When I got to the newsstand, I hesitated. I'd come this far. Maybe it would be a good idea to continue on to Fred and Ethyl's and eat a proper lunch for once.

"There she is," Ethyl said when I walked in. "Where's Ol' Blue Eyes?"

"I was just about to ask if you'd seen him."

She laid a hand over her heart when the meaning of my words registered. "Aw, that's tough. Sorry, girlie. I thought you two kids were a match."

"So did I." I dropped into a seat at the communal table.

"Lunch is on me today." She sized me up, adding, "and you'd better finish it or you're gonna disappear into thin air."

It was one of those freakishly warm days that sometimes arrive out of nowhere in mid-March, exposing the pasty limbs of the locals and inspiring way too much kissing on the street. By the time I returned home, I just wanted to draw the shades and crawl into bed.

The phone began to ring as soon as I opened the door.

"Hello?"

Click.

This time I knew better than to hurl the receiver against the wall. I'd only just replaced it.

When the unseasonable weather held, I determined I should take advantage of it. The sunlight would be good for me. So would some physical activity. I resolved to take daily walks on all the side streets between Second and Avenue B, starting with Fourteenth. By the end of the week, I'd wrap it up down on Houston.

Maybe I'd see Hank's truck.

But it was nowhere to be found along the sidewalks of the East Village. By now his work could have taken him anywhere. I might never find him.

I did, however, find Ray Devine. A scrap from one of his old billboards—ironically, just the "Healthy" panel from the "Healthy, Wealthy, and Wise" campaign—still fluttered at the corner of Eleventh Street and First Avenue.

I leaned against a wall and took him in. *God, Ray,* I silently addressed the picture. *If only you were healthy.*

That was when I realized I hadn't even begun to mourn the loss of Hank. I was still mourning Ray.

Tears formed in my eyes and rolled down my cheeks. An ancient bag man pushing an overloaded grocery cart approached me for a handout, but he begged my pardon and continued down the street as soon as he saw my face.

Then I got even crazier, if such a thing was possible. I began to make daily pilgrimages to see Ray, even though the temperatures had plummeted back into the twenties and some punk band, posting handbills for its upcoming gig, usurped the billboard and obscured half his image.

The handbills were what finally snapped me out of it. This was ridiculous. And self-destructive. And no matter how much Ray's death might have affected me, I still knew I'd been right to end the relationship, no matter how hard it had been at the time. I could never have wound up the way Lark would be soon enough, married to a man who was decades my senior; wondering every day if he would cheat on me the way he'd cheated on the previous wife.

I took a deep breath. It was time I got unstuck and went about the business of my future, whatever it turned out to be.

I looked at Ray for one last time, bidding him a wordless goodbye before returning home to Ninth Street.

When I got there, Billy Moody was waiting for me on the front stoop.

Oh crap, I thought. I looked awful—much too skinny; my hair a quasi-Afro due to the stiff wind blowing off the East River; not enough makeup to enhance the face of a far younger woman. "What are you doing here?"

"Making a last-ditch effort to salvage some sort of . . . rapprochement." He gazed into my eyes, seemingly impervious to my ravaged appearance. "And I know you asked me to back off, but—I'm sorry. I just can't help it."

"I . . . don't think I want you to help it."

I unlocked the front door, and he followed me up the stairs and into my apartment. I watched as he wandered from room to room, his eyes ultimately coming to rest on the photograph of me with Elinor Ann, taken so long ago that I'd been his age at the time.

That's the Dana Mayo you should have gotten involved with, I thought but didn't say.

"I have your shirt," I told Billy, reaching for where it still hung on the bedpost. By the time I turned around, he was right in front of me, slipping his arms around my waist and holding me close. He felt so good, I had to suppress a whimper.

"Listen, Dana. I swear I never meant to screw up your life the way I did."

"You didn't screw it up. I have free will. I'm the one who screwed it up."

He sat on the bed and reached for my hand, pulling me down next to him. "Tell me what happened."

I had to laugh. "Do you really need to ask? You were in room 2611, too, you know."

"No—after that. With that guy."

"I decided I had to be honest with him. So I told him what I'd done."

"You did?" His smile was one of pure joy. "That's awesome!"

"Oh yeah. Worked out just great. Haven't seen him since."

"No, you don't understand. If you and I had been a one-nighter, you would've been able to keep it a secret. But you couldn't. That means you love me." There was that blinding smile again, this time tinged with unmistakable pride.

"But—"

But wait a second. Maybe Billy was right. Maybe I did love him.

Well, there was one surefire way to find out.

He took my face in his hands and kissed me for something like three years. "I wish you'd take me seriously, Dana."

"I have a feeling I'm about to do just that."

But Puny had other plans. He slinked out from underneath the bed and flopped at our feet.

"Wow," Billy said. "You weren't kidding when you told me he looked like Biddy." He smiled again. "See? More proof that we're meant for each other."

Damn, I thought to myself. *This boy is so sweet, and so noncynical, and so endlessly, ridiculously adorable. Why would I even try to resist him?*

There it was. Why had it taken me all this time to figure it out? I was Ray now, and Billy was my—well, me. And all the selfish mistakes and bad decisions I'd made in the past would be—well, replaced with a brand-new bumper crop of selfish mistakes and bad decisions, but at least I wouldn't waste years of my life regretting not seeing it through.

"Billy?"

"Yes?"

"I love you."

"You'd better."

The problem with saying you loved somebody was that it was impossible to stop once you'd done it, especially the first time. We must have repeated the words a thousand times before finally drifting off to sleep.

But by then it was undeniably true. Our night in Brooklyn had been a mere prelude to what happened between us in my bed that night. When I opened my eyes the next morning, I marveled at the difference between the despair I'd been living with for the past few weeks and the exhilaration that coursed through me now. Everything would turn out all right. I was sure of it.

Until I went to open the blinds and looked out the window onto Ninth Street. Hank's truck was parked at the far curb, and he was getting out of it. He raised his head and our eyes locked.

Swell, I thought. Now *he decides to make eye contact.*

CHAPTER TWENTY-EIGHT

NATURE CALLS

gasped so loudly that Billy stirred and turned on his side to face me. "What are you doing over there?" He grinned and pulled back the covers. "Come here. I've got a present for you."

"Not now."

My tone made him sit up.

"My—that guy is here," I explained, grabbing my jeans from the back of a chair. "He just got out of his truck. I—I don't know what to do."

The buzzer on the intercom blared.

"I'll be right down," I called into the speaker, not pushing the button that would allow me to hear Hank's response—or, god forbid, the one that would unlatch the front door.

"Billy, I don't know what's going on. We haven't spoken in weeks. I don't even know where he's been for all that time."

"Do you want me to hide in the closet?" His expression made it clear he found the prospect more than a little titillating.

"Are you serious? I've been living in this apartment for over twenty years. Do you know how much junk is jammed into that closet?" Including a wedding dress, which could easily cause him to jump to erroneous conclusions.

"How about under the bed, then?"

I just looked at him.

"Twenty years. I get it."

I pulled on yesterday's sweater and stepped into a pair of flip-flops. "Just . . . sit tight while I find out what he wants?"

He nodded, and I tore down the stairs, zipping my fly en route.

Hank broke into a wide smile when I came into view. I cracked the door to the vestibule just wide enough for us to talk, but not enough to grant access. He could *not* enter the building.

"Dana, I'm—I'm so sorry. I don't know what got into me that I thought we couldn't work things out." He leaned in and kissed me.

"I'm sorry, too." He had no idea.

"Listen—I got someplace I been wanting to show you. Could you . . . ?" He looked over his shoulder in the direction of the truck.

"Oh. Uh, absolutely. But can you give me a minute to get myself together? I only just woke up." I knew I desperately needed a shower. In fact, if I opened the door all the way, I was certain Hank's smile would disappear immediately.

"You go ahead and take all the time you need," he said, moving toward me. He could *not* come through that door.

I eased my foot up against the jamb. "You know what would be great? Could you maybe go over to the deli on Second and pick me up a cup of coffee?"

"You got it."

"And a toasted sesame bagel? With a schmear?"

"Anything you want." He kissed me again. "Man, I missed you, Dana. But I reckon I can wait a little longer."

Finally I was able to let my guard down. The time it would take to toast that bagel just bought me a shower.

———

Billy was dressed and staring out the window when I got back upstairs. "Nice truck," he said.

"Listen, I'm sorry. I never thought I'd see that guy again, and—well, he seems to want to talk. I think I owe him that much."

"So do I."

That was a relief. "He wants to take me someplace, too." But where, exactly, did Hank want to take me? His new renovation project, I supposed. "I think it's only right that we try to reach some kind of . . . resolution. Closure. Whatever you want to call it."

"Of course it is."

"You really don't mind?"

He crossed the room and put his arms around me. "It's the least you can do. Hell, it's the least *I* can do—I just stole his girl, didn't I?"

"I am *so* glad you're a reasonable man."

After the fastest shower I'd ever taken, I put on a fresh pair of jeans and a different sweater and went over to the bed, where Billy was reclining against the pillows, watching me. Before I could say goodbye, his guarded expression made me hesitate.

"Are you sure you're okay with this?"

"I'm sure. But—Dana?"

"Yes?"

"I did just steal that guy's girl, didn't I?"

Oh, Billy. Billy Billy Billy.

I kissed him one last time and went down to the street.

Hank was waiting on the passenger side of the truck with my breakfast. He handed it to me, then unlocked the door.

"Thanks," I said, getting in as quickly as I could and holding my breath until he was in the driver's seat. I was sure we were under observation. "Where are we going?"

"You'll see."

He drove up Third and made a right onto Tenth Street. "Listen, Dana, I—"

"I'm sorry."

"That's what I'm supposed to be saying to you. Wasn't right, me taking off the way I did."

"Well, I was hardly . . ."

He rested a hand on my thigh. "Let's not get into a big old conversation about who did what to who, okay?"

When I turned my head to assess Hank's expression, he squeezed my leg and smiled at me. What had become of the furious man who'd made me re-create every graphic moment of my night with Billy? Which, to be fair, had aroused me no end at the time—until it was over, at which point he'd promptly disappeared off the face of the earth. What had caused him to change his mind about me?

And why, why, *why* had it taken so long for him to change it?

"Went over to our favorite restaurant for dinner last night." He chuckled. "I'll tell you, your pal Ethyl sure gave me an earful."

So that was the catalyst.

"Soon as she told me how you were doing, I knew I had to see you right away." He stopped at the red light on Avenue C and turned to me. "Look, Dana—here's the thing. I ain't happy about what you done, but heck—least you were honest with me. Can't hardly say the same about myself." He shook his head. "Maybe if I'd been straight with you sooner . . ."

"Yeah, that might have been . . ."

What? Mitigating? Would knowing Hank's real identity have made a difference? Or was what happened in Brooklyn, and last night, unavoidable?

I took a sip of tepid coffee as the light turned green. Hank made a left and parked in front of a squat building nestled between two tenements. Its facade was covered by a faux brick face in a bilious shade of brownish green.

"Ain't much to look at from the outside," he said as we got out of the truck.

Inside was a whole different story.

"What *is* this?" I asked, craning my neck as I took in the cavernous empty space. It was a wreck, with years of grime covering every surface, but I could see its potential. The ceiling rose even higher than the ones in the brownstone, except in the rear third of the building, where mirror-image staircases on opposite walls led to an open second story. Light filtered in from a bank of filthy windows positioned above the entrance.

"Best guess is it was built as a synagogue, but over the years—well, you name it: revival hall, dry goods emporium, after-hours club . . ." He pointed to a door at the far end. "There's an enclosed office space underneath the loft that's perfect for a bedroom. And a little patio out behind that."

The door burst open, and Dinner came trotting over to greet me. I squatted down to say hello, and he promptly absconded with what was left of my bagel.

"Hey!" I called after him.

Hank grinned. "Told you he was sneaky."

"That you did." I turned in a circle, taking in the room a second time. "Hank, this place is—"

"A whole heck of a lot of work. But at least it's all ours."

"It's—excuse me?"

"You could have your painting studio up there," he said, gesturing toward the open loft. "Living area over on the right, kitchen and bath on the other side, where the pipes are . . ."

"Wait—what did you just say?"

He came over and wrapped his arms around me. "Our place. Closed the deal about a month ago. Wanted to surprise you."

But I surprised you first.

"So, what do you say, Dana? Feel like playing house with me?"

Oh, Hank.

I stood there for a while, swaying back and forth in his arms, digesting his words and trying to come up with some of my own.

"This is all—"

Just what I've always wanted, I thought but didn't say. A handsome, devoted boyfriend who forgave the most flagrant of sins and surprised me with freestanding real estate. I looked up at the loft and pictured myself there, the western light illuminating the painting on my easel, Dinner sprawled at the foot of one staircase, Puny by the other, Hank applying sealer to the walls of exposed brick. . . .

Or was it too late for all that?

"Hey—you're speechless." He laughed. "Ain't never seen you like this before."

"I think I'm on sensory overload. Seeing you again, and this place, and . . ."

And Billy. Couldn't forget Billy.

"I understand. I just asked you to make a mighty big decision."

It's a much bigger decision than you realize, I thought but didn't say.

I turned and put my hands on his shoulders. "Listen—would it be okay with you if I took a little while to think things over?"

He raised an eyebrow. "What's there to think about?"

What, indeed. "It's just—well, so much has changed in the past hour, I can't quite wrap my brain around it yet."

He hugged me, and I breathed in his wonderful Hank smell.

"Take all the time you need, Dana. We'll be right here waiting for you."

Now what? I thought as I walked down Tenth Street toward home. I'd run out of my apartment so fast, I'd forgotten to take my cell phone, but it didn't matter. Elinor Ann couldn't help me make this decision. Nobody could. Not Tom-Tom, certainly not my parents . . .

I sighed. *This is what happens when you're left to your own devices at too early an age,* I thought to myself. *You never do get the hang of being a grown-up.* And now I was on my own, and somehow I'd have to figure out the right thing to do.

Unless maybe God . . .

I recalled my father's favorite adage: There is no God; there's only nature—human nature.

When I walked through my front door, Billy was gone, and his shirt no longer hung from my bedpost. I looked for a note—on the pillow, on my desk, the bathroom mirror—but when I didn't find one, I went to turn on the computer. Maybe he'd sent me an email after he'd gotten back to his apartment.

Maybe he hadn't. I'd been gone for quite a while.

The phone rang before I had time to check.

"Hello?"

"*There* you are! You're certainly not an easy person to get hold of lately."

"Oh—hi, Mom. Yeah, I've been . . . out a lot." Crisscrossing the streets of the neighborhood searching for a truck, mostly.

"I just wanted to find out your flight information so we'll know what time to expect you on Friday."

"I'm supposed to be getting in just after three."

"Good. That's well ahead of happy hour." She paused. "Now, have you given any more thought to bringing that young man of yours?"

"I'm . . . still thinking. Although at this point, I'd be surprised if there were any seats left on the plane."

"Oh dear. That's certainly a possibility."

"But Tom-Tom and I will be flying down together. And he lined up a rental car, so you won't have to come to the airport."

"Splendid!"

In the background, I could hear my father asking what was splendid.

"Mom? Could you put Dad on for a second?"

"Really? Right now?"

"Why not?"

"Well . . . you're going to be seeing him in just a couple of days. . . ."

But as I'd recently learned, even one day was no guarantee. Everything could change irrevocably in far less time than that. "I know. Put him on anyway, would you?"

She covered the receiver with her hand, and, after a muffled conversation, my father's voice came through the line.

"Hey there, kiddo!"

"Ready for the big birthday bash?"

"You know it. And I think it's just terrific that you and your half brother are traveling partners. You'll like him, I promise."

"Dad—listen. I don't know why I didn't tell you this a long time ago, but . . . well, Tom-Tom and I have known each other for quite some time. Like, since my college days. He's been like—well, like a brother to me."

And a daddy, when the need arose.

"He's—what did you say? You've known each other *how* long?"

"Years. Decades."

"Is that so?" He was obviously tickled to hear the news. "It's good to know somebody up there is keeping an eye on you."

"Yeah. It is." I looked up at my bulletin board. Someone—Billy—had affixed a Post-it note to the bottom of Ray's Valentine. Underneath the flowery, cursive *you* were the words, *should be with me.*

"So I guess that means I can finally stop checking up on you," my father said.

"Huh? What are you talking about?"

"Oh, you know."

"No, I don't know."

"Sometimes I get to wondering how you're doing up there. So every once in a while I just . . . pick up the phone and hear for myself."

The hang-up calls. Oh my god.

"Dad, that's—"

Utterly crazy. But kind of sweet.

But definitely more crazy than sweet. I walked over to the bed in a daze and sat down, just in case my knees buckled. "That was you on the phone? All those times?"

"You know how it is. A father worries sometimes. New York can be a tough town, kid. Especially for a good-looking gal out on her own."

Huh, I thought. *Tom-Tom's right. We're definitely not the Cleavers.*

But my father was right, too. This could be a tough town. And it was nice to know somebody was checking up on me all those years, even though I'd never, ever have guessed who was doing it.

But it wasn't just him, though. Or Tom-Tom. Elinor Ann had come to my rescue too many times to count. Ray had told me he loved me and made my life perfect, at least for a little while. Vivian had provided me with the career I'd always hoped for. Hank had bought me a house—an actual, incredible house. And Billy—

Oh, Billy. Billy Billy Billy.

"Dad, there's just one thing I don't understand. Why in the world didn't you just stay on the phone long enough to ask me how I was?"

"Ah, you're young. I'm sure you've got better things to do than jaw with your old man."

"I don't know about that. But—Dad? I really am doing okay up here. Honestly." *And I've finally—finally—figured out how to proceed with my future,* I silently added. *No matter how messy and disastrous it turns out to be.*

"Glad to hear it, kid. So I can stop keeping tabs on you?"

"Yeah, Dad. You don't have to worry about me anymore."

CHAPTER TWENTY-NINE

FLYING BLIND

A chorus of groans went up from the passengers when our pilot announced we were seventeenth in line on the runway. Tom-Tom's were among the loudest. I could hear him—all the way in the back of the plane, right next to the lavatory—from where I sat in the fourth row.

"Boy, is he going to need a drink when we get to Florida," I said.

"Then I'm buying. It was real nice of him to switch places with me."

"I'll say. When I found out there was only one seat left on the flight, I should have known it would be the worst one." I pulled the *Times* from my purse and rifled through the second Arts section until I located the crossword puzzle.

"So . . . which one of us gets to solve it?"

"Neither." I smiled and turned the page around to reveal the byline. "We've already solved it."

PUZZLE BY DANA MAYO AND W.W.W. MOODY

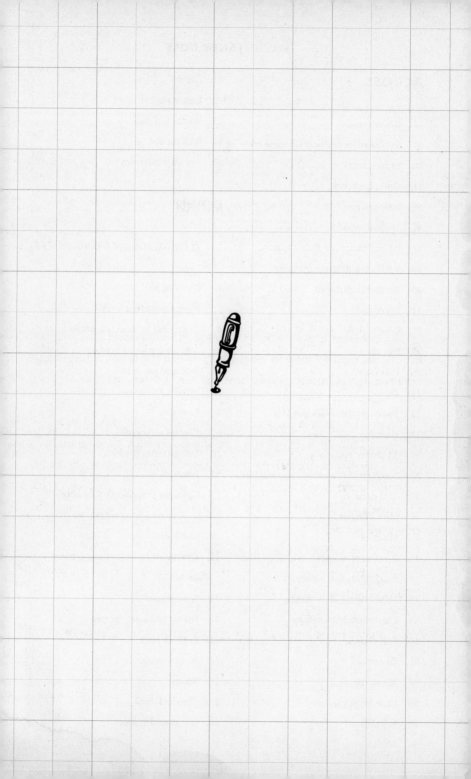

ACROSS

1. Driver's seat
5. Symbol of longevity in Japanese art
10. Express buss?
14. Quito quencher
15. Held sway
16. That's a wrap
17. It's less on a driver than a spoon
18. Works in a different medium
20. Band of Englishmen
22. Saved seat?
24. Boxer, briefly
25. Not state
26. Late state
28. Blows
31. You might get a kick out of it
32. Honey
33. 38-Down, essentially
37. Second half of a noted Pope line (var.)
40. Cold comfort?
41. Mister Roberts
42. Watches
43. Partners of monsters in a 1998 film title
44. Stocking stuffer, perhaps
45. Sister city to San Francisco
49. Claustrophobe's challenge
50. End of days?
51. Operator
56. Accounts
57. Look longingly
60. Hibernia
61. Revolt
62. Depression, of a sort
63. Bombs in a club
64. Rich deposit
65. Fire off a 39-Down

DOWN

1. #13 on AFI's Greatest Film Villians of All Time
2. Diva's excess
3. Night terrors from WWII
4. Tough class for Teen Talk Barbie
5. Area known for its beaches
6. Extended sentence
7. Whiffenpoofs' lack
8. Essential
9. On pins and needles
10. One of 150 in the Bible
11. Polish off
12. Container that doesn't hold water
13. _____ Suzuki, Bond wife in "You Only Live Twice"
19. One-third of a Major League crown (abbr.)
21. Ground swell
22. Romeo and Juliet, for two
23. Prufrock poet
27. Bad for business
28. Brews
29. The third man?
30. It's covered in sheet

32. It might be flipped in anger
33. Keen
34. Abstainer's alternative
35. Part of the Tootsie Roll family
36. Caesurae
38. Muck
39. Modern account
43. Celebratory
44. Clutches
45. Held the paper on
46. Harry's daughter
47. Elevated digs
48. Spaces spaces
49. They might appear on blackboards
52. Phrase for those who shall remain nameless
53. Act against organized crime
54. Overindulge
55. Anonymous way to sign a Valentine
58. Practice in 45-Across
59. Squelch

(solution on following page)

PUZZLE SOLUTION

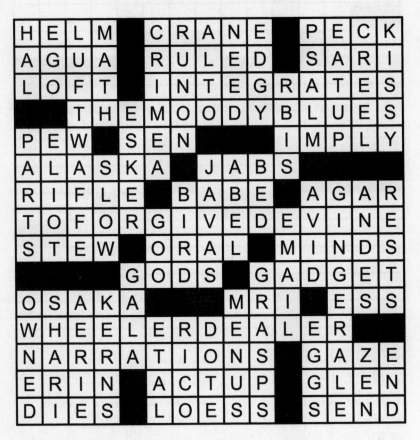

Puzzle © Peter W. Mitchell and Janet Siefert

ACKNOWLEDGMENTS

First and foremost, heartfelt thanks to my own personal gridmeister, Pete Mitchell, who provided not only the grid, but more than a few of the clues, for the puzzle on page 325 (or my Web site, if you're holding an ebook). Equally heartfelt thanks to the lovely and talented Vica Miller, who invited me to read at her literary salon, and to my agent, Molly Lyons, who was open-minded enough to attend a literary salon showcasing the work of unpublished authors.

Many insightful readers have given me support over the years, but special mention is due to Maureen Brady and the writers in her advanced fiction workshops, who provided invaluable feedback—notably Laurie Silver, who asked to keep reading even when she was no longer required to do so. Thanks to my editor, Kerry Donovan, who shepherded me through the publishing process with unflagging good cheer, and her team at NAL.

Thanks to all my friends in crossworld, especially my fellow Brain Cell Killers: Nousheen Afshani-Wezorek and Joe Wezorek; Carmen and John Dreyer; Carol Ezeir and Ned "Eduardo" Robert; Will Irving; Sharen McKay and Keith Yarbrough; Bill Sullivan; Virgil Talaid—and to my beloved Dougs, Ashleigh and Heller.

Thanks to my endlessly supportive family: my mother, Margaret, and the late Harry Siefert (who may be the only father on the planet who was thrilled when his daughter married a drummer). My sister, Joan Siefert Rose; her husband, Jim; and my dear nephs, Andy and Ian. Any and all Gosses, Luwisches, Zawises, and Stows. And to those people who might as well be family: Vykie Whipple and her boys; my Camp Oneka girls; Amy Lipman; Ellen Yampolsky; and Henry and Linda Kellerman. And to the late Michael J. Campo—wish you were here.

Finally, a special thanks to my paragon of a husband, Edgar, who never stopped believing in me (despite formidable odds to the contrary).

Photo © Chellise Michael Photography

Janet Goss lives in Greenwich Village with her husband, Edgar, and their spoiled-rotten behemoth of a cat, Gomez. She is currently working on a new novel that will be published by New American Library in 2013.

CONNECT ONLINE

www.janetgossbooks.com